KILL ME
TOMORROW

Look for these exciting Western series
from bestselling authors
William W. Johnstone and J.A. Johnstone

The Mountain Man
Luke Jensen: Bounty Hunter
Brannigan's Land
The Jensen Brand
Smoke Jensen: The Early Years
Preacher and MacCallister
Fort Misery
The Fighting O'Neils
Perley Gates
MacCoole and Boone
Guns of the Vigilantes
Shotgun Johnny
The Chuckwagon Trail
The Jackals
The Slash and Pecos Westerns
The Texas Moonshiners
Stoneface Finnegan Westerns
Ben Savage: Saloon Ranger
The Buck Trammel Westerns
The Death and Texas Westerns
The Hunter Buchanon Westerns
Will Tanner, Deputy US Marshal
Old Cowboys Never Die
Go West, Young Man

KILL ME TOMORROW

WILLIAM W. JOHNSTONE
AND
J.A. JOHNSTONE

KENSINGTON
PUBLISHING CORP.

www.kensingtonbooks.com

KENSINGTON BOOKS are published by

Kensington Publishing Corp.
900 Third Avenue
New York, NY 10022

Copyright © 2024 by J.A. Johnstone

PUBLISHER'S NOTE
Following the death of William W. Johnstone, the Johnstone family is working with a carefully selected writer to organize and complete Mr. Johnstone's outlines and many unfinished manuscripts to create additional novels in all of his series like The Last Gunfighter, Mountain Man, and Eagles, among others. This novel was inspired by Mr. Johnstone's superb storytelling.

All Kensington titles, imprints, and distributed lines are available at special quantity discounts for bulk purchases for sales promotion, premiums, fund-raising, educational, or institutional use. Special book excerpts or customized printings can also be created to fit specific needs. For details, write or phone the office of the Kensington Special Sales Manager: Attn. Special Sales Department. Kensington Publishing Corp., 900 Third Ave., New York, NY 10022. Phone: 1-800-221-2647.

The K with book logo Reg. U.S. Pat. & TM Off.

Library of Congress Control Number: 2023949857

ISBN: 978-1-4967-4611-5

First Kensington Hardcover Edition: April 2024

10 9 8 7 6 5 4 3 2 1

Printed in the United States of America

KILL ME TOMORROW

Chapter 1

Deputy U.S. Marshal Colton Gray walked into the Country Kitchen soon after the owner, Art Givens, opened for breakfast. The previous night had proven to be one hell of an evening for the young lawman and he felt the need for a solid breakfast before he reported to his boss, Marshal John Timmons.

"Good mornin', Colton," Art greeted him cheerfully. "You want your usual?"

"Good mornin', Mr. Givens. Yes, sir, I'll have the usual." He sat down at the long table in the middle of the little restaurant.

"Marthy," Art called out to his wife in the kitchen, "Colton Gray wants his usual breakfast." Her name was Martha, but Art always pronounced it as "Marthy." He poured a cup of coffee and took it over to Colton then. "I heard about the shootin' in the Reservation last night. Heard that Hank Penny got killed and Cecil Stark was wounded. I heard they was after some feller that escaped from prison and he did the shootin'. Was you mixed up in that?"

"Yes, I was involved in it, too," Colton replied.

"Well, I'm glad to see you're all right," Art said. "I'da hated to lose a customer. Is that feller back in jail?"

"No, he's dead," Colton answered.

"Did you shoot him?" Art asked.

"No, sir, I didn't. He was shot by a man named Casey Tubbs, who just happened to be at the right place at the right time."

"Casey Tubbs," Art repeated. "Is he another lawman?"

"No," Colton answered politely, although he was beginning to get a little weary of answering Art's questions about the incident. "Casey Tubbs is half owner of the D and T Cattle Company, a cattle ranch over in Lampasas County."

"Well, I'll be . . . How did he . . . ?" Art was interrupted when another customer walked in the door and he went to greet him.

When Martha brought Colton his breakfast, he could hear Art telling the new customer about the shooting. She always made sure she brought his order out and said good morning to the young deputy marshal. She knew he rented a room at Rena Bramble's boardinghouse and his meals were included in his rent. But he always showed up at the Country Kitchen one morning a week when he was in town and he always ordered pancakes. She often wondered if her pancakes were that special, or if Rena's were that bad.

Colton exchanged greetings with Martha and turned his attention to his bacon and pancakes, although he could not rid his mind of the turmoil caused by the happenings of the night just past. He replayed the picture in his mind once more, remembering the helpless feeling as he had stood weaponless, staring at Buck Garner's pistol aimed point-blank at him. A mere second after he heard Garner cock the hammer back, Casey's rifle spoke and Garner collapsed without ever pulling the trigger. For a brief moment, Colton had not been certain he had not been shot. And when he saw Garner fold up and sink to the floor, he realized that Casey Tubbs had saved his life.

His first emotion after it happened was naturally gratitude and he'd expressed that feeling to Casey. It was only afterward, after he had taken the bodies of Buck Garner and Deputy Hank Penny to the undertaker, and Cecil Stark to the doctor, that he thought about the irony of the incident. Marshal John Timmons had placed Colton on full-time duty to bring a pair of bank robbers to justice. The two outlaws were unique in that they were two old men who were expert in pulling the wool over their victims' eyes and escaping with thousands of dollars. To make matters worse, they had become quite famous all over the state of Texas. They were especially popular for their ability to vanish completely after a holdup. Colton Gray was the only lawman who suspected the two old men were not old men at all, but were younger men in disguise. He was alone in this theory because eyewitnesses all testified that they were convinced the two robbers were actually old men, who had little left to live for. Consequently, they were not reluctant to take chances. They had become especially popular with the poor class of folks who were struggling to make it, if only because the two old men seemed to pick on banks that were out to grab land from those who could no longer make their payments.

To complicate Colton's dilemma, through a series of unlikely happenings, he had become quite friendly with Casey Tubbs and Eli Doolin, men he suspected to be these two outlaws. He had even stayed overnight at the D&T Ranch on occasion. In the beginning of the old-men holdups, it seemed that Eli and Casey were in the same town, either the day before or the day after the old men struck. To Colton, that was just too much coincidence to accept. He had reported to his boss, Deputy Timmons, that he felt strongly that the elderly robbers were younger men in disguise. But he had not confided that he also had a strong suspicion that they might be Casey and Eli, not young men, but not as old as "Oscar" and

"Elmer," as the old men were called. Adding to his suspicions was the apparent wealth of the two partners and their reputation for helping out the not-so-successful ranches. How could that apparent wealth possibly come from the yearly cattle drive?

All these questions had been contributing to Colton's confusion about the two characters for some time. Last night's incident gave him another question he had no answer for: He had stood facing certain death at the hand of Buck Garner, but Casey Tubbs shot Garner before he could pull the trigger. Casey had shown up from nowhere to save Colton's life. He had no business there at all. And had he not shot Buck Garner, Colton would be dead. The only man who suspected Casey and Eli were the two old outlaws would be dead. Was he wrong in his suspicion of the two? There was too much evidence to make him believe that he was mistaken. What were Eli and Casey doing in Waco yesterday, anyway? After his meeting with John Timmons, he decided to check by the Mc-Clellan House Hotel to see if they had checked out. He couldn't help wondering if there might be a bank robbery in town today.

"Is your breakfast all right, honey?" Martha Givens asked when she filled his coffee cup again. "You look like you're doing some serious thinking."

"Oh, yes, ma'am, Miz Givens. It's just fine as usual," Colton answered. "I guess my mind is far away somewhere. I need to get finished and get to work." He downed the last of his coffee and got up from the table, leaving the money for his breakfast on the table.

"Mornin', Colton," Ron Wild, Timmons's clerk, greeted him when he walked into the marshal's office. Then without getting up from his desk, Ron turned his head to yell through the open door behind him. "Marshal, Colton's here."

"Well, send him on in," a call came back, so Colton walked

back into the office. "Good mornin', Colton. You ready to go back to work?"

"I reckon so," Colton answered. "Too bad about Hank Penny. I'm sure you hated to lose him. He was a good man." He made it a point to say that, although he remembered cursing Hank the night before when Hank had ordered him to walk in the front door of the saloon to draw Buck Garner's fire, while he chose to sneak in the back.

"Yes, sir, he was a good man," Timmons agreed. "It's gonna be hard to replace him. I reckon we ought to be thankful we didn't lose you last night, too. That was a downright stroke of luck you didn't get shot down when you walked in the front door of the Dead Dog Saloon. Didn't you know Garner would be waitin' for one of you to walk in that door?"

"Yeah, I knew," Colton answered.

"Have you got a death wish or something?" Timmons asked.

Colton hesitated before answering. He didn't want to speak ill of the dead, but he was tired of wearing the rookie label that Timmons continued to burden him with. "I went in the front because Hank told me to. He was the boss, so I did what he said."

Timmons picked up on the little touch of chafing in the young deputy's tone, so he said, "Cecil's gonna be all right. He wasn't wounded as bad as he thought. He got lucky and he said you handled yourself like an old professional." Then Timmons changed the subject and started talking about keeping Colton in town for a while, since there were no reports having to do with the old bank robbers.

That talk changed abruptly when Ron walked into the office and handed Timmons an envelope. "This just came from the telegraph office," Ron said.

Timmons opened the envelope and read it, then looked up at Colton. He handed him the telegram and said, "Looks like

I was wrong. I reckon you're gonna be travelin' again. Your two old bank robbers hit the Farmers Bank in Huntsville yesterday. Damn it!" He cursed and smacked his hand down hard on the desk. "I was truly hoping those two old geezers had retired after that last job in Fort Worth."

Colton continued staring at the telegram in his hand, unable to believe what it said. Huntsville was a hundred and thirty miles from there. Casey and Eli were there in Waco yesterday. These two men in Huntsville had to be copycat robbers. Either that, or he had to be dead wrong about Casey and Eli, and he was still not ready to admit that.

"It doesn't say they were apprehended," Colton finally said.

"No, it doesn't," Timmons said. "Get down there and see what you can find out. Maybe they left a trail to follow." He paused, then added, "But they never do." He shook his head, clearly aggravated to hear the two old gents were back in business. "The sheriff down there is Robert Joyner. He'll help you if he can, but he ain't much for workin' outside the city limits."

"I'll be on my way down there just as soon as I can get my horses and some supplies ready to travel," Colton said.

"Good huntin'," Timmons said, sincerely meaning it. He was sick of chasing after the two old men.

A ride of three and a half days brought Colton to the town of Huntsville, a town he was familiar with, even though he had never actually been within its city limits before. It was well known by all Texas lawmen as the Huntsville Unit of the Texas State Prison. He walked his horse, a bay gelding he called Scrappy, slowly down the main street, passing the Farmers Bank on his way to the sheriff's office. He pulled up in front of the sheriff's office and dismounted, looped

Scrappy's reins loosely around the hitching rail, and went inside.

"Sheriff Joyner?" he asked the man seated at the one desk in the office.

"Yep, I'm Sheriff Joyner. What can I do for you?"

"Sheriff, I'm Deputy U.S. Marshal Colton Gray of the Waco District Office. We got your telegram about the robbery of the Farmers Bank."

The sheriff grinned and replied, "I figured we'd get a visit from one of you boys when you found out who robbed the bank." He got up from his chair and reached out over his desk to shake Colton's hand. "Bob Joyner, Deputy, how can I help you?"

"I've been following these two outlaws for a good while now," Colton explained. "So I'd appreciate everything you can tell me about the robbery and I'd like to talk to the people at the bank. I'm looking for anything that might help me get on their trail." He couldn't help being curious about the sheriff's grin, which kept growing and growing as Colton spoke. When he paused, the sheriff enlightened him.

"I'm gonna do better than that," Joyner declared. "I'll let you talk to the two bank robbers. You see, Colton—ain't that what you said your name was?" Colton nodded and Joyner continued. "Those two slick outlaws finally picked the wrong town to try their little masquerade holdup. Alvin Williams, one of the tellers, got suspicious of 'em and said he was gonna send for me. So one of 'em whipped out a revolver and shot him. Hell, everybody in town heard the shot, includin' me and my deputy. They ran out the north road at a gallop. We had a posse of five men after 'em in fifteen minutes. We ran 'em to ground seven miles north of town." Joyner shrugged and said, "They just picked the wrong town for their little show."

"I reckon," Colton replied. He remembered that Timmons had commented that Joyner didn't operate outside the city limits. He would have to tell Timmons that Joyner extended his authority for seven miles. "What makes you think the two men you arrested are the same two old men that have escaped arrest for so long?"

"Oh, there wasn't any doubt about that," Joyner insisted. "But you see, they ain't really old men like they pretend to be. They were wearin' disguises to make 'em look like old men. I've got the disguises they were wearin', hangin' on those coat hooks over there on the wall. You can take a look at 'em." He pointed to the far wall. "They're actually two brothers, name of Earnest and Stanley Simpson. They're part of a whole damn litter of Simpsons that live back in the woods near Crockett. And they stay in trouble pretty much all the time. I've run two or three of 'em out of town before. They're all bad, but the four brothers are the worst. I've had both of the other two in jail for raising hell in one of our saloons. Maurice and Derwood, I told 'em not to set foot in this town again if they didn't wanna take up residence in the Huntsville Unit of the Texas State Prison. I'll take you back in the cell room and you can talk to Stanley and Earnest if you want to."

"Yes, sir, I'd like to talk to them," Colton said, and walked over to the wall hooks to see what Joyner said were their disguises. He was already sure Earnest and Stanley were copycat robbers, so everything he had in mind to do now was simply to confirm it. He started with the disguises. There were two large rain slickers hanging on the wall and a couple of battered old hats. There were also two identical fake gray beards, complete with big noses and eyeglasses that were frames without lenses. To keep from insulting Sheriff Joyner, he didn't comment on the disguises, but simply asked, "Can I talk to them now?"

"You sure can," the sheriff replied, and led him through the door to the cell room, where they found the two Simpson brothers lying on their cots. "Wake up, boys," Joyner said.

"You got a deputy U.S. marshal, come all the way from Waco to talk to ya." They both sat up to stare at Colton. "I just wanna ask you a couple of questions," Colton told them. "All right?" Neither man replied, so he continued. "Do you know who Bryan Dawkins is, down in Austin?" As he expected, there was no change in the dull expressions on their faces. "He's the president of the Cotton Growers Bank." Stanley and Earnest looked at each other to exchange confused expressions. "How 'bout Travis Bradshaw in Fort Worth?" Colton asked then, and received the same puzzled response. "Bradshaw and Lane, Cattle Buyers," he added to give them another clue, still with no response from the two brothers. So he turned to face Sheriff Joyner and said, "That's all I need, Sheriff, I 'preciate your indulgence. I expect you already have them set for trial, so there ain't nothing you need from the U.S. Marshal." He led the sheriff back into his office.

"You gonna want to talk to Horace Winter now?" Joyner asked. "He's the president of the Farmers Bank."

"No," Colton replied, "that won't be necessary." The disappointment was immediately apparent in Joyner's face and Colton knew the sheriff must have been hoping for a greater measure of public recognition for capturing the notorious "old-men bandits." But Colton knew as soon as he saw the disguises Stanley and Earnest wore that they were not the real Oscar and Elmer. The real old-men bandits wore the kind of makeup that had to be scrubbed off. "No," Colton repeated. "I'm gonna get outta your way now and I wanna thank you for your cooperation. I'd like to congratulate you, too, on a job well done when you responded so fast to the robbery of the Farmers Bank and captured the robbers. But I'm afraid those two in your cell room aren't the pair of old men who have been hitting banks and other targets in other parts of Texas."

"But they were wearin' those disguises with the gray beards and all to make 'em look like old men," Joyner protested.

"I know," Colton explained patiently. "But the two disguises are identical, and they just hung the glasses on their ears. Not much difference than tying bandanas around their faces. But you still did a first-rate job of catchin' the robbers. The mayor and the town council oughta be happy about that."

"Yeah, I reckon they are," Joyner allowed. "You pretty sure those two ain't the real old-men bandits?"

"Yes, sir, I'm pretty sure," Colton replied. "But if we don't have any more robberies by the two old men, then I might be wrong." He extended his hand. "Thank you for your help, Sheriff."

Joyner shook his hand. "Sorry you had to make the trip for nothing. You take care of yourself, young fellow."

"You do the same," Colton returned, and took his leave. Outside, he paused to decide what he was going to do. He had arrived in Huntsville in the middle of the afternoon, too late to catch the noontime meal at the typical restaurants. He refrained from asking Sheriff Joyner which saloons offered food, for fear the sheriff might send him to a rotten trough because he ruined his claim-to-fame story. He had to rest his horses before starting back to Waco. He remembered passing a nice little creek just short of town, maybe three or four miles north. So he decided to go back to that creek and rest the horses there. He had plenty of bacon left and coffee, as well as some hardtack, so he might cook himself some dinner and then start out for home. That settled, he climbed aboard Scrappy and started back out the north road. He knew that he had just wasted half a week to ride down here to confirm what he knew beforehand was a useless trip. Now he was going to waste another half a week going back.

As he rode past the last of the small houses and farms close to town, he thought about his two unlikely friends. Casey and Eli, or Elmer and Oscar, as they were called on special occasions, he thought. "Come on, Scrappy," he insisted, "you know damn well those two do-gooders are the old-men bandits. I just ain't found enough evidence to prove it yet." Even as he made the statement, he was not sure he really wanted to find that evidence. In spite of himself, he could not help admiring the way they continued to perform their old-men routines and took the money without shooting anyone. And then, their willingness to help the poor rancher who's down on his luck, how could you not admire men like that?

Chapter 2

"Eli, I've been thinkin'," Casey Tubbs announced when he came out on the front porch with his cup of coffee to join his partner. They had just enjoyed another fine supper prepared by their cook, Juanita Garcia. This time of the year, after the cattle had been taken to the railroad, the evenings were quite pleasant on the porch.

"Is that a fact?" Eli responded. "Well, maybe if it ain't anything important, it won't hurt your head too bad. Maybe Juanita can wrap a bandage around your head. Then if that don't stop it, I'll take you over to Lampasas to see the doctor."

Accustomed to Eli's nonsense, Casey ignored it. "Matter of fact, I was thinkin' about the bank in Lampasas—"

That was as far as he got before Eli interrupted him. "Whoa now! I thought we had us a rule not to mess with any banks too close to home. And Lampasas ain't twenty miles from here."

"I never said nothin' about robbin' the dang bank," Casey said. "But I was thinkin' about how hard we've worked to build this ranch back to where it was when it was Whitmore Brothers, and you and I was just a couple of their cowhands. And doggone it if we ain't built it to where it's bigger'n they was. D and T Cattle Company is the biggest cattle ranch in this part of Texas. But you know what? D and T ain't got no bank connections anywhere. Whitmore Brothers did."

"That may be so," Eli said. "But what do we need with bank connections, anyway? We run our business on a cash basis." He paused to look around him as if someone might hear. "Other people's," he added. "We don't need no loans."

"I ain't talkin' about loans, Eli. I'm talkin' about bank connections, the kind you have when you're the biggest customer the bank has. The kind that makes the bank wanna do things to please you. We might decide to take an interest in that little town when we get tired of robbin' banks. It'd be nice to have some influence in the town. Besides that, it wouldn't hurt to get some of this cash we've got stuck in every hidin' place we can find in this house, into the bank. I swear, there ain't no way to keep all our money hid from Juanita much longer."

Eli paused at that point to give it some serious thought. He was not so sure about the necessity of having "bank connections," as Casey called them, but he was concerned about the accumulation of cash. Juanita was pretty bad about wanting to clean their rooms fairly often. It wouldn't be good for her to stumble on some of those bureau drawers whose bottoms were lined with bundles of fifties and hundreds. "You're right about that," he finally said. "She might decide to give the house a good cleanin' sometime when we're gone somewhere. I know we can trust her to keep her mouth shut about it, but I'd druther she didn't know how much we've got hid around here. 'Course, it might be just our luck, if we put it in the bank, that the bank would get robbed."

"I reckon that's the chance you take," Casey said. "I think in our case, it's worth the risk."

"How much do you think we ought to put in the bank?" Eli asked.

"Well, the last time we counted it, after we sold the herd, we had close to one hundred thousand. Everybody knows we keep operatin' money in the safe in the study, but nobody knows how much is in there, or in that other safe in your bedroom. We're gonna need a good chunk of that to keep our full crew on, like we promised, but we could still put thirty-five thousand in the bank. That oughta get us a high spot on the customer list on a little ol' bank like First Bank of Lampasas. Whaddaya think?"

Eli stroked his chin and gave it some thought. Maybe it would be one step toward becoming legitimate and respected businessmen. "What the hell," he remarked, "it ain't our money we're riskin', anyway. Let's ride down to Lampasas in the mornin' and talk to the bank."

"Done," Casey said. "I think it's a step in the right direction. We'll tell Juanita we're leavin' early in the mornin' and tell Davy to saddle Smoke and Biscuit first thing."

After an early breakfast, they rode out on a little trail that led to the wagon road to the town of Lampasas, planning to make it a one-day trip. With thirty-five thousand dollars in Casey's saddlebags, they figured to reach the bank during the midmorning hours by alternating the horses' gait between a walk and a lope. It was actually a few minutes before ten o'clock when they rode past the stable on the north side of town. So they decided to go straight to the bank and get that business taken care of first. Then they would come back to the stable and leave their horses there to rest while they found a place to have some dinner. They figured it was worth the daily rate at the stable not to have to keep an eye on the horses while they walked around town. And they could take their saddles off and give them grain and water, too.

The First Bank of Lampasas, an unimpressive white frame building, was located on the corner of Main Street and River Road. There were no horses tied at the hitching rail in front of the bank. It appeared to be a good time to have business inside. They tied their horses, Casey pulled his saddlebags off the gray gelding, and they went inside.

"Good morning, gentlemen. How can I help you?" Teller Marcus Smith greeted them cheerfully.

"Good morning," Casey answered him, equally cheerful. "Who can we talk to about openin' an account?"

"That would be Mr. Bennett," Marcus answered. "He's the president of the bank. I'll get him for you." He left his cage, walked to an open office door, and disappeared inside.

Casey and Eli couldn't help grinning at each other, both thinking the same thing, since they had been in that situation before. This time, however, they wouldn't have to try to talk like ancient old men, and Eli wouldn't have to pretend he had to go to the outhouse. "Don't slip up and call me Elmer," Casey warned him.

"Kinda hard not to," Eli replied. "The name just seems to fit you better than Casey."

Marcus came back out the door then, followed by a smiling man, who walked up to them with his hand extended. After he shook hands with both of them, he said, "I'm Malcolm Bennett. Marcus said you were inquiring about opening an account with us."

"That's right," Casey said. "My name's Casey Tubbs and this is Eli Doolin. We're partners in the D and T Cattle Company, about twenty miles north of Lampasas."

"Yes, I've heard of the D and T," Bennett said. "Used to be the Whitmore Cattle Company, right?"

"That's a fact," Casey replied.

"We never did any business with Whitmore," Bennett said. "I think they did all their banking with one of the banks in Waco."

"You're a lot closer to the D and T, so Eli and I thought, why not do our bankin' with somebody close to home."

"Well, we certainly appreciate that," Bennett remarked.

"We'll be happy to work with you any way we can. What is it you have in mind? Loans?" This was an all-too-familiar routine with farmers and ranchers looking for money to keep their heads above water.

Casey looked at Eli, then back to Bennett. "We don't need a loan, Mr. Bennett. We were hopin' we could open an account so we'd have a safe place to keep some of our extra money. You know, like a checkin' account."

"Of course, you can," Bennett responded at once. "We'd be happy to have D and T as a checking account, or a savings account, whatever you need. How much do you want to open it with?"

"We brought thirty-five thousand. Is that enough to open an account?" Eli couldn't resist asking.

"Yes," Bennett said at once. "Come right into my office and I'll open your account right away. You say you have the money with you?"

"Yes, sir," Casey answered as he and Eli followed Bennett into his office, "right here in my saddlebag."

"We'll have to count it, of course," Bennett said when Casey started pulling the banded stacks of fifties and hundreds out of the saddlebag and laying them on the desk. *And I thought this was going to be a slow day,* Bennett thought. *The way it started, I thought nothing was going to happen.* "Excuse me just a moment," he said, then went back to the door to call to the tellers. "One of you come in and help me verify a money count." When another young man hurried into the office, Bennett said, "You met Marcus, this is James Woodley. James, this is Mr. Doolin and Mr. Tubbs. They have decided to entrust us to do their banking."

It took some time to count the stacks of money, one bill at a time, and both Bennett and Woodley counted the whole thirty-five thousand. Luckily, they both ended up with the correct amount. Bennett produced a large sack from his desk drawer and Woodley began putting the money in it while Bennett did the paperwork. "I'll sign the papers and give you a receipt for all this, and I've listed Casey Tubbs and Eli Doolin as the only persons authorized to write checks or make withdrawals. Now I'm going to put your money into the safe. Would you like to see the time-release safe we have?"

Casey looked at Eli and got a shrug of indifference. "No, I reckon we've taken up enough of your time already," Casey said. He glanced out at the lobby. "Looks like you're gettin' kinda busy, anyway."

"Well, I certainly want to welcome you to our banking family," Bennett said, and shook their hands again. "I hope we'll enjoy a long and prosperous relationship."

They walked back through the lobby, where there were a few people in line at Woodley's cage, and Marcus was talking to two gray-bearded old men in the middle of the lobby, one of them leaning on a cane. They seemed to be upset about having to wait to see Bennett, Eli interpreted from their arm motions. But Marcus paused to say, "Thank you, Mr. Doolin and Mr. Tubbs."

Outside, they found two more horses at the hitching rail and Eli stopped dead still. "What's got into you?" Casey asked. "You look like you saw a snake."

"I got a feelin'," Eli started.

"Well, maybe if you don't try to use your brain . . ." That was as far as he got before Eli stopped him.

"Just shut up and listen," Eli said. "There's too many things that don't add up. Them two old men that young teller was talkin' to. When one of 'em dropped his walkin' stick and he bent over to pick it up, I thought something looked kinda strange about him. In the first place, he bent over and grabbed that walkin' stick off the floor quick as a twelve-year-old. But the thing that started me thinkin' was when he reached down, I thought I saw his hairline move on the back of his neck. He had white hair, but I swear I think I saw a little strip of black hair peekin' out from under it. And now I'm lookin' at two horses at the rail that weren't there before. And that ain't all. Didn't we tie our horses at this end of the hitchin' rail, closest to the front door? Now they're slid down the rail and two new horses are at this end."

He didn't have to say more. Casey caught on immediately. "Son of a . . ." he started, thinking that surely this could not be happening. But when he replayed the scene of the two old-timers talking to the young teller, he understood why it had struck Eli the way it had. And now, he had to admit that he wasn't sure that he and Eli weren't being copied by two other outlaws. His first reaction was one of indignation to think that two outlaws were copying their originality and likely alerting all banks to be watchful for the two old men. His next thought was the same one Eli had at that moment. Those two old men were waiting to go into the office to talk to Malcolm Bennett, and their thirty-five-thousand-dollar deposit was sitting on Bennett's desk.

They turned around and started to go back inside the bank, but Eli asked, "What if we're wrong? We'd sure look like a couple of fools. I only got a quick look at what I thought was dark hair under the white hair. It mighta just been a dark scar or something."

"Maybe," Casey said, having second thoughts about rushing back inside. "You're right, if we're wrong, we'll look like a couple of fools. If we're right, we might start a gunfight in there. Why don't we just wait outside here and see what happens inside? We can stand ready for 'em, if they do rob the bank. Might be a good idea to loosen the cinches on those two saddles, too—give us a little advantage."

Eli thought that a good idea as well, so they quickly stepped up to the horses and loosened the cinches on both the double-rigged saddles. That done, they took positions on both sides of the bank door and waited.

"What are we gonna do if we're wrong and those two old fellows come out to get on their horses?" Eli asked.

"Tell 'em they'd best check their cinches because somebody had loosened ours," Casey said. Eli was about to comment on that, but was interrupted by the report of two gunshots from inside the bank. They both drew their six-shooters and flattened their backs against the wall on each side of the front door.

After a brief moment with the sounds of angry voices and a scream from the one woman inside, the front door was flung open and the two "old-timers" burst through them, one was carrying the sack from Bennett's desk, the other a similar sack from the teller cage. Taking no notice of the two armed men plastered against each side of the door, they ran to their horses and jumped in the saddle with one foot in the stirrup and a hand on the saddle horn. They were promptly dumped on the ground as the saddles turned upside down. In a state of total shock, the two bank robbers found themselves flat on their backs, staring up at the business ends of a couple of Colt .45 Army revolvers.

Malcolm Bennett burst through the door then, followed by James Woodley and Marcus Smith. All three stopped, stunned by the sight of the two robbers on their backs, under their horses, and Eli and Casey standing over them with their six-shooters threatening. Bennett almost dropped to his knees to give thanks, but came to his senses in time to tell his tellers to go back inside to watch their cash drawers. Then he quickly picked up the sack containing the thirty-five thousand dollars.

"Send somebody to get the sheriff," Casey said.

"No need to," Bennett replied, still amazed that his two new customers had just thwarted a bank holdup. "Here comes Deputy Millican. He must have heard the shots."

Deputy L. R. Millican pushed through the small group of spectators who had accumulated by then. Surprised by the scene he walked into, he was about to ask Casey and Eli to put their guns away. But he saw Bennett standing there, so he asked, "Trouble in the bank, Mr. Bennett?"

"You can certainly say that," Bennett replied. "These two tried to rob the bank, and if it hadn't been for Mr. Doolin and Mr. Tubbs, they would have escaped with a substantial sum of money."

Millican pulled the pistols out of each robber's holster before telling them to get on their feet. He looked at Casey and Eli, who still held their guns on the two robbers. "That was a pretty good way to stop 'em," he said. "What made you think they were gonna rob the bank?"

"Just got a feelin' when we saw 'em inside," Eli answered. "Something didn't look right." To demonstrate, he reached over and grabbed a handful of the robber's hair closest to him. When he pulled his hand back, the whole gray wig came with it, revealing dirty black hair. "I didn't see any reason for two fellows to dress up like somebody else to go to the bank, unless they was plannin' on doin' somethin' they didn't wanna be remembered for."

"The old-men bandits!" Bennett and Millican exclaimed at the same time.

"Stopped at the First Bank of Lampasas," Malcom Bennett proclaimed when he realized, "by two of the bank's fine customers."

"I can't wait to tell the sheriff," the deputy said. "The U.S. Marshal in Waco is gonna wanna hear about this, too." He addressed Casey and Eli then. "Would you gentlemen walk these two over to the jail with me so I won't have to tie their hands up?"

"Sure," Casey said, since he could see the sheriff's office and jail up the street half a block away. They herded the two would-be bank robbers to the jail, and on the way Millican took the opportunity to find out exactly who Casey and Eli were, so he could make a full report to the sheriff. "Where is the sheriff?" Casey asked after the prisoners were locked in a cell.

"He went out to his farm this morning," the deputy replied. "He'll be back this afternoon. You fellows leavin' town now?"

"No," Eli answered him. "We were plannin' to rest our horses and find us a place to have some dinner before we go back to the D and T. Matter of fact, we were thinkin' about leaving our horses at the stable while we're in town, so we can look around a little bit. We ain't spent much time in Lampasas. You want us to take your prisoners' horses to the stable for you."

"'Preciate the offer, but I'll take 'em and I'll tell Harvey to charge the sheriff's office to take care of your horses. We oughta at least do that for you, since you two captured the bank robbers for us."

"Why, that's right neighborly of you," Casey said.

"And since you say you ain't that familiar with Lampasas, I could recommend the hotel dining room for your dinner," Millican said. "That's where I eat."

"That sounds like a good idea," Casey remarked. "Why don't we take the horses and all go to the hotel to eat. You can be our guest, Deputy Millican."

"That's mighty kind of you," Millican replied, "and I'd be happy to join you, but the hotel doesn't charge me for my meals. That's part of my employment package."

"Hell, that's even better," Eli said. "Let's go get the horses." They went back to the bank then and walked the horses to the stable, where they left Smoke and Biscuit with Harvey Frost, along with the prisoners' horses. From there, they went to the hotel to eat.

They found L. R. Millican to be a quiet, serious-thinking young man, whose first name was Leander. He said his friends nicknamed him "Lee."

"What made you wait outside the bank today and set up

that ambush for those two robbers, instead of runnin' for the sheriff?" he asked. "They'd already shot a couple of times inside the bank. They might have come out with their guns blazin'.."

"Well, I don't know about Eli, but I had thought about that very thing," Casey answered. "We worked hard for that money and I knew it was still on Mr. Bennett's desk. Then, when they came out the door, I saw both of 'em was holdin' a sack in one hand. So I figured they were gonna have to holster their guns to have a free hand to grab the saddle horn. And I was damn sure I could pull the trigger faster than one of them layin' on his back, tryin' to get his gun outta the holster. And I figured Eli would take care of the other one."

Millican nodded his head as if acknowledging that made sense. Casey didn't divulge the main reason they made sure they stopped the pair in their tracks. And that was because of the aggravation they felt to see someone attempting to take a free ride on their stagecoach.

"At the sheriff's office, we've been hearin' a little bit about the so-called old-men bandits," he said. "Do you think these two you captured today are the same two who have been hitting those other banks?"

"I seriously doubt it," Casey found himself forced to say. "These two coyotes today were wearin' cheap disguises to make 'em look like old men. From what I've heard, the genuine old-men bandits ain't wearin' disguises. Accordin' to the eyewitnesses, they really are two old men. Ain't that what you've heard, Eli?"

"That's my understandin'," Eli replied. "At least, that's the talk around Waco." Eli was thinking the same thing he knew Casey was thinking. This business at the bank today might soon be happening all over the state of Texas, with any number of dim-witted saddle tramps thinking it an easy way to rob a bank. And if that was the case, no matter how good their disguises were, the banks would be on guard as soon as they walked in the door. Things at D&T were going along fine right now, but there would be tight times to come. There always were, and then they might have to go back to their usual source of capital. So, what were they going to have to do then? Start wearing dresses and long blond wigs?

After their dinner, they said so long to the deputy. He carried a couple of dinner plates back to the jail for his new guests while Casey and Eli took a walk around town, just to see how much the town had grown. They ended up with a stop at a saloon called Big Red's, where they had a couple of shots of whiskey, corn for Casey and rye for Eli. Then it was back to the stable to get their horses and a long ride back to the D&T Ranch.

Chapter 3

"Speak of the devil," Ron Wild uttered when Colton Gray walked into U.S. Marshal John Timmons's office in Waco.

"What's that supposed to mean?" Colton asked Marshal Timmons's clerk. "It's a three-and-a-half-day ride to Huntsville. Did you expect me back any sooner?"

"No, it's just funny you showing up today and we got a letter today from Lampasas. They ain't got telegraph over there yet and they've got two old men that tried to rob the bank last week. So I wouldn't be surprised if you don't have to get right back on your horse and go question those two. Marshal Timmons is adamant about checking on every one of those robberies."

"Lampasas?" Colton asked, thinking the little town wasn't very far from the D&T Ranch. His first reaction was that the bank robbery there had to be another case of copycats, because Casey and Eli wouldn't operate that close to home. "You think he's gonna send me over there?"

"He was talkin' that way this morning," Ron replied.

"Well, I'll go on in and give him my report on the Huntsville pair." He passed on through Ron's little outer office and stopped to knock on Timmons's open door.

Timmons looked up when he heard him. "Come on in, Colton. I was just lookin' at your next assignment."

"Lampasas?" Colton asked as he reached out to put his written report on the marshal's desk.

"Yeah, that's right," Timmons said. Familiar with Colton's detailed written reports, he picked up the several-page report, glanced at it, then laid it back on his desk. "Just tell me what it says and I'll read it later," he told Colton. "You don't look all that excited, so I'm guessing the two weren't the real thing."

"That's right," Colton replied, "they weren't even close." He told Timmons about the two brothers, Stanley and Earnest Simpson, and their two identical fake disguises. "They looked like masks you'd buy your kids for Halloween," he said.

Timmons picked up the letter he had been holding when Colton walked in. "This came this morning. It's from the sheriff's office in Lampasas. They had a holdup at the bank there by two more copycats. But these two must have had better disguises than the ones you described in Huntsville, because they thought they really were two old geezers until they stopped them." He paused to look up at Colton and smiled. "You oughta get a kick out of this next bit," he said, and then read from the letter. "The two robbers escaped from the bank with an undisclosed amount of money, but were ambushed outside the bank by two residents of Lampasas County, a Mr. Eli Doolin and Mr. Casey Tubbs, two of the bank's customers." Timmons paused then, still holding the letter. "Ain't that the two fellows you bumped into in Fort Worth when you went in the Dead Dog Saloon after Buck Garner? One of 'em saved your life, you said."

"That's right," Colton replied, "Casey Tubbs." He didn't say anything further because he was stunned by the news. *Casey and Eli captured the two bank robbers? What in the world are they up to?* he thought. *How did they know the bank was going to be robbed?*

"I know it might seem to you like we're just like a little dog runnin' around in a circle, chasin' his tail," Timmons said. "But I'm sendin' you over to Lampasas to look into that bank holdup. My boss wants all those copycat robberies investigated. I believe he thinks those two old bank robbers really are younger men in disguise." Timmons's boss was U.S. Marshal Quincy Thomas, Chief Marshal of the Western District.

So now, Colton thought, *your boss and I have at least one thing in common. We both know the old bandits are really younger men in disguise.* His problem still remained, however. He was ninety percent certain that Casey and Eli were the real old-men bandits, and he was reluctant to find the evidence that would give him the ten percent proof he was lacking. The fact that Casey had saved his life had severely complicated his desire to uncover any more evidence against him.

His thoughts were interrupted when he heard Timmons ask, "You got any problem with that?"

"What? No, no problem. You just caught me thinkin' there for a moment. I'll try not to let that happen again," he joked. "I'll head over that way in the morning. Any chance I can pick up my expense money today from the trip to Huntsville?"

"I don't see why not," Timmons replied. "Stop back by this afternoon and Ron oughta have it for you."

"I 'preciate it," Colton said. "I need to buy a couple of things I'm runnin' out of." He walked out of the office and paused long enough to tell Ron he would be back to pick up his check. The usual rate when going to make an arrest was six cents a mile and ten cents a mile when he brought a prisoner on the return trip. He got nothing for the return trip if he didn't bring a prisoner back. Since these trips Timmons was sending him on didn't involve an arrest and transporting a prisoner back, Timmons authorized payment both ways at six cents a mile. Colton had figured the amount he was due, after the standard twenty-five percent cut that the marshal got out of every deputy marshal's expenses, would net him eleven dollars and seventy cents. He could buy the supplies he needed with that and have a little left over.

His next stop was the stable, where he was greeted by Horace Temple.

"Howdy, Colton, did you have a good trip? I forgot where you said you was goin'."

"Howdy, Horace," Colton returned. "Huntsville, I rode down to Huntsville. It was just a routine trip that wasn't worth the trouble. I'll leave my horses with you tonight, but I'll see you early in the mornin' and head out again." He paused when he had another thought. "I changed my mind. I'll pick up my horses after breakfast. Where I'm headin' is gonna take a day and a half, anyway, so I might as well eat breakfast before I go."

"That sounds like the smart thing to me," Horace said with a chuckle. "Where you headin' this trip?"

"Lampasas," Colton replied. "You know where that is?"

"Can't say as I do," Horace said. "I've heard of it, or maybe I've just heard of Lampasas County."

"It's a small town in that county, but I've never been there," Colton said. "I was hopin' you could tell me how to get there. I took a look at the map in the office, so I know the general direction from here. Reckon I'll stumble across somebody who can direct me." He had thought about riding over to the D&T Ranch first. He was sure they could tell him how to get to Lampasas, but he preferred to talk to the people at the bank before he talked to Casey and Eli.

Horace helped him unload his packhorse and put his saddle and packs in a corner of one of the stalls. "Much obliged," Colton said, then pulled his rifle out of the saddle scabbard, put his saddlebags over his shoulder, and remarked, "See you in the mornin'." He left the stable and walked to the boarding-house, which was about a quarter of a mile away.

"Well, I see you're back in town," Rena Bramble sang out to him when she saw him walk down the front hall on his way back to his room. "Glad to see you back all right. Dinner's gonna be ready in about fifteen minutes. Give you time to wash up, if you need to."

"Yes, ma'am," he responded. "I'm glad to be back. Whatcha cookin'?"

"Beef stew," she answered, "and it's a good thing we cooked enough to feed a hungry young man like you." He walked on back to his room and she went back to the kitchen. "Better put a few more potatoes in that stew, Gracie. Colton showed up."

After dinner, Colton told Rena he would be leaving again after breakfast and would be gone for possibly a week. Then he told Gracie, a middle-aged widow, that he needed to wash a shirt and some of his underwear and socks. And he asked her if she thought there was time for them to dry, if he hung them on the line that afternoon. He felt pretty sure there was plenty of time to dry clothes, but he figured if he played dumb, she'd take care of them for him. She reacted just as he thought she would and told him to bring her the dirty clothes and she'd take care of them.

"I can't ask you to do that," he protested.

"Nonsense," she replied, "just bring me the dang clothes."

"If you're sure you don't mind," he said. "It sure will help me out. I've gotta go back to the office. Then I have to go buy some supplies, so I'll have something to eat while I'm gone." His conscience started bothering him, however, and by the time he came back with his dirty clothes, he felt so bad that he gave her a dollar, along with them.

"A dollar!" she exclaimed. "That's way too much for doing that piddling little amount of clothes, even if I was gonna charge you anything to wash 'em. And I know for a fact, they don't pay deputy marshals that much money. Hell, Rena wouldn't charge you but twenty-five cents to throw your little bit in with her other wash."

"Yeah, but I need to have my stuff washed today. I can't wait for her to do the wash." He stuck the dollar in her hand. "Besides, I'd just like to do something nice for you."

"Bless your heart," she responded. "Well, then, I'll take the dollar and I'll thank you for being so thoughtful." She chuckled then and asked, "Are you sure you're mean enough to be a law officer?"

"Sometimes I wonder myself," he said, and gave her a smile. "I'd best get going." He walked out the door.

"I'll have it ready for you before suppertime," she called after him. He didn't turn around, but threw his hand up to acknowledge the message. *If I was ten or twelve years younger,* she thought, *I'd throw you down and smother you, right here in the hall.* "I reckon I'll have to settle for washing your underwear," she said when he was out of earshot.

"What did you say, Gracie?" Rena asked as she came out of the dining room.

"Oh, nothing," Gracie said. "I was just mumbling to myself."

"You better be careful with that stuff," Rena teased. "That's a sign of old age."

"I've already seen enough of those signs today," Gracie said.

Unaware of a spark he had rekindled in Gracie's memory, Colton picked up his expense money at the office, and with the money he already had, he bought the supplies he thought he might need for his trip the next day. After taking the supplies to the stable to put in his packs, he spent a good part of the rest of the day asking people if they knew the road to Lampasas. Then it occurred to him to go to the post office and they might know. They did, so he walked back to the boardinghouse, since it was almost time for supper, anyway. When he went to his room to leave his rifle and saddlebags, he found his clean laundry folded in a neat little stack in the middle of his bed.

"Well, I reckon I don't have any excuse for not takin' a bath now," he muttered.

After breakfast the next morning, he went to the stable to get his horses and rode out of town on the road to San Antonio. After about a mile, he turned onto a little cross trail he knew as the old Comanche Trail and headed west. It was the trail that would take him straight to the D&T Cattle Company, if he stayed on it long enough. On this trip, however, he would be turning onto another trail he had passed before without really noticing it. On the lookout for a narrow wagon track that forked off the Comanche Trail where one lone pine stood as a marker, Colton pulled Scrappy to a halt and dismounted when he spotted it. He walked over to the tree and found the rough sign fashioned with two boards lying on the ground, face down. He turned it over with the toe of his boot to read LAM-PASAS 30, with an arrow pointing the way. After propping the sign up against the tree, so it could be seen, he climbed back up into the saddle, intending to cut that thirty miles closer to twenty before camping for the night.

He came to a nice-sized creek after riding what he esti-mated to be a little short of ten miles. Seriously doubting he would find a better spot, he turned off the trail and rode up-stream, until satisfied his camp was far enough from the wagon road to be unnoticed. There were enough trees along the creek to provide firewood and hide a small campfire, so he unloaded his horses and let them go to water. He soon had his fire going and water heating in his coffeepot while he sliced some bacon to fry. Some hardtack and dried peaches and that was going to be supper. He planned on getting invited to supper tomorrow night for a meal cooked by Juanita Garcia at the D&T Cattle Company. He didn't figure to spend more than half a day in Lampasas, just long enough to let them know that the U.S. Marshal responded to their report of the bank robbery.

After a peaceful night, he was awake with the first light of day the next morning. He saddled Scrappy and loaded the packsaddle on the sorrel named Joe and got under way. It was only a little over twenty miles to Lampasas. The horses could make that without stopping, but he preferred to give them a rest before he reached Lampasas. So he would stop and make himself some breakfast before he reached town.

Colton tied his horses at the hitching rail in front of the sheriff's office and walked in the door to find a slender young man seated at the desk.

"Can I help you, sir?" the young man asked.

"Sheriff Denson?" Colton asked.

"No, sir, I'm Deputy Sheriff Millican. Sheriff Denson won't be in this morning, but I'll be glad to help you with whatever you might need from the law."

That was not good news to Colton. He paused a moment to think about it, then pulled his vest aside so Millican could see the badge on his shirt. "I'm Deputy U.S. Marshal Colton Gray. We got a letter from Sheriff Denson that said you had an attempted bank robbery by two outlaws dressed up as old men. Marshal Timmons sent me down here to question the two men you have in custody to see if they might be the original two old men." He shrugged, then asked, "When will Sheriff Denson be back?"

"The sheriff's out of town," Millican replied, "and he might not be back tonight." Colton thought the deputy looked like he didn't really want to tell him where the sheriff was. Then Millican said, "But you can still question the prisoners. Sheriff

Denson left me fully in charge while he's gone. I can give you all the details of the attempted holdup and the subsequent arrest." He released a short chuckle and claimed, "Heck, I'm the one who really wrote the letter and Sheriff Denson just okayed it. I can take you to talk to Malcolm Bennett at the bank, if you need to talk to him."

"Well, Deputy Millican, I think that's what we should do. Whaddaya say we get started?"

"Fine," Millican responded. "What do you want to do first?"

"What are the names of the prisoners?" Colton asked. "That wasn't in the letter."

"I'm sorry about that. I didn't even think of it, but Sheriff Denson wanted me to get it in the mail right away. They're two men we've arrested before for disorderly conduct, Coy Pope and Leroy Johnson. But they were wearing disguises and wearing old hats, and one of 'em was using a cane. Honestly, they were made up so good that I wasn't surprised that Mr. Bennett, the president of the bank, couldn't tell who they were." He hesitated when he heard what he had just said. "Of course, I doubt that Malcolm Bennett would have known those two, even without disguises."

Colton didn't say anything for a moment. Millican had just told him everything he needed to know to satisfy Timmons and everybody else with even half a brain that Coy Pope and Leroy Johnson were not the infamous old-men bandits.

"Deputy Millican, the reason I'm here is to see if your two prisoners could possibly be the two old men who have robbed banks all over the state and a cattle buyer's office in Fort Worth. And I doubt your prisoners are those two old men."

"To be honest with you, I seriously doubt it myself," Millican said.

"Let me talk to them to make double sure," Colton said. "Then I'd like to hear how the attempted robbery was performed in the bank and how you made the arrest."

"Right," Millican replied, and paused when he thought about it. "That's a more interesting story than the actual attempted robbery."

Colton went into the cell room and talked to the two prisoners. It was an interview that lasted only twenty minutes before he was satisfied that his doubts about them as his suspects were accurate. He explained to Millican that the fugitives he was seeking were actually two really old men, or younger men disguised so well that it was impossible to tell they were not who they appeared to be. Their usual approach was to pretend they were seeking the services of the bank, to deposit money, instead of gettin' any money from the bank. Millican listened with sincere interest and had to agree that Coy Pope and Leroy Johnson definitely did not fit that profile.

"So," Colton continued, "did you make the arrest? Your letter said they were apprehended by two local citizens."

"That's right," Millican answered. "I made the official arrest, but it was two of the bank's actual customers who took them under control for me."

"How'd they do that?" Colton asked. "Did they see 'em runnin' outta the bank with the money?"

"No, Mr. Doolin and Mr. Tubbs were in the bank and got suspicious of 'em, so they decided to wait outside to see if their suspicions were correct," Millican said. He then went on to describe the ambush Casey and Eli set up and the loosening of the robbers' saddle cinches, which caused him to chuckle again at the thought of it. "I heard the two shots fired in the bank, so I was already on my way up there. But when I got there, Coy and Leroy were flat on their backs, their saddles hangin' upside down, and Mr. Doolin and Mr. Tubbs were standin' over them with their revolvers aimed at them." He shook his head and chuckled again at the picture of the incident as it returned to his mind. "They even marched 'em to the jail with me." Thinking Colton wasn't getting the full unlikeliness of Eli and Casey's involvement, he emphasized,

"And these two gentlemen own the biggest cattle operation in the county, D and T Cattle Company."

"Yeah, I heard of 'em," Colton said.

"Mr. Bennett at the bank told Sheriff Denson he oughta give Mr. Doolin and Mr. Tubbs honorary deputy badges," Millican said.

"Maybe so," Colton remarked. *Casey and Eli would love that,* he thought. He wondered what Millican would think if he told him that Casey had saved his life when he shot Buck Garner in the Dead Dog Saloon. He decided not to tell the deputy sheriff about that incident. "I think I'll go to the bank now and see if I can have a word with Mr. Bennett. I'd like to let him know the marshal department is interested in protecting his bank. But I wanna tell you it's been a pleasure talking to you, Deputy Millican. I appreciate you takin' the time to give me all the information on the robbery."

"Happy to do it," Millican replied. "Sorry those two in there didn't turn out to be the big game you were huntin'." He walked outside with Colton. "You want me to go with you to see Mr. Bennett?" Colton thanked him, but said that wouldn't be necessary. So Millican pointed down the street and said, "Yonder's the bank right down there."

"Obliged," Colton said, and took Scrappy's reins and led his horses to the bank. He paused at the hitching rail while he tied the reins and looked at the front door of the bank and created a picture in his mind. He imagined Casey with his back flattened against the wall on one side of the door and Eli on the other side. He couldn't help but grin when he thought of how surprised the two robbers were when they fled the bank and jumped for the stirrup and the whole saddle turned upside down, landing them on the ground. He shook his head to clear it of the comical scene and walked into the bank.

There was only one customer at the two teller windows, so he stepped up to the one who was not busy. His name plate said MARCUS SMITH.

"Good morning," Marcus greeted him.

"Mornin'," Colton returned. He showed his badge and said, "I'm a deputy marshal out of the Western District Office in Waco and I'd like a word with Mr. Bennett, if he's available."

"Are you here about our attempted bank robbery?" Marcus asked. Colton said he was. "I'll go tell Mr. Bennett you're here," Marcus said, and went at once to Bennett's office. Colton followed, but stopped ten or twelve feet short of the door. In a few seconds, Marcus came back out the door and Bennett was right behind him.

"I'm Malcolm Bennett, Deputy," he said. "You need to talk to me?"

"Yes, sir, just briefly about your recent attempted holdup. My name's Colton Gray. I'm a deputy U.S. marshal out of Waco. I've been to the jail and talked to the deputy sheriff and the two suspects who attempted the holdup. I just wanted to check in with you in case you had anything to question or add to what I've learned from Deputy Millican."

"Did he tell you who actually captured the two robbers after they ran out of the bank with two sacks of money?" Bennett asked, a wide smile creasing his face.

"Yes, he did," Colton replied, "Casey Tubbs and Eli Doolin. They're partners in the D and T Cattle Company, not far from here, right?"

"That's right. They were leaving when the two bank robbers came in and they thought there was something fishy about those two men. So they waited for them outside the bank, just in case. They had just deposited a large amount of money with us and it was still in a sack on my desk. That money was what the robbers ran out with, that and some cash out of the teller cages. They would never have gotten away with that much money if they hadn't stormed into my office before I had time to put it in the safe. We were lucky nobody was shot. They fired a couple of shots in the ceiling when Marcus and James tried to block their exit. They didn't know what was waiting for them outside." He shook his head and chuckled again.

This was a totally new experience for Colton. Accustomed to the bitter wreckage left behind after a bank holdup with the shocked manager or angry president and the terrified employees and customers, and sometimes wounded or killed bystanders, this one seemed more like a comedy. There was no point in his staying in Lampasas any longer. Actually, there was no point in Timmons sending him over here in the first place. He knew before he got here that the two men who tried to rob the bank were not the real old-men bandits. But it had afforded him an excuse to visit the D&T Ranch again, since Casey and Eli had managed to get themselves involved. So he would take his leave now and head for the D&T.

"I won't take up any more of your time," he told Malcolm Bennett. "I think I've heard everything I need to know. Your two bank robbers will be held in the jail awaiting trial by a circuit court. I imagine you'll be called to testify. Thank you for your time and the information."

"You're welcome, Deputy Gray," Bennett responded. "Come back to see us anytime."

Chapter 4

As he walked out of the bank, he noticed the clock on the wall was just approaching noon. He acknowledged it with a low growl in the pit of his stomach. Good timing, he thought, he could find some dinner here in town and take his time going to the D&T. He didn't want to get there too early, because he wanted to be invited to supper and that was usually followed by an invitation to sleep in the bunkhouse, or maybe the main house. As for dinner right now, he didn't ask Millican or Bennett for a recommendation for a good place to eat. He was afraid he might have gotten an invitation to join one of them for dinner. So he would just take his chances. There was a hotel in town and he thought he remembered seeing a sign that said DINING ROOM over one of the outside doors. Hotel dining rooms were usually a fairly safe bet, so that's where he went.

It wasn't a bad decision. The food wasn't great, but it was good and the servings were ample. And the most conversation he had to put up with was one word from a seemingly bored waiter who came around once in a while with the coffeepot and asked, "More?" After dinner, he started out for the D&T at a leisurely pace. The trail he followed held close to the river and when he was about halfway there, he came to an especially pleasant little clearing where a sizable creek joined the river. He decided to stop there and let his horses rest and graze in the grassy clearing. Still feeling full from the heavy meal he had eaten at the hotel dining room, he sat down with his back against a tree to watch his horses graze. As he sat there, he realized what a fine lazy afternoon this day had become, and since he was purposely killing time, he let himself relax. Before long, he could feel his full stomach pulling down on his eyelids, so he didn't fight it.

He didn't know how long he had been asleep, but he would have slept longer if Scrappy hadn't decided it was time they moved on. The big bay gelding woke him with his muzzle nudging his chest. "You tryin' to tell me you're ready to go, boy?" Colton said as he scratched the bay's ears. "All right, I reckon I did get a little bit lazy, but I sure had a fine nap." He had even been dreaming. He didn't remember what the dream was about, but he did remember that Casey and Eli were both in it. "I swear, Scrappy, I hope to hell I ain't gonna be dreamin' about those two outlaws. It's bad enough worryin' about 'em when I'm awake. I wish Timmons had dumped this damn job on somebody else."

Being honest with himself, he had to admit that he did not want to find that conclusive evidence that would tie those bank robberies to Casey and Eli. He had to confess that he liked the two ol' cowhands, and to make matters worse, he owed Casey for his life. But he really believed he was eventually going to find evidence to convict them, if he kept searching. And he was going to keep searching, because that was his job as a deputy marshal.

"Colton Gray, Deputy U.S. Marshal!" Eli Doolin sang out when Colton rode into the barnyard. "Everybody who's on a wanted paper better run for cover." He walked out of the barn to greet Colton. "What brings you out to this part of the country, young feller?"

"My boss sent me out here where the real outlaws are," Colton replied in spirit with Eli's japing. "He said I could arrest the first person I run into 'cause they're all guilty of something." He stepped down from the saddle as Davy Springer and "Smiley" George walked out of the barn after Eli. They both said howdy to Colton. He returned their greetings, then said, "I had to ride out to Lampasas and I couldn't go back to Waco without stoppin' by to say hello to the D and T cowhands."

"What did you have to go to Lampasas for?" Davy asked.

Surprised he had to ask, Colton said, "Why, to investigate that attempted bank robbery they had over there a week or so ago." None of the three responded, and both Davy and Smiley wore questioning expressions.

"Somebody held up the bank in Lampasas?" Smiley asked.

"Somebody tried to," Colton answered, "but they didn't get away with it." He was still met with blank expressions.

"Well, I reckon that's a good thing they didn't get away with any—" Smiley started, but was interrupted by Colton.

"Wait a minute!" Colton exclaimed. "Are you tellin' me you don't know anything about a bank holdup in Lampasas?"

Smiley and Davy looked at each other, obviously clueless. Colton then looked directly at Eli, who met his gaze with a sheepish expression and shrugged his shoulders. It was hard for Colton to believe that Casey and Eli had made no mention of their takedown of the two bank robbers. As unlikely as that seemed, there must have been a reason not to tell the crew about the incident. So he decided not to inform the crew, at least until he talked to Eli and Casey in private about it.

"I thought you'd hear about that holdup, since it was attempted by two men who dressed up in disguises like the two old men who have been robbin' banks and gettin' away with it. They were apprehended right outside the bank, so if you've put any money in the bank in Lampasas, it's still there," Colton explained. He saw an immediate sigh of relief on Eli's face and decided he was going to get to the bottom of this.

"Well, we're glad you rode over to see us, since you were that close," Eli said. "You might as well stay here tonight. I'll tell Juanita that you'll be havin' supper with us. Casey will be tickled to see you stopped by. He oughta be back anytime now. He went out with Monroe and the boys to move part of the herd to some new grazin' closer to the river."

"'Preciate the hospitality," Colton said. "I was hopin' I'd get an invite to try some more of Juanita's cookin'. Not that I've got any complaints about your cookin', Smiley. I recall that last time I stayed in the bunkhouse, your cookin' was pretty doggone good."

Smiley laughed and said, "I ain't no competition for Juanita's cookin'."

"Come on," Eli said. "Davy and I'll help you take care of your horses. You can leave your packs and saddle right in that first stall. We'll let you sleep in the main house with us, since we ain't got anybody in the guest room, even if you are a lawman." He waited for the chuckle, then continued. "Juanita will be glad to see you again. She thinks you're a fine young man. I told her she didn't know you like me and Casey do."

Colton laughed and said, "Well, I've always thought Juanita was a fine judge of character."

They got Colton's horses and packs taken care of and were just coming out of the barn again when Casey Tubbs and Monroe Kelly rode into the barnyard. "Colton Gray." The words fell out of Casey's mouth as soon as he saw him, not ready for the surprise.

Eli quickly stepped up and said, "Look who stopped in to visit. He said the bank over in Lampasas had an attempted robbery, but they caught the robbers and put 'em in jail."

"Is that a fact?" Casey recovered at once. "Well, we're always glad to see ya, Colton. You're stayin' for supper, ain'tcha?"

"Yep, I sure am," Colton said. "Eli already invited me and all we need is Juanita's okay. And then there are a couple of things I'd like to talk to you about."

"Let's get on up to the house then," Casey said. "It ain't that long before supper and we need to make sure Juanita has enough for an extra plate." When they walked in the kitchen door, they found that Juanita was already working on extra food. Her husband, Miguel, saw Colton when he first rode up to the barn, so Juanita started making preparations for extra food at that time.

"Supper be ready in twenty minutes," Juanita said. "You want to eat in dining room?"

"Nah," Casey said. "No need to go to that extra trouble. Colton's like family, he can eat in the kitchen like we always do. Ain't that right, Colton?"

"That's right, Juanita," Colton responded. "To get one of your meals, I'd eat it on the back steps if you wanted me to."

Juanita blushed prettily and Miguel said, "Wife gonna be hard to live with now." And everybody laughed.

"Twenty minutes," Casey said, "that'll give us time to have a little shooter before we eat. Holler when supper's ready, Juanita." He led the way to the study, which served as their office. "We don't keep but two choices here, Colton. Maybe you remember, corn or rye." Eli didn't wait and poured himself a shot of rye. Casey poured one corn and waited for Colton to nod before he poured another. "Here's to everything workin' out the way it's supposed to," he said, and then they tossed the whiskey back. That done, Casey stated, "You said you needed to talk to us about something."

"Nothing serious," Colton said. "Let me just start by saying this ain't strictly a social call on my part. I was sent down here to investigate that attempted holdup at the bank in Lampasas. We got a letter from the sheriff about the holdup and in it they wrote about the capture of the two bandits by you and Eli. So

Marshal Timmons told me to check with you two while I was down here and get your version of the story. It's as simple as that. Now, I've already got a pretty good picture of the capture of the two robbers—Mr. Leroy Johnson and Mr. Coy Pope, for your information—from Deputy Millican and Malcolm Bennett. And I have to say I wish I coulda been there to see it. The only question I have is why are you tryin' to hide it? Nobody here at the ranch knows what you did, do they? I picked up on that talking to Smiley and Davy. I'll be careful not to mention it, if you don't want your men to know what a couple of hell-raisers you are," he joked.

Casey looked at Eli and shrugged before he answered. "You know, I don't reckon there's any real reason. We talked about it on the ride back from Lampasas. You see, it ain't been that long since me and Eli was just a couple of the crew workin' Whitmore's cows. Since we were lucky enough to build this ranch back up again, one of the biggest jobs we've had is gettin' the men to get used to us as the owners. And coming home after that little to-do in Lampasas, we thought that sounded like some of the nonsense we mighta got mixed up in back when we was just thirty-dollar-a-month cowpokes. So we just decided not to say anything about catchin' those two drifters when they wasn't lookin. That ain't the kinda thing the owners of a ranch like ours would do."

Colton considered what Casey said, and while he thought the incident at the bank would have only provided some entertainment and probably admiration for their bosses, he supposed it was a legitimate excuse. Whatever their reasons, they were their own.

"Just tell me what happened," Colton said, "so I can see if it's the same as the deputy sheriff and the president of the bank said. I expect you know you'll be summoned to testify when they hold the trial for those two."

"Dang!" Eli exclaimed. "I hadn't thought about that. We coulda just as well told 'em the night we came back."

Casey shrugged. "Yeah, I reckon the word will get out about that."

"Why don't you go ahead and tell me how it happened," Colton said. "What made you think they weren't the real old men?"

"'Cause you could see they was wearin' disguises," Eli replied. "They weren't really old men a-tall."

"You think the 'real old men' are, in fact, old men and not two younger fellows wearin' disguises?" Colton asked, watching Eli's expression closely for any signs of discomfort.

Eli shrugged. "That's what I've heard, but that don't mean it's so. Hell, them two birds we caught mighta been the big deal, for all I know. The fact of the matter is, those two were tryin' to run off with our money, just like Malcolm Bennett musta told you. All we knew at the time was two fellers came into the bank wearin' disguises. And we couldn't think of no good reason for somebody to put on a disguise to go to the bank, and move our horses to get theirs closer to the door. That's why Casey and me decided to wait to see if they were up to something 'cause we had just come outta Bennett's office after leavin' him a sizable deposit. And it's a good thing we waited. We couldn't afford to lose that money and we couldn't take a chance on waitin' for the sheriff to catch them. We figured whether those two are the old-men bandits or not is your problem. We don't care how many banks they rob, as long as they don't come after our money again."

Colton couldn't suppress a chuckle. "I swear, Eli, that's the longest speech I've ever heard come outta you." He looked at Casey and asked, "You got anything to add to that, or do you think he covered it all?"

Casey chuckled, too. "I think he covered it all."

Colton had a pretty complete picture of the circumstances inside the bank that led up to Casey and Eli's decision to take matters into their own hands. The one factor they didn't mention that he felt played a prominent part in fueling their takedown of the two robbers was their anger at them for trying to cash in on their creation. He could imagine their desire to punish Coy and Leroy. Colton was surprised that the two were not shot on the scene. He gave one firm nod of his head and said with a grin, "Good. Now tell me about how you fixed their saddles up and landed 'em on their backs under their horses' bellies."

Before Casey could answer, Juanita came to the door and told them supper was ready. "I'll tell you about the ambush while we're eatin'," Casey said.

They went back in the kitchen and sat down at the table, and as he had said, Casey started telling Colton about loosening the cinches on the two robbers' saddles, then waiting on each side of the front door of the bank with their backs pressed flat against the wall.

"We was worried that they might see us," Eli said.

"And we heard two shots fired inside the bank," Casey said, "so we didn't know if they were gonna come out shootin' or not."

"We didn't have no time to think about it, anyway," Eli commented, "'cause they come bustin' through the door right after we heard the shots. They didn't look right or left. All they was thinkin' about was jumpin' on their horses and headin' outta town."

Meanwhile, during this running account of the incident, Juanita, stone-faced as usual, went about filling their coffee cups, passing the bowls around, and spooning out servings. And Miguel, seated at the far end of the table, kept his face buried in his plate. Colton couldn't help wondering why Eli and Casey saw fit to discuss the issue in front of Miguel and Juanita if they had chosen not to tell the men about it. When Juanita went to take some empty bowls to the sink on the porch, he mentioned his surprise that they talked so freely in front of her and Miguel.

"Oh, they don't pay no attention to what you're talkin' about, unless you call 'em by name and say something directly to 'em," Casey told him. "It's about the same as havin' a couple of dogs in the house." He quickly added, "I don't mean no disrespect. I just mean they don't pay no attention to what you're sayin'. And even if they did, they don't ever talk to the hands workin' the ranch."

"If you say so," Colton said. "But I figure Juanita is one sharp lady. I'd bet she hears every word. She just doesn't care what you're talking about." She came from the stove with fresh coffee at that moment. Her lips tightened into a tiny smile and she winked at him as she filled his cup.

"Maybe you're right," Casey said. "But even if you are, she probably wouldn't tell any of the men what we talk about, anyway. You shoulda seen the look on those two drifters' faces when they grabbed them saddle horns and jumped in the stirrup, and that saddle just turned upside down. Flat on their backs, while they were tryin' to figure out what happened, me and Eli was standin' over 'em, guns cocked and ready to blow 'em to hell. Right, Eli?"

"It'da served 'em right if we had," Eli answered.

Now, there's an honest reaction, Colton thought, still betting that the two bandits were bitterly angered by the sudden crop of copycats springing up all over the territory. They finished supper and Casey suggested that they should take a drink of likker and smoke a cigar out on the front porch, seeing as how the evening was so pleasant. Colton thanked Juanita for the fine supper on such short notice and she rewarded him with a sweet smile and told him she expected to cook his breakfast in the morning.

They passed a pleasant evening on the porch, an evening that could have been awkward for all three men, since Colton was still convinced he was in the company of the notorious old-men bandits. And Casey and Eli were well aware of his suspicions. Had they known how reluctant he was to find ir-refutable evidence of their guilt, they might have felt more at ease. The basic fact of the situation was they had become friends while being on opposite sides of a line drawn in the sands of law and order. As far as the bluffing game of chance the two bandits played with the young lawman, Casey knew that he drew a wild card when he saved Colton's life when he shot Buck Garner moments before Buck intended to shoot Colton.

Juanita prepared a big breakfast the next morning and the men took the time to enjoy it. Colton thanked them all for their hospitality and Juanita for the supper and breakfast. Casey and Eli walked down to the barn with Colton while he saddled his horses. Some of the men who had not yet ridden out to their assigned jobs gathered around Colton to say howdy. Colton looked at Casey, grinned, and asked, "You gonna tell 'em?"

"Nah, hell, they're late gettin' out to their work already," Casey answered. "Maybe we'll tell 'em tonight, if they put in a good day's work."

"Tell us what?" Sam Dunn asked.

"Nothin'," Eli answered him, "if you don't get the work done."

"What's he talkin' about, Colton?" Sam asked.

"He'll have to tell you that," Colton japed. "You'd be sur-prised what your bosses have to do to keep this ranch run-nin'." He climbed up on Scrappy and thanked them again for their hospitality, then turned the bay toward the front gate and the old Comanche Trail. Just as he reached the gate, he met another rider coming in. It was no one he had ever seen be-fore, so he just nodded and said, "Mornin'." The stranger re-turned the greeting and Colton nudged Scrappy into a trot.

Back at the barn, Davy Springer asked, "Who's that comin'

in?" He was still watching Colton as he rode away and saw the rider Colton just passed.

Everybody turned to look and Monroe Kelly said, "Looks like Gary Corbett."

"It is Gary," Smiley George said. He had known him longer than anyone on the D&T. But they all recognized him right away, since they had seen him at that distance many times before on the recent cattle drive to Dodge City when he was the trail boss. "Wonder what he's doin' here?" He turned toward Casey as if he might know.

"Beats me," Casey said. "I ain't got no idea. Maybe he's comin' to visit you. He mighta got to missin' you." He joked because Smiley used to be Gary's chuck wagon cook before he went under when the cattle market sank. But Corbett was trying to get his cattle business started again since the market had recovered. Casey hoped he wasn't coming to try to get Smiley to go back to work for him. He glanced over at Eli, and when he met his eye, he figured Eli might be thinking the same thing. And neither he nor Eli knew of another cook to replace Smiley.

All the men still there at the barn waited for Corbett to ride in, since they had all gotten to know him on the cattle drive. So he got a cordial greeting when he rode into the barnyard. "Good mornin', men," he returned. "Ain't nobody workin' today?"

"We were just leavin'," Monroe Kelly answered him. "We were just waitin' to see if you'd got lost."

"It wouldn't be the first time," Corbett japed in return.

They all said howdy as Corbett stepped down; then Monroe, acting in his position as foreman, said, "All right, boys, let's get to work." They went to their horses and in a few minutes were gone, leaving only Smiley and Davy at the barn with Corbett and the owners.

"Davy, take care of Gary's horse," Eli said. Then he asked, "What brings you over this way, Gary?"

"I just thought I'd come talk to you and Casey about something," Corbett answered.

Both Eli and Casey recognized the tone in his voice. They had heard it a few times before, so Casey said, "Well, let's go on up to the house. Me and Eli was just fixin' to have one more cup of coffee after we walked down here to see Colton Gray off. He's a deputy marshal we've gotten to know. That was him you passed goin' out the gate—"

"I can put a pot of coffee on real quick, if you want it," Smiley interrupted.

"Thank you just the same, Smiley," Casey said, "but Juanita's probably made a new pot and she gets a little testy if you make her waste coffee."

"I'll talk to you later, Smiley," Corbett said, and followed Casey and Eli up to the house. They went in the back door, and when they walked through the kitchen, Juanita asked if she should make a pot of coffee. "Yes, ma'am," Casey said, "if you don't mind."

They went on through to the office. When they sat down in the office, Casey asked, "How are things goin' at your ranch, now that you're startin' up again?"

"Good and bad," Gary answered. "I'm sure you and Eli have already guessed why I came to see you. Let me start out by sayin' the money you boys paid me to trail boss that herd made a helluva difference and it gave us a good start. But we found out we need a lot more to get where we need to be by brandin' time. I've gotta hire more men, if I'm gonna have a chance to build a herd to drive to market this year. I know where I can get some good men, but we haven't got the money to pay 'em. And that's just the men. Never mind everything else we need to buy. Well, I went to the bank, but they won't loan me a dime. You know my brother, Jack, came to help me out while I was drivin' your cattle to Dodge. He decided to stay and together we were gonna build my ranch back up. We were plannin' to use the money Jack got for his farm in Anderson County to cover the payroll and supplies we needed. But the bank wants to foreclose on my land if I don't pay off my mortgage by the first of next month. They won't wait till after we sell the cattle. They want the land. That's what they want." He dropped his head and shook it slowly back and forth, his pride suffering sorely. "I wouldn't have come to you with this problem, but I knew you've helped other damn fools down on their luck. I've been to two other banks, but they're all the same."

"How much do you need to pay your land off?" Casey asked.

"I owe them two thousand dollars," Corbett said. "I bought it for eight thousand and I had it paid down to two. With the herd we've built so far, we could pay that off, but they won't wait for it. They say the market could go broke like it did before."

They were interrupted then when Juanita came to the door and announced that the coffee was ready and asked if they wanted it in there. "Yes, please, Juanita," Casey answered. When she went to fetch it, he asked Corbett, "Will two thousand dollars take care of what you need, if that just pays off the loan?"

"From what I've figured, two thousand oughta get us by," Corbett said.

They paused the discussion when Juanita returned with a large tray holding cups and the coffeepot. Accustomed to Casey and Eli's preference for black coffee, she asked Corbett if he wanted sugar for his and he said no, so she poured it and took the pot back to the stove. As soon as she left, Corbett said, "I know you boys ain't in the money-loanin' business, but if you saw fit to loan me the money, I'd expect to pay you some interest, higher than what the bank would charge, I reckon."

"You're right," Casey said, "we ain't in the money-loanin' business, but we'll try to help a friend whenever we can." He glanced briefly at Eli, who responded with the slightest hint of a nod, so he continued. "We ain't forgot you took that herd of cattle to Dodge for us when me and Eli had to go on ahead of the herd—"

Corbett interrupted to remind him, "Yeah, but you paid me damn well for the job."

"We paid you what it was worth to us," Casey said, "and you did a good job. But like I said, we ain't in the money-loanin' business, so there won't be interest charges. We don't know how to figure that stuff, anyway. Two thousand is what you say you need, but that just pays off the loan. I expect five thousand would be closer to takin' care of what costs you've got comin' up. Am I right?"

"Well, yeah, you're right, but I have to think about payin' you back," Corbett said. "How long would I have to pay you back?"

"We won't worry about that until you get yourself in the shape you wanna be in. Then you tell us when you'll pay us back. How would that work for you?"

Corbett had to pause to take a serious look at each one of them. It suddenly struck him that they might be having him on. Moments before on the edge of his chair, he sat back now and exhaled his frustration. "You fellows are messin' with me, ain't you? I shouldn'ta come beggin' for a loan. I don't know what I was thinking." He got up from the chair.

"Whoa!" Eli exclaimed. "You ain't gonna leave without your money, are you?" It was enough to make Corbett pause. "You ain't even drank your coffee."

"You came at the right time," Casey told him. "We totaled up the money we had left from the cattle sale after the expenses were paid. It came to a nice little total of five thousand dollars and we were fixin' to take it to the bank tomorrow. I think we druther loan it to you and know you put it to good use. Right, Eli?"

"You bet," Eli said. "I'll go get it out of the safe." He went out the door on his way to his bedroom, where they kept a safe with considerably more than five thousand in it. Drained emotionally, Corbett sank back down on the chair.

"Which bank is holdin' your title?" Casey asked while Eli was gone.

"Citizens Bank of Mexia," Corbett said.

"*Mexia?*" Casey reacted. "You picked one a long way from home."

"It sure is," Corbett reacted immediately, "and I'll be ridin' over there tomorrow." He hesitated before saying, "If you're really gonna loan me that money. But it wasn't a matter of pickin' one so far away. It was the fact that they were the only bank that would give me the loan I needed and they charged more interest than any of the other banks. But I wasn't left with much choice. They had me over a barrel."

Eli returned then with a sack filled with the neat stacks of paper money. He dumped it out on the desk to be counted. Corbett was almost beside himself with the excitement of getting that sum of money. They counted the money and verified that if was, indeed, the right amount. Then they put it back in the sack and tied it with a string and Casey handed it to Corbett, who was still at a loss for words. It had happened so suddenly and so unexpectedly that he wasn't prepared for it.

"I swear," he finally managed, "I don't know what to say. I was desperate when I rode in here. I'll pay you back just as soon as I can. Don't you want me to sign some papers or something?"

"A handshake will do," Casey told him. "You just be sure you get that title to your land back in your hand. From what you tell me about that bank, I wouldn't trust 'em for a minute. You know that town has two banks and I ain't ever heard nothin' bad about the other one."

"I tried the other one," Corbett said. "They didn't give me the time of day. Don't you worry, though, I won't give Citizens Bank a cent till I get my deed and my loan papers in my hand. I think my horse has had enough rest now, so I'm gonna get on the trail back home. I can't wait to tell Jack that thanks to the D and T, we're still in business."

"I expect you'll maybe have a little visit with Smiley before you ride out, seein' as how he worked for you before he came here," Casey said. "Eli and I would appreciate it if you'd tell him that sack you're totin' is a bunch of books we loaned you on how to run a ranch profitably."

"I understand," Corbett said. "I 'preciate the books."

Casey and Eli stood on the porch and watched him walk toward the barn. "I think maybe Oscar and Elmer might like to meet the folks down at the Citizens Bank of Mexia," Casey said. "Whaddaya think?"

"It sounds like the kinda bank they like to visit," Eli said.

Chapter 5

They had not really planned to bring Elmer and Oscar out of retirement so soon after the recent rash of copycat bank robbers. But after their decision to put thirty-five thousand dollars of their money in the bank in Lampasas, and then the five thousand they generously donated to Gary Corbett, their supply of cash on hand was less than they had become comfortable with. Thinking it always best to have the cash on hand, they decided it was time to make another withdrawal. It had been their policy since the beginning to strike only those banks that showed no love for the down-and-out cattle rancher. Citizens Bank had certainly earned that reputation. And for that reason, Eli and Casey could imagine how desperate Corbett must have been to even approach Moss Blanchard, the president of the bank. It was even more of a mystery to them that Blanchard had agreed to loan him the money. The only reason that made any sense was the probability that Blanchard had an interest in acquiring some of the land west of Waco. There was already some talk about the railroad's future interest in opening up that part of Texas. Whatever the reason, Casey and Eli were certain of one thing, Citizens Bank of Mexia was no friend of the cattleman.

So the planning began when the original and genuine old-men bandits would ride again. They were not total strangers to the town of Mexia, having staged a train robbery there over a year before. The bank holdup would have to be done by Elmer and Oscar, with no help of any kind from Casey and Eli, as was the case in the railroad robbery. Casey and Eli had made too many acquaintances in the little town when they were scouting the train job. After this job on the bank, it would be the same as a confession of guilt if the lawman investigating the robbery was told that Eli and Casey were in town anytime close to the same day. This was especially true if that investigating officer was Colton Gray, and chances were that he would be sent to look into it.

"That means no supper at Bertha's and no after-supper drink at Henry's," Casey said, recalling the husband-and-wife businesses right next door to each other.

Mexia was fully one hundred and thirty-five miles from the D&T Ranch, so they were going to have to tell the crew, as well as Juanita and Miguel, that they were going to have to go to Waco for a meeting with their financial backers. As usually was the case, these meetings sometimes lasted for a couple of days. But they were important to ensure the financial backing of the ranch. As far as the job they were actually going to do, they spent quite a bit of time discussing how it should be attempted. Now, since there had been a rash of copycat holdup attempts, there was the definite possibility that the banks might be more suspicious of two bumbling old men who wanted to see the safe. Their old routines that worked before might be suspect now. They needed something new, but what?

Maybe it was time to abandon the two old men, since so many amateurs were trying to cash in on their creation. But the trouble with that was they had become so expert at creating their disguises—and they didn't know anything else to try. And they were not ready to tie a bandana on and go in with guns blazing, then flee the scene with everyone in town shooting at them. They felt more confident and actually safer in their disguises as Elmer and Oscar, and they spent the rest of that day trying to come up with a new idea. By suppertime that night, they were still at an impasse. Later that evening in the study, Casey came up with a new idea. They decided there were some changes needed in their disguises, however, and they were going to have to rehearse their approach, but it might work.

"Hell, I figure we've got a fifty-fifty chance of makin' it work. But if we don't, we'll go out in a blaze of glory," Casey predicted.

"Fifty-fifty," Eli repeated. "That might be a little high, but what the hell?"

They started working on the changes necessary for their costumes right after breakfast the next morning. Juanita wondered what they were working on in the bedroom with the door closed and they told her they were working on some important papers that had to do with the ownership of the ranch. It took quite a few trials before they figured out a way to make Casey look like a humpback. With the summer coming on, it no longer made sense to wear the heavy shirts under the oversized dusters. So Casey wore nothing but his undershirt under the duster. And for his deformity, they used a denim laundry bag, stuffed with towels, underwear, and socks. They tied it in place on his left shoulder with the drawstrings around his neck. With the duster over it, they decided it passed for a humpback, if you didn't look too closely.

"It'll have to do," Eli said. "I can't think of anything else to try."

The only alteration to Eli's costume was some towels stuffed into his trousers to give him a little more belly. Casey looked at him and shook his head. "How come I get to be the humpback? If this damn sack slips off my shoulder, we might as well shoot each other." He got serious then. "I reckon this is what we're goin' with. If you think we're crazy to try it, just tell me now and we'll say to hell with it."

"We've come this far with Elmer and Oscar," Eli told him. "We might as well try a different way to rob a bank. I think people see what you tell 'em they're seein'. So I'm all in."

"All right, then, we'll pack all this stuff up and head back east in the mornin'," Casey said. The rest of the day was spent overseeing the operation of the ranch. They informed Monroe Kelly, their foreman, that they were going to be gone for about a week, maybe a little longer, for some important meetings in Waco. By this time, Monroe was accustomed to the occasional meetings his bosses traveled to, so he was no longer curious about them. The only person who found the meetings strange was Juanita. Casey and Eli always took extra clothes with them to wear when they attended these meetings, but she never actually saw what extra clothes they took. She always offered to help them pack, but they always said it wasn't necessary. She found it odd that they never gave her any clothes to wash when they returned from their meetings. Consequently, she had her suspicions about their meetings, which she didn't even confide to Miguel. She figured it was their business, and if they wanted her to know, they would tell her. She told Miguel the same thing when he asked if she knew what they packed in their bags.

They left the D&T headquarters the following morning, planning to make the ride to Mexia in three and a half days and hit the bank the morning after that. They had decided to push the horses hard on the trip to Mexia, with no comfort stops in Waco, as was their usual custom when going through that town. Depending upon the success of their trip, they would stay overnight at the McClellan House Hotel and have supper in the hotel dining room in celebration. Possibly Eli would celebrate further with Frances afterward, if she would be inclined to negotiate a cheaper price for her favors. On their previous engagement, Eli had generously given her a hundred dollars, a decision made in a moment of drunken exuberance. It was when they first got back to Texas after their introduction to a life of crime. Casey had said he was a damn fool, but Eli insisted it was the best one hundred dollars he had ever spent. This time, passing by Waco, they camped beside the Brazos River at noontime to rest the horses. They pushed their tired horses another twenty miles before stopping for the night at a creek that looked to be a popular camping spot, judging by the many remains of old campfires. It offered good grass and water, so they added their ashes to the others.

At first light the next day, they were on their way again, their destination the little creek a mile or so short of the town of Mexia. It was the creek where they had left their pack-horses while they rode into town to hold up the train. And it was the place where they changed out of their disguises after the holdup. They were not sure they would recognize the little creek when they struck it, because trees and bushes had been given lots of time to grow. They were both certain that it was the same creek when they did come to it, however. They rode their horses down the middle of the creek about a hundred and fifty yards from the road before they came to the small clearing where they had made their camp before. They rode up out of the water then, dismounted, and started searching for any signs of recent camps. Ordinarily, when making camp, they would have ridden upstream from the road, but when they made this camp, they went downstream, thinking other campers would think upstream best.

"Nobody's been here since we were here," Eli said. He remembered about where they had built their fire and found some weeds growing up through the ashes.

"I reckon we couldn't ask for better than that," Casey said.

"Let's unload the packhorses and get started with the disguises."

"We might as well tie the ropes to the same two trees we used before, so they can get to the creek for water," Eli said.

They changed into their old baggy trousers and tucked the legs into their boots. Then they stuffed wads of the rags and towels in the legs to give them a lumpy look. Eli had to get Casey's hump bag situated on his left shoulder, then stuff the bag until satisfied with the size of his deformity. When they were confident that Casey really looked like a humpback, they each went to work transforming their faces into those of two old men with the application of the dark salve. Next came the whiskers and the mustaches, and finally, the gray wigs, adjusted and tested, until they were satisfied they were looking at Elmer and Oscar.

"You ready, Oscar?"

"I'm ready, Elmer," Eli answered.

The night before, they had tried practicing what they were going to say, just as if acting in a play. But they gave up on it because they were afraid they couldn't remember their lines. So they decided they had a better chance if they just said whatever came naturally.

With hopes that no one stumbled across their camp before they returned, they rode back up the creek, cautiously approaching the road to make sure there was no one in sight. Then they turned back on the road toward town. The thought occurred to Casey that they were leaving tracks of four horses approaching the creek, but only two horses coming out of it. *I hope no eagle-eyed outlaw don't come along and notice that*, he thought.

"Where the hell is this bank?" Eli asked as they came to the first buildings of the town.

"Beats me," Casey said. "When we were here before, I didn't even notice if they had a bank or not. I wasn't thinkin' about anything but the railroad track."

"Yonder it is!" Eli exclaimed. "Right on this end of town, Citizens Bank of Mexia."

"That's good," Casey said. "We won't have to ride down the whole length of the main street when we leave." There was a hitching rail in front of the bank, but they decided to tie the horses up at the rail in front of the doctor's office next door. This was in case they suffered an accident with their costumes while trying to mount or dismount. On the ground, after no dislodging of any of their stuffing, they proceeded to walk the short distance to the bank.

According to the clock on the wall over the teller cages, it was eleven o'clock when they walked inside. Like many banks of that size, it had two tellers. Only one of them, Adam Rich, had a customer, but he cashed the customer's check and wished him a good day. Fred Fancher, the other teller, had been watching the two old gentlemen who just came in. "Hey, Adam," he whispered when Adam's customer walked away. "You can have the next two customers."

Adam looked toward the door then. "You're always more popular with the old geezers and I think I've gotta go to the outhouse, anyway."

"Yeah, but you're much better working with humpbacks," Fred insisted, lowering his voice even more, since the two old men started walking toward them. "Too bad, Adam, they picked you."

"Good morning, gentlemen," Adam greeted them. "How can I help you?"

"See there, Oscar," Casey said, using his best impression of an old coot's voice, "he called us 'gentlemen.' He must be talkin' 'bout me 'cause if he knew what a bounder you are, he mighta just throwed us out the door."

"The hell you say," Eli came back. "My money's as good as anybody's."

Trying to hide his impatience, although not very well, Adam asked, "Is there something I can do for you?"

"Yeah, sonny," Eli replied. "I got some money I wanna put in this here bank. Can you handle that for me?"

"You want to open an account?" Adam asked.

"Ain't that what I just said?"

"You want to open an account," Adam repeated. "How much do you want to open it with?"

"All of it," Eli answered.

"The bank manager, Mr. Blanchard, will have to do that," Adam said. "I'll go tell him you want to open an account."

"You do that, sonny, before I change my mind," Eli said.

"You stay here, Adam," Fred spoke up, having just been struck with a worrisome thought. "I'll go get Mr. Blanchard." He left his cage and hurried across the lobby to Moss Blanchard's office. The door was closed, but he didn't bother to knock and rushed right inside.

Caught having a jelly biscuit with a cup of coffee, Blanchard almost spilled the coffee. "Damn it, Fancher, knock when that door's closed! What do you want?"

"I'm sorry, sir, but I got a feeling that we've got that trouble you were telling us about yesterday."

"What are you talking about, Fancher? What trouble?" Blanchard insisted.

"Those old-men bandits who have hit some other banks in Texas. I might be wrong, but I swear we've got two old coots out there right now who sure fit the description of the two you were telling us about."

That got Blanchard's attention right away. "Why do you think that? What did they say they wanted?"

"They say they want to open an account. At least one of them wants to. When Adam asked how much he wanted to open it with, the old buzzard wouldn't show him any money. And he got right cross about it, so Adam told him you'd have to open an account. And I said I'd go tell you, but what I really wanted to do was warn you."

"Well, you did the right thing," Blanchard said, fully as worried as Fred was now. He got up from the desk and went to the door, opened it a crack, just far enough to let him peek at the teller cages. "Damn!" He swore after watching the two old men at Adam Rich's cage. "They sure as hell look like that pair I've had described to me. I haven't heard anything about one of 'em being a humpback, though." He continued watching them while he tried to decide what he should do. "Two decrepit-looking old geezers," he finally decided, "I'll just be damned if I'm gonna let them walk out of my bank with any of the bank's money. We'll find out if they're up to anything or not right away." He closed the door again and went directly to a closet, where he kept a double-barrel shotgun. He checked the gun to make sure it was loaded. Then he sat back down at his desk and laid the shotgun on the desk close to his hand. "All right, now go back and bring the two gentlemen to see me and we'll show 'em right away that this bank ain't no easy target."

"You want me to tell Adam to go get the sheriff while they're in here talking to you?" Fred asked.

Blanchard hesitated a moment to consider it. "No," he said, "just in case we're jumping to the wrong conclusion. We ought to be able to handle two old buzzards like them, anyway. Bring 'em on in here." He opened a desk drawer and placed his jelly biscuit inside and waited. In about half a minute, he heard them approaching, so he stood up behind his desk to greet them. "Come in, gentlemen," he said when Fred led them into the office.

Both old men balked when they saw the shotgun lying on the desk at Blanchard's right hand.

"Whoa!" Casey blurted. "What's goin' on here? What you fixin' to do with that shotgun? Ain't this a regular bank?" He looked at Eli and said, "I don't know, Oscar, there's something funny goin' on here. I'm takin' my money somewhere else."

Realizing he had let his imagination get the best of him and blaming Fred for starting it, Blanchard quickly tried to explain. "My apologies, gentlemen. I should have removed that shotgun from my desk before you walked in. The reason I have it there is because of a recent rash of attempted bank robberies by two old men, or robbers dressed up like old men. And when Fred saw you two elderly gentlemen, he just let his imagination run away with him. I hope you won't hold that against us for just being careful. I'm sorry we insulted you."

"You thought we was them bank robbers?" Casey replied. He looked at Eli and repeated it. "They thought we was bank robbers, Oscar." He chuckled delightedly, then looked back at Blanchard and said, "I ain't insulted. Makes me feel kinda proud somebody thinks me and Oscar ain't just waitin' for the undertaker." Back to Eli again, he said, "Fine pair of bank robbers we are. We ain't even wearin' a gun." He opened his duster and pulled it open far enough to expose his waistline and the absence of a gun belt.

Chuckling with him, Eli opened his duster and revealed his absence of a gun belt, but not high enough to reveal the twenty feet of clothesline wrapped tightly around his chest. "You reckon we got so old we forgot to bring a gun with us to rob the bank?"

"Most likely, we just forgot that we was goin' to the bank to rob it," Eli said.

"I want to thank you for taking our mistake so kindly," Blanchard said, "especially the shotgun on my desk."

"Heck, that shotgun told me that you folks ain't gonna let nobody just walk in here and take the money," Casey told him. "So I want you to take care of my money."

"Show him your money, Elmer," Eli said. "We're takin' up too much of their time."

"Don't you worry about that at all," Blanchard said, then paused, surprised when Casey reached in his pocket and pulled out a sizable roll of money and placed it on the desk. "Do you know how much you've got there?" Blanchard asked. "We'll count it, of course, but do you know how much you've got?"

"Yes, sir, near as I remember, there's three thousand dollars there," Casey said. "That's enough to open an account, ain't it?"

"Oh, it surely is," Blanchard said at once. "I'll fill out the forms right away. Perhaps you'd like to read over the forms before I start filling them out."

"Yes, sir," Casey said. "I'd like to look 'em over, but I can't read."

"That's no problem," Blanchard said. "It's just a lot of legal stuff that tells what the bank will do for you. I'll fill it out for you and all you'll have to do is sign it, or make your mark, and you'll be a part of the Citizens family." He looked at Fancher, who was still standing there watching. "You can go on back to your cage now, Fred, I'll take it from here."

That was enough to get another chuckle out of Eli. "Is that where you have to keep that young whippersnapper? In a cage?" He poked Casey with his elbow and Casey laughed, too.

"I don't reckon this bank is big enough to have one of them fancy safes with the time lock on it," Casey said.

"That's where you'd be wrong," Blanchard said. "Our safe is one of the finest safes made. It has a time lock that I can set for any time of day. Take today, for instance, I set the time lock when we closed yesterday for ten o'clock. And it wouldn't make any difference if you knew the combination or not. That safe wouldn't open until ten o'clock this morning. And I can change that combination if I'm afraid somebody might have seen me opening it."

"I swear," Casey said, "that truly is a wonderment. I can't hardly believe there's folks smart enough to invent somethin' that'll do that." Both Casey and Eli held their breath and waited, both thinking, *There it is, there's the bait, come on, take it.* It seemed a long time coming, but Blanchard finally took it.

"Would you like to see our safe?" Blanchard asked.

"We ought not take up any more of your time," Eli said. "You most likely got a lot more important things to do than to show a couple of old saddle tramps how far things have come since we was born."

"Nonsense," Blanchard insisted. "There's nothing more important to me than to show a new customer how we safeguard his money." *Especially when he opens an account with three thousand dollars and hasn't even asked if he'll get any checks,* he thought. "Let me give this money a quick count and we'll go put it in the safe. All right?"

"All right!" Casey responded excitedly. He and Eli stood quietly while Blanchard counted the roll of bills Casey had brought. Just as a test of how dishonest the man might be, Casey had actually given him three thousand and twenty dollars. Blanchard proved to be as contemptible a crook as Gary Corbett had said he was when he announced that the count was three thousand on the money.

"If you're ready to see the safe, you can come with me and watch me put your money in it," Blanchard announced, and led the way across the lobby into the back of the bank, where the safe was located. Eli almost grunted involuntarily when Blanchard was not quite so gifted with sleight of hand when he slid the extra twenty off the stack of bills and stuffed it in his pocket as he went through the doorway to the back room.

"Well, here she is," Blanchard said proudly, "and she's built right into the wall, so nobody's likely to be draggin' her out of here. We'll open her up and put your money inside. Then we'll go back to my office and I'll give you a copy of the deposit." He turned to face the safe, keeping his back to them as he entered the combination.

Eli took advantage of Blanchard's efforts to block their view of the combination. Casey quickly opened the top of his duster enough for Eli to reach inside the sack on his shoulder and pull two Colt six-shooters, wrapped in rags, from Casey's hump. Unaware of the rapid hustle going on behind his back, Blanchard took his time dialing the combination. While Eli stood behind Blanchard with his pistol aimed at his head, Casey reached inside Eli's duster and quickly worked away at the clothesline wrapped around his chest. In no more than a few seconds, he managed to loosen it into one large coil, big enough to drop down to the floor, so Eli could step out of it.

Hearing the soft sound of the clothesline hitting the floor, Blanchard turned around, his wide smile freezing in place when he stared at the business end of Eli's six-shooter in his face.

"You make a sound and you're a dead man," Eli said matter-of-factly.

In that moment, Blanchard was so deeply in shock that he was incapable of making a sound, which worked nicely with his assailants' plans. Casey quickly pulled Blanchard's hands behind him and tied them with one end of the clothesline. Then when Blanchard started to speak, Casey stuffed a ball of rags in his mouth and tied it in with a bandana.

"Set down, or get knocked down," Eli told him, motioning toward the floor. "Now, over on your belly." Blanchard got the message and rolled over on his stomach. Casey tied his feet together, then tied his feet to his hands behind him.

With Blanchard out of the way, the two bandits went to work pulling rags, towels, old socks, and pieces of blankets out of their trousers and replacing it with money from the safe. Worried that one of the tellers would come back there at any moment, they both concentrated on stuffing the bag on Casey's shoulder with money in an effort to fill the space their two pistols had occupied before. They figured they could walk out with their pistols unnoticed under their dusters and stuck in their belts. Then if they needed them, if things went wrong, they would have them handy. When they decided they looked reasonably close to the two dumpy-looking old men who had walked in, they quit stuffing the money in their clothes.

As a final gesture, Casey took the roll of three thousand he had given Blanchard and put it under his hat. "You ready?" he asked, and Eli said he was. So Casey looked down at a mortified Blanchard and said, "It was a pleasure doin' business with you. You can keep the twenty for your trouble."

They walked out of the back room and started a casual walk toward the front door. They were halfway across the lobby when Fred Fancher called out to them, "Wait a minute, gentlemen, you haven't signed your new account form yet, or gotten your checks!"

"That's a fact," Casey said. "Mr. Blanchard ain't filled it out yet, so we're comin' back after we get some dinner."

"You said you were hungry and you wanted to go first today," Adam said. "Why don't you tell them to hold up a minute and you'll go with them?"

"I would, but 'hold up' is a term we don't use in the bank," Fred joked. "Besides, I ain't sure I could keep my dinner down, if I had to look at those two eating."

"Did you see Blanchard go back to his office?" Adam asked.

"No. I suppose he's still back in the safe room," Fred answered. "Or maybe he went out the back door to go to the outhouse. When I went to tell him about those two old men, I caught him having a jelly biscuit and a cup of coffee. Maybe he had to go get rid of it."

Outside the bank, Eli and Casey walked unhurriedly next door to the doctor's office and Smoke and Biscuit waiting at the hitching rail. "I hope I don't spoil this whole thing by lettin' my hump slide down my back" Casey said. "That's what it feels like it wants to do." He placed his foot in the stirrup and pulled himself up into the saddle very carefully.

"I swear," Eli remarked, "watchin' you climb on that horse, you convinced me you're as old as you look." They turned their horses away from the rail, both men watching the front door of the bank, expecting it to be flung wide open and one or both of the tellers screaming about the robbery. But all remained peaceful around that end of the street and no one took more than a casual notice of two old men riding out on the road to Waco.

Chapter 6

They met no one on the road before they reached the creek, where they left the road, which they felt very thankful for. Because that meant there were no witnesses to report seeing two old men on the Waco road. They rode down the creek and found their packhorses waiting, and no sign that anyone or anything had happened upon their camp. "I hate to say it, but I swear, I don't think anything coulda gone off more perfectly," Casey declared.

"I wish you hadn't said it," Eli responded. "You probably just jinxed the whole deal."

"Jinxed or not," Casey insisted, "everything happened just like we planned it."

"Yeah? Well, I ain't gonna brag about it till I get outta this rig I'm wearin' and wash all trace of this mess off my face."

"Me too, I reckon," Casey said, "but before I do that, I wanna get all this money put away in our packs."

"Yeah, I reckon that is best," Eli agreed, so they busied themselves with the task of hiding the generous sum of money they had been able to stuff inside their clothing and walk out of the bank with. "How much you reckon we got?"

"I ain't got no idea," Casey replied, "but I'm certain we came away with a little more than three thousand." Then he removed his battered old hat and caught the wad of bills that fell off his head, getting a chuckle from Eli. "You reckon any of this money is part of the five thousand we gave Gary Corbett?"

"I hadn't thought about that," Eli replied. "I don't know if he said he was comin' over here right away or not. He was awful anxious to get his loan paid off, though."

"I hope to hell he did. I'd hate to run into him on our way back."

"If we do, we'll have to give him another five thousand to keep his mouth shut," Eli joked, "or shoot him." They both laughed at the thought. It was easy to joke about the caper, now that it had been completed with such success. The graveyard humor helped to relieve the tension that had mounted during the tense moments standing before that open safe, stuffing the money into their trousers and shirts. Most of that money now went into the laundry sack that had formed the hump on Casey's shoulder, but there was still a great deal that was stowed in their saddlebags.

After the money was put away, they began the process of removing all signs of the two robbing old men, Oscar and Elmer. As they had done before, when they had robbed the mail car of the train, they took off their baggy old clothes and went into the creek with washcloths and a bar of soap to remove all traces of their elderly characters. Close at hand, their two gun belts lay on the creek bank, with their Colt .45 revolvers within easy reach.

The lobby of the Citizens Bank of Mexia was the scene of a large gathering of curious spectators, soon after the word rang out that the bank had been robbed. Not only that, but it had been robbed by the notorious old-men bandits, making it all the more fascinating. The town had no full-time sheriff, but Adam Rich had run to summon Jack Myers, the blacksmith and acting sheriff. Myers was in the process of trying to recruit a posse to go after the bank robbers, even though it had been a fairly lengthy time between now and the time they fled the bank.

Fred Fancher had gone in search of Moss Blanchard when he failed to return to his office. He found him bound and gagged, lying face down beside the open safe. To make matters worse, not one of the spectators had seen which road the two old men took out of town. Close to a nervous breakdown, Blanchard was berating Myers and all the spectators for their lack of interest in forming a posse.

"I understand how you feel, Mr. Blanchard," Myers said. "But the fact of the matter is, they've got too big a start on us to think about catchin' up with 'em. And in the first place, nobody noticed which way they went when they rode outta town. We don't know if they headed to Waco or Huntsville. So we ain't got much chance of ever seein' those old boys again."

"Damn it!" Blanchard fumed. "You're supposed to be the sheriff. It's your job to go after bank robbers. Are you just gonna do nothing?"

"I ain't the sheriff," Myers reminded him. "I'm just the *acting* sheriff because there ain't nobody else in town who'll do it. I don't get paid to be sheriff. Maybe you men on the town council oughta think about that at your next meetin'. I don't understand why you took those two old fellers back to show 'em the money in your safe, anyway."

"That's not the point," Blanchard insisted. "They robbed the bank. That's the only point."

Myers scratched his head, as if confused. "Are you sure they robbed you? Both your tellers saw them when they left the bank and they said they didn't see 'em carryin' anything when they walked out."

"Do you think I tied myself up?" Blanchard demanded. "They stuffed the money in their clothes and just walked it right by my tellers' noses."

Myers shrugged, his thoughts already shifting to the two horses he had to shoe that morning. "I'm sorry you got robbed, but there ain't nobody who'll volunteer to ride on a posse because they know there ain't a chance we'd ever catch up with those two. And there ain't no point in me goin' after 'em by myself, because I believe they're right. Best thing you can do is contact the U.S. Marshal in Waco or the Texas Rangers. Maybe if they catch 'em, you can recover some of the money."

"Thanks, Jack, thank you for your help," Blanchard said sarcastically. "Come and see me if the bank can ever help you."

"Right," Myers said, and turned to leave. *You ain't much help if you ain't got any money,* he thought as he walked out.

With all traces of Elmer and Oscar either packed away or washed off, Casey and Eli rode back up the creek once again to the road. They paused there briefly to take a look at the most recent tracks on each side of the road. Their tracks were still the freshest along with a few heading into Mexia. But most important was the fact that there were no recent tracks of a posse leaving Mexia. This brought a level of comfort to the two bank robbers, since they had not been sure they would have heard a posse on the road when they were back at the camp. It was a hundred and fifty yards down that creek and a posse would have had to be extra noisy to have been heard. So they were free to start back at their leisure, if they wanted. But both men felt the need to push their horses to make the forty-five miles to Waco by noon the next day. Then they would give the horses plenty of rest in Waco, while their masters were enjoying the comforts of the McClellan House Hotel and Dining Room. They decided to camp that night at the same place they had camped on the way to Mexia. It had been a good campground with everything they needed, as far as water, grass, and wood for a fire, and it would only leave them twenty miles to go to Waco the next morning.

It was a little past suppertime when they reached the creek

and rode up it to the same spot they had camped at before. With nothing for dinner that day but a couple of pieces of beef jerky, they were ready to fry some bacon and dried apples and hardtack to soak up some coffee. "And tomorrow we'll eat like the owners of the D and T Cattle Company are supposed to eat," Casey said.

"Served by the lovin' hands of sweet Frances," Eli added.

"Wonder if we might run into our good friend Colton Gray," Casey remarked. "I'd just as soon we didn't, but maybe we'd best decide why we're in Waco, so we'll both tell the same story."

"We could most likely save him a little time," Eli suggested. "We could tell him he needs to get on that horse he calls Scrappy and get on over to Mexia, 'cause the two old men have robbed another bank." He chuckled, then added, "Poor ol' Colton, you know they'll send him down there to talk to Blanchard and his tellers. But it ain't no tellin' how long it'll be before the marshals find out about it. We could save 'em a heck of a lot of time and he might get over there while all our tracks are fresh enough to follow."

"Wouldn't it be easier to just tell him it was us and surrender?" Casey japed.

"I suppose it would," Eli continued, "but it wouldn't impress his boss as much as it would if Colton went to Mexia and figured it all out himself."

Feeling pretty contented with the way things had turned out on their trip to Mexia, they finished off their simple meal, then decided to find out exactly how much they had profited from the day's work. They brought their saddlebags and the denim sack over beside the fire so they could see a little better, then dumped the money out on Casey's bedroll. They sorted it out in stacks according to the denomination: tens, twenties, fifties, hundreds, etc. Then they started their count, and when they finished, they felt even more content with their day's work. The count, not including their original three thousand, came to a total of $38,105. They were especially happy to see that they had covered the thirty-five thousand they had deposited in the bank in Lampasas. They were set for a while again. "I'd drink to that," Casey said, "but we ain't got any whiskey. We'll have to drink to it tomorrow night."

They picked up all the money and tucked it away again in their saddlebags and the one denim sack, which Casey threw up against his saddle to use as a pillow. "I don't want you to get too used to that," Eli said, and rolled his jacket up to use as a pillow. Then he put a couple of pieces of wood on the fire before he sat down again. They talked for a little while, but it wasn't long before they both pulled off their boots and stretched out on their bedrolls. It was a peaceful spot there beside the creek, and soon the conversation stopped, replaced by the sounds of the horses moving around near the water and the crickets calling to each other.

"Evenin', boys." The gruff voice broke through the quiet of the peaceful night. Casey and Eli were both jerked out of their near slumber to look right and left before focusing on two dark images on the other side of the fire. "Looks like we disturbed your sleepin' and we didn't wanna do that. Ain't that right, Merle?"

"God's own truth, Jeb," his partner answered. "We didn't wanna disturb you fellers a-tall." They stepped forward into the light of the fire, and Casey and Eli could see that they both had one hand resting on their gun handles. "Ya see, this little spot is kinda our private campin' ground. Most ever'-body knows that. I take it you two fellers is strangers, just passin' through."

"You're right, we didn't know that you owned this piece of ground beside the creek," Eli said. "You know, there weren't no signs or nothin'."

"Don't nobody own it," Jeb blurted. "It's just who got it

first and that's us. But maybe we could work somethin' out with ya."

"Yeah, that's the civilized thing to do," Casey said. "What did you have in mind?"

"Whatcha totin' in them packs?" Jeb asked.

"Oh, those packs?" Casey answered. "They're totin' cash money, over thirty-eight thousand dollars, fresh outta the bank." Both Jeb and Merle were stunned, not sure they had heard correctly. Eli was little better off. "But you don't have to worry about that," Casey continued. "We ain't allowed to trade any of that. What do you boys need? We've got some bacon left and some crackers. We'll trade you some of that."

Jeb and Merle were totally confused. "You ain't sayin' you're totin' that much real cash money, are you?" Merle asked.

"That's exactly what I'm sayin'," Casey replied, "over thirty-eight thousand dollars of it. We counted it this evenin'. Didn't we, Eli?" Eli didn't answer and Casey continued. "But we can't trade a penny of it. Ain't that the damnedest thing?" He waited for their reaction, but they seemed to be unsure what was going on. "So, how about some bacon and then you go along and leave us in peace?" Casey asked, his hand resting casually on the boot he had removed before.

"We wanna see the money," Jeb demanded.

"Nope, sorry, can't do that," Casey answered. "Ready, Eli?"

"I reckon," Eli replied, somewhat unsure.

At the end of their wits, the two robbers did what they came to do and reached for their guns, only to come up short when Casey and Eli fired first. "Damn!" Eli swore when both men collapsed, shot in the chest. "I thought you had gone plumb loco. Why in the world did you tell those two we had all that money?"

"I was pretty sure they were plannin' to kill us for our horses and whatever else we had," Casey explained. "So I thought I'd try to stall 'em a little while to give myself some

time to pull my boot closer up beside me. And I was hopin'
like hell that you were doin' the same thing."

Eli considered Casey's reasoning, then said, "Well, it obviously worked." He paused, then added, "On all three of the
simple minds, includin' mine. It sure made 'em hesitate before they pulled those weapons. But I went after my boot, too.
It was lucky we didn't both shoot at the same one, though."
This was the first time it had really paid off, but they had
picked up the habit of taking their guns out of their holsters
and sticking them in one of their boots when camping on the
trail. When accosted by a gunman, he was not as apt to shoot if
you reached for a boot, instead of your gun belt and holster.
They both claimed to have been the one who thought of that,
but actually Colton Gray had told it to them.

The peace and quiet of the popular camping site by the
creek having been effectively destroyed, the two bank robbers pulled their boots on and disposed of the two bodies.
With no notion of digging a grave, they first found their horses
and used them to drag the bodies away from the creek. Then
they propped the two bodies up against a couple of trees in a
sitting position as if they were talking and left them for someone else to find. They had no interest in searching the bodies,
for they had no desire for anything they might have. Through
with the bodies, they then removed two cheap saddles from
their horses, and after looking the horses over, they decided
they weren't worth the trouble they'd be. So they took their
bridles off and let them go free.

By the time they were finished with the brief history they
shared with Jeb and Merle, it was well after midnight and into
the early-morning hours. It was impossible to regain the peaceful sleepy mood they had enjoyed before, but they tried to
sleep again with eyes straining to stay closed and ears on alert.
Both men passed out from fatigue, shortly before dawn.

* * *

Once again, they were aroused from their sleep, this time by the bright morning sun shining directly in their faces. "I swear," Eli said, sitting up and looking at his watch, "we're gonna sleep half the day away. We'd best get movin' if we're gonna make it to the hotel by dinnertime."

That thought was sufficient to rouse Casey out of his blanket, too, so they proceeded to break camp and get ready to ride. When they rode away from the camp, the two horses they had set free the night before followed along behind until they reached the road. Then they lingered beside the creek when Casey and Eli left it and took the road to Waco.

They reached the McClellan House Hotel a little after noon and decided to go ahead and check in, since the dining room was just opening for dinner. Clark Wright, the hotel clerk, greeted them cordially, and they rented two rooms for the night. Clark gave them each a key and they put their rifles and saddlebags in their rooms, plus some items from their packhorses, including a denim laundry bag. Trusting that no hotel employee would be snooping in their rooms, they then took their horses to the stable, where they left them in Horace Temple's care until the next morning.

Back at the hotel, Clark looked up in time to see Casey and Eli walk through the lobby on their way to the dining room. He reached in the drawer where he had placed a note and took out the envelope. After he wrote a few more lines on his note, he put it back inside the envelope and sealed it. Then he walked out on the front porch, where the hotel owner's twelve-year-old son was sitting in one of the rocking chairs.

"Tommy," Clark asked, "you wanna earn a nickel?" The boy got up from the chair and came to him immediately. "You know where the U.S. Marshal's office is behind the courthouse?" Tommy said he did. "I want you to take this envelope over there and give it to this man. That's his name on the envelope. If he isn't there, give it to whoever is and ask them to give it to him. All right?"

"All right," Tommy answered, and took the envelope. Clark reached in his pocket, pulled out some change, and gave him a nickel.

It had been a dull morning for Colton Gray. He never liked working out of the headquarters office, anyway, and he just got back from delivering a summons to a witness in an upcoming trial, one of his least favorite jobs. "I got nothin' else," he told Ron Wild, "so I'm going to dinner." On his way out, he almost bumped into young Tommy Gains, who was coming into the building.

"Can I help you, young man?" Colton asked, figuring the boy was lost.

"I got a letter for this man," Tommy said, and held the envelope up so Colton could read the name on it.

Colton looked at the envelope and read his name. " 'Colton Gray'? That's me. Who sent it?"

"Mr. Wright at the hotel," Tommy answered. "He said you'd give me a nickel when I gave it to you."

"He did, huh?" Colton responded, and dug a nickel out of his pocket and gave it to him.

"Thank you, sir," Tommy said, a wide grin almost reaching from ear to ear as he turned and ran back to the hotel.

Knowing what it had to be, Colton opened the note and read: *Colton, Casey Tubbs and Eli Doolin checked into the hotel this morning.* It was signed simply, *Clark*. Then there was a P.S.: *They went into the dining room at 12:30.*

Colton smiled. He had asked Clark to let him know if Casey and Eli registered at the hotel. The reason was because he wanted to know when they were away from their ranch, especially if they were in Waco. He still found it highly coincidental that they were there during the attempted arrest of

Buck Garner in the Dead Dog Saloon. The reason he gave
Clark Wright was that Casey and Eli had shown him so much
hospitality whenever he was over in Lampasas County, he
wanted the opportunity to repay them whenever they came to
Waco. So, if they just went into the dining room at twelve-
thirty, he had plenty of time to catch them. He gave a few seconds' thought toward whether he should join them, or not let
them know he was aware they were here. He decided to let
them tell him why they were in town.

"Well, hello, Colton," Thelma Townsend greeted him.
"Are you going to have dinner with us today?" It was a rare occasion when the young deputy marshal ate at the hotel, since
he lived at Rena Bramble's boardinghouse.

"Howdy, Miss Townsend," Colton replied. "I thought I
might join two friends of mine I see sittin' at a table." He nodded toward a table near the back of the dining room.

Thelma followed his nod with her eyes. "You're a friend of
Casey and Eli?" she asked, making no effort to hide her surprise.

"I've stayed a couple of nights at their ranch, the D and T
in Lampasas County, when I had to go over in that part of the
state. So I thought I'd join 'em for dinner."

"I'da thought you mighta come to arrest 'em," Thelma said
with a laugh.

He laughed with her, then said, "I'll just walk on back, and
if they don't invite me to sit down, then I'll arrest 'em."

"Uh-oh, look who's comin' here," Eli said when he glanced
up and saw Colton Gray walking toward them.

"Who is it?" Casey asked, unable to see without turning
around.

"Colton Gray," Eli said. "You suppose he suspects something?"

"No," Casey said. "How the hell could he?" He turned
around then and greeted him with a great big grin. "Wouldja
look what the cat dragged in? Howdy, Colton."

Colton returned the grin. "I declare, they'll let anybody in here to eat now. I better ask Miss Townsend if she knows who you two are."

"Ask who?" Eli asked.

"Thelma," Colton answered.

"Oh," Eli said. "Is that her name, Townsend? Well, set down and join us. You ain't ate yet, have you?"

"Nope, I thought I'd have myself a fancy dinner today," Colton said, "but I didn't know I'd have such high-class company as the owners of the D and T Cattle Company. What are you two fellows doin' in town?"

They were saved from having to make a quick answer when Frances arrived at that moment to interrupt. "Howdy, Colton," she greeted him. "Are you here to arrest these two, or are you wanting to eat dinner?"

"I'll have dinner, Frances, and I'd like to pay for theirs, too. I owe these two gentlemen so much more than that. And I'm not just talking about their hospitality when I show up at their ranch at suppertime."

"'Preciate what you're sayin', Colton, but we can't let you do that," Casey responded. "It never amounted to much if Juanita had to throw a couple more potatoes in the pot. We're always glad to see you. Besides, I don't remember how long it's been since I read a newspaper, but I ain't heard nothin' about deputy U.S. marshals gettin' big pay raises."

"That ain't no problem," Colton insisted. "I always keep a little sum of money back for entertainin' important people. Then it doesn't matter how many times I show up at the D and T Cattle Company at suppertime, I can always say, 'Remember, I bought your dinner at the McClellan House in Waco.'"

Her patience wearing thin, Frances stated, "Keep up this nonsense and it's gonna be too late for you to eat. You get a choice, Colton, which do you want?"

"I'll have what they're eatin'," Colton replied. "It looks

pretty good." She went to the kitchen to fix his plate and he was ready to change the subject. "So, what brings you two into town today? Business or pleasure?"

"Oh, maybe a little bit of both," Casey answered after a pause. Colton couldn't help but notice that Eli was always prone to let Casey handle most of the questions he asked. And then he expounded on Casey's answers. Sometimes he suspected that Eli, like himself, didn't know the answer until he heard it from Casey. "The only way we can keep up with what's goin' on in the cattle market is to talk to some of the investors here in Waco, since the telegraph is here."

"That's a fact," Eli said, taking the cue. "We wouldn't have to take so many trips if the telegraph was closer to our ranch." He chuckled then. "All work and no play ain't no good for your health. So, as long as we gotta come to town, anyway, we might as well stay in the hotel, eat some fancy food, and have a drink or two."

"I don't see anything wrong with that," Colton said.

Frances arrived then with Colton's plate and filled everybody's coffee cup. All three turned their attention to their food for a few minutes before Casey asked a question. "What have they got you doin' now, Colton? You workin' in the office now, instead of in the field like you were doin'? I'll bet you'd like it better if you were back chasin' after the bank robbers."

"I have to admit you're right about that," Colton answered. "I don't care much for the little jobs you do workin' in the office. But it's just a temporary assignment. I'm still assigned to chase after the old-men bandits, but they've been layin' low lately. There are still some copycats that show up, but they're not the real bandits."

"I expect you'd really like to catch up with those two," Eli suggested.

"I don't know," Colton answered honestly. "Sometimes I wish they'd just quit the game while they're still ahead."

"Well, if they're as old as everybody says they are, I don't see how they can go much longer before they're done," Casey said. "What do you think? Do you think they're as old as the witnesses say they are?"

"I can't say," Colton replied. "I ain't ever seen them."

The conversation soon returned to what Casey and Eli had planned for the rest of the day. Casey claimed it depended on which cattle traders were in their offices, and if they could find out what predictions were for the future markets. But they planned to be back at the hotel for supper, if Colton wanted to join them. Colton said that was fine. He would plan on it. Then he took his leave, since he was supposed to be at the office if he was needed. He paid Thelma for the three dinners on his way out.

Chapter 7

"Oh, Colton," Ron informed him when he walked back into the office, "Marshal Timmons wants to see you right away."

"Why," Colton asked because Ron looked as if it was urgent. "What's up?"

"He'll tell you," Ron said. So Colton shrugged and went into Timmons's office.

"You wanna see me, boss?"

"We just got a telegram from Mexia," Timmons said. "Your two old men held up the Citizens Bank of Mexia yesterday morning. They got away with over thirty-eight thousand dollars."

Timmons had taken to referring to the two bandits as Colton's "two old men," which didn't sit too well with Colton. He had no choice but to ignore it, so he asked questions. "Anybody shot?"

Timmons said there was no report of shots fired.

"Was there a posse?"

Again, the answer was negative.

"Did anybody even see which way the robbers fled?"

"No, damn it, Colton, it was just a telegram!" Timmons exclaimed. "The bank was robbed. It was the two old men. And they got away with a helluva lot of money. It's your job to find out all the details of the robbery, so get your junk together and get over to Mexia. Maybe this time you can find a trail."

"I'll be there in the mornin'," Colton said. "I'll leave here as soon as I can get my horses ready." He left at once for the stable to pick up Scrappy and his packhorse. He needed some supplies, so he stopped to buy them, and then he headed for the boardinghouse to get some clean clothes and let Rena and Gracie know he was going to be out of town. On the way, he made one stop at the hotel dining room to ask Thelma to tell Casey and Eli he couldn't join them for supper because he had to go to Mexia.

"Be sure to tell them *I had to go to Mexia*," he stressed. He had an idea they might be able to guess why.

On his way to his room at the boardinghouse, he found himself wondering from which direction Casey and Eli had come to Waco that morning. He had automatically assumed they had come from their ranch in Lampasas County. They might just as well have come from east of Waco. He was not ready to give them credit for the robbery until he investigated it, but he would not be surprised if it turned out to look like the work of his two friends.

"If you're just gettin' here for dinner, you're too late," Rena told him when he walked into the kitchen, where she and Gracie were cleaning up.

"If you're hungry, I can scrape something up to put in your stomach and maybe hold you till supper," Gracie offered.

"Thank you, Gracie, but I ate dinner at the hotel," Colton said.

"Oh?" Gracie took offense at once. "You decided you wanted some highfalutin kind of food for dinner today, huh?"

"You know very well that the food they serve at the hotel ain't anywhere close to being as good as your cookin'. As a matter of fact, I was walkin' out of the office a little before noon, on my way here, when I got a message that the owners of D and T Cattle Company wanted to meet with me. They were in the hotel dinin' room, waitin' for me, so I didn't have much choice."

"The D and T Cattle Company, huh?" Gracie questioned, not completely convinced he wasn't making the whole thing up. "What business did they have with a deputy marshal?"

"They happened to be involved in an attempted bank holdup at the bank in Lampasas and they had to be summoned to be witnesses in the trial," Colton said. "They had a lot of questions about it."

Gracie considered that for a moment, then seemed to accept it, so he told them he was on his way out of town again and wouldn't be there for supper. "I've gotta go to Mexia to investigate a bank robbery over there yesterday. I don't know how many days I'll be away. Depends on what I find over there."

Rena slowly shook her head back and forth. "My goodness," she uttered, "sometimes I wonder if I oughta charge you a little bit less than my other guests. It seems like you miss half the meals you've paid for in your regular rent."

"Don't you worry about that," Colton quickly assured her. "My rent is more than fair. And it's just an extra-special treat when I can make it home for a meal."

"Oh, he's good," Gracie said. "You be careful out there. Have you got any clean socks and underwear?"

"Yes, ma'am, I'm all set. Thanks to you. So I'll see you when I get back." He left them then to pick up a few things from his room, which he put away in his packs. Then he climbed up into the saddle and headed for Mexia.

It was still fairly early in the afternoon when Colton set out on the road. A little better than forty miles, he would have made it in one day, if he could have started early in the morning to Mexia. At least he could arrive at the Citizens Bank by opening time in the morning, anyway. There was a popular camping spot about halfway there on a nice creek, which he might normally take advantage of. But since he was starting so late in the day, he decided to bypass that spot and push his horses a little farther than that twenty miles. His horses were well rested, so he was sure they were up to it, as long as he was not too demanding on the pace.

Maybe I'll stop and give 'em a little rest, before stopping for the night, he thought. With that in mind, he increased the big bay gelding's pace by alternating it between a walk and a trot. That way, he figured to cut some of the time it would take to reach that popular camping spot.

The sun was getting pretty low in the sky when he spotted the line of trees that signaled the creek he was thinking about. He also noticed a number of buzzards circling high over the trees. He turned Scrappy off the road and followed the path upstream to the grassy clearing beside the creek. Although he was close to the buzzards circling overhead, at least whatever attracted them wasn't there in the campground. So he relieved his horses of some of their burden and let them go to water and graze in the clearing. While the horses were resting, he looked around the campsite. It had obviously been used re-cently—judging by the tracks of horses and the ashes of a re-cent campfire. Also obvious was what appeared to be two tracks of something being dragged through the bushes that grew around the edges of the clearing. He glanced up at the buzzards and realized the tracks led in that direction. The ob-vious explanation popped into his mind at once and he drew his Winchester '73 from his saddle sling as a precaution. Then he followed the trail through the broken bushes into a patch of short oaks.

He didn't walk very far before he heard the noisy screech-ing of the buzzards fighting over what was left of two men who looked like they were sitting at the base of two trees. Since he felt certain there was no one else still around the camp, he fired a couple of shots to scare the birds off the bodies. There was not a great deal he could tell about the victims. Most of their clothing had been torn away in the buzzards' panic to get to the meat. The unfortunate men were still wearing their gun belts, but there were no guns in the holsters. The screeching scavengers soon returned, so he backed away to let them continue the banquet. Looking around a little more, he found two cheap saddles and a couple of bridles. So whoever prepared the feast for the noisy birds appeared to have let the horses go free. He had to wonder if this had anything to do with the robbery of the bank in Mexia. There was enough left of them to tell him they were not the two old men. He concluded that they were a couple of no-name drifters who might have made the mistake of trying to rob someone who was not easily taken advantage of. He could not stop his mind from creating a picture of two drifters coming upon a camp of two old men, who might have just robbed the bank in Mexia. The two drifters would not necessarily know the two old men had a fortune and would attempt to kill them for their horses, losing their lives in the process. Then the two old men would continue on to Waco and check in the McClellan House Hotel. He pictured Casey and Eli sitting at the table in the hotel dining room.

"What direction did they come from to get to Waco," he asked the gentle wind rustling the oak leaves, "east or west?" That fact alone could end his uncertainty.

He went back to the creek and made a small fire with the pieces of unburned branches and limbs left by the last fire built there. Once he got it going, he put some water in his little coffeepot to boil and dropped enough grounds in it for one cup of coffee.

"I'm gonna sit here and have one cup of coffee," he told

Scrappy when the big bay wandered over to see what he was doing. "And then you're gonna have to take me about ten more miles before we camp for the night."

It was just before ten o'clock in the morning when Colton rode into the town of Mexia after a ride of about eight and a half miles from the small stream he had found to camp beside. "Well, that's handy," he said to Scrappy. "The bank's right on this end of town." He had been to Mexia before. There were two banks in town, but he didn't remember which one was on this end. He was hungry, but he decided to get down to business right away, so he pulled his horses up in front of the bank and stepped down. While he was looping his reins over the rail, a young man coming down the boardwalk stopped at the door to the bank.

"If you're coming to rob the bank, you're too late," Adam Rich remarked. "We've already been robbed."

"I'll keep that in mind," Colton replied, and stepped up on the boardwalk.

With one hand on the door handle, Adam pointed to a CLOSED sign on the door and said, "We're closed. I'm one of the tellers."

Colton showed his badge. "I'm Deputy U.S. Marshal Colton Gray. I came over from Waco to see what I can find out about your bank robbery."

"Oh, well, I guess you want to talk to Mr. Moss Blanchard. He's the president of the bank," Adam said.

"Yes, I do," Colton said, "but I want to talk to you, too, and any other tellers. What is your name?"

"I'm Adam Rich. There's one other teller and his name's Fred Fancher. He and Mr. Blanchard are both inside. Come right on in." He opened the door and held it for Colton. When they went inside, he saw Blanchard and Fred talking near the door to the back of the bank. They stopped at once when they saw Colton with Adam. Blanchard started to ask, but Adam spoke first.

"Somebody's finally responding to our crisis, Mr. Blanchard. They sent a Texas Ranger to come and investigate."

"Well, I'm glad somebody in law enforcement got the message," Blanchard said, and stepped forward to shake Colton's hand.

"Sorry to meet you under these circumstances, Mr. Blanchard. I'm not a Texas Ranger, though. I'm a deputy U.S. marshal out of Waco. I got over here as quick as I could to try to find out all I can about the actual robbery. And hopefully, I can catch up with these outlaws."

"From what I've heard," Blanchard said, "the law hasn't done much of a job in catching these bandits. They walked out of here with over thirty-eight thousand dollars, after sticking a gun in my face."

"Tell me about that," Colton said. "Where were you when they stuck a gun in your face? And where were Mr. Rich and Mr. Fancher?"

"I was in the safe room in the back," Blanchard said.

"With both of the robbers?" Colton asked.

"That's right, with both of the robbers," Blanchard answered. "And Rich and Fancher were in their cages, I suppose."

Colton turned to the two tellers. "Did you both know Mr. Blanchard was in the safe room with the robbers?"

Adam and Fred exchanged glances, and Adam answered, "Well, yes, we knew they were back looking at the safe. We saw them go back there."

Colton turned back to Blanchard then. "How is it you took two strangers with guns back to your safe?"

"They didn't have guns before I took them back to show them the safe," Blanchard insisted.

"Where do you think they got them when they went back to the safe?" Colton asked.

"I don't know where the hell they got them," Blanchard blurted, obviously losing control. "They were in my office just before we went in the back. They didn't have any guns then. Tell him, Fred, you were in there with us. They opened up those filthy rags they were wearing for dusters so we could see they weren't wearing any guns. They danced around like it was the funniest joke they ever heard." He glared at Fancher for confirmation, and Fred said that was what happened.

"But somewhere between the office and the open safe, they found two pistols," Colton declared. "Let's forget about that for a minute. Describe the two old men." When none of the three seemed anxious to lead, Colton said, "Anybody, what did they look like?"

"They looked like old men," Fancher volunteered. "I don't know how else you could describe them." Rich nodded his agreement and Blanchard did the same.

"They looked like old men," Colton repeated, "and not like somebody dressed up like old men?"

"No," Rich replied. "They were really old men. One of 'em was a humpback."

"A *humpback*?" Colton responded in surprise. That was something new for the original old-men bandits. Then it struck him. "I think we found out where they got the guns." He was met with questioning looks from all three, so he explained. "One of them had a big hump on his back, right?"

"It wasn't really a hump on his back," Blanchard said. "It was more like a hump on his shoulder. His left shoulder," he remembered then, recalling the image of the deformed man. "It made his left shoulder look like it was way higher than his right shoulder." He looked in Adam's direction for confirmation. Adam agreed with him.

Colton was forming the picture in his mind's eye as well, and in his picture, he saw Casey Tubbs with a made-up hump on his shoulder. He could think of no particular reason to go to the trouble of creating the fake deformity except to hide two six-shooters.

"I believe that's where they hid their weapons," Colton said, "until they got back there and you opened the safe."

"I don't know," Blanchard balked. "I didn't see them pulling any guns out of his hump. If I had, I would have hesitated to open the safe."

"Think back," Colton said. "There wasn't one time when you turned your back on them after you got to the safe room?"

"Nope," he answered right away, but then remembered. "Wait. I turned my back to them when I actually opened the safe. I couldn't let 'em see the combination. But that was only for a few seconds. They wouldn't have had time to pull two guns out of his hump."

"I think they would have," Colton said. "I can only guess how they made that hump on his shoulder, maybe a sack stuffed with something." He paused to think, then asked, "Did you find anything left behind in that room after they left?"

"There were some wads of cloth and old towels or something on the floor back there, but that was all," Fred offered.

"That was the stuffing that made the hump," Colton said, almost silently applauding the imagination exhibited by the two bandits. "They replaced it with money from your safe to provide the stuffing. I'll bet you and Mr. Rich didn't see them carrying any money when they left. Did you?" Both Fred and Adam answered that they did not.

Back to Blanchard, he said, "I'm assumin' they tied you up while they emptied your safe." He pointed to the clothesline lying on the floor. Blanchard confirmed his assumption. "One of 'em was probably wearin' it wrapped around him somehow," Colton said, recalling a holdup when they had done that before.

He felt that he had a complete picture of the holdup, with the exception of one minor detail, so he thought it necessary to have that for his report as well. "When they came into the bank, did they have any money with them? To open an account or something?"

"That's the craziest part about the whole thing," Blanchard was quick to respond. "They wanted to open an account with three thousand dollars. That was the reason I let them watch me open the safe, to put that money in it."

"Based on the information you've given me, I can tell you that your bank was hit by the genuine old-men bandits. I know that doesn't make you feel any better, but these two outlaws work to a recognizable pattern. First they look like they really are old men with nothing to lose. They usually bring cash with them as bait. And although they threaten, there are never any shots fired. They never harm anyone, except financially." He could see that there was nothing more they could tell him, so he asked, "Anybody see which way they left town or see what kind of horses they rode?"

"Nobody's claiming to have seen 'em leave the bank," Blanchard said. "I tried to get Jack Myers to form a posse to go after them. He's the acting sheriff, but he wasn't interested. I think he had some horses he wanted to shoe."

"I'll be goin' to talk to him next," Colton said. "He's the one who sent the wire to us. I wanted to get the facts of the robbery from you folks first. And I reckon that's all I need to know, here at the bank. Our office has already wired the other district marshals about the robbery, so all we can do now is hope we get a lead on the two robbers. I wish I could give you some news that's more encouraging, but all I can do is promise you that every lawman in the state wants to catch up with these two. Thank you for the information." He left them and headed for the blacksmith's shop.

He found Jack Myers repairing a wagon wheel at his forge

when he pulled Scrappy to a halt and dismounted; Myers greeted him with a friendly howdy.

"Understand you're the acting sheriff here," Colton said.

"That's right," Myers responded. "I act like the sheriff when somebody needs one, 'cause we ain't got one. Are you lookin' for the sheriff or the blacksmith?"

Colton chuckled in appreciation of Jack's attempted humor. "I reckon this mornin' I'm lookin' for the sheriff. My name's Colton Gray. I'm a deputy U.S. marshal out of Waco and I rode over here in response to that telegram you sent about the bank robbery."

"I swear," Myers said, "I didn't expect anybody would show up that fast. Did you stop at the bank already?"

"Yep, I stopped there first to hear how the robbery went down," Colton answered.

"I reckon ol' Moss Blanchard most likely did some belly-achin' about how I wouldn't get a posse after 'em."

"He did mention that," Colton allowed. "I figured you must have had a reason."

"I don't suppose he told you the whole story of that bank robbery," Myers replied. "I mean, when you tell it like it really happened."

"I'd really be interested to hear that version of it."

"In the first place, nobody even knew they'd been robbed till after the two old men had long gone," Myers said. "Blanchard took those two outlaws back to the safe room and opened the safe for 'em. They tied him up and gagged him, and then they strolled back through the lobby. Adam and Fred, Blanchard's tellers, saw 'em leavin'. They said the old men weren't carryin' anythin' with 'em, so they just waved goodbye. They didn't know they were wavin' goodbye to the bank's money, too. So Adam and Fred just kept on workin' till they started wonderin' how long Blanchard was gonna stay in the back room. So one of 'em went lookin' for him and that's when they found out they'd been robbed. So after all that time, that's when they sent somebody to get me. I went to the bank right away and started questionin' everybody in the crowd that had gathered when they heard there was a holdup. There was not one soul who said they saw two old men come out of the bank. It was like they had never even come to town. Nobody had noticed two old men on horseback, let alone which way they rode outta town. Blanchard kept tellin' me to get up a posse and go after the robbers. I tried to tell him we didn't know what direction to ride after 'em, and even if we did, they had too much head start on us for us to ever catch up with 'em." He inhaled deeply and concluded. "And that's the fact of the matter."

"Well, I'll tell you, Mr. Myers, I've been trying to track these two men down for quite some time now and your version of the robbery sounds typical of every bank they rob. Oh, they may come into the bank with different approaches. This is the first time I've heard of 'em disguising one of 'em as a humpback, but they always have some little act that fools the bank. So, at this point, I'm in the same fix you were in. I ain't got a notion about which way they went when they left here. I've got a theory I'm workin' on about where I might find them, so I'll keep working on that until I strike an honest-to-God trail that'll lead me to them. I thank you for your information. I'm gonna head back to Waco, but first I'm gonna see if I can find something to eat. Can you recommend any place here in town?"

"Bertha's," Jack said with a chuckle. "You can't go wrong there. If you want some company, I'll go with you. I was about ready to quit for dinner, anyway, and when I saw you ride up, I was afraid it was gonna be something to make me late."

"I'd enjoy the company," Colton said. "I feel more confident in your recommendation, since you're willing to risk it yourself, anyway." So he waited while Jack put some tools away and put up his GONE TO DINNER sign.

"You can leave your horses right here, if you want to," Jack said. "We can take the saddles off and tie 'em by the water trough. Or you can let 'em graze behind my shop. There's good grass back there between the shop and a little creek. You don't have to worry about 'em. We can see 'em from Bertha's."

"That sounds like a good idea," Colton said. "I think I'll let 'em graze." He pulled off Scrappy's saddle and Joe's pack-saddle. Then he hobbled them to keep them from wandering while he and Jack were at Bertha's. It was right next door to a saloon, but Colton didn't notice the name of the saloon until they walked past it and he read the sign over the door. "'Henry's,'" Colton read aloud. "Any chance Henry's married to Bertha?"

Jack chuckled. "That's a fact." He led Colton into Bertha's, which was a much smaller building than the saloon next door. The dining room held only one long table with place settings for up to twenty people. At present, there were six diners occupying the benches.

"Brought you a new customer, Bertha," Jack said to a rather large woman with a bandana wrapped around her forehead to keep the sweat out of her eyes. She was ladling out potatoes from a large bowl into the plates of the six diners, who were all gaping at the tall young man with the blacksmith.

"Well, set him down, Jack, if you can find a vacant place," she japed. "Whaddaya want to drink, young feller?"

"Coffee, please, ma'am," Colton replied, and he and Jack sat down at the table.

"I declare, Jack, where'd you find such a polite young man?" Bertha asked.

"He's a deputy marshal come to town to investigate why so many people are windin' up dead after eatin' at Bertha's place," Jack said.

"I been wondering that myself," Bertha came right back. "Better tell him he ain't gettin' none of these potatoes till he turns his plate over." Colton turned his plate right side up and she dropped a huge spoonful of potatoes on it. "Meat and biscuits are on the table, honey. I'll bring you some beans and a cup of coffee."

He didn't get away without having to answer questions about the reason he was in Mexia, although he tried to claim the reason was he had heard how good the food was at Bertha's. So he came to see for himself. In fact, it wasn't bad, but it wasn't as good as Gracie's. When the people at the table realized that he really was a deputy U.S. marshal, they naturally figured he could be in town for only one reason. So there were many questions about the old-men bandits, which he answered politely. By the time he left, there was a handful of people who were impressed by the cleverness of the two old men who had robbed the bank. They wished him luck in tracking down the colorful old geezers.

Chapter 8

After he said goodbye to Jack Myers, Colton started back to Waco. With nothing to go on whatsoever, he decided he might as well assume that the two bandits were actually Casey Tubbs and Eli Doolin and try to put himself in their place. Thinking like he thought they might, he knew he would not ride all the way to Mexia in disguise. He would want to find a place to change into his disguise that was close to town, a place secret enough to leave his packhorse while he went to the bank. He had ridden possibly a little over a mile from town when he came to a nice little creek. He remembered crossing it on his way to Mexia that morning, but had thought nothing of it. This time, he pulled his horse to a stop while he considered the advantages, as well as the disadvantages. As Casey and Eli, he would have to leave his packhorse with his other clothes while he went into town. How safe would that be? To find out, he would have to ride up the creek.

He would not want to leave any tracks showing he left the road, so he rode upstream, remaining in the water. As he moved slowly up the creek, he looked at the creek bank on both sides for any sign of a horse leaving the water. The trees that lined the creek were plenty thick enough to hide a horse, but there was no evidence for a hundred yards of a horse leaving the water. Then it occurred to him that it might be smarter to go downstream from the road. If you were concerned that someone might decide to camp there, you might think they would choose to make their camp upstream from the road crossing. So he turned his horses around and went downstream, but had the same results as he had upstream after riding the same distance.

It would have been a good place for my camp, he thought, looking at the forest on both sides of the creek. He started to turn around and go back to the road to Waco, but it looked like the ideal place to change into the old-men bandits. So he continued on, picking out a low bank forty or fifty yards farther ahead as his limit. When he reached it, he started to turn around again, when he caught sight of a clear hoofprint on the low bank. He knew he was right!

He rode up the creek bank to a small grassy plot in the trees and dismounted. It didn't take long for him to find many tracks, especially those where he guessed two packhorses were tied with ropes long enough to permit them to reach water. This was it! This was where the two bandits had changed into their disguises and left their packhorses while they took a short ride into town to rob the bank.

He thought hard on the matter, to think of the disadvantage of this camp. It might be too close to town in the event there was a posse hard on his tail as he raced out of town. If that was the case, he might not have had the time to ride up this creek to get his packhorse. *Unless*, he thought, *I was so confident in my ability to buy enough time to walk out casually and go unnoticed by people on the street that no one saw which way I left town.*

Add to that the idea that Casey and Eli might have known the town really had no sheriff, so a posse would be slow in forming and maybe not at all. They may have figured they could change out of their disguises right there a mile or so out of town. Like two Shakespearean actors, he thought, playing the roles they created. "I know it's you! I just can't prove it!"

Everything he had found pointed toward Eli and Casey.

This camp he found on the creek told him that the bandits came from the direction of Waco, and beyond that, possibly Lampasas County. And when they fled Mexia, they returned to Waco. And his two friends from the D&T Cattle Company arrived in Waco yesterday morning, according to Clark Wright's message. And they went to the dining room at twelve-thirty. That rang another bell in Colton's mind. That would be about right for a twenty-mile ride from that campground where he found the two bodies yesterday. Maybe that was what happened to the two dead men. Maybe they had been unfortunate enough to try to hold Casey and Eli up.

"Damn!" Colton swore in frustration. To him, everything seemed to point straight at Casey and Eli, but anybody could have killed those two men at the campground. His whole case against them was built on coincidence without a shred of evidence. He hesitated to take his theory to his boss. Marshal John Timmons was totally convinced that the two robbers were truly two ancient old outlaws who had decided to go to their graves in a storm of blazing gunfire. Colton knew that Casey and Eli planned to live the good life that money could buy for a good many years to come.

"Unless I can catch 'em in the act," Colton announced to the bay gelding, "and that ain't gonna be easy."

He considered riding all the way back to Waco without camping overnight. It was only forty miles, but it was already the middle of the afternoon and he would have to stop and rest his horses at least once. It would make him pretty late getting there, too late to leave Scrappy and Joe at the stable. And Eli and Casey may have stayed in Waco only one night. They said it would depend on what information they could find that day. They claimed it had to do with the price of cattle, but who knows what they were in town for?

No sense in killing my horses.

* * *

He rode into Waco at about ten o'clock the next morning. His first stop was at the McClellan House Hotel, where he found Clark Wright at his usual place behind the reservation desk.

"Morning, Colton," Clark greeted him. "You're too late for breakfast and too early for dinner. What can I do for you?"

"Mornin', Clark. I just got back in town. I got called out to check on a bank robbery in Mexia, so I thought I'd stop by to see if my friends from Lampasas County had checked out while I was gone."

"Mr. Doolin and Mr. Tubbs," Clark replied, "no, they haven't checked out yet, but they only rented their rooms for two nights. So I expect they'll be checking out sometime this afternoon, after dinner, probably."

"Good," Colton said. "I'll go take care of my horses and check in at the office. Then maybe I'll surprise 'em in the dinin' room at dinner."

"They might be in their rooms. You want me to send word up there that you're back?"

"No," Colton said. "I'd rather surprise 'em when they're eatin'. It's kind of a joke we like to pull on each other."

"Right," Clark replied. "If I see them before they go to the dining room, I won't tell them you're back."

"Good, 'preciate it, Clark. I'd better go take care of my horses now. Have a good day."

"You do the same," Clark responded.

Colton rode to the stable then and turned his horses over to Horace with instructions to give them both some extra grain. "They worked hard," he explained. From there, he went to the marshal's office, where he went through his whole investigation with Timmons. When he had finished, Timmons asked if he thought the two robbers at the Citizens Bank were the real thing, or another pair of copycats.

"There ain't no doubt in my mind," Colton told him. "They were the real thing. Their disguises were realistic and they even came up with a new gimmick, one of 'em was a humpback. All three of the bank people, Mr. Blanchard and both of his tellers, were sure they were really old men."

"That business about the humpback bothers me, though," Timmons said. "Maybe they're not the two original bank bandits. If the men at the bank were sure they weren't wearin' disguises, then we might have another pair of old men that decided to get in the game."

His comment caught Colton off guard. He hadn't thought about the humpback causing a problem. He had assumed that the fact one of them was a humpback on this robbery might make Timmons realize they were faking everything and they were still fooling the bankers. To Colton, that was a dead giveaway that they wore disguises.

"No, sir," he had to say, "I still think they're younger men wearin' disguises."

"I know you're hangin' on to that belief, Colton, and that's even after you've seen holdup suspects wearing disguises from several other banks. It's just too hard to really make yourself look that old and keep your disguise from falling apart when you have to move and be active."

"Well, sir, I'll write up my complete report on my investigation tonight and give it to you in the mornin'," Colton said. "It'll show why I'm still leanin' toward the theory that these two men are masters at disguising themselves—"

"You and your written reports," Timmons interrupted him. "Just tell me what you found that makes you think they're faking their ages."

"For one thing, I found the location of a camp up a creek about one mile west of Mexia. It was well hidden, about a hundred and fifty yards from the road that runs between Waco and Mexia. From the tracks I saw in that camp, it looked like they had two horses tied between two trees. I think the two outlaws rode east on that road, stopped at that camp just short of town, then rode into town to the bank, leaving their pack-horses in the camp. Then I think they went back to that camp after they robbed the bank to get their packhorses. And since they got away without anybody chasin' 'em, they mighta even got rid of their disguises right there at that camp. I wouldn't be surprised if they had. They've sure got the gall to risk it. But, anyway, they got back on the road and headed west."

"'Headed west'?" Timmons echoed. "Headed toward Waco? You think the two old bandits are here in Waco? Is that what you're saying?"

"I don't know if they are or not," Colton said. "I just think that they came this way after the holdup. If they stopped here, that would have been two days ago. I plan to go check the register at the hotel to see who checked in on that date." He didn't mention the fact that he already knew of two men who checked in on that date, but he wasn't ready to name Casey and Eli as his suspects yet. "I also think the two robbers spent the night before at a popular campground, twenty miles east of Waco."

"What makes you think that?" Timmons asked.

"I found the bodies of two men, half eaten by buzzards near that camp, and I figure they musta tried to jump our two old men and found out they weren't old men. Granted, it coulda been the other way around, but I'd bet it wasn't. And just to be sure, I'll check the Reservation to see if any big-spendin' saddle tramps have shown up." He paused and then said, "Of course, there's also the possibility they didn't stop in Waco. They might have ridden around it and gone somewhere else."

Timmons considered what Colton had just speculated, before he decided what to do about it. "Well, it sounds like you've got plenty to check on, doesn't it?" he asked, still skep-tical of the young deputy's reasoning. "Go check with the hotel before you go to the Reservation."

"Right," Colton said, and left the office.

Timmons followed him out, as far as the outer office, but stopped at Ron Wild's desk. After Colton went out the door, Timmons looked at Ron and shook his head. "Sometimes that boy drives me crazy. He comes up with some of the damnedest ideas."

As far as Colton was concerned, his day could now be spent on trying to gather information to confirm his suspicions. He had been afraid that Timmons was going to assign him more office work. As Timmons had ordered, however, he would check with Clark Wright at the hotel to see if any other two men had checked in when Casey and Eli had. Then he would hope to join the two owners of the D&T for dinner. At least he hoped they would have dinner at the hotel before they headed back to the ranch. There was also the possibility that they might decide to visit the Reservation before leaving town. With the amount of cash he suspected they were carrying, however, he was more inclined to believe that they would not risk the Reservation.

Colton was correct in his assumption that Casey and Eli had no interest in anything the Reservation had to offer on this particular day. They had stayed an extra night in the hotel, supposedly to rest up from the rather demanding trip to Mexia and back. And there was also the matter of Eli's desire for the opportunity to spend some time with Frances. After picking up their horses at the stable, they came back to the hotel, where they planned to eat dinner before vacating their rooms and packing up their possessions on the horses. They approached the dining room door just as Thelma was turning the sign around to the OPEN side.

"Howdy, boys," Thelma greeted them. "I thought you were checking out this morning. You going to stay with us a while longer?"

"No, ma'am," Casey answered. "We're leavin'. We just thought we'd travel better with a good dinner in our bellies."

"Well, we can sure fix you up with one," Thelma said. "Sit down wherever you like and Frances will take care of you." They walked on back to the table they usually picked, if it was not occupied, and since they were the first customers to arrive, it wasn't. "I'll tell Frances," Thelma said, and went into the kitchen.

It was only a matter of seconds before Frances came out of the kitchen with two cups of coffee. "There's my two favorite customers," she said in greeting them. "I wasn't sure you'd be here for dinner today. Thought you might have gone after breakfast."

"We thought about it," Eli said, "but we thought we'd like one more look at your smilin' face before we started back."

"Oh, that's so sweet," she gushed, and patted his hand. "I'm gonna go get your plates ready. I'm not even gonna ask you what you want."

Casey sat silently watching the extra-flirty performance Frances put on for Eli, and when she went back to the kitchen, he spoke. "You gave her another hundred dollars, didn't you?"

Eli just shrugged and made a face.

"You son of a gun. She's playin' you like a fiddle."

"Sweetest music you've ever heard," Eli said with a smug grin.

"I ain't sure we can continue to afford your love life just workin' cattle alone. We're gonna have to keep our part-time jobs," Casey said. "Speakin' of which, look who's comin' in the door."

Eli turned to see Colton Gray walk in the dining room. He came straight back to their table.

"Whatcha say, Colton?" Casey called out. "You gonna have some dinner?"

"I thought I might catch you two in here," Colton answered.

"I hate to have to tell you this, Deputy, but you're runnin' a little bit late," Casey told him. "You were supposed to meet us here night before last."

"I left word with Miss Townsend that I wasn't gonna make it to supper," Colton said.

"Thelma told them, Colton. Don't let 'em kid you," Frances said, just coming out of the kitchen in time to hear his reply. "Are you gonna eat?"

"Yes, ma'am, I thought I would. If it's all right with Mr. Tubbs and Mr. Doolin, I thought I'd join them."

"Set yourself down then," Eli told him. "We ain't particular who we eat with. Are we, Casey?"

"Not by a long shot," Casey replied. "How come you didn't make it the other night?"

"I got called outta town," Colton answered, knowing the two of them had a pretty good idea why. "I was sent over to Mexia. The old-men bandits hit the Citizens Bank over there."

"I swear," Eli responded. "That's hittin' kinda close to home, ain't it? Mexia, that little town ain't but forty or fifty miles from Waco."

"More like forty," Colton said, suspecting it was unnecessary to tell Eli.

"Well, what happened?" Casey asked. "Did they get away with robbin' the bank, or did you catch 'em?"

"They got away with it. I just went over there to try to figure out if it was the real old men, or just another couple of copycats, like the pair you took down in Lampasas."

"Which was it?" Casey asked.

"They were the genuine old-men bandits, in my opinion," Colton answered. He paused while Frances placed his dinner before him and filled his coffee cup.

"You'd think the sheriff over there coulda got up a posse and gone after 'em," Eli commented. "You know somebody musta seen 'em runnin' outta the bank and jumpin' on their horses, like those two in Lampasas."

"You'd think so, wouldn't you?" Colton agreed, while thinking, *You know damn well there ain't no sheriff in Mexia.*

"So they got away again," Casey declared. "I feel sorry for the people who lost money in the bank. It's too bad the law doesn't even have any idea who those old coots really are."

"Oh, I didn't say that," Colton couldn't resist suggesting. "We have suspects that we're watchin'."

"You do?" Eli responded. "Who do you think they are?"

"Why, you and Casey," Colton said.

A frozen moment of dead silence followed, with no response from Casey or Eli, until Colton finally threw his head back and laughed. They both roared out in nervous laughter then, in respect for his pulling a joke on them.

"I swear, you had me there for a minute," Casey said. "I thought for sure you had been chasin' after that pair of bank robbers so long that you'd gone plumb loco."

"Hell," Eli said, "I thought I musta lost my memory, if I didn't even remember robbin' the bank. But the worst part was I couldn't remember where I hid all the money we stole."

"What's so funny over here?" Frances came to investigate. "Thelma and I heard you laughing, all the way back in the kitchen."

"Oh, it wasn't that much," Casey told her. "Colton just told us he found out me and Eli are the old-men bandits."

They continued to laugh about it, but the fact that Colton chose to make a joke about it was enough to cause a spark of concern in Casey's mind, which he wasn't comfortable with. He wondered if Colton might still harbor some thoughts about the possibility as he had in the beginning, when he and Eli always seemed to be in the area of every holdup.

Maybe I shot the wrong man, he thought, *when I shot Buck Garner that night in the Dead Dog Saloon, instead of Colton Gray.* Even as he thought it, he knew he could not have lived with himself if he had shot Colton.

As far as Colton was concerned, that night in the Dead Dog Saloon placed a tremendous load of debt upon his conscience. Standing unarmed, facing Buck Garner, his six-shooter cocked and aimed at him, he was seconds away from his death when Casey placed a rifle round in the center of Garner's chest, saving the life of Deputy U.S. Marshal Colton Gray. He owed Casey for his life. How could he repay him by arresting him and sending him to prison? He felt guilty for playing this joke on him and Eli just now.

Even worse, he did not miss the looks on Casey's and Eli's faces during that frozen moment after he cracked his joke. Although it lasted for only a moment, it seemed to him that he had struck a raw nerve, which only contributed to his feeling of their guilt. Then he reminded himself, as he had done before, an expression of shock is not evidence. He still had no solid indisputable evidence of their guilt, so he could not make charges. And he found himself grateful for that, and yet he also felt compelled to search for that solid evidence.

The few moments of uneasiness faded away when Colton asked how things were getting along back at the D&T. Casey and Eli started talking then about the raising of cattle and how well their crew of cowhands were managing their larger herds.

"Eli and I aren't gonna have much time to make these visits to Waco durin' the rest of the year. Oh, once in a while," Casey reconsidered, "but that's about it. We've got a young crew, but they're growin' right proper."

"How 'bout you?" Eli asked Colton. "You gonna just continue to be assigned to jump up and run every time there's a bank robbery?"

Colton chuckled because Eli accurately described his occupation, ride to the crime after it's too late to do anything about it. "I don't know, Eli, I reckon so. I wish to hell my boss would switch me back to regular duty, though. I think I'm ready to go back to deliverin' summonses or transporting prisoners or ridin' with a posse. But I guess I'm stuck until John Timmons—he's my boss—decides he wants somebody else to do my job."

"Anytime you're workin' out west of Waco, drop by the D and T, you're always welcome," Casey told him. He looked at Eli then and said, "And I reckon we'd best get started back that way ourselves, partner. We've got a ways to go."

"You need some help gettin' your stuff outta your hotel rooms?" Colton asked, and wasn't surprised when they insisted there wasn't that much to carry. He shook hands with both of them and wished them a good trip home, then left them to say goodbye to Thelma and especially Frances, who hated to see Eli go. As he walked back toward the marshal's office, he found himself hoping they were packing enough money home with them, so they wouldn't need any business trips in the near future.

Casey and Eli got all their possessions out of their rooms and checked out of the hotel. Then they packed their packhorses, all the while looking over their shoulders, thinking they might spot Colton watching from the corner of a building somewhere.

"That son of a gun knows we robbed that bank. I just know he does," Eli said. "When he made that crack that he knew it was us, I just about soiled my britches. I thought he was dead serious, until he laughed."

"You might be right," Casey said. "I don't know for sure, but I wouldn't be surprised if he ain't figured it out. But you know what? I wouldn't be surprised if he ain't done nothin' about it because I saved his life. I just can't figure what he's gonna end up doin' about it. I wouldn't be surprised if we retired from the bank-robbin' business. That would be the end of anybody lookin' for us."

Back at Marshal John Timmons's office, Colton was reporting his findings to his boss. "You checked the hotel and there wasn't any two men that checked in there two days ago?" Timmons asked.

"That's right," Colton said. "Oh, there were two that checked in on that day, but they were two co-owners of one of the biggest cattle ranches in West Texas. I didn't find any evidence of any two men throwing money around in the Reservation, either." That was the truth. He did not find any evidence of it. The fact that he didn't look for any, he left out of his report. "I have had to come to the conclusion that the two suspects in the Citizens Bank holdup might have come to Waco, but they didn't stay, and went on, probably west of here." That was true, too, for all intents and purposes.

Timmons was not happy with the report, but there was really nothing about it that he could refute. He had to admit that Colton had done a credible job investigating the bank robbery, and his theories made sense. But theories alone didn't put suspects in jail and he hadn't identified the perpetrators, so he didn't know who to arrest. At this stage in the game, the old men were winning, and that didn't sit very well with John Timmons.

Chapter 9

"You wanna see me, boss?" Colton asked as he rapped on John Timmons's door. Ralph Barkley's trial in the killing of Pete Sardis in the Texas Rose Saloon ended in a guilty verdict the day before, so Colton figured his summons to report to Timmons had to do with that. "You want me to transport Ralph Barkley to the Huntsville Unit?"

Timmons responded with a tired smile, then said, "No, I'm sending Cecil Stark down to Huntsville with the prisoner. I'm sending you up to Tyler."

"What's in Tyler?" Colton asked.

Timmons's smile widened slightly. "Something more in your line of expertise," he said. "There's been another Farmers Bank held up. This one in Tyler. Just got the wire today, two old men robbed them of twenty-seven thousand dollars, shot one of the bank employees, and rode outta town scot-free. Your old-men bandits have gotten busy again already. And that ain't but a week after you followed them here from Mexia. So I reckon they decided to turn right around and go back in that direction."

"Copycats," Colton said at once, because he knew Casey and Eli had gone back to the D&T Ranch. They had not had enough time to go home, then turn around and get to Tyler. Tyler was a hundred and thirty miles from Waco, and the

D&T was another ninety miles added to that. "The person who got shot, is he dead?"

"Yes, that's what the wire said."

"Copycats," Colton repeated.

"Why do you say that?" Timmons asked.

"Because the real old-men bandits aren't into killing," Colton said matter-of-factly.

"How the hell do you know that?" Timmons asked, losing his patience. "Men who rob banks are prepared to do anything it takes to get what they want, and will kill anybody who threatens to stop them. You need to get it in your head that you're not trying to apprehend people who go to church on the days they aren't robbing other people."

"I'm just sayin' that the original old-men bandits are not conscienceless killers. I think they will avoid takin' a life if they can," Colton tried to explain, but he knew he was wasting his time.

"Just go up to Tyler and investigate the damn holdup," Timmons said. "That's what you're good at. Then at least we'll have all the information in our files."

"Right, I'll leave right away," Colton said, thinking if he tried to defend his opinions any further, he might be out of a job. He went out the door then, and when he was passing Ron's desk near the outer door, Ron shook his head slowly.

Colton whispered, "Who sent the wire?"

"The sheriff," Ron answered, "Roy Whitley. Good luck."

"Much obliged," Colton returned. It was early in the afternoon, so he thought he would start for Tyler now, instead of waiting until morning. With that decided, he began his usual procedure for leaving town, with his first stop the stable to get Scrappy and Joe. After going through his packs to see what he was short of, he went to Humphrey's General Merchandise to buy what he needed. Then it was a quick trip by the boardinghouse to let Rena and Gracie know he would not be there for supper and for a number of days after that. After promising both of them that he would be extra careful, he departed Waco, figuring he could make it halfway to Corsicana before stopping to camp for the night.

He pushed his horses a little more than he normally would, but he had to go a few extra miles before he found good water. As a result, he came to the little community of Corsicana before he was ready to rest the horses. When he had left Waco, he had thought to find some place to buy his breakfast in Corsicana, but he didn't see any place among the few shops that sold breakfast. Seeing a public watering trough, where a man was watering a mule, he stopped to let his horses drink.

"Mornin'," he greeted the man, who paused to take a good look at him.

"Good mornin'," the man returned the greeting.

"I'm just passin' through Corsicana on my way to Tyler," Colton said, "and I'd like to find a place to buy some breakfast. But I don't see any place that looks like that kind of business."

"There ain't no place like that in Corsicana," the man replied, and pulled his mule back from the trough, turned, and led the mule back in the direction Colton had just come from.

"Much obliged," Colton called after him, wondering if the whole town was that friendly.

I should have asked him if he knew Marshal Timmons, he thought, recalling the marshal's snide attitude toward him ever since he gave his assessment of the two old men, and it was opposite Timmons's. The more he thought about it, the more he resented the fact that the trip he was on was just another waste of his time: three and a half days to Tyler, three and a half days back, plus any time spent investigating.

He was convinced that it was just Timmons's way of getting rid of him for a while. He pulled his horses away from the trough and rode out of the little town, on the road to Tyler, all the while thinking how tired he was of making useless trips.

It was close to suppertime when Colton rode up the main street of Tyler, looking for a hotel if there was one. He passed two banks, but was only interested in the one with the sign that identified it as the Farmers Bank. There was a hotel just past it called the Texas House, so he pulled up there.

"I'm not sure," he answered when the desk clerk asked him how many nights he planned to stay. "One, maybe two, depends on what I find out."

"You in town about the bank robbery?" the clerk asked, noticing the badge Colton wore. "Deputy Marshal Gray," he added when he looked at Colton's signature on the register.

"Matter of fact," Colton answered. "Where can I find the stable?"

"It's on the street behind us, near the end of that street, you get a cheaper price if you tell Jesse you're stayin' in the hotel."

Colton nodded, then asked, "What kind of risk am I takin' if I eat supper in your dining room?"

The clerk laughed. "Less than anywhere else in town. We've got a pretty good cook. They'll be open for supper in about thirty minutes."

"Good," Colton said. "I'll go take care of my horses first, then I'll try out your dinin' room." He hesitated, then said, "Maybe I oughta let the sheriff know I'm in town first."

"Sheriff Whitley usually takes supper in the hotel dining room," the clerk said. "You could catch him back here."

"That sounds like a good idea. I'll go ahead and take care of my horses first." The clerk gave him his room key and he went outside, pulled his rifle out of the scabbard, then took it and his saddlebags upstairs to leave in his room. He rode three blocks to a side street that took him over to the street behind the hotel and the stable, where he made arrangements with Jesse Trotter to take care of Scrappy and Joe. Like the clerk at the hotel had done, when Jesse saw Colton's badge, he asked if Colton had come to town because of the bank robbery. Colton admitted that he had.

"That was a terrible thing," Jesse said. "They shot Albert Davis and he never made a move to stop 'em, Randolph White told me. Randolph's one of the tellers."

"Who's Albert Davis?" Colton asked.

"Albert was the bank guard," Jesse answered. "But Randolph said he never went for his gun or anything, because those two fellers had their guns out before anybody knew what they was about."

"Yeah, those things happen, and like you say, most of the time there ain't no reason for it," Colton replied, not interested in a thirdhand report and therefore anxious to end the conversation. "I'd best get goin'. I wanna try to catch the sheriff tonight."

"If he ain't at the jail, you can likely catch him at the hotel dinin' room," Jesse suggested.

"Much obliged," Colton said, and took his leave.

When he got back to the hotel, the dining room was open, so he walked in and was greeted by the manager. "Good evening, sir. Welcome to the Texas House Dining Room. Can I ask you to leave your firearm here at the desk while you're dining with us?"

"You can ask, I reckon, but I think I'd prefer to keep it on me," Colton answered, and pointed to his badge. "I'm guessin' that's the sheriff I'm lookin' at sittin' at that table in the back. Is his gun here at the desk?"

"My mistake," Ed Leonard said. "My eyes got caught on your sidearm and I didn't even notice the badge until now. No offense."

"None taken," Colton replied. "I think I'll ask him if I can join him. All right?"

"Of course," Ed said. "I hope you enjoy your supper. Tonight's special is pork chops."

"Sounds good," Colton said. "I don't get that very often." He walked on back to the table where Sheriff Roy Whitley had his face almost buried in the plate before him. He glanced up only when Colton asked, "Sheriff Whitley?"

Whitley glanced up then, but said nothing, until he looked Colton over thoroughly. "Deputy U.S. Marshal Colton Gray," he announced. "Right?"

"That's right," Colton answered.

"Charley said you'd be lookin' for me," Whitley said.

"Who's Charley?" Colton asked.

"Charley Post, the desk clerk in the hotel. He told me you checked in. Have a seat." Colton pulled a chair back and sat down. "Are you up here about our bank robbery?" Whitley continued. "From Fort Worth or Waco?"

"Waco," Colton answered. That was all he had time to say at that moment because a young lady arrived to ask if he was going to eat and he said he was.

"My name's Daisy Dean and I'll be takin' care of you. Are you gonna want the special?"

Colton said he would.

"You want coffee?"

He said he did.

"It'll be right out," she said, and went to fetch it. She returned with his meal very quickly.

"I know you were not able to stop them from gettin' away with the money, twenty-seven thousand dollars was what I was told. Were you able to give chase at all?" Colton asked.

"Oh, yeah, I got up a posse and we chased after 'em. The trouble was, I didn't find out soon enough to have much of a chance to catch 'em. It was just a piece of bad luck. You know where the stable is"—he waited for Colton's affirmative nod—"on the north end of town. Well, that's where I was when we heard the shot. Me and Jesse Trotter was tryin' to figure out what was ailin' my buckskin geldin'. The Farmers

Bank is down near the south end of town. There wasn't but one shot fired and it was inside the bank. Like I said, we heard it, but we weren't sure it really was a shot. We stopped and listened for a while, but we didn't hear another shot, so we figured it was nothin'. Then a little bit later, we heard the yellin' that the bank was robbed. 'Course I went a-runnin' then and everybody was yellin' that it was them two old-men bandits and they rode outta town to the south, on the river road. I had to saddle another horse, my buckskin was still ailin', but I asked for volunteers and I got four of the boys to go with me and we went after 'em. They was long gone. We followed 'em for a couple of miles till they left the road and went into the river and that's where we lost 'em. We searched for quite a ways, but we never found where they came outta the water. It's a sorry story, but that's what happened."

"Like you said," Colton said, "you just had a bad set of circumstances. You did what you could." He was satisfied that he had heard all that the sheriff could tell him. "I appreciate you tellin' me what you could. I'll go see the bank manager in the mornin' to get a picture of what happened during the actual holdup. I'm sorry to hear about the bank guard. So I reckon the only thing to do now is go to work on these pork chops before they get cold."

Whitley chuckled. "That's just what I was thinkin'." So they turned their attention to the task at hand and there was no more conversation for a while. Daisy kept the coffee coming until both men begged her to stop.

"Are you staying in the hotel?" Daisy asked Colton, and he said that he was. "Then I'll expect to see you in the morning for breakfast. Right?"

"I expect so," Colton answered. "What time do you open for breakfast?" She told him six o'clock and he said, "I'll probably see you around seven. I might sleep in a little later in the morning, since I've gotta wait for the bank to open."

She smiled sweetly. "Then I reckon I'll see you at seven."

"I reckon," Colton answered.

"Mr. Newgate and the others are usually at the bank at eight, even though they don't open till nine," the sheriff informed him.

"Much obliged," Colton said. "I'll call on him about eight then. It was a pleasure to meet you, Sheriff Whitley." He got up to leave. "It was a pleasure to meet you, too, Miss Daisy. Do I pay you for my supper?"

"You pay Ed at the desk," she replied, "and the pleasure was all mine."

"Too bad he's only in town for a day, ain't it?" Ed said to Daisy as they watched Colton go out the door.

"Hell yes," she answered, and went back to the table to check on the sheriff.

After breakfast at seven, Colton absorbed another great quantity of coffee and conversation with Daisy before going to the Farmers Bank. As Whitley had said, the door had the CLOSED sign hanging on the shade behind the glass panel. He knocked on the door until someone came, pulled the shade aside, and pointed to the sign. They started to leave, but he knocked again, causing the person to look at him and he held his badge where they could see it. The person hesitated, apparently asking someone what to do; then he unlocked the door and opened it. Colton walked inside to be confronted by the manager and two tellers.

"Good mornin'. I'm Deputy U.S. Marshal Colton Gray, out of the Waco District Office. I'd like a little bit of your time to talk about the bank robbery. I hope it's not an inconvenience right now, but I thought it would be less trouble for you before you were open."

The older man and obvious manager shrugged and replied, "I guess it doesn't really make much difference. My name is

Ted Newgate. I'm the manager. These two gentlemen are Randolph White and Gerald Baker. They work as tellers. We had one other employee, a guard, his name was Albert Davis, and he was killed during the holdup."

"If you would, Mr. Newgate, could you tell me how the whole robbery went down. I'm here because it was reported as another bank holdup by a couple of robbers who appear to be old men."

"These were clearly not old men that robbed us." Newgate was adamant in his judgment. "Although they attempted to disguise themselves as old men, their disguises were ridiculous, almost juvenile. It was a real piece of bad luck for the bank when they happened to come in." He paused to say, "And, of course, for poor Albert." He continued then. "I had just gone in the back and opened the safe when I heard the noise in the lobby. I came out here to see what the disturbance was and saw the two robbers with their guns out, cleaning out the tellers' cash drawers into a bag. When they saw me, they ordered me to go open the safe. The safe was already open and I told Albert to stay there and make sure nobody went near it. Well, one of them, the one with the gimpy leg, stayed out here in the lobby and held his gun on Randolph and Gerald."

"What do you mean by 'gimpy leg'?" Colton asked.

"One of them was lame or something," Newgate said. "I noticed it more when they were running away. He could walk all right, but he dragged one foot on the floor every time he took a step. I think it was his right foot." He turned to his tellers for help.

"It was," White said. "It was his right foot. He never picked it up when he walked." Baker agreed.

"Anyway, he stayed in the lobby, guarding Randolph and Gerald," Newgate went on, "and his partner marched me into the back room, where the safe is. I didn't know whether to call out to Albert that we were coming in or not. I was afraid he might draw his weapon and we'd all be in the middle of a gunfight. Since the robber already had his gun out, I figured Albert had better sense than to pull his weapon. I was right, Albert just froze when we walked into the room, but that lowdown piece of trash panicked. When he saw Albert, he just shot him down. Then his partner must have panicked, too."

"That's when I thought he was gonna shoot us," White said. "He told Gerald and me to go back there or he'd kill us."

Newgate continued his remembrance. "They both went kinda crazy then and drag-foot asked his partner why he shot Albert. And his partner said because he had a gun. And dragfoot said they had to get out of here because the sheriff would hear that shot. Then he ran over to the safe and grabbed a couple handfuls of money and stuffed it in the bag with the other money. His partner reached in and got some, too, but they were afraid the sheriff was coming. So they ran out and closed the door behind them. I was told they knocked a woman down who walked in front of the bank door when they ran for their horses."

"So they didn't clean you out of all your money, right?" Colton asked.

"We made a count and came up with twenty-seven thousand dollars missing," Newgate said. "That's a helluva lot. I don't know if you're aware of it or not, but our sister bank was recently hit by bank robbers, the Farmers Bank in Huntsville."

"Yes, sir, I'm familiar with that robbery," Colton replied. "I talked to Horace Winter, the manager down there. They were more fortunate than you folks, because the sheriff was able to act quick enough to capture those bandits. They made a similar report on the disguises, too. Those two are awaitin' trial. I'd like to track down the pair that robbed your bank and killed your guard. When I leave here, I'm gonna see if I have any better luck pickin' up their trail."

"I surely wish you luck, Deputy, but I don't know how much of a chance you have. They've been gone for the most part of a week."

"I don't know till I give it a try," Colton said. "'Preciate you takin' your time to tell me what happened. I'll get outta your way now."

"Good luck, Deputy."

"Thank you, sir." He walked out of the bank and headed back toward the hotel. He had all the information about the robbery he figured he would get, so there was no useful purpose in staying any longer. He decided to make one more stop before leaving town, and that was at the telegraph office at the railway station to update his boss.

Chapter 10

"Yes, sir, Deputy, what can I do for you?" Rob Green, the telegraph operator, asked when Colton stepped up to the window.

"I need to send a wire to Marshal John Timmons at the Waco District Office," Colton said.

Green handed him a pad and pencil. "Just write it out on this pad. I sent Marshal Timmons a wire just last week from Sheriff Whitley. You must be in town on account of that bank robbery at the Farmers Bank."

"That's a fact," Colton replied.

"Do you think it was really those two old men who have been robbing banks all over Texas?" Green asked.

"No, as a matter of fact, I don't," Colton replied. Just a couple of copycat bandits who think the bank will be more likely to hand over the money if they think they're the original old-men bandits.

He wrote out the message and handed it to the operator. It read: *Investigated robbery STOP Copycat bandits as suspected STOP Will track their escape for as long as worthwhile STOP Will contact later STOP Deputy Gray.*

He had a pretty good idea that his telegram would likely cause Timmons's head to explode and might finally cost him his job, or at least get him transferred to some god-awful post. But he no longer cared. He was tired of investigations with no arrests—and he had thought about a couple of interesting things about the robberies of these two Farmers Banks. While he was sitting in the hotel dining room, drinking a final cup of coffee that morning, he recalled a conversation with Sheriff Robert Joyner in Huntsville after he had gone into the cell room and talked to the two Simpson brothers who had attempted to rob the bank. Joyner had said they were two of four brothers who were just part of a snake nest of Simpsons that lived in the forests near the little settlement of Crockett. Joyner said he had never ventured into the little group of three cabins huddled around a larger cabin that used to be a store on the bank of Cat's Eye Creek, halfway between Crockett and the Angelina River. The store had been owned by old Thaddeus Simpson, whose customers were all cousins, aunts, and uncles, all with the name of Simpson. And if you were a lawman, you just never had a reason to go there.

Thinking about it now, he wondered if the two men who robbed this bank in Tyler might possibly have the last name of Simpson. What if the two brothers of Earnest and Stanley Simpson, now locked in the Huntsville jail, decided to strike another Farmers Bank in retaliation for their brothers' arrest? Sheriff Whitley and his posse chased the two bank robbers south, along the Angelina River. Were the robbers running back to Cat's Eye Creek, near the settlement of Crockett?

As he approached Jesse Trotter's stable, he had to clear his mind for a moment and ask himself if his imagination had run completely out of his control. He had just come up with another one of his theories based on no factual evidence, as bad or maybe worse than his theory on Casey and Eli.

"I can't help it," he muttered. "It makes sense to me and I'm gonna at least see if I can follow those two where the posse left off."

"What's that you said, Colton?" Jesse asked as the deputy marshal walked up.

"Nothing," Colton answered. "I was just talkin' to myself."

Jesse chuckled. "I reckon that's a habit you can pick up pretty easy bein' a lawman. Me, I talk to the horses and mules. It's when they talk back is what spooks me." He chuckled again. "You come to get your horses?"

"Yep, I'm gonna check outta the hotel and head outta town," Colton answered. "I've done about all I can do here."

"Well, it's been nice doin' business with ya," Jesse said, "and come see me if you're back this way again."

"I'll sure do that," Colton said, and paid Jesse what he owed. Then he rode back to the hotel and checked out of his room. He gave a casual thought toward delaying his departure until after dinner in the hotel dining room, especially being served by Daisy. It was tempting, but it would be too long to wait for the dining room to open for dinner. So he threw his saddlebags up behind the saddle, dropped his rifle back into the saddle scabbard, and climbed aboard his horse.

Colton rode the narrow trail that led to the south, after leaving Tyler, to follow the river and the escape route of the two bank robbers.

There were a good many tracks on the trail, but he was able to identify those left by the sheriff's posse, even after several days. For they were deeper and spaced farther apart, since they obviously left town at a gallop. There were five of them, counting the sheriff, so he had to assume the tracks of the outlaws were hidden by those of the posse. After a couple of miles, he came to the point where they left the trail and went toward the river. He followed the posse's tracks to the bank of the river, where they stopped. He stopped as well and stepped down from the saddle and walked down to the water's edge, where he was able to see the two outlaws' tracks for the first time. There were no boot prints around the tracks, which told him the members of the posse had not dismounted to look at the tracks of three horses entering the water. So the two outlaws evidently had one packhorse with them.

All the tracks told him a story that differed from the one Sheriff Whitley had told him. For the tracks of the posse went no farther along the river, as Whitley had said. In fact, they left the riverbank and returned to the road, at which point, they turned back toward town. The picture Colton had now was the posse riding two miles at a gallop, wearing their horses out in the process. Then when the outlaws went into the river, the posse decided to call it quits, probably justifying it by saying the outlaws had too much head start. There was no sign of any attempt to find out if the outlaws crossed to the other side or took to the water to hide their tracks.

Colton noticed that the water didn't appear to be too deep at that point, so he climbed back on Scrappy and forded the river. He saw the outlaws' tracks leaving the water on the other side. Up the bank they led, so he followed them and they led him to another trail beside the river, this one a smaller one, a game trail. He could see right away that the Simpson brothers, as he had already begun calling them, preferred the cover that the game trail offered. He imagined this was especially true, since they were carrying twenty-seven thousand dollars.

The tracks he followed were several days old, but they were still evident, with only occasional newer tracks showing up for short distances before disappearing—evidence of how few people used the game trail. Finally he came to a campsite, their first since leaving Tyler. His horses were ready for a rest as well, so he rode over to a spot between the game trail and the river and prepared to make something to eat while the horses rested. He was not sure of the distance to Crockett, but he guessed it to be in the neighborhood of seventy-five miles. And he also guessed the Simpson brothers would make it in two days. But if what Sheriff Robert Joyner told him was true, the Simpson clan lived somewhere between Crockett and the Angelina River. It might not be easy to find.

He went on for another sixteen or seventeen miles before stopping for the night, but switched over to the wagon road on the other side of the river when the trail he followed crossed over. It was close to noon when he forded the river again, so he thought about stopping pretty soon to rest the horses. He followed the road for only a quarter of a mile before he saw a log building beside the river up ahead, and what appeared to be a crossroads a little way beyond it. As he got a little closer, he realized that it was possibly a store or a trading post, because he could see a sign nailed to a post on the front porch. And there was a hitching rail out front, so he pulled Scrappy to a stop and dismounted. He read the sign: THOMPSON'S STORE.

Colton took a cautious look all around him before climbing three steps to the porch, then walked inside the store. A long counter ran the length of the store on one side, while the opposite wall was made up of shelves. There was no one in the store, but by the time he walked up to the counter, a man appeared in the open doorway at the back of the room. "Sorry, friend," he said, "I didn't hear you come in. I just slipped into the kitchen to eat a little dinner with my wife. What can I do for you?"

"It's time for me to rest my horses and fix myself something to eat, too," Colton replied. "So there ain't no use to interrupt your dinner. I'll take care of my horses and come back after you finish your meal."

"No need to do that," the man said. "Clara can just stick my plate in the oven and keep it warm. This ain't the first time I've been caught in the kitchen." He just noticed Colton's badge then. "My name's Sam Thompson, Marshal. I wouldn't wanna hold you up, if you're in a hurry to get somewhere."

"I'm a deputy marshal, Mr. Thompson. Colton Gray's the

name and I am looking for somebody, but it ain't so urgent that it should interrupt a man's dinner. You go ahead and eat and I'll come back after I build a fire and fry up some bacon. There are a couple of things I need to buy from you, so your time won't be a total loss."

"I've got a better idea," Sam said. "Why don't you eat dinner with us and we can talk while we eat."

"That's mighty neighborly of you, Sam, but I wouldn't wanna be the cause of you gettin' hit on the head with a fryin' pan after I leave here."

That brought a laugh out of Sam loud enough to cause his wife to come into the store to see what was going on. A little woman, who looked to be dealing quite comfortably with middle age, Clara looked at the young deputy marshal with an appraising eye.

"I didn't mean to interrupt," she apologized.

"You ain't interruptin'," Sam said. "I was trying to invite Colton, here, to eat dinner with us, and he's sayin' he'd rather eat some bacon he'd cook."

"Colton Gray, ma'am. I didn't say any such thing. I just don't want to pop in on you like that, and you with no warning."

Clara's face broke out in a great big smile. "Oh, so that's what this discussion is about. Well, I can settle this in a hurry. I cooked too much, to begin with, and I hate to give so much to the hogs. So you're invited to eat dinner with us."

"I really couldn't put you out like that," Colton insisted. "If you really have enough to spare, how 'bout if I buy dinner from you, just like I would in a hotel or restaurant?" He glanced at Sam, who was enjoying the negotiations between the two.

"All right," Clara said. "We'll charge you for dinner. Sam, charge him a nickel for one dinner."

"Oh, no," Colton protested at once, "that would be like an insult to your cookin'."

"All right, then," Clara came back. "Sam, charge him a hundred dollars for one dinner." She smiled at Colton and said, "You can pay me next time you come this way again."

He couldn't help laughing. "All right, we'll settle for that, if you're really sure you'll have enough. But I'll have to take care of my horses before I can eat. So please go ahead and start without me." He paused to give her a little grin and said, "That'll give you a little time to do whatever you ladies do when you say you've cooked too much."

"Oh, he's too smart for his own good," Clara remarked as Colton went out the door.

After he took the saddles and packs off his horses and left them by the river behind the store, Colton came back inside to find Sam waiting to escort him into the kitchen, where he found a place set for him at the table. "Honest to goodness," Clara said, "I don't think that corn bread I put in the oven before we started to eat is ever gonna get done. We might need a new stove." She couldn't keep the smile off her face, however. Halfway through the meal, she took the corn bread out of the oven.

The chance meeting with Sam and Clara was not only a pleasant dinner, it was also an extremely critical source of information in his search for the men who robbed the bank in Tyler. Sam's father had built the store on the Angelina River when Sam was a baby. So Sam had lived all his life in the same county. And when his father died twelve years ago, Sam took over the store. Consequently, when Colton asked if he knew where Cat's Eye Creek was, Sam hesitated before he answered with a question: "Are you interested in findin' the Simpsons?"

"Well, let's put it this way," Colton answered. "I think I'm interested in findin' two of them."

"Would it be the two brothers who passed through here last week?" Sam asked.

Colton felt as if he had been stunned. It told him that his wild hunch had been correct. He had, in fact, been tracking the two Simpson brothers all the way from Tyler.

"Yes," he answered Sam. "I've been trackin' them from the bank they robbed in Tyler."

"They robbed the bank?" Sam found it hard to believe.

"And killed the bank guard," Colton added.

"Evil," Clara blurted, "the whole nest of them is evil." She looked at her husband and said, "You wondered who they stole the money from when they came in the store and bought all those dried apples and crackers."

"How much did they steal from the bank?" Sam asked.

"Twenty-seven thousand dollars," Colton said. "It's the killing of the guard that was the worst, though. He didn't even make a move against them. They shot him because he was wearing a gun."

"I heard the two older brothers are going to prison for trying to rob the bank down at the Huntsville Unit," Sam said. "That shows you how smart that inner-family breeding is, rob the bank where the prison is. So you're goin' after Maurice and Derwood now. Well, Colton, you'd better be damn careful. Those Simpsons are like a nest of roaches."

"I intend to be," Colton responded. "You could help me tell 'em apart, if you would. I know their names are Maurice and Derwood now, but I don't know which one goes by which name. Which one has the gimpy leg?"

"That's Derwood," Sam said. "His brother Earnest ran over him with a wagonload of logs." He shook his head when he thought about his next question. "Colton, are you sure it's a good idea to go into Cat's Eye Creek lookin' for those two worthless roaches? I think it would be a whole lot wiser to go into that nest with a company of marshals or Texas Rangers.

There's a Simpson growin' on damn near every bush up that creek, and they're all cousins, the husbands and wives, too— all cousins."

"I 'preciate your concern," Colton said, "but it would really help me if you could tell me how to get to that place from here."

"I can, if you're dead set on committing suicide. It ain't that hard to find. It's the gettin' out again, that's tough. I reckon you saw that trail just beyond my store that runs back across the river," he began.

"Yeah," Colton said, "I saw it. It didn't look like much of a road. Where does it go?"

"If you take it back across the river to the east, it'll take you to Nacogdoches, after about fifteen miles. But if you go west on it, it'll take you to the Neches River after about ten miles. It you stayed on that trail, it would take you to Crockett, but you'll take another trail to the north after you cross the Neches. Follow that trail for about a mile and you'll come to Cat's Eye Creek, and back down that creek, there ain't nothin' but Simpsons."

"I'd at least like to scout out their place, and then I might decide you're right and I'll have to get some help before I try to make an arrest." He gave Clara a big smile and said, "If this is my last meal, I sure came to the right place."

"You be careful," she told him.

"I will," he said, "and just to show you how careful I'm gonna be, I wanna buy some coffee and flour and some molasses, if you've got any. And I'm gonna put fifty cents for a down payment on that hundred dollar dinner I just ate."

"We'll just settle that up next time you drop by," Clara said. When he was ready to go, he packed his purchases away and said goodbye. They stood on the porch and watched him until he rode up to the cross trail, turned right, and rode out of sight.

"A right fine young fellow," Clara said. "I surely hope he knows what he's doing."

"I'm afraid if he goes ridin' down that creek wearin' that badge, he won't have a chance to get to the old man's house," Sam remarked. "Somebody will take a shot at it before he gets halfway."

With much the same thought in mind, Colton hadn't ridden more than a mile or so when he reached up and removed his badge from his shirt and put it in his pocket. *No point in giving them a target to shoot at,* he thought.

After a couple hours, he came to the Neches River and decided to give his horses another rest. It was too early to think about camping for the night, but he had ridden the horses another ten miles. According to Sam Thompson's directions, he was now within a mile of Cat's Eye Creek, after he crossed the river. So he thought it a better idea to rest and water the horses on this side of the river. He had encountered no other traveler on the trail between the two rivers, but he decided to go down the river a little way from the trail, so that's what he did.

After his horses were rested, he rode back to the trail and forded the Neches River. Once across, he was surprised to find a line of tree-covered rolling hills, in contrast to the mostly flat terrain on the other side of the river. He followed the narrow trail along the river until he came to what he was sure had to be Cat's Eye Creek. It was a wide creek running between two hills that formed a hollow and he assumed the Simpson conclave he searched for was at the end of the hollow. He could readily appreciate Sam's remark about the difficult part of his mission being the slim odds of getting back out of the camp, once he got in.

Colton had no doubt that he would pass more than a few shacks and cabins on his way to the end of the hollow. He also had a pretty good idea he would never make it to the end of the hollow. But he had reached the tree-covered hills that formed the hollow, so he rode past the creek, until reaching a good place to leave the trail and climb up through the trees.

About three-quarters of the way to the top of the hill he stopped when he found a good place to leave his horses. He got his field glass out of his saddlebag, drew his rifle from the saddle sling, and went the rest of the way on foot.

When he reached the top of the hill, he had to go down the other side for about ten yards before he could see the creek below. He could now see several rough cabins scattered along the creek, but he was not over the end of the hollow yet, where there was supposed to be a cluster of three or four cabins. So he moved farther along the hill until he reached the back of the hollow, which was formed by another hill. And there were the four cabins sitting on three sides of a small pond, formed from the creek.

He put his field glass to his eye to get a closer look. One of the cabins was a good bit larger than the other three, no doubt the original store, built by the old man. There was a corral, but no barn, a smokehouse, and an outhouse. There were children playing around the pond, but he saw no adults until the outhouse door opened and a man came out, still buttoning up his britches.

Is that Maurice or Derwood?

He had no way of knowing, since he had never seen either of them. Then he reminded himself that he knew it wasn't Derwood because this man didn't have a gimpy leg. This was not going to be easy, or even possible, but at least he had found the rats' nest.

He sat there, high above the Simpson stronghold, honestly wondering if he hadn't created an impossible situation for himself, and knowing that every decision he made from that moment forward might mean life or death. His thoughts were interrupted then when the door of the big cabin opened and a woman came out and banged on an angle iron. Supper was ready, he assumed. Some of the children ran toward the cabin. Then the door of one of the other cabins opened and two men came out and walked to the big cabin. One of them dragged his foot on the ground when he walked.

Chapter 11

He felt sure he was looking at Derwood Simpson, unless there was another one with a gimp leg. Peering through the field glass, he tried to get a good look at him and especially the man walking to the cabin with him. He wanted to recognize him when he saw him again. Colton's mind was racing to put what he was seeing into logical assumption. No one else followed the two men out of the smaller cabin to go to supper—no wives, no children. Maybe none of the four brothers were married and they slept in that cabin, but ate their meals with the old man. And now, there were only the two brothers left to use the cabin. So the other man had to be Maurice. He was looking at the two men who robbed the bank!

Colton wondered if the old man had any idea how much money his two sons had in that little cabin. *I would bet not*, he thought, *for then he would demand a share of it.* The question to be answered next was, what are they going to do with the money? If they didn't plan to share it, why did they return home with it? Maybe it's not in that cabin, after all. Maybe they hid it somewhere until they decided what to do with it. Or he could be wrong and the old man might have it. Whatever, he told himself, the odds of him going into that hornet's nest to arrest them were one hundred percent against him coming out alive. His only option was to watch them and maybe get a chance to arrest them if they came out of the nest.

He wanted to recover the money if possible, but the capture of the two men was the priority. So he remained there and waited until the two of them came out of the big cabin. And he watched while they sat on the edge of the small porch and smoked a cigar. He was too far from them to hear what they were saying, but from all the yawning and scratching he saw, he guessed they were talking about retiring for the night. They got up from the porch and one of them yelled something back toward the open door. Then they walked back and went inside the small cabin again.

"That's right," Colton said, "be good boys and go to bed, and I'll be back in the mornin'."

The sun was already sinking behind the rolling hills to the west and he knew he had best lead his horses down the hill while there was still enough light to see his way. He would have liked to stay where he was and watch the cabins in the hollow all night. But his horses had to have water, so he had to go back down the hill to the river to make his camp.

"You reckon we oughta tell Pa about the money?" Derwood asked his brother.

"Hell no," Maurice answered at once. "We tell him about all that money and you know damn well he'll want at least half of it. We're the ones who had the guts to walk into that bank and get it. Besides, we brought him them dried apples and crackers he likes and gave him ten dollars, to boot. He ain't got no cause to complain. And now, me and you have got enough money to live in style. We'll do like Stanley and Earnest said they was gonna do after they robbed that bank at Huntsville. We'll get outta this blame hollow and go to Nacogdoches and buy us some fancy clothes, take us a room in a hotel like the high-class gents we're gonna be."

"Don't you reckon there might be some lawmen out lookin' for the two men that robbed the bank in Tyler? I wish you hadn'ta shot that guard in the bank."

"Hell, we couldn't take no chance on him drawin' that pistol he was wearin'," Maurice insisted. "Whaddaya think he was there for? That was his job to stop us, so there weren't no sense in givin' him a chance to do it." He grinned at his brother. "It's just the luck of the draw he ended up dead and we ended up with more money than we've ever seen before. So I say let's go spend it. Whaddaya say?"

"That's what I say, too," Derwood said, "and let's go in the mornin' before somebody goes pokin' around in this cabin and finds that money."

"Right after breakfast," Maurice said.

"Right after breakfast," Derwood confirmed. "We'll tell Pa we're gonna ride down to Huntsville to see if we can find out where Stanley and Earnest are."

"Yeah," Maurice replied, "good idea. He oughta appreciate that we care enough about 'em to wanna find out."

Colton made it a point not to linger at his camp by the river the next morning. He got his horses ready to go, and then he revived his fire only enough to make a small pot of coffee to go with some jerky for breakfast. As soon as it was light enough to see his way, he killed his camp and rode back up the hill again to his surveillance position over the hollow. He left his horses at the same spot as he had the day before just in time to hear the summons ringing up from the angle iron that breakfast was ready. He hurried along to see if he could confirm that Maurice and Derwood were still there. If they were, he couldn't say, because he didn't get to his spot in time to see them go into the big cabin.

So he settled down and waited, his thoughts returning to the same subject that dominated his mind since the night before. How could he slip into that camp, capture the two brothers, and ride out with them and the money? Looking across the hollow at the other hill, he stared hard at what appeared to be a narrow passage and wondered where it led. Maybe there was a way to get to it from the other side of the hollow and he could slip into the back of their cabin during the night. Then slip them out again without raising an alarm. He didn't like the odds for success. Then he noticed two horses saddled outside the corral.

Somebody's planning to ride this morning, he thought.

He waited, anticipating the best, for if the two brothers were leaving the hollow this morning, he might have a reasonable chance of arresting them. After what seemed an exceptionally long time to eat breakfast, they walked out on the porch. One of them, Derwood, stopped, and while holding the door open, he continued to talk to someone inside the cabin. Colton could imagine there were last-minute reminders or requests having to do with a trip the brothers were going to take. Derwood released the door and someone inside closed it. Then he and Maurice returned to their small cabin, but not for long, for they came right back out, each one carrying their saddlebags.

Bet they're taking the money with them!

Colton had to move fast now. He had to get back down from the top of that hill and find a place to wait for them to ride out of the hollow formed by Cat's Eye Creek. He hadn't a clue as to how long it would take them to ride out the length of the creek. Not only that, he had no notion of which way they would turn when they reached the river, north or south. Whichever, the most important task he had at the moment was to get down to the river before they reached it. He ran, almost recklessly, down through the trees to the place where his horses were tied and sprang into the saddle. Riding as fast as he dared, he retraced his route of half an hour earlier until he reached the bottom of the hill and the confluence of Cat's Eye Creek and the Neches River. There was no sign of the two brothers. Not sure if that was good or bad, he rode across the wagon road beside the river, into the cover of the trees between the road and the water. Once he was sure he couldn't be seen, he watched and waited.

A period of perhaps a quarter of an hour passed before the two riders came up from the path beside the creek. Almost to a point of dismay a few moments earlier, Colton now exhaled a breath in relief. Evidently, the two had stopped to exchange some conversation with some cousins on their way. They turned onto the road, heading south. Colton remained where he was until they were just about to slip out of sight. He knew he couldn't lag too far behind them because it was not that far to the east-west crossroad and he had to see if they turned toward Crockett or Nacogdoches.

If at all possible, he wanted to catch them when they were not in the saddle. Because if it became a chase, they could split up and he would definitely lose one of them. And he wanted them both, so he dropped a little farther back after he saw that they crossed the river and headed toward Nacogdoches. That meant they would come to the Angelina River and Thompson's Store after about ten miles. They had stopped there on their way to Cat's Eye Creek. He wondered if they would stop there again. He didn't expect them to stop before they got to the store. He imagined it was a novel experience for the two outlaws to have plenty of money to buy whatever they desired. And that might be incentive enough for them to stop at the store. While trying to keep his eye on the two riders he followed, he would speed up occasionally until he could catch sight of them again. Then he would drop back before one of them took a notion to look behind them. Finally, on one such occasion, he caught sight of the river and Thompson's Store just beyond.

So, what's it gonna be, boys? Colton wondered. *Are we gonna have a formal introduction at the store, or am I gonna have to follow you all the way to Nacogdoches?*

He reined Scrappy back to lessen the chance of being seen and waited a few minutes before rounding a curve in the trail that temporarily blocked his view of the riders. When he rounded the curve, he saw the two brothers turn their horses off the trail and head toward the store. That gave him the opportunity to nudge Scrappy into a fast lope, since their view of the road behind them was now blocked.

When he reached the path to the store, he pulled up to take a look before proceeding. He saw both horses tied at the hitching rail in front of the store. There were no windows in the wall on the side of the store facing this direction. He remembered then, that was the wall across from the counter and it was all shelves. That was a fortunate happenstance for him, since he could ride in a gentle lope right up to the side of the store without being seen or heard from inside.

He had a difficult situation to handle, so he paused briefly to determine his best chance for making an arrest without injuring Sam or Clara Thompson. He preferred not to attempt to arrest the two Simpson brothers inside the store because of that possibility. If he waited until Maurice and Derwood came out of the store, and confronted them, he'd likely be facing two men in a quick-draw contest. Then he remembered Casey and Eli's method of evening the odds.

Deciding that was his best option as well, he dropped Scrappy's reins to the ground, knowing the horse would stay there till he returned. Then he got the two pairs of handcuffs he always carried out of his saddlebag and hurried around to the front of the building, where the horses were tied. Working as quickly as he could, he loosened the cinches on the outlaws' saddles. Then he positioned himself at the corner of the building, his six-shooter in hand, cocked and ready to fire.

There was nothing to do now but wait and hope the loose saddles worked as well for him as they had for Casey and Eli.

Inside the store, the two Simpson brothers were buying some things to eat when they stopped a little farther up the trail to rest their horses.

"You got any more of them dried apples?" Derwood asked.

"I sure do," Sam answered, always in a courteous manner when dealing with any of the Simpsons. "How much do you want?"

"How much did I get the last time we was here?" Derwood asked.

"You got two pounds," Sam answered.

"That was about right," Derwood allowed, "so give me two pounds again." He looked at his brother and said, "You better order you some, if you want any, 'cause I'm gonna eat all of them two pounds."

"Gimme two pounds, too," Maurice said to Sam. "Then I won't have to eat ol' drag-leg's apples." He received a punch on his shoulder for his insult, which he countered with a slap on the back of Derwood's head.

Sam waited patiently for the two simpleminded brothers to finish shoving each other back and forth before he asked, "Will there be anything else today?"

"No, reckon not. How much I owe you?" Maurice asked, and when Sam told him, he pulled out a roll of money and peeled off a couple of dollars. Sam gave him his change and thanked him. Then he went through the same routine with Derwood, happy to have been paid for their items. Sometimes all he got in payment was a story that they were a little short right then, but they would come and pay him when they had the money. Sam suspected that the promise to pay was because the old man knew he needed a place to get supplies, so he told his sons not to take what they wanted without paying

Sam. If they had to steal what they wanted, then go to Crockett or someplace else.

Outside the store, Colton heard Sam thanking them for their business and the sound of their boots as they walked out the door. He backed away from the corner of the building to make sure they didn't see him standing there. Derwood came out first. He walked down the steps and went straight to his horse. Holding a sack with his purchases in one hand, he gathered his reins in the other and grabbed the saddle horn. Then with a foot in the stirrup, he hopped up in the saddle, but the saddle slid over with his weight to leave him hanging on the side of his horse. Colton realized that he had not loosened the cinch enough to cause the saddle to turn upside down. He was hanging helpless, however, so Colton hurried over and pulled the pistol out of his holster.

Meanwhile, Maurice, who had walked around Derwood's horse to get to his, and therefore had his back to Derwood, was unaware of his brother's problem. And before Derwood could yell, Maurice stepped up in the stirrup and promptly landed on his back under his horse.

"You just lie right where you are," Colton told Maurice. "You're both under arrest for the Farmers Bank robbery in Tyler and the murder of the bank guard." Maurice reacted by reaching for his six-shooter, and Colton didn't hesitate to put a round into his shoulder.

"You shot me!" Maurice squealed.

"I saved your life," Colton replied frankly. "You were fixin' to make a big mistake. You only get one mistake. The next one you make gets a shot in the head."

Then Colton quickly grabbed Maurice's boots and dragged him out from under his horse and flipped him over on his stomach, ignoring the wounded man's howling protests. The deputy marshal pulled his prisoner's hands behind his back and locked them together with his handcuffs; then he relieved Maurice of his six-shooter.

He turned his attention to Derwood, still hanging sideways on his horse.

"It weren't me that shot that bank guard," Derwood told him.

"Shut up, Derwood!" Maurice groaned, his shoulder throbbing.

"Is that a fact?" Colton replied as he got Derwood's foot loose from the stirrup. "Well, maybe the judge will give you a reward for turnin' your brother in." He released his foot and Derwood dropped to the ground, where Colton immediately gave him the same treatment he had given Maurice, flipping him over on his stomach and cuffing his hands behind his back. "Now, you two just lie there and make yourselves comfortable and I'll see if I can't tighten your saddles up a little before we ride." He looked up at Sam and Clara Thompson, now on the porch and gaping wide-eyed at the unusual arrest.

"Sorry for the little disturbance, folks. We'll be on our way shortly."

Sam shook his head in amazement. "I swear, I never thought I'd ever see you again." He looked at Clara and added, "Alive, anyway." Back to Colton then, he asked, "How far do you have to take them? All the way back to Tyler?"

"No, that's farther than I want to transport 'em without a jail wagon," Colton told him. "I'll drop 'em off at the jail in Nacogdoches and hold 'em there till we send a wagon to transport 'em. Besides, I wanna have the doctor take a look at that shoulder wound before it gets infected. How far is Nacogdoches from here?"

"From my store, it's sixteen miles," Sam replied.

"That's about what I figured," Colton said. "So the next order of business is to see how much of that twenty-seven thousand dollars is left to take back to the bank." Sam and Clara continued to watch while he straightened the saddles again and tightened the cinches. Then he went through their saddle-bags and searched the packhorse, finding what appeared to be the biggest part of the stolen money. Satisfied that he would have most of the money to return to the bank, he completed the search by going through the pockets of the two prisoners.

"Hey, that's my personal money," Maurice protested when Colton pulled a sizable roll of bills from his pocket.

"Right," Colton replied. "I'll put it with the bank's money in case we need to borrow some from you to help make up what the bank has lost. I know they'll appreciate it."

"What will you do with all that money?" Clara wondered. "Put it in the bank in Nacogdoches?"

"I could arrange to do that," Colton said, "but I expect I'll just take it straight back to the bank in Tyler. That way, they'll have it, or most of it in two days. No tellin' when they'd finally see it, if they had to make all the transfers and such."

When he was ready to ride, Colton tied his prisoners' horses on lead ropes to follow behind him. As an extra measure of precaution, after he helped them into the saddle, he tied their feet together under their horses' bellies, so they wouldn't take a notion to dismount. As a last item to check off, Colton tucked Derwood's sack of dried apples and crackers in between a couple of his packs and promised he could have some of them when they stopped to water the horses.

Sam didn't mention it, but he was aware of and appreciative for the fact that Colton made no mention of the bank money the Simpson brothers had spent in their store. When Colton said a final farewell to the Thompsons, Maurice spoke up.

"Mr. Thompson, would you tell our pa what happened to me and Derwood? Tell him we done what the marshal said. We robbed the bank in Tyler and we was plannin' to split it with him. But the marshal's got all the money and he's takin' it back to Tyler after he leaves us in the jail in Nacogdoches."

The attempt was so obvious that Colton, Sam, and Clara all found it impossible to keep from smiling. Sam and Clara both looked at Colton and shook their heads. Sam answered Maurice's question. "Sure, I'll try to get word to him, Maurice."

Colton led his caravan out to the east following the trail to Nacogdoches. It was still early in the day and he had only sixteen miles to transport his prisoner. So he hoped he could get everything worked out with the sheriff and a doctor in town and maybe get started back to Tyler before it got too late in the day.

It was just past noon when Colton led his caravan through the streets of Nacogdoches on his way to the city jail. It had been some time since he had been in the town, but he remembered that Sheriff John Freeman had been a very cooperative man. That one occasion had been when Colton had been sent to transport a prisoner back to Waco for trial. He pulled his train up in front of the sheriff's office, dismounted, and opened the office door and looked in, while keeping one eye on his prisoners. They weren't likely to try to run, since their hands were cuffed behind them and their feet were tied together, but he saw no sense in being careless. He knew the man sitting at the sheriff's desk. It was the sheriff's deputy, but he couldn't recall his name right away.

"Deputy Marshal Colton Gray," the man said, and got up to greet him.

"How ya doin', 'Slim'?" Colton replied, remembering his name just at that moment: Slim Asher. "Sheriff Freeman gone to dinner?"

"Yep, you just missed him. What you got out there?"

"Two men who robbed the Farmers Bank in Tyler," Colton said. "I need to jail 'em here until either I or somebody else can be sent down here with a jail wagon to transport 'em back to Tyler for trial. I'm sorry I didn't get here early enough to catch the sheriff. I'd like to get 'em off my hands so I can get started back to Tyler with the bank's money."

"I don't see no problem with that," Slim said. "We can go ahead and lock 'em up and you can go tell the sheriff what's goin' on."

"One of 'em's got a bullet in his shoulder and he needs to see a doctor," Colton said. "It doesn't seem to be too bad, but he's doin' a lot of complainin' about it."

"Sheriff Freeman will most likely tell me to take him to see Doc Portman this afternoon," Slim remarked. "Ought not be no trouble. Let's go ahead and get 'em off those horses and lock 'em up. Then you can go over to the German's and catch the sheriff. He always eats there. He'll be surprised to see you."

"That would sure help me," Colton said. "Maybe I could get something to eat while I'm there. I 'preciate it, Slim, I surely do. I'm already overdue to get back to Waco and I've got to go to Tyler before that."

So he and Slim pulled the Simpson brothers off their horses and marched them into a cell before Colton took the cuffs off them. He gave Slim their names and the fact that they were wanted for robbery and murder of the bank guard and gave him this warning: "Slim, they're stupid as two cow pies, but they've got no conscience about killin' any livin' thing, whether it's a cockroach or a bank guard. So always keep that in mind."

"Thanks for the warnin'," Slim said. "I'll be careful. They're all locked up now. You go find the sheriff and I'll lock the office up while I take their horses to the stable."

"Thanks, Slim. Good seein' you again," Colton said, and headed down the street to the restaurant Slim pointed to, which had a sign saying ZIMMERMANN'S.

He tied Scrappy and Joe at the rail in front of the restaurant, happy to see the two large windows in the front of the building, because he thought he might be able to keep an eye on his horses while inside. He realized how hungry he was when he smelled the food as soon as he opened the door. It was a smell mixed with a touch of alcohol and he realized the place was also a saloon. Standing just inside, he paused there while he looked over the room, until he spotted John Freeman sitting alone at a small table close to the bar that ran the length of one side of the room.

When he paused to take a sip of coffee, Sheriff Freeman glanced up at the tall young man approaching him. He thought he should recognize him and then he remembered when he saw the badge.

"Deputy Marshal Gray," he greeted him. "You lookin' for me?"

"Howdy, Sheriff," Colton replied. "I just left a couple of prisoners with Slim that I need to leave with you till I can get back down here with a jail wagon."

Freeman invited him to sit down and recommended the food if he hadn't already eaten dinner.

"I figured I'd try it out, since Slim said it was one of your favorites," Colton said, and sat down. Zimmermann's son, Christoph, brought him a plate of food and a cup of coffee, and Colton gave the sheriff all the information about the two prisoners he had left in his jail.

"You tellin' me you rode back up in that hollow they call Cat's Eye Creek and arrested two of them Simpson boys and you rode back out alive?" Freeman asked.

"No," Colton answered. "I arrested them after they came back out of that hollow. Like I said, at Thompson's Store."

"Oh, right, you said that. It'da been outright suicide to go in there alone. It ain't the first time we've had trouble with some of that Simpson bunch across the river over there," Freeman commented. "But we ain't had none of 'em that's tried to rob a bank yet. You say they dressed up like them two old men that's been hittin' the banks?"

"Well, they tried to dress up like 'em, but it wasn't a very good job. Then they shot the bank guard and got away with a lot of money. Most of it I've recovered and I'm on my way back to Tyler with it as soon as I finish this fine dinner. What is it, anyway?"

"I don't know," Freeman said. "They just fix one recipe a day. That's why Christoph didn't ask you what you wanted to have. He just brought you your food. I quit askin' what they fixed long ago. It's all good."

Colton found that he had to agree, so he finished eating, thanked the sheriff again for his cooperation with the marshal service, and was soon on his way to Tyler.

He left Nacogdoches on the same road he had come from Tyler on. The only difference was, on his way down, he had left the river road where it veered to the east to reach Nacogdoches while he had followed the Simpson brothers to Cat's Eye Creek. He planned to reach Tyler in two full days of travel. Since he didn't get away from Nacogdoches until after dinner, he thought to arrive in Tyler close to dinnertime on the second day of travel. He figured that would work out well for him because the bank would still be open. He could return the money and get a verification from the bank on whatever amount was left and possibly head back to Waco the next morning. Now that he thought about it, he decided it might be a good idea to wire his boss as soon as he got to Tyler, to bring him up to date on his whereabouts.

He could imagine that Timmons had already fired him. But he didn't care, he had arrested the men who had robbed the Farmers Bank and recovered the bank's money, at least most of it. And to his way of thinking, that was what a deputy marshal was supposed to do. The only guilt he felt about his performance of his job was his reluctance to find damning

evidence that proved Casey and Eli guilty of the old-men robberies. Then he brought his mind back to the present.

"At least I didn't have to go down into that hollow to try to
arrest Maurice and Derwood," he told Scrappy. "I'da never
come out of there alive." He could laugh about it now, knowing he was done with the Simpsons.

Chapter 12

"Who is it, Marge?" Doc Portman asked.

"It's Slim Asher, Doc," his housekeeper answered. "He's got a fellow with a gunshot wound in his shoulder."

"A prisoner?" Doc asked.

"I expect so," Marge answered. "He's got him in handcuffs."

"Damn, right when I'm eating supper. Why do the surgery patients always show up when you're trying to eat? All right, take him in my surgery. I'll be there in a minute. Then you might as well put some water on the stove." He took his fork and stuffed several large bites of food in his mouth, then washed it down with the last half of his cup of coffee, then followed Marge to his surgery. "You got a shoulder wound patient there, Slim?" he asked the deputy when he walked in the room.

"Yep," Slim replied. "Sorry to bother you at suppertime. I was gonna wait till in the mornin', but he was bellyachin' so much about how he was in pain that Sheriff Freeman said take him to see you."

"Well, let's have a look. You gonna behave yourself if we take those handcuffs off?" he asked Maurice. "We need to take your shirt off, but I don't have to take it off. I can just cut the sleeve off."

"I won't cause you no trouble," Maurice said. "I just want that bullet outta my shoulder."

"All right, then, let's get right to it. Slim, take his cuffs off."

Slim unlocked the cuffs, but removed only the one on the wounded arm.

"What's your name?" Doc asked.

"Maurice."

"All right, Maurice, let's take your shirt off. Then I want you to lie down on this table on your back and we'll have you fixed up in a jiffy."

After a quick look at the wound, Doc was true to his word. The bullet had avoided the bones and settled in the muscle. Anxious to get back to another cup of coffee and maybe a slice of pie, Doc cut the bullet out in short order. He packed the wound with a thick bandage and told Slim to bring Maurice back the next day to change the bandage.

To Maurice, he said, "I don't think that wound's gonna give you much trouble at all. Just try to keep it as clean as you can." He helped him get his shirt back on. "He's all yours, Slim."

He left Marge to clean up the surgery and returned to the kitchen. Maurice didn't wait to be told, he turned and walked out of the surgery, not stopping until he went out the front door, the one handcuff dangling from his one cuffed wrist.

"What did you do with your scalpel?" Marge asked when she walked through the kitchen carrying the bucket of water she had used to clean his instruments.

"Whaddaya mean?" Doc asked.

"Your scalpel you just used," she answered. "What did you do with it?"

"I didn't do anything with it. What are you talking about?"

"You did something with it," she insisted, " 'cause it's sure not in the surgery anywhere."

"What are you talking about?" Doc repeated, finally concerned enough to get up from the table and go back to the surgery. She followed him and watched while he duplicated the search she had just made. When he, too, came up with no scalpel, he said, "It couldn't have walked out of here by itself."

His statement caused her to walk to the front door and look out at the front yard. "Doc," she called to him. She could still hear him mumbling to himself in the surgery as he searched once more. "Doc," she called again, with still no response from him. "Doc!" She fairly yelled it this time.

"What?" he yelled back at her as he came out of the surgery. She pointed to the dark form of a body lying in the front yard. "Oh, dear Lord," Doc blurted, and hurried out into the darkness. "Oh, dear Lord," he uttered again after a hasty examination. "It's Slim."

"Is he dead?" she asked with a gasp.

"He's dead, all right," Doc answered her. "His head was hit hard with something that cut his eye, probably those handcuffs." He pictured the prisoner walking out of the door with the one open cuff dangling from the hand that was still cuffed. "Then he sliced his throat with my scalpel. Damn," he murmured, picturing it. "Take his feet and help me carry him back to the porch. Let's at least get the poor man out of the yard. Then I'll go find the sheriff."

The doctor's house was almost a quarter of a mile from the edge of town, not far enough for Doc to hitch his horse to the buggy in this instance. He would be at the sheriff's office walking before he got his buggy hitched up. When he got to the jail, he found the sheriff's office locked up, so his only option was to try the saloons. Fortunately, he found him in the first one he checked.

The sheriff was standing at the end of the bar talking to Fred Murphy, the owner of Murphy's Saloon. He looked up, surprised to see the doctor.

"Hey, Doc," Sheriff Freeman said. "Was you in your office about an hour ago? I sent Slim up to see you with a prisoner."

"That's why I've come lookin' for you, John. I was there and I took a bullet out of that outlaw you sent Slim with. Get hold of yourself, because I've got some damn bad news to tell you." He told him the terrible circumstances of his deputy's death by the hand of the despicable Maurice Simpson. As Doc expected, the sheriff, as well as Fred Murphy, were stunned.

It took a minute or two before either man could speak. "He's on the run," Sheriff Freeman said, trying hard to make himself think what to do. "Did he take Slim's gun?"

Doc said there was no gun belt on Slim's body.

"Damn Simpsons!" Freeman blurted. "I'd best get back to the jail. He's liable to be tryin' to break his brother out, too." He started for the door, but stopped right away. "No, he ain't. He's runnin' for it, back to that hollow they live in. I need a posse to go into that hollow."

He picked up the spittoon at his feet and banged on it with the butt of his gun until he got the attention of everyone in the crowded saloon. Then he made the announcement of the terrible murder of Deputy Slim Asher and the foul scum who did it. And he asked for volunteers to track Slim's killer down. Slim was well liked in the town, so Freeman got a dozen who answered the call right away.

"It's twenty-five or more miles to that hellhole he lives in, so you need to take somethin' you can eat and your blanket to sleep on. We'll meet back here in front of Murphy's in thirty minutes."

There was a mass exodus of the twelve volunteers, which caused mixed emotions on the part of Fred Murphy. He had considered Slim Asher a good friend, but still it was hard to watch a dozen hard-drinking customers up and walk out and the evening so young. He received a slight reprieve, however, when Ransom Ford came back in the saloon, looking for the sheriff.

"I can't go," Ransom complained, "somebody stole my horse!"

"Stole your horse?" Freeman asked. "Where was he?"

"Right out front," he replied. "He was tied at the hitchin' rail with all the other horses to choose from. And the sorry dog picked my dun to run off with."

"Damn!" Freeman swore. "How long were you here before Doc came in and told us about Slim?"

"Half hour, I reckon, give or take a minute or two."

The sheriff was trying to estimate how much head start Maurice had on his posse. "If Simpson stole your horse the minute you got here, he wouldn't have but thirty or forty minutes' head start. We need to get goin' right now!"

He ran to the stable to get his horse saddled as quickly as he could, ignoring his advice to the others about bringing food. When he returned, he pulled up in front of Murphy's, pulled his six-shooter, and fired a couple of shots in the air to motivate his volunteers. It took fifteen or twenty minutes longer before he counted eleven men, on horseback, ready to ride.

"Don't shoot my horse!" Ransom Ford called after them as they rode west, out the road to Crockett. In an effort not to think of the abuse his dun gelding might be enduring at the moment, and trying to think what was in his saddlebags, he went back inside the saloon to order a drink of whiskey.

Ransom was halfway right in his assumption that his dun gelding was being worked overly hard as his hooves pounded the dark road before him. But it was not the road west to Crockett. It was the road north to Tyler. The thought of breaking his brother out of jail had never entered Maurice Simpson's mind. The single thought that dominated his thinking was the knowledge that Deputy Marshal Colton Gray had possession of the money stolen from the bank. He was on his way back to Tyler tonight. And he was alone. To Maurice, it was an opportunity to recover the entire sum of the robbery—with no splits to anyone else. It was too bad about Derwood. The poor drag-leg, rotting away in prison, but the money was rightfully his alone. He had killed the bank guard and he had taken a shot from the deputy marshal. Derwood had done nothing but accompany him.

He was counting on the fact that the lawman was not pushing his horse as hard as he was pushing this dun he was riding. But he had enough sense to know not to force the horse beyond what it could do. So his plan was to ride the horse at a fast lope to work away at the head start the lawman had, then rein the horse back to a walk when it showed signs of failing. By that time, he needed to ride no faster than a walk, anyway, because of the darkness.

He had to be careful not to pass by the lawman's camp in the dark. So every source of water he came to, whether creek or stream, he stared into the darkness of the trees beyond the road, searching for the telltale signs of smoke or sparks. Once he found him, the rest should be easy, for the lawman could not know that he had escaped. There would be no reason for him to think he might be in danger of being attacked.

The unsuspecting target of Maurice Simpson's attack was at that moment some four miles ahead, finishing the little bit of coffee he had left in his small coffeepot. He took the coffeepot down to the edge of the quiet little creek to rinse it out and then walked back to put it in his packs. He had decided to start out as soon as he woke up in the morning and would make his breakfast when he stopped to rest his horses. So his cup and frying pan went back into his packs as well, the frying pan after he scrubbed it out with sand from the creek bank. He thought about the two Simpson brothers and figured they probably had a better supper than he had.

"If I didn't have all this money I'm carryin'," he confided to Scrappy, "I'd take an extra day to go to Tyler and hunt for something to eat besides bacon and hardtack." When he stopped there to make camp, he saw deer signs all along the creek bank. *If they show up in the morning before I leave, it's going to be hard not to shoot one,* he thought. He knew he couldn't, though, because he wanted to turn that money over as soon as possible.

He didn't even know the exact amount, since he hadn't cared enough to count it. He'd let the bank tell him how much was there. Whatever the amount, however, he had to make sure it was protected. He had met no one on the road since he left Nacogdoches. He had learned from experience that didn't mean there weren't people watching the road for the unwary traveler.

When he was ready to sleep, he prepared his dummy by wrapping an old blanket he carried for the occasion around several clumps of bushes he formed as best he could to make the shape of a body. He positioned his decoy back away from the campfire so that it was halfway in the shadow and halfway in the firelight. Then he took his blanket roll and the saddle-bags filled with the money, along with his Winchester, and went down close to the creek with his horses.

He figured if he was visited that night, it would most likely be some two-bit rustlers who would try to sneak off with the horses. So he decided to sleep where he could protect them. To make sure they didn't decide to wander off somewhere, he put each of them on a lead rope that would give them enough slack to go to the water, but not any farther. Scrappy would normally stay close to him, anyway, but he decided not to leave it to chance. With the thought that he was being overcautious in preparing his camp for an uninvited guest, he unrolled his bedroll, pulled off his boots, and crawled in, unaware of the desperate threat only an hour away. He lay there for only a few minutes before he was sound asleep.

Maurice could see a dark line of trees up ahead of him that told him he was approaching a creek or a stream. Maybe this would be the one, he thought. Because if it wasn't, he was beginning to think he may have passed it in the darkness. Surely, he would have caught up with the lawman by this time.

"Damn you, don't you quit on me," he cursed the dun when it stumbled slightly. While he had no compassion for the horse, he was concerned, however, with the possibility of finding himself on foot. So he reluctantly dismounted and started walking, leading the weary horse. As he approached the creek, he saw no sign of a camp, but he knew he had no choice but to stop and let the dun get water and rest. It was only then that it occurred to him that he was hungry. He stopped the horse and looked in the saddlebags for something to eat, but there was nothing. That only made his stomach feel as if it could cave in.

"Damn you," Maurice cursed the dun again, as if it was the horse's fault. He could hunt. He had weapons, but he was reluctant to use them, for fear he was close enough for the man he chased to hear his shot. Even if he found game to hunt, he didn't have what he needed to skin, butcher, and cook the meat. Almost angry enough to take a bite out of the horse, he led the dun off the road and up the creek a ways so as not to be seen from the road while the horse rested.

Maurice had gone about twenty yards up the creek when he suddenly heard a horse inquire up ahead of him and his horse answered. Reacting at once, he drew the Colt Peacemaker he had taken off Slim Asher's body and prepared to defend himself. But there was no further sound for several minutes as he knelt on one knee and peered into the darkness of the creek beyond him. Nothing was moving except a slight stirring of the leaves, the result of a gentle breeze. Suddenly he caught the flash of a small flame through the trees and he realized it was from a dying campfire.

I found him! The thought almost made him shout it. Angry at the horse moments before, he now felt like kissing him. He dropped the horse's reins and began to move slowly along the creek bank in the direction he had seen the flame, until he reached a small clearing. The fire was on the other side of it, close to the bushes. And between the fire and the bushes, Deputy Marshal Colton Gray was sound asleep, thinking the Simpson brothers were locked up in jail. Beyond the camp, he saw the movement of two horses down by the water. It couldn't be better.

Maurice was right. Colton was sound asleep, but then he was suddenly yanked out of his slumber by the explosion of five consecutive rounds from Slim Asher's Colt Peacemaker, which tore five holes into the old blanket wrapped around the clumps of bushes. With no time to think, Colton came out of his blanket, grabbing his rifle as he charged up the bank. He cranked a cartridge into the chamber as he ran toward his as-sailant, who was now hurriedly trying to reload his pistol. Hearing Colton cock the rifle, the man turned to face him.

"Simpson!" Colton exclaimed in shock.

When Maurice slammed the cylinder closed, with still only three cartridges loaded, Colton squeezed the trigger, placing one round in the middle of the frantic man's chest. He cranked in the next round, while Maurice staggered backward to stum-ble over the fire, pulling the trigger to strike an empty cylin-der. His last dying effort sent a live round into the ground at his feet.

Colton walked over to the body and shifted Maurice's legs off the fire before his pants started to blaze. They were al-ready smoking. Colton started to kick some dirt on them to make sure, but when he looked down, he remembered he didn't have his boots on. And his big toe was poking out of a hole in his sock.

He turned his attention back to the dead man lying there and asked, "How the hell did you get here?" The next ques-tion was even more worrisome: "What the hell am I gonna do with you?" Obviously, he had escaped from the jail somehow.

Should he bury him, leave him for the buzzards, take him to Tyler with him, or take his body back to Nacogdoches? "First thing is to put my boots on," he muttered, since he was now aware of some tender spots on his feet that he hadn't noticed when he was first flushed out of his bedroll.

When he went back to the bedroll, the first question he had asked was answered when the weary dun horse walked slowly up from the creek. "Somebody's missin' a horse," he said. He decided he should go back to Nacogdoches in the morning, even though he really wanted to return that money safely to the bank in Tyler. Sheriff Freeman had suffered a jailbreak and needed to know what had happened to Maurice Simpson. And a stolen horse needed to be returned to its owner. Plus, he would like to know if Derwood was out on the loose somewhere, although he felt he would have been with Maurice if he had escaped, too. At any rate, it would be a lot shorter to take Maurice's body back to Nacogdoches than to continue on to Tyler with it. Since it was not always easy to predict the hard state of rigor mortis—it varied with temperature, and different people—he figured he'd better get the body ready to ride tonight.

What he wanted to avoid was loading Maurice across the saddle if rigor had set in while he was lying flat and his body had set up like a rigid pole. He wanted a U-shaped body to hang over the saddle. So he looked around for a log, but there was none. He considered draping him over the saddle that night before the body got too stiff to bend. But if he did that, the weary horse would have to bear the weight all night, and he didn't want to do that to a horse already overworked. Then he got an idea that he thought might work, so he saddled his horse, picked out a young pine tree, and rode Scrappy up beside it.

Holding on to the tree, he climbed up to stand on his saddle while he tied his rope around the trunk as high as he could reach. When that was done, he took the coil of rope off the dun's saddle to secure the tree, once he had it where he wanted it. He then tied the loose end of his rope around Scrappy's breast and started leading the bay gelding toward another tree he had picked out to be his anchor.

Scrappy seemed to understand what his master wanted, so he set to the task and the young pine had no choice but to bend over in that direction. When Colton reached the anchor tree, the top of the young pine was about four feet from the ground. Satisfied with that, he quickly tied the tree down, securing it to the other tree. It seemed to him that he was going to a hell of a lot of trouble to transport a body. But he didn't like the idea of trying to tie a body like a stiff log across the saddle.

Maurice wasn't a big man, but every corpse was deadweight and a pain to deal with. Colton hefted it up on his shoulder and hung it over the bent-over pine. He rolled the body over on its belly, and the arms and legs hung down limply, almost touching the ground. *Perfect,* he thought. To make sure the arms and legs continued to hang straight down after rigor set in, he took a piece of the rope and tied it between the feet and hands.

"In the mornin', I'll just hang him on the saddle of his horse and he oughta ride just fine," he told Scrappy.

He stood there, looking at the corpse hanging over the pine tree, thinking how much work it had taken to accomplish it. It occurred to him then that he could have simply placed the corpse at the base of one of the trees and tied his feet and hands together to accomplish the same thing.

Feeling like an idiot, Colton looked Scrappy in the eye and said, "We're gonna keep this thing about bending the tree over just between you and me. Right?"

He pulled the saddles off his horse, as well as the dun that

Maurice rode, then went back to bed to catch a couple hours' sleep before sunup.

He awoke the next morning just as the first rays of light penetrated the tree-covered creek bank. He had already planned to ride before thinking about breakfast, so he started immediately to ready his horses for the trip back to Nacogdoches. After he saddled Scrappy and Joe, he saddled the dun and looked the horse over to see if he had recovered from his hard ride the day before. He seemed okay, so Colton said, "Let's see if we can get your rider off that tree."

The body was already into the first stages of rigor mortis with definite stiffness and some discoloration, but was not into the putrefaction stage yet, so there was no odor. He decided to untie the young pine from the larger tree, thinking the pine might rise up a little bit, making it easier for him to pull the body off, right onto his shoulder. The pine, however, had more spring in it than he figured. When the rope fell away, the tree immediately started to straighten gradually and then it seemed to recover completely, resulting in the hurling of the body like a stone thrown by an ancient catapult.

Colton had no words to cover his amazement at his seeming stupidity. The sight of Maurice's flying corpse would remain in his memory forever, and at the moment, he could not imagine an occasion when he might relate the occurrence to anyone else. He continued to rewind the coil of rope, while staring at the bank of bushes the body looked to have landed in, halfway expecting Maurice to come walking back out of them. The whole incident was so crazy that he wondered if he might be dreaming.

"No such luck," he announced, and walked over to tie the rope back on the stolen horse's saddle.

Then he led the horse toward the bushes he saw Maurice land in. He found him, his body still in a bent-over position, lodged between two tall bushes about shoulder high. Thank-

ful for any help the corpse gave him, he simply walked between the two bushes, bending only slightly to get under the
body. He straightened up next, lifting the body off the bushes,
and walked out of the thicket. He carried the body over to the
dun and unloaded it onto the saddle. As a precaution, he tied
the hands and feet together. Satisfied the corpse would ride
well, he climbed on Scrappy and started back the way he had
come the day before. *I better telegraph Timmons,* he thought.
He's probably crapping pinecones by now.

Chapter 13

"Uncle John!" Gordy Pugh yelled when he stuck his head in the office door. "Look, comin' down the street!"

Sheriff Freeman didn't get up from his desk at once. Gordy, the sheriff's fifteen-year-old nephew, who had been helping out at the jail since Slim Asher was killed, was an excitable young boy.

So Freeman asked, "What is it, Gordy? What's comin' down the street?"

"It's the deputy marshal that left the Simpson brothers here!" Gordy answered. "And he's got somebody with him!"

That was enough to lift Freeman out of his chair. "Colton Gray?" he asked, not expecting an answer because Gordy had already run back into the street.

Freeman plopped his hat on his head and went out the door after his nephew. Gordy was right. It was Colton Gray, and the somebody with him was a corpse draped across the saddle of a horse he was leading. Freeman walked forward to meet him.

"I got something I think belongs to you," Colton said when he pulled his horse to a stop beside the sheriff.

"Colton," Freeman acknowledged. "Who've you got?" He went to the body. "Maurice Simpson!" he blurted when he saw the face. "I figured that mighta been where he went after we rode all the way to Cat's Eye Creek. But by then, you were long gone. I reckon he found you." He grabbed a handful of Maurice's hair and pulled his head up to stare again at his face. "I'm glad you killed him 'cause if you'da brought him back here alive, I'da shot him." He walked back to stand beside Colton's stirrup. "He killed Slim."

"Damn," Colton swore. "That's sorry news to hear. I know that had to hit you mighty hard. How'd it happen?"

"Slim took him to see Doc Portman, and Doc cut the bullet outta his shoulder. Then when they was ready to go, Maurice stole Doc's scalpel. He hit Slim in the head with the hand-cuffs. Then he cut his throat wide open."

"Damn," Colton swore again. "All this happened yesterday, right after I rode out of town? And he came after that bank money I was takin' to Tyler. Where'd he get the horse?"

"That belongs to Ransom Ford. He stole it right in front of Murphy's Saloon while I was inside raisin' a posse to go after him. If I'da had sense enough to know he'd go after the money, instead of holin' up in that hollow with all the rest of them Simpsons, we mighta had a chance to run him down. Serves the son of a cockroach right that he caught up with you." The sheriff exhaled forcefully and shook his head.

"I shoulda thought he'd go after you," Freeman said. "I reckon I was thinkin' I finally had enough men to ride into that hollow. Hell, all the men left when they saw us comin'. There weren't nobody in any of them shacks up that creek— but women and young'uns."

"He came sneakin' into my camp last night," Colton said. "I shot him, and when I saw who it was, I figured I needed to bring him back here, so you'd know what happened to him. Now that you've told me how Slim got killed, I reckon Der-wood didn't have anything to do with it."

"No," Freeman said. "Derwood's still in the jail. I was

tempted to make him pay for Slim's murder, but that ain't the way a sheriff's supposed to run his office."

"Now that you've seen this body, I'd like to get rid of it," Colton told him. "Then that fellow can have his horse back."

"We can take care of that for you," Freeman said. "My temporary deputy can handle that. Gordy, lead this horse over to Wilton Johnson's place and tell him that corpse is a city-paid burial with no headstone. Tell him you have to take the horse back to the stable. It belongs to Ransom Ford. Can you remember all that?"

"Yes, sir, Sheriff," Gordy replied respectfully.

Colton stepped down from the saddle, untied the lead rope, then handed the dun's reins to the boy. "I thought I was young for a lawman," he commented as Gordy led the horse away.

"That's my nephew, Gordy Pugh," Freeman said. "He insisted he wanted to help me out around the jail, since Slim's gone. I reckon I never realized how much Slim did until he weren't here no more, and he's just been gone one day."

"Is Derwood givin' you any trouble?" Colton asked.

"No, I reckon not," the sheriff answered, hesitated, then added, "The mayor and the city council ain't too happy about feedin' him three meals a day for however long he's gonna be in our jail. They're complainin' that he's Tyler's problem in the first place and not ours."

Colton could see that it really was a problem for Freeman, so he decided to help him out. "I'll take Derwood off your hands," he said. "I don't mind transporting one prisoner without the use of a jail wagon. Since he's gonna end up going to trial in Tyler, anyway, I'll take him with me when I leave this afternoon. Would that help the situation any?"

"It surely would," Freeman replied, "if you're sure you ain't takin' too big a risk. I mean with you carryin' all that money with you."

"If you don't tell anybody," Colton joked, "maybe they'll think the only thing I'm transportin' of any value is Derwood. If you can get him ready to go after dinner, I'll take him with me. But I'm gonna have to rest my horses before I start back. So I'm gonna take 'em to the stable while I'm in town. I think I'd better send my boss a telegram to let him know where I am. I saw a hardware store back there. I need to pick up a couple of things there, and then Derwood and I can take a little ride."

"You wanna go back to the German's for dinner?" Freeman asked, his day having been greatly improved by Colton's decision to take Derwood Simpson out of his jail that afternoon.

Colton said he was going to suggest that himself. "Whaddaya think? Meet you at Zimmermann's in about an hour?"

"That'll be about right," Freeman answered. "Tell Highsmith that the sheriff's department will take care of any charge for your horses."

"I'll do that," Colton replied. "'Preciate it." He stepped back up into the saddle and turned Scrappy toward the north end of the street, where the stable was located.

"Howdy, Deputy," Ralph Highsmith greeted him. "I saw you when you rode by here a little while ago. Was that the Simpson brother who killed Slim Asher and escaped?"

"Yep, that's who that was," Colton answered. "Are you Mr. Highsmith?"

"I am," he replied, "Ralph Highsmith, this here's my stable. What can I do for you?"

"Colton Gray, Mr. Highsmith. I'm fixin' to turn around and head back to Tyler, but I need to rest my horses for a spell. So I'd like to leave 'em here while I'm in town, take the saddles off 'em, and give both of 'em a portion of grain. Sheriff Freeman said to tell you, he'd pay the charge for that." He waited for Highsmith to nod his understanding; then he went on.

"When I leave here, I'm takin' the other Simpson brother with me. So I'll be takin' the horse he rode in on. I know there are some charges for those horses. I don't expect the sheriff to pay for them. I expect to pay those charges with the horse that Maurice rode in on. Fair enough?"

"I expect so," Highsmith japed, smiling. "One five-year-old gelding in exchange for one night's lodgin' and feed? You drive a hard bargain, young fellow."

"I reckon I'm not in this business to get rich," Colton said. "And I don't feel like messin' with an extra horse on this trip."

"Well, you got a deal," Highsmith said. "I'll take good care of your horses for ya and I'll put your saddle and your packs in one of the back stalls. Nobody can bother 'em back there."

"'Preciate it," Colton said. He thought it better not to tell Highsmith that there was about twenty-seven thousand dollars in his saddlebags. For the short time the saddlebags would be in the back stall, he felt the risk was small. So he left the stable and walked down to the telegraph office and sent a wire to Marshal Timmons. Then he walked back to Zimmermann's Saloon to meet Sheriff Freeman.

"You came back to see us," Christoph Zimmermann said in greeting when Colton walked back to join the sheriff. "I thought you were leaving town yesterday."

"I did. I got halfway to Tyler," he exaggerated, "and got to thinkin' how good that dinner was yesterday, so I turned around and came back to see if you folks cooked like that every day."

Christoph laughed. "Pretty much, I reckon," he said. "It brings the sheriff back most every day."

"Is my prisoner eatin' this good every day?" Colton asked Freeman.

"No," Freeman answered. "He ain't eatin' this good, but he ain't eatin' bad. The hotel dinin' room provides the meals for the prisoners in the jail. I got him his dinner before I came over here to meet you. He knows he's gettin' ready to go to Tyler this afternoon."

"You didn't tell him I'd be takin' the bank's money back with us, did you?"

"No, I didn't tell him anything about the money," Freeman said. "He didn't ask me anything about the money."

"If he asks me about it, I'm gonna tell him I left it here in the bank," Colton said. "If he asks you about it, I'd appreciate it if you'd tell him the same thing. I figure there ain't no sense in givin' him an even bigger reason to try something."

After another satisfying dinner at Zimmermann's, Colton went back to the stable to get the horses, and Freeman went to the jail to make sure Derwood was ready to travel. When Colton got to the jail, Freeman brought Derwood out of his cell and Colton handcuffed his hands behind his back. Derwood said nothing until they walked him outside. Then he remarked, "That ain't my horse. That's Maurice's horse."

"That's all right," Colton told him. "Maurice don't care if you ride him." He was sure that Ralph Highsmith had kept the better of the two horses for himself. He couldn't blame him for that.

"I druther ride my horse," Derwood complained. "He's a better horse than Maurice's."

"I understand," Colton said. "Your horse is a better horse than Maurice's. But your horse developed a split hoof when you and your brother rode into town, so he wasn't ready to go."

"Oh," Derwood responded. "I didn't even notice when he did."

"Don't worry about it," Colton assured him. "Mr. Highsmith caught it right away and he's gonna take good care of your horse, so don't worry."

"I 'preciate it," Derwood said. "I'll be comin' back to get him when I get outta jail."

Sheriff Freeman stood grinning as he listened to the conversation between Colton and the simpleminded outlaw, until he decided to contribute. "Looks like you're all set to go, Deputy Gray," he said. "I'll wire Waco and tell 'em you left all that money Derwood and Maurice stole here in the bank in Nacogdoches."

"Thanks a lot, Sheriff," Colton played his part. "I'm glad I won't have to worry about that money on this trip." He took hold of Derwood's elbow to help him up and said, "Stick your foot in that stirrup." Then he lifted him up into the saddle, and for the second time in as many days, he left Nacogdoches and headed for Tyler.

"Telegram from Deputy Gray, boss," Ron Wild announced as he walked in Marshal John Timmons's office. He handed Timmons the telegram and waited to see his reaction.

"Telegram?" Timmons responded, thinking it was long past the time he expected Colton back in Waco. "Where's it from?" he asked Ron as he took the wire.

"Nacogdoches," Ron answered.

"Nacogdoches?" Timmons reacted as Ron expected. "What the hell is he doing in Nacogdoches? I sent him to Tyler!" He ripped the envelope open and read the wire: *Leaving Nacogdoches today with one prisoner and money from Tyler bank holdup STOP Second suspect killed on road to Tyler yesterday forcing return to Nacogdoches STOP Anticipate arrival Tyler in two or three days STOP Should arrive Waco three and a half days after that STOP Deputy Marshal Colton Gray.*

"Nice of you to drop us a line, Deputy Gray," Timmons muttered as he continued to stare at the telegram as if he expected it to say more. "Maybe you'll explain to me why the hell you went to Nacogdoches when I told you to come home." He crumpled up the telegram into a ball and threw it at his trash can.

Ron walked over and picked the telegram up from the floor and deposited it in the bin Timmons had aimed at. "Sounds like he might have arrested one of the bank robbers and killed the other one, and recovered the stolen money," he said.

Timmons didn't want to hear any defense of Colton Gray's actions. "The man can't seem to follow orders. He just takes off in any direction that fancies him without thinking there must be a reason for orders."

Ron left his boss to stew over his frustration with the seemingly unpredictable young deputy marshal. Colton was different from the other deputies, but he was fearless, and usually competent. The only negative his boss could truly find to criticize Colton was the fact that he had not been fortunate enough to catch the real old-men bandits. And he maintained that they were two younger men in disguise, when Timmons and the bank employees who were robbed by them were certain they were not. Timmons always swore that the truth of his belief was proven by every incident of copycat bandits and their flimsy disguises.

Colton knew he was not going to find any better place to camp on that first leg of the journey to Tyler than the spot he had stopped at the night before when Maurice paid him a visit. He didn't anticipate any problems with Derwood, since he wouldn't tell him he was camping where his brother was killed. To make sure he didn't get a clue, Colton planned to camp just short of the little clearing where Maurice shot up his old blanket. When he came to the creek, it still looked like the perfect campground. So he led the horses off the road and went up the stream about three-quarters of the way he had before. He pulled to a stop and announced, "I think this'll do for the night."

He dismounted and looked around to decide where he would build his fire and where he was going to situate his prisoner. When he had decided, he untied the lead rope but held on to the reins for Derwood's horse. "Derwood, I think it'd be a good idea to explain how this business with you and me is gonna work. I intend to make this trip as easy on you as I can. But I know if I was in your place, I'd be thinkin' about what I could do to escape, and I'd be lookin' for the first opportunity. Since I gotta figure you're thinkin' that way, I have to make sure you don't get that chance. Now, I'm gonna help you down off your horse and I'll unlock one of your wrists, so you don't have to hold your hands behind your back. But that'll just be until I handcuff your hands around a tree so that I can set up the camp, build a fire, and cook us something to eat. While you just sit and watch, I might add. Now, if you make any attempt to get free before your cuffs are locked around that tree, the procedure is simple. I just put a bullet in your brain. The reason I don't shoot you just to cripple you is simple, too. It's too much trouble transportin' a wounded prisoner and I get paid just as much for bringin' in a dead one. It's just common sense."

Derwood listened with great interest and he spoke for the first time since they left town. "Is that the way you killed my brother?"

Colton paused a moment, then said, "Your brother committed suicide. I never arrested him. He tracked me down and sneaked into my camp when I was asleep and emptied his handgun into a blanket he thought was me. When he found out it wasn't me, he reloaded and turned around, and when he saw me, he came charging at me. So I helped him commit suicide. I put a .45 bullet in the middle of his chest. So, you see, it's a different situation with you and me. I'm willin' to make it easy on you, but make no mistake, I will shoot you if you make one wrong move. Do you believe me?"

"I believe you," Derwood answered.

"Good, that's the first step in makin' this a decent journey for you." He reached up and grabbed his arm and helped him out of the saddle. "I think we'll set you down by that little tree over there," he said, pointing to a little oak tree. Then, still holding his arm, he walked him over to the tree, unlocked one cuff, and quickly pulled his hands on both sides of the tree, then clamped the cuff around his wrist again. Leaving him there to watch, he went about the business of taking care of the horses. Then he cut wood and built a fire to cook their supper.

When the bacon and the hardtack were ready, and the coffee was made, Derwood complained. "I don't think I can eat too good with my hands around this tree."

"Well, I wouldn't expect you to," Colton said. "I picked up a little something at the hardware store for you. I almost forgot it." He went to the packs on the ground and pulled out a six-foot length of small chain and a padlock. He reached down and pulled one of Derwood's boots off, then wrapped the chain around Derwood's ankle several times as tightly as he could pull the chain. "It's too easy to slip your foot outta your boot," he explained as he looped the other end around the tree, brought it back to the ankle, and fastened it with the small padlock. Then he unlocked one of the handcuffs again. "There you go, your hands are free to eat and you've got room to move around to get comfortable."

When Colton went about the business of the supper, as skimpy as it was, Derwood took the opportunity to test his confinement. He was disappointed to find that no matter how hard he strained, he could not pull his foot out of the chains.

After giving up on that, he strained again in an effort to break the chain, but found the chain too strong. The padlock proved to be just as impossible. He couldn't force it open, and he didn't have anything to try to pick the lock with, even had he known how to pick one. So he surrendered to his predicament. Unnoticed by him while in the testing of his restraints, Colton kept a constant watch out of the side of his eye to see if he had any success. He was quite pleased with the idea he had come up with spontaneously.

When bedtime came, Colton asked, "You need to get rid of some of that coffee you drank before you turn in for the night?"

Derwood said that he did. "But I don't wanna go right here if I gotta sleep next to this tree."

"I don't blame ya," Colton said. "Stick your hands out in front of you." When Derwood did that, Colton quickly closed the open handcuff around his wrist again. "Your hands are in front of you now and you can still take care of business as soon as I unlock your foot. I'll even escort you to the place of your choice, long as it ain't too far."

"I ain't gotta do nothin' but pee," Derwood said, already convinced that Colton would not hesitate to shoot him, if he showed the slightest sign of resistance. He walked only a few yards away from the tree, with Colton at his back, his Colt in hand. After Derwood relieved himself, Colton repeated the procedure with the chain and the padlock, then helped him make his bed.

The night passed without incident and the routine was continued the next morning, the only difference being the fact that Derwood urinated next to the tree, since he wasn't going to sleep beside it again. They continued on with no trouble from Derwood at all and arrived in Tyler at noontime on the third day after leaving Nacogdoches.

* * *

"Well, I'll be . . ." Sheriff Roy Whitley started when he looked out his office window and spotted the young deputy marshal riding up the street, leading another rider with his hands cuffed behind his back. "Danged if he didn't track 'em down and he got one of 'em." He slapped his hat on his head and hustled out the door to meet him. "Colton Gray!" Whitley exclaimed. "I didn't figure I'd be seein' you any time soon. Is that one of the pair that robbed the bank?"

"That's a fact," Colton answered. "This is Derwood Simpson. He's one of the men who pulled the holdup, but he says he ain't the one who shot the bank guard. He said that was his brother, Maurice. It oughta be easy enough to see if he's tellin' the truth. Just let the folks at the bank take a look at him." He didn't bother to explain that they surely knew which brother shot the guard, the one with the drag-leg or the one with two normal legs.

"The other one get away?" Whitley asked.

"No, unfortunately, he's dead," Colton said. "Couldn't be helped."

"Was you able to recover any of the money they stole?" Whitley asked.

"I think I recovered almost all of it. I don't think they had time to spend much of it. Ain't that about right, Derwood?"

Derwood responded with an indifferent shrug.

Colton went on, "I wanna drop Derwood off in your custody while I take the money back to the bank. Then I'll check back with you. All right?"

"I've got a cell I've been savin' for him, right up front, close to the office," Whitley said. "You go along to the bank. I know Ted Newgate will be mighty happy to see you."

"You reckon it's too late to get him something to eat? We were so close to gettin' here that I didn't stop for dinner."

"You ain't too late," Whitley said. "The hotel dinin' room will be open for an hour yet. They feed my prisoners."

"Good, I'll stop on the way and tell 'em they got a prisoner to feed. You need some help takin' Derwood inside?"

"I don't think so," Whitley replied, and gave Derwood a stern look. "You gonna cause me any trouble?"

"No, sir," Derwood answered meekly. Colton reached up and helped him down from the saddle and gave Whitley the key to his handcuffs. He waited a few moments until the sheriff took Derwood inside before continuing on to the hotel dining room. A brief stop there with Ed Leonard, who was happy to accommodate him, as well as offer to save some dinner for him, no matter how long it took him at the bank.

With his prisoner and himself taken care of, as far as dinner was concerned, Colton proceeded to the bank, the saddlebags filled with money on his shoulder. Gerald Baker, one of the tellers, recognized him. "Howdy, Deputy, I see you're back in town. What can I do for you?"

"I reckon I need to talk to Mr. Newgate," Colton replied.

"I'll tell him you want to talk to him," Gerald said. "He's suffering one of his headaches today and hasn't been seeing many customers."

"I'll try not to take up much of his time, but it's kinda important," Colton said.

Gerald went to Newgate's office door, which was closed. He rapped lightly and waited until he was invited in. He returned after a brief moment with Newgate following him out the door.

"Deputy Marshal Gray," Newgate said, "is this a matter of some importance, or could it wait possibly until a later time?"

"I reckon I'll leave that up to you," Colton responded. "I'm kinda anxious to get rid of all this money that was stolen from your bank, but I guess I can hold on to it for another day or two." He patted the saddlebags on his shoulder.

"My money!" Newgate blurted. "You recovered the stolen money? How much of it? Come on in my office!" He grabbed his arm and pulled him toward the door.

"I don't know exactly how much I've got," Colton said. "I didn't count it, but judging by how much is in here, I'd guess most of it's still here. I don't think those two robbers had a chance to spend very much."

"We'll find out right now," Newgate said. "Baker, you come in here, too, and help me count it."

"I'm gonna need some kinda paper when you're done with the countin'," Colton said, "verifyin' the amount I turned over to you."

"Of course," Newgate said as he emptied out the saddle-bags, his headache evidently having flown away. "I assume you caught the outlaws who stole the money and shot poor Albert Davis."

"Yes, sir, I did. They were two of four outlaw brothers from down near Nacogdoches. I just turned over one of the two who robbed you to Sheriff Whitley to hold for trial. The other one I had to shoot. I'm pretty sure he was the one who shot Albert Davis." He didn't say anything more, since Newgate and Gerald had both started counting.

Gerald finished first and wrote his total on a piece of paper. Minutes later, Newgate finished and wrote his total down. Then they placed their totals on the desk and they matched. A warm smile broke out across Newgate's face. "Twenty-six thousand nine hundred and fifty dollars," Newgate announced. "They only spent fifty dollars of the twenty-seven thousand! It's a miracle!" He looked directly at Colton and declared, "*You're* a miracle!"

"Yep, that's what my boss calls me," Colton said, thinking about the chewing out he was going to suffer when he reported back to Timmons.

"Sheriff Whitley thought you were wasting your time when

you left here," Gerald remarked. "He said those two outlaws would vanish from the face of the earth."

"I got lucky, I guess," Colton said. "Could you give me some kinda verification that I turned over that amount to the bank now? Mr. Leonard, over at the hotel dinin' room, said he'd save a plate of dinner for me. So I don't wanna make him hold it too long."

"Yes, indeed," Newgate replied. He sat down at his desk and wrote a statement saying Colton had turned over that amount to the bank. He had Gerald sign it; then he signed it. He used the bank's official seal on it. "There you are, Deputy Marshal Gray, and we thank you."

"Thank you, sir," Colton replied, and left to go to the dining room. They had just turned the OPEN sign over, but he went in, anyway. Ed saw him come in and he waved him on over to a table by the kitchen door.

Daisy came from the kitchen carrying a plate of food and a cup of coffee. "Hello, Deputy Gray. Minnie put this plate of food in the oven for you."

"Would you tell her I appreciate it very much," Colton replied. "I was afraid I was gonna miss eatin' one of her fine meals."

"I'll tell her you said that," Daisy said. "She'll be tickled. We heard you tickled Ted Newgate when you brought that stolen money back to the bank."

Her comment surprised him. "How'd you know that?" he asked, since he had only just come from the bank.

"Sheriff Whitley came to eat dinner and picked up a plate for a prisoner in the jail. He told us the prisoner was one of the two men who robbed the bank. He said you brought him in and brought the bank's money back, too."

"Just part of the job," Colton tried to say modestly. "That's what deputy marshals do."

"Well, Ed said for me not to charge you anything for your dinner," Daisy said. "Have you got enough coffee?"

"You folks are mighty nice to a man who was just doin' what they pay me to do. And I thank you very much. Now, the least I can do is get on outta here so you folks can finish cleanin' up. Thanks again, Daisy." He ate quickly, then got up and headed for the outside door, stopping briefly near the front desk to thank Ed for the complimentary dinner.

Chapter 14

Outside the dining room, he stepped up into the saddle, wheeled Scrappy from the hitching rail, and led the horses down to the stable, where he had left Derwood's saddle horse with Jesse Trotter.

"You gonna leave your horses here, too?" Jesse asked.

"I hadn't planned to," Colton replied. "But I swear, I've already used up so much of the day, I've a good mind to stay over tonight and get an early start in the mornin'. You've talked me into it, Jesse. I'll leave my horses with you tonight and see you in the mornin'." *Maybe by then you'll have heard I brought the bank's money back and won't charge me for boarding my horses,* he thought.

He pulled his saddlebags and his rifle from his saddle and started walking back to the Texas House Hotel to get a room. "I feel like I've earned a good night's sleep in a bed, a good supper, and a decent breakfast before I start back to Waco and report to Marshal John Timmons," he announced. He wondered if he should send Timmons another telegram to tell him about the successful closing of the case. "I've spent enough money on telegrams," he decided. "He'll find out everything when I get back."

"Howdy, Deputy Gray," Charley Post greeted him when he walked into the hotel. "I heard you were back in town."

"Yep," Colton replied, "word gets around pretty fast, don't it? I'd like to rent a room for the night."

"Sure thing," Charley responded. "I can put you in the same room you had before, if that's all right."

"That would be fine," Colton said. "First floor, close to the dining-room door. Yep, that'll be fine. I'll be leavin' right after breakfast in the mornin', so I'll go ahead and pay you for the room." He took his key from Charley and went to his room to leave his saddlebags and his rifle. Then he went back to the sheriff's office to check with Sheriff Whitley.

"You have any trouble with your new prisoner?" Colton asked Whitley.

"No, not a bit of trouble," the sheriff answered. "You musta took all the fight outta him. He ain't said nothin' but 'yes, sir' and 'no, sir.' He seemed surprised when I brought him his dinner. I reckon he thought I wasn't gonna feed him."

When Derwood saw Colton, he got up from the cot he was sitting on and came over to the bars. "How long do I have to stay here?"

"I don't know, Derwood," Colton answered, "until a circuit judge gets here, I reckon." He looked at Whitley and asked, "Do you know when that might be, Sheriff?"

"I have to notify 'em that I have a prisoner for trial and they'll tell me when I'll have a judge show up. Right now, you're the only prisoner I'm holdin', so I don't know when you'll be tried."

"If you'll let me go, I'll go back to Cat's Eye Creek and I won't cause no more trouble for anybody," Derwood said.

Whitley exchanged glances with Colton before he answered. "We can't do that. That ain't the way it works. You pulled a crime and you have to pay for it. Don't matter if you're sorry for doin' it or not. The good thing you got goin' for you is you didn't kill that bank guard, so maybe the judge might give that some consideration."

"Oh, okay," Derwood said, and went back to his cot to sit down again.

"You just don't cause me any trouble and it won't be so bad," the sheriff told him. "A cot and three meals a day. That ain't too hard to get used to."

Colton and the sheriff walked back into the office. "Damned if he ain't kinda pitiful," Whitley said. "I hope he ain't gonna be here a long time waitin' for trial."

"I can understand how you feel," Colton said. "I'm kinda sorry I arrested him, but he and his brother had the bank's money."

"Here are your bracelets," Whitley said, and he picked up Colton's handcuffs from the desk and handed them to him. "You don't wanna forget them. You stayin' in town tonight?" he asked, since Colton didn't have his horses with him.

"Yep," Colton replied. "I figured it was gettin' a little late in the day to start out for Waco, so I'm gonna wait and start out in the mornin'. And I'll pull into Waco around dinnertime Friday."

"You gonna eat supper in the hotel dinin' room?" Whitley asked.

"Yeah, I thought I would," Colton replied. "You wanna join me?"

"If you ain't particular who you eat with," Whitley answered.

"I'd welcome the company," Colton said. So they agreed to have supper together when the dining room opened its doors at five-thirty.

He left the sheriff's office then and returned to the hotel, where he planned to take advantage of the hotel's washroom. He felt like soaking his body in a tub of hot soapy water and shaving the start of a beard he didn't want the bother of. He didn't like admitting it, even to himself, but Daisy Dean, the spunky little server in the dining room, seemed to be a little more flirty each time he ate there. If she continued her teasing ways tonight, he was going to tell her he stayed over an extra night just to see if she was really interested in him, or just a flirt. He'd let her know he was staying in the hotel that night and see if that affected her teasing. He would have preferred not to take supper with Roy Whitley that night, but he didn't want to be impolite to the sheriff. Whitley seemed to be a fairly sharp individual. He might realize that two's company and three's a crowd. At any rate, he wanted to spruce himself up as best he could so he didn't always look like he'd just crawled out from under a log.

So he heated some water on the stove in the washroom and filled a tub with it. With a washrag and a bar of lye soap, he scrubbed everywhere he could reach. When he had finished and put on his clean shirt and underwear, he felt like it was worth the trouble to feel so clean, whether anyone else appreciated it or not.

He went to the dining room just as the clock struck five-thirty and was among the first few diners to arrive. Ed Leonard, the dining-room host, met him at the door and welcomed him in. "Good evening, Deputy Gray, glad to see you back to eat with us. Any particular place you wanna sit?"

"I'm supposed to meet Sheriff Whitley for supper, so why don't you just put me at his usual table."

"Right," Ed replied, "in the back, close to the kitchen door. Sit yourself down and Daisy will be there in a minute to get you started with some coffee."

A few minutes later, Daisy appeared in the kitchen doorway to see how busy she was going to be. When she saw Colton sitting at the table closest to the kitchen, her face bloomed into a contented smile and she walked over to greet him immediately.

"Colton Gray!" she gushed. "I thought you might have left town after dinner today. I'm glad you decided to stay a little longer. Are you staying in the hotel tonight?"

"Yes, I am, as a matter of fact," Colton answered. "I had

planned to leave after dinner today, but I decided I had to have one more meal with you folks here in the dinin' room."

"Well, we'll see if we can't make it hard for you to leave tomorrow, too," Daisy teased. "We were kinda getting used to having you around. We're gonna miss you when you're gone." She gave him a naughty smile and winked. "I'll bet you've got a little gal back in Waco wishing you'd hurry up and come home."

He felt himself flushing. "Nope, no little gal waitin' for me," he insisted. "I reckon I can't stay in one place long enough to get to know a woman."

"I bet I know you," Daisy said, then asked, "Are you ready to eat?"

"I told Sheriff Whitley I'd meet him here for supper, so let's wait till he shows up," Colton said. "You could start me off with a cup of coffee, though."

"You betcha!" she said, and spun on her heel to return to the kitchen. When she returned, she was carrying two cups of coffee. She set them on the table and nodded toward the front door. "Here comes your supper companion now. He'll say, 'That better be my cup of coffee or I'll close this place down.'"

Whitley walked purposefully back to the table. He looked at Daisy and said, "That better be my cup of coffee or I'll close this place down." He pulled a chair back and sat down. Daisy winked at Colton. He returned it with a wink of his own. "Well, Colton, I see you got all slicked up for your ride back home," Whitley went on. He stroked his chin with his thumb and forefinger. "Even shaved," he remarked.

"I was gettin' kinda scruffy," Colton replied, "and I was afraid Daisy wouldn't serve me if I didn't clean up a little." He glanced up to meet her sweet smile for his remark. Then he said to Whitley, "You look like you slicked up a little yourself."

"Glad you noticed," Whitley said. "I went to the barber-

shop after I left you and got a shave and a haircut. I always try
to look sharp whenever there's somebody from the marshal's
office in town."

Colton graced him with a chuckle. He was thinking, however, that the sheriff was in an unusual casual mood. He hoped
he wasn't thinking about hitting the saloons after supper for a
few drinks, still celebrating the arrest of the bank robbers and
the return of the money. Glancing at Daisy, Colton thought of
other, more pleasant ways to spend his last evening in town.
And what was encouraging to him was that, based on her comments and subtle glances, he was sure she felt the same.

There was no perception on Whitley's part of the obvious
attraction between the deputy marshal and the dining-room
server. He continued to rattle on about how he had so much
hope for the future of the town and what a great place it was to
raise a family. Colton waited him out, exchanging patient
glances with Daisy whenever she was at their table to bring
coffee or simply passing by, until there was no reason to sit
there any longer.

It was then that Colton learned the reason for Whitley's attitude.

Daisy had picked up the dirty dishes from the table and
taken them to the kitchen, when Whitley confided, "I enjoyed the supper with you, Colton, and I'd walk out with you,
but I'm gonna set here to say a few words to Daisy, just the
two of us." He made a wide grin for Colton. "I asked Daisy to
be my wife earlier this afternoon and she said she would." He
watched Colton's shocked reaction for a long second before
continuing. "We've been bouncin' back and forth for almost a
year before I finally got up the nerve to ask her and she said
yes. Ain't that something?"

Colton was speechless for a few seconds. When he did find
his voice, he could only say, "Yes, sir, that surely is something."

"As smart as you are, you most likely figured there was

something going on between me and her," Whitley said, "as much time as she spent at our table."

"Right," Colton said, "I did think about it." *And I took a bath and shaved*, he thought. "But I figured that was business between you and her, and none of my own." He got up from the table then. "When's the big day?"

"That's what we're gonna talk about tonight," the sheriff replied, still grinning like a baboon.

"Well, I wish you the best of luck," Colton said. "I think I'll stop in that saloon on the corner and have a drink to your long and successful marriage." *Then I'll have a couple more to the sincere wish that I don't stay stupid all my life.*

"Everything all right?" Ed asked when Colton stopped at his desk to pay for his supper. "Did Daisy take good care of you?"

"She sure did," Colton replied, "and the food was as good as usual. I got just what I needed."

"Well, I'm glad to hear that," Ed responded, although it struck him as an odd remark. "Will you be eating breakfast with us in the morning?"

"I expect so," Colton said. "I'll be leavin' here in the mornin', but I'll most likely eat breakfast before I start out for Waco."

"Good. We'll look forward to seein' you. Have a good evening." Colton nodded in reply and went out the outside door to the street. Ed walked back to the table where Daisy was talking to Whitley.

"Nice enough young fellow," Ed remarked.

"Yeah, he is," the sheriff replied. "He's a heckuva good lawman, too. Said he was goin' to have a drink or two at that saloon on the corner before he turned in. I didn't think about it till after he left, but I didn't ask him which corner. Maybe I shoulda asked him if he was talkin' about Cobb's Crib. I don't wanna have to go over there tonight." He looked at Daisy and winked. "Tonight's too nice a night to spoil by havin' to go over and break up a bar fight."

"I expect he can handle himself," Ed said. "He strikes me that way. Anyway, Cobb's is at the other end of the street."

Colton walked out on the street and paused to look at the town closing up for the day. The sun was settling down on the low hills west of the town, leaving it with just enough warmth from the day to make it a comfortable evening. He decided he'd take a walk, so he started toward the north end of the main street, looking at the different shops as he passed, most of them closed. About halfway down the street, he started feeling a little better about himself, even to the point where he could laugh about it. Thinking back, he couldn't really recall where he'd made a complete fool of himself in anything he had actually said to Daisy or Whitley.

Hell, they'll make a wonderful couple. Maybe have a dozen little deputy sheriffs, he decided.

When he reached the end of the street, he crossed over to walk the other side back to the hotel. The building on the corner was obviously a saloon, since it was the only one with horses tied at a hitching rail in front. "'Cobb's Crib,'" he read the sign aloud.

Wonder what that's supposed to mean? Owner's name is Cobb? Either that, or it stands for corn, like in a corncrib. Maybe all they serve is corn whiskey?

He decided he'd go in and have that drink he threatened to have, back in the dining room. He reached up and removed his badge from his shirt and dropped it in his vest pocket, preferring not to call attention to it.

He stepped inside the batwing doors and waited for a few seconds to allow his eyes to adjust to the dim interior of the saloon. He counted eight men standing at the bar and several tables with two, three, or four occupants. Back in one corner of the room, there was a large table hosting a five-player card game. Colton was surprised to see so many customers on a weeknight. He walked over to the bar and filled a gap in the line of drinkers, who all turned to look him over. The bartender, a short little man with long gray sideburns on an otherwise bald skull, stepped over to face him.

"Whaddle you have?" Moe Trace asked.

"I'll take a shot of whatever you're pouring at the bar," Colton answered.

"This is corn whiskey," the bartender said as he put a glass on the bar and poured a shot.

"I would have guessed that it was," Colton said, and tossed it back. He paused to let the burn cool, then asked for another. "Why do they call this place Cobb's Crib?"

The bartender shrugged. "'Cause the owner is Jackson Cobb, so he can call it whatever the hell he wants."

Colton guessed the bartender must be asked the question so many times that he was sick of answering it. So Colton said, "Well, it's a good name for a saloon, easy to remember."

The bartender grinned. "Yeah, I reckon it is. Is your name Gray?"

"Yes, it is. How'd you know that?"

"'Cause I ain't never seen you in here before," Moe said, "and I know there ain't but two new people in town today. One of 'em's a bank robber and the other one's a deputy U.S. marshal. Last I heard, the bank robber's still in the jail, so I figure you're Deputy Marshal Colton Gray. My name's Moe Trace, and I'll bet you've already figured it out that I'm the bartender."

"Almost, Moe, I'm still workin' on it," Colton japed; then they both chuckled.

"You gonna be in town a while?" Moe asked.

"No, I'm leavin' in the mornin' to go back to Waco," Colton said.

"Good riddance," a muffled voice said down at the end of the bar.

Colton ignored it, but Moe took offense. "Who said that? Was that you, Ike Antley? You ain't got no call to disrespect a lawman that caught that pair of robbers that ran off with the money in the bank and brought the people's money back to the bank. He didn't have nothin' to do with your brother, Lemuel, going to prison for cattle rustlin'." He turned his attention back to Colton then. "Deputy, them two drinks you just had are on the house, and I'll pour you another'n if you're ready for it."

"You don't have to do that, Moe," Colton said. Moe held both hands up in a gesture to stop him, so Colton said, "I thank you for the two shots, but that's all I came in to have. I'm sorry I disturbed the peace in here. I'll thank you again and I'll be on my way."

"Good riddance," Ike repeated, not as muffled this time, mistakenly thinking the young deputy was a little shy of a direct confrontation. When Colton ignored the insult a second time, Ike sought to enhance his own reputation. "How 'bout a couple of free drinks for the people who buy your damn whiskey all the time, Moe?"

That was enough for Colton. "All right, damn it, that's about enough out of you. It's time you shut your mouth while you're still ahead."

All the conversation around the bar suddenly stopped while everybody close to the bar waited to see what Ike was going to do. Clearly, the young man was accustomed to giving orders when he was wearing a badge. But he wasn't wearing a badge now. And without the badge, he was just another whiskey-drinking big talker. At least this was the line of reasoning that Ike Antley chose to follow. So he said, "I'm tellin' you to get your sorry butt outta here right now, or get ready to use that sidearm you're wearin'."

Colton turned and looked at him in disbelief. "You're callin' me out? For what reason? Because I told you to shut up? You think that's worth dyin' for?" All the while, he kept moving toward him, until Ike started backing up, his hand on the handle of his six-shooter. Finally Ike could back up no farther when his back hit the wall.

"All right," Colton said, "we'll draw. You ready?"

"We ain't but a foot apart!" Ike blurted.

"So what?" Colton demanded. "We can still draw and be guaranteed we won't miss. I'll count to three and we'll draw. Ready?"

"No, hell no, that's crazy," Ike protested. "You're crazy and I ain't drawin' against a crazy man."

"That's the first sensible thing that's come outta your mouth," Colton said. Knowing what to expect from Ike, he moved as if to turn away—and Ike suddenly went for his gun. Colton reacted instantly, jamming his elbow under Ike's chin and grabbing Ike's gun hand with his hand. A struggle for only a couple of seconds ensued as Colton forced Ike's gun back down into the holster, then squeezed Ike's trigger finger until the gun went off, firing a bullet out of the holster and into Ike's boot. Ike howled in pain and Colton drew the weapon out of the holster when Ike let go and limped over to a chair to try to get his boot off.

Colton walked back by the bar and handed the pistol to Moe. "I'm sorry I was the cause of a disturbance, Moe. You can give this back to Ike after I'm gone." He paused, then added, "Although I'm not sure he's got enough sense to own one. Thanks again for the whiskey." Once outside the saloon, he wasted very little time walking back to the hotel, in case Ike had steam enough left to hobble out the door after him. He could have continued his leisurely pace of before, had he known the trouble Ike was having back in Cobb's Crib.

While Ike was suffering a great deal of pain, his bullet had gone all the way through his foot, and had lodged in the thick sole of his boot. The problem was, he could not get the boot off his throbbing foot. When the bullet went into the boot sole, it had evidently pulled part of his sock into the sole with it and Ike couldn't pull his foot out. It was only after someone told him to pull his foot out of his sock—and leave the sock—that he freed himself from his boot. As soon as his foot was free, he limped to the bar and demanded his pistol. Moe handed it over and Ike limped out the front door, leaving a spotted trail of blood behind him. He was too late, however, for Colton was nowhere in sight.

As he stood there on the boardwalk in front of the saloon, staring down the dark empty street, he was suddenly aware of the sounds of laughter coming from inside the saloon. He knew what they were laughing about and he temporarily forgot the throbbing in his foot as the anger of his humiliation took preference. He stomped back inside the saloon, walking on his heel and one boot, to discover his other boot sitting on the bar.

"I reckon you learned that it ain't healthy messin' around with a deputy U.S. marshal," Moe told him when he snatched his boot off the bar. "You reckon you'd better go up and let Doc Beard take a look at that foot?"

"What for?" Ike replied. "The bullet went clear through. He ain't gotta dig it outta my foot, and I ain't gonna pay him to wrap a rag around it. Louella can do that. Can't you, darlin'?" he asked her, since she seemed so interested in his wounded foot.

"Maybe Doc Beard might give you something that'll keep it from gettin' infected," Moe said. "Louella don't know nothin' about that."

"Hell, all she'd have to do is pour a little whiskey on it and wrap a rag around it," Ike said. "And I'd pay her the same thing that Doc would charge."

"Yeah, I can do that," Louella volunteered.

"Of course, you'd have to do me one more service that I wouldn't ask Doc Beard to do," Ike informed her. "More along your regular line of work."

"I'll be doggone," Louella said, "you're gonna have to pay double then."

"Time and a half," Ike said. "You oughta gimme a better deal 'cause I'm wounded." He waited for her answer.

"Oh, all right," she caved in. "I'll bandage your foot for you and give you a discount on my usual rate, just because you were dumb enough to call a deputy marshal out. You're lucky he didn't kill you. He just shot you in the foot to teach you a lesson. Let me hunt up some rags and we'll go back to my room."

Ike didn't dispute her words because he knew she was right. He had pretty much made a fool of himself.

Colton Gray, a young man who had also come very close to making a fool of himself earlier that night, unlocked the door to his room at the Texas House Hotel. He felt very fortunate that he had not blundered any further in his interpretations of Daisy Dean's smiles and remarks.

And thank goodness Roy Whitley had confessed his and Daisy's plans before I totally stuck my foot in my mouth, he thought. Thinking back on it now, he could actually chuckle about it. His thoughts shifted over then to one Ike Antley, and whether or not there was a potential there for more trouble. He felt there was a very good possibility that he might have embarrassed Ike to the point where he would seek retaliation. And Ike quite possibly might have heard him comment that he was going to start back toward Waco in the morning.

"Never a good policy in a situation like that to let your adversary know when you were leaving and what road you would be traveling," he said aloud. He just might have set himself up for an ambush in the morning, with his shooting of Ike Antley's foot.

An assassination was a very easy crime to commit. Find a good cover spot anywhere along your target's line of travel. Set the front sight of your rifle on his chest and pull the trigger. Unfortunately, the only way to avoid becoming the victim is just pure blind luck. And that's something Colton didn't like to count on. To play it safe, he could leave Tyler on the south road out of town for five or ten miles, then cut back north to strike the road to Corsicana. If Ike was planning an ambush, he wouldn't likely set up and wait for him that far out of town.

To hell with it, Colton thought, *I'll decide if it's necessary in the morning.*

He realized he was ready to get a good night's sleep, so he hung his gun belt on a chair beside the bed, where it would be handy if there was an occasion to need it. Then he stripped down to his underwear, blew out the lamp, and crawled into bed. He was asleep within a few short minutes after his head hit the pillow.

He was suddenly awakened by something; he knew not what. Groggy from being jerked from a deep sleep, he knew only that it was late. He didn't hear another sound in the hotel. Then he realized what had awakened him when he heard a light tapping on his door. Alert then, he reached over and pulled his Colt .45 from the holster. He tiptoed to the door, but stood beside it, instead of standing in front of it. There it was again, the tapping.

This time, he answered, "Yes?"

"Colton?" the soft voice answered.

"Daisy?" he responded, and unlocked the door. "What's the matter? What's wrong?"

"Can I come in?"

He opened the door and looked to see if there was anyone

with her. She slipped inside the room and closed the door behind her.

"Nothing's wrong. I know you're leaving tomorrow morning and I don't know if you'll ever be back in Tyler again. So I wanted to spend a little time with you before you go."

"Daisy," he replied, "I don't understand. Roy Whitley told me at supper that you and him are getting married. Isn't that right?"

"Yes, we are getting married. We've been courting for a long time and I truly love Roy. So when he asked me to marry him, I said yes."

"But if you truly love him and you've accepted his proposal of marriage, don't you think it's wrong to spend time in my room with me?"

"Why?" she asked. "We're not getting married until Sunday. I'm not married now."

Chapter 15

Colton awoke the next morning to realize he had slept much later than he had intended. He quickly assaulted the chamber pot under the bed, then frantically began to pull his clothes on. When he found his watch, he was relieved to find he still had time to get to the dining room before it closed for breakfast. He was still confused about what had happened last night. One look at his bed prompted him to try to put it back in some semblance of a peaceful night's sleep. He only took time to splash some water on his face from the basin on the dresser. Tossing the door key beside it, he picked up his rifle and his saddlebags and left the room, then walked the short distance down the hall to the dining-room door.

Ed met him when he walked in. "Good morning, Deputy Gray. I expected you a little earlier. Sheriff Whitley was gonna try to catch you before you left town, but he was called away."

"Mornin'," Colton said, then thought, *They know! They all know!*

He parked his rifle and saddlebags over behind Ed's desk, then walked back to Whitley's usual table, which had already been cleared. He pulled out a chair on a side of the table that would permit him to see people coming in the door and sat down.

In the next instant, Daisy came out of the kitchen. "Well, good morning, sleepyhead. We expected to see you in here as soon as the door was open, since you said you were leaving us today."

"Good mornin'," he responded, not sure what else to say. "I overslept."

"You look like you need your coffee," she said. "I'll get you a cup right away and I'll tell Minnie you're here. She's making pancakes this morning and she wanted to make yours special with some real maple syrup." Before he could ask why Minnie wanted to make his special, Daisy popped back into the kitchen.

"Ed Leonard said Sheriff Whitley was here, but he left already. I reckon he thought I'd be here a lot earlier than this," Colton said when Daisy came back with his coffee.

"Yes, he waited for you for a while," Daisy said. "Then he decided to go ahead and take breakfast plates back to the jail for his prisoners. He said he's got two now, so he thought he wouldn't make 'em wait any longer for breakfast."

"Two?" Colton responded. "He must have arrested somebody last night, because there wasn't anybody in the jail yesterday but Derwood Simpson."

"Didn't you hear the shots last night?" Daisy asked. He shook his head. "We heard 'em here. We were cleaning up the kitchen and dining room. The sheriff was here, helping us empty the coffeepot, so he went to see what the shooting was about. He didn't come back last night, but when he came in this morning, he told us what it was. It was some trouble where it usually is, at Cobb's Crib." She paused then and waited for some response from him, an expectant smile on her face. When he didn't respond, she said, "Cobb's Crib," in an effort to remind him. "Where you shot Ike Antley in the foot last night."

"He shot himself in the foot," Colton corrected her. "I just helped him. But what's that got to do with the shots you heard late last night?"

"The sheriff said Ike and another fellow got into an argument over that woman that works there, and Ike pulled his gun and shot him in the leg."

"So he put Ike in jail, did he?" Colton asked. When she nodded yes, he thought, *That takes care of my little ambush problem.* It would make for a more leisurely ride back to Waco. He sat there, working on his first cup of coffee for a little while. Then when Daisy came back with the pot, Minnie came with her carrying a plate with a stack of crispy brown pancakes and some bacon. She had decorated the top pancake using maple syrup and butter to form a smiling face. She set the plate down on the table and stepped back to enjoy his reaction. He stared at the stack of pancakes, knowing they were anticipating his reaction. But he couldn't make anything out of the mess of syrup and the thin strip of bacon on top.

"Well, if that ain't something," he remarked, stalling for time. Then he figured it must be a smiling face, so he gambled and said, "It looks just like you, Minnie."

Both women laughed delightedly. "Minnie said you'd say it looked like me," Daisy giggled. "I said you wouldn't know what to make of it."

"We just wanted to let you know we enjoyed meetin' you, Colton," Minnie said. "And we hope you have a nice trip home."

"Come back to see us," Daisy added, "if you're ever back this way again."

"You can count on that," Colton said. "I don't think I've ever had a send-off this nice before. Most places, folks are just glad to see me go."

"If they're on the wrong side of the law, I expect," Minnie said. "Come on, Daisy, let's let him eat before those pancakes get cold."

They left him to eat his breakfast, and he ate every bite, to make sure Minnie thought he enjoyed it. When he finished, Daisy brought the coffeepot, in case he had room for more; he told her that he had best get going. She placed her hand on his and gave it a little squeeze. He whispered, "Thank you, Daisy. I wish you the best that life can offer."

She smiled and whispered, "I'll never forget you, Colton Gray." Then she did an about-face and returned to the kitchen.

He paid Ed for his breakfast, picked up his rifle and saddlebags, and started for the stable.

"Mornin', Colton," Jesse Trotter called out when he saw him approaching. "I expected to find you waitin' for me to open up this mornin'."

"Yeah, I shoulda been here that early, but I got behind, and everything I did seemed to put me further behind. I need to saddle up, then go by the sheriff's office before I ride out. If I don't get goin' pretty soon, it'll be time to make camp right here in the street."

He settled up with Jesse and rode to the jail, where he found Whitley standing out on the little porch before his office door.

"Thought I'd stop by and let you know that I'm officially leavin' your town," Colton said.

"I swear," Whitley responded. "I thought you must have already gone when you didn't show up for breakfast this mornin'. What happened? You have a rough night, last night?"

"No, I wouldn't call it that," Colton replied. "Just for some reason, I didn't wake up this mornin' when I usually do. I just made it to the dinin' room before they closed."

"Did the women take care of you?" Whitley asked.

"Yes, sir, they certainly did," Colton answered. Then quick to change the subject, he said, "I heard you arrested Ike Antley last night."

"Yeah, he's in jail. He got in an argument with Jay Wilkerson and pulled out his pistol and shot him. You might be interested to know they were arguing about Luella spending too much time takin' care of Ike's foot." He grinned then and said, "I was wonderin' if you were gonna tell me how Ike got his foot shot. I heard Moe Trace's version of it. I figured that was pretty much the real story." He chuckled. "Sounded to me like you mighta saved ol' Ike's life."

"I just wanted to check with you before I left town to tell you about the incident at Cobb's Crib. I thought about telling you right after it happened last night, but I knew you and Daisy were meetin' to talk about your weddin'. So I didn't think this business with Ike Antley was worth interruptin' you."

"I 'preciate that, Colton. Thanks again for the job you did for the bank, and I hope you have a good trip back home."

They shook hands, and then Colton climbed up into the saddle and rode out on the road to Corsicana and Waco. He was afraid it would take a while before his brain would ever regain its balance after this business in Tyler.

He had originally planned to arrive back in Waco around dinnertime on Friday before his delay in leaving Tyler. And after an uneventful three-and-a-half-day trip, he still managed to pull into the stable in Waco before suppertime on Friday. He very much wanted to report in before the weekend, since he had been gone for so long. He left most of his packs with Horace Temple, taking only his dirty clothes, his saddlebags, and his rifle. Then he went straight to the marshal's office to report in, before John Timmons left for the day.

"Colton Gray," Timmons's clerk pronounced solemnly when he walked into the outer office. "Glad to see you. Let me tell Marshal Timmons that you're here. I know he's anxious to see you." He got up from his desk and hurried to the marshal's office door. "Excuse me, sir, I know you're trying to get away from here a little bit early today, but Deputy Gray just walked into the office."

"Gray," Timmons pronounced the name in the same tone he might report a plague. "So he's come back, after all. Send him in, Ron." He leaned back in his chair, crossed his arms across his chest, and waited.

"Yes, sir," Ron said, and went back to get Colton. "Marshal Timmons said come on in." Then he whispered, "Good luck!"

Colton nodded and walked back to the office.

"Deputy U.S. Marshal Colton Gray," Timmons announced. "I'm happy you could find the time to report into this office today. You know, Gray, I have twelve deputy marshals under my command in this office. Eleven of them go where I send them, do what I tell them to do, and report back when they've completed the job. And then I have you. Your assignment, since you've been working exclusively on the old-men robberies, was to go to Tyler to investigate the robbery there of the Farmers Bank. Three and a half days up there, spend a day investigating, three and a half days back, that's a total of eight days. Do you know how many days you've been gone?"

"No, sir, I don't, but I can probably come up with the total for you, if you give me a minute to count 'em."

"Never mind that now," Timmons stopped him. "The point is, why didn't you return to Waco when you were through with the investigation? Instead, I get a telegram that you are going to try to pick up the trail of the robbers, where it was lost by the posse."

"Well, sir, I had a strong feeling about a family of outlaws named Simpson that hole up in a hollow called Cat's Eye Creek."

"You had a feeling?" Timmons asked. "You went chasing down the Angelina River on a feeling?"

"A hunch, I reckon, but I felt pretty sure if I found Cat's Eye Creek, I'd find the two Simpson brothers who robbed the bank. And I thought that was more important than reporting right back to Waco."

"Why were you in Nacogdoches?" Timmons asked.

"That was the closest place with a jail and a telegraph," Colton answered. "I was about to say that I was right about the Simpson brothers. I was able to arrest them and recover almost all of the bank's money. I dropped the outlaws in the jail to hold them for a jail wagon to transport 'em to trial, while I took the bank's money back to Tyler. That's why I wired you from Nacogdoches." He paused then, waiting for Timmons's reaction.

Timmons didn't say anything for a minute while he glared at Colton. He was desperate in that he did not want to concede to his young deputy that following a lead and making an arrest was more important than strict obeying of orders.

Finally he spoke again. "Gray, what you don't understand is that no unit of law enforcement can be effective without strict discipline. And that means following orders to the letter, no matter what your personal feelings may be. You were lucky this time, but you can't ignore direct orders and continue to wear that badge. Consider this a final warning. Take the weekend off and think about whether or not you would like to continue to serve Texas as a deputy marshal. Report back Monday morning and wear some old clothes. This office needs painting."

"Yes, sir," Colton said while biting his tongue to keep from telling him where he could stick his paintbrush. He turned and left the office to find Ron waiting in the hallway door for him.

"I heard most of it," Ron said as Colton walked past him. "Maybe this will teach you a lesson. You can be punished for arresting the bank robbers and returning the stolen money."

"I reckon I'm just a slow learner," Colton said. "See you Monday, when I get a chance to show you I'm a worse painter than I am a deputy marshal." He picked up his rifle, saddle-bags, and his dirty clothes and headed for Rena Bramble's boardinghouse. For some reason, he felt a hankering for a nice home-cooked meal by Gracie and a good night's sleep in his own room.

"Gracie!" Rena called out when Colton walked in the front door. "Our wandering boy has come home." She smiled delightedly when she saw him cringe in reaction to the "wandering boy" label.

Gracie came out of the kitchen immediately to greet him as well. "My goodness," she agreed, "it is him. It's a good thing you didn't rent his room out, after all." She stood and looked at him, her hands on her hips, and shook her head. "I expect I'd better peel a couple more potatoes for supper. You are here for supper, aren't you?"

He shook his head slowly, unable to think of any answer appropriate to counteract their teasing. "Yes, I'm here for supper, and it better be worth the money I'm payin' to eat with you," he said. That riposte was the best his tired mind could come up with at the moment.

Gracie sensed he was troubled about something, so she said, "You go along and wash up for supper. It'll be ready in about twenty-five minutes."

"Yes, ma'am," he replied. "I'll be ready."

He walked back down the hallway to his room, propped his rifle in the corner, and his saddlebags in the one chair. He decided it would be best if he shaved, since he hadn't since the night before he left Tyler. That thought triggered another memory and it occurred to him that Sheriff Roy Whitley and Daisy Dean were going to tie the knot the day after tomorrow. *He's getting himself a hell of a woman*, he thought. *I hope they enjoy a long and happy marriage.* He picked up the water pitcher from the bowl on the dresser and went to the pump to get some water to clean up with.

When he heard Rena's little bell announce that supper was ready, he went to the dining room to join the little group of boarders. "Well, looks like we've got a guest for supper to-night," Howard Boyd joked.

The others at the table said hello and welcomed him back. They all turned their attention to the loading of their plates, and once that was accomplished, there was time for conversation. Melva Birch, an elderly widow who had lived with Rena for several years, asked Colton where he had been.

"I had to go up to Tyler," Colton told her. "If you don't know where that is, it's a little town northeast of here, about a hundred and thirty miles."

"What did you have to go up there for?" Howard asked. A single man a few years older than Colton, Howard worked in the post office. "You have to go pick up a prisoner and bring him back here for trial?"

"No," Colton replied. "A couple of fellows held up the bank and I was sent up there to investigate the robbery."

"After it was already robbed?" Howard asked. "What's the sense of that? That's lockin' the barn door after the cow's run away, ain't it?" He paused to make sure everyone got his point, but then had another thought. "It weren't them two old-men bandits, was it?"

"No," Colton answered, "it wasn't them, but the reason I was sent to investigate it was because it was two outlaws dressed like the old men. But they were just copycat bandits."

"If they robbed the bank and got away, I guess it don't make no difference if they were the genuine old-men bandits or not."

"I reckon not," Colton replied, "but they didn't get away with it. They were tracked down and arrested before they had a chance to spend the money."

"So they weren't the real old-men bandits," Howard continued, apparently fascinated by the two nearly legendary robbers. "It might notta been so easy to track 'em down, if it hadda been the real pair."

"I expect you're right," Colton said, willing to give him that.

Howard was not satisfied, however. "Those two old men are pretty slick when it comes to robbin' the little banks. You don't never hear about 'em knockin' over one of them big national banks, like that new Wells Fargo Bank in Fort Worth. They got guards and three or four tellers and other folks workin' in that bank. And even if they was to rob 'em, they'd have a Wells Fargo special agent sent down here to investigate it and track those two old men down before they knew what hit 'em."

"You may be right," Colton said. "Those Butterfield Line and Wells Fargo detectives are pretty sharp men. It might take that before they're stopped—"

"I don't know a whole lot about bank detectives," Gracie interrupted. "But if you two keep talking until those beans get cold, don't come complaining to me about it."

Chapter 16

At another table, some distance from Waco in Lampasas County, at approximately the same time, another discussion about the new Wells Fargo Bank in Fort Worth was under way. This one had a more meaningful impact upon the two people exploring it. Before the name of Wells Fargo entered the conversation, there was more serious discussion regarding the topic of retirement from the banking business.

"We talked about this before," Casey Tubbs remarked, "and how we would know when it was time to quit."

"Well, D and T Cattle Company is in pretty good shape right now," Eli Doolin stated. "But how do you know when you've got enough money? One thing I know for sure is that we've gotta stop bein' everybody's Santa Claus. We've been mighty lucky we ain't been caught, up to now. You know Colton Gray thinks we're Elmer and Oscar. You know he does. He just ain't been able to prove it yet."

They paused their discussion when Juanita came into the study to ask if they wanted coffee. "I cook a peach pie this morning, so you could have with your coffee," she said. "You want?"

"I want," Casey answered. "I think that's what I need right now more than anything else I can think of."

"Me too," Eli said.

Juanita's broad smile was evidence of how pleased she was by their reaction. "Good," she said. "I go fix."

When she left to fetch the pie and coffee, Casey looked at his partner and grinned as he shook his head in amazement. "We've come one helluva long ways from the time when you and me was just the two oldest cowhands workin' on this ranch."

At the time when they decided to rob that first bank, they had no future prospects beyond riding the grub line, looking for a job with another cattle ranch. But there were no jobs for cowhands because the cattle market had collapsed. So they figured they had little to lose. If they were unsuccessful as bank robbers, at least they would get meals and a place to sleep in prison. They didn't feel the loss was that great, if they were caught.

Things were different now. Their criminal careers had been so successful that they had been able to rebuild the Whitmore Ranch and rename it the D&T Cattle Company. They had re-hired all the young cowhands and built the ranch into the biggest in the area. They had money in the bank, as well as in their private safe. So now, there was much to lose if Casey and Eli were caught.

Monroe Kelly was a promising young man, and he was doing a good job as their foreman. But he was not mature enough to run the D&T Cattle Company as it now stood, should Casey and Eli get sent to prison. He held that thought when Juanita came back into the room carrying a tray with pie and coffee. He felt the responsibility then for Juanita's and Miguel's lives as well. When Juanita left the room again, he asked Eli to share his thoughts on the matter regarding Frank Carter.

Eli scratched his head to awaken his thoughts. "Well, like we said, D and T is buyin' most everything we need from

Carter General Merchandise, 'cause it's in Little Bow and that ain't but four miles from us. That beats the hell outta havin' to go to Lampasas for supplies. Frank's a good man. Does right by us. 'Course, we're the only reason he was able to keep his business. It was mighty poor luck when that little bank he had a loan with in Fort Worth got bought out by Wells Fargo. And Wells Fargo is callin' all loans payable immediately, if they're overdue."

"I expect Wells Fargo has been lookin' to put a bank in Fort Worth to add to their string of banks in the southwest," Casey speculated, "wantin' to be the biggest in the country. You know why Frank told us all about it. Too many people we helped have shot their mouths off about us helpin' them out of financial trouble. I swear, Eli, if we keep up our outlaw business, we ain't gonna have to wear disguises to look like them two old men. We've got to stop before we go to the bank one time too many." He took a big bite of peach pie and washed it down with a swallow of coffee. "Frank don't owe that much, but we've got to stop sometime."

There was another reason both men were anxious to retire from the bank-robbing business, but neither man had wanted to express it, afraid the other one would no longer trust his resolve. Eli decided to make his feelings known.

"I think you're right," he said. "We've got to stop sometime and I think that time is right now. Frank Carter owes six thousand dollars. Let's bail him out and get back to raisin' cattle for a livin'. We've always robbed the banks that were takin' advantage of the farmer and the rancher, figuring they oughta be punished. But most of the small banks ain't like that, and I don't cotton to robbin' the honest bankers. It's a little late to be sayin' that, I reckon. But they ain't like the big national banks, like Wells Fargo, that wanna own all the land where the railroad's supposed to go."

Casey didn't say anything for a few moments as he just

stared at his partner. "I reckon we both feel the same way about robbin' the small-town banks. It feels like we're stealin' directly from the folks who trusted the bank. And that ain't a good way to feel. I'm ready to quit, too. I've been thinking about this thing ever since we talked to Frank Carter about his problem. We can afford to give him the money he needs, but I'd feel better about the shape D and T Cattle Company is in if we had one more good haul. What do you think about Oscar and Elmer makin' a visit to the new Wells Fargo Bank in Fort Worth for one last withdrawal before we retire?"

"The thought appeals to me," Eli said. "That way, I believe we'd be stealing money from all the Wells Fargo Banks and not the Fort Worth bank."

"All right, we agree on it," Casey said. "One last bank holdup and we bury Elmer and Oscar for good. Right?"

"That's right," Eli responded, "one last time." They shook hands on it. "We're gonna have to come up with a real good plan for this one. It's gonna be hard to beat the trick we used in Mexia, but I'm sure they've passed the word around about the humpback."

"There ain't no deadline on it," Casey said. "We'll take a little trip to Fort Worth and see what the new Wells Fargo looks like. They might make it a much bigger bank than whatever Frank said the name of the old bank was. We might have to worry about a lot more people workin' in there."

"We might even decide we ain't even gonna try it, if it don't look like we got a dang good chance of pullin' it off," Eli said.

"That's a fact," Casey agreed. "I ain't interested in havin' my picture took, layin' on a board in front of the bank. I kinda like livin' the life of a partner in a major cattle operation."

"You know what would be a real treat to do in Fort Worth?" Eli asked. He waited for Casey to inquire what. "To get us a room at the Woodward House Hotel."

Casey grinned in response. "That would be something,

wouldn't it? I expect Emma Woodward don't expect to ever see the two of us again. And Pearl, she was sure one fine cook. What was that other lady's name? Oh, yeah, Rose, I remember now. I would enjoy seein' those folks again."

"I don't see why we couldn't stay there if they've got an empty room," Eli said. "There ain't no reason to think they would connect us with a bank robbery. We'd just be in town on business, like a lot of other people. Besides, I'd bet those ladies wouldn't tell anybody if they knew it was us that robbed the bank. Hell, let's do it."

"All right, we'll do it," Casey said, still grinning with the thought of surprising Emma and the others. "When do you wanna go?"

"Well, pretty soon, I reckon, but I suppose we'd best go by and talk to Frank Carter and give him his money before we go. We might all be startin' out to Fort Worth at the same time."

That remark sparked an idea in Casey's mind. "You know, that's a pretty long trip from here to Fort Worth. We could save Frank from havin' to take that ninety-mile trip to pay off his loan. We could do it for him. Tell him we'll act as his representatives and make sure it's legally taken off the books. That'd give us a chance to see what's what with the new bank without them gettin' suspicious at all."

"I swear, that's a darn good idea, even if I ain't the one who thought of it," Eli said. "We'll go see Frank Carter tomorrow and make his day for him."

The last campaign of the old-men bandits was officially launched with a four-mile ride into Little Bow to Carter General Merchandise. When Casey and Eli walked into the store, Frank Carter was quick to give them a warm welcome.

"Mornin', Casey, Eli," he greeted them, "what can I get for you this mornin'?"

"Nothin', I reckon," Casey answered. "We didn't really

come to buy anything this mornin'." The disappointment registered immediately on Frank's face, but was replaced just as quickly by Casey's next statement. "We came to tell you that we've decided to make you a no-interest loan of six thousand dollars to pay your debt to Wells Fargo Bank." Frank's cheeks flushed and he was speechless.

"The terms are as follows, you have a hundred years to pay us back, at which time the full amount of six thousand dollars is due, just like it is now with Wells Fargo."

For a moment, Frank was confused. Overjoyed at first, he hesitated then. "Wait, what? It's due in full when?"

Casey and Eli laughed. "A hundred years," Eli said. "Do you need more time than that?"

Frank was speechless again when he realized what they were saying. "I don't understand. You fellows are *giving* me the money? That doesn't hardly seem fair. I thank you from the bottom of my heart, but I expect to pay you back sooner than that. If it wasn't for you two building D and T Cattle Company up to the size it is now, I wouldn't even be in business. If things keep going the way they have been, I expect to be able to pay you for the loan. I'm picking up business from Gary Corbett, and he told me you fellows helped him get started again. I appreciate you loanin' me the money and I'll be happy to pay you back."

"Well, you're an honorable man," Casey said. "You just handle the loan any way that suits you best, but take as much time as you need. Eli and I would be happy to take care of that business with the bank for you, if you want. That's a long ride up there to Fort Worth. And it just so happens that Eli and I have business to take care of in Fort Worth. We're headin' up that way tomorrow. Be gone about a week. If you'll give us any paperwork you have on the loan and the person's name you talked to, we'll pay it off and bring you the signed papers. And you won't have to ride all the way up there to take care of it."

"I swear, I don't feel right about askin' you to take care of all that for me. I can't believe you'd offer to," Frank said.

"No trouble a-tall," Eli assured him. "We're gonna be up there, anyway. Might as well help out a neighbor."

"I declare," Frank exclaimed, "you two fellows are a god-send! I can't wait to tell Alice about this. Wait right here and I'll get the papers outta the office." He was back in a few minutes' time with the loan papers. "It's the Wells Fargo Bank," he said as he handed them to Casey. "Least that's what it is now. It was the Fort Worth Investment Bank when I took out the loan and the man I dealt with was Edwin Polk." He didn't catch the sudden look of shock in Casey's eyes or the exchange of disbelief between Casey and Eli.

After almost dropping the papers, Casey forced himself to carry on as casually as he possibly could. The Fort Worth Investment Bank was the bank that had tried to cheat Emma Woodward out of her property in Fort Worth. And Edwin Polk was the low-down scoundrel behind it all. It resulted in the robbery of the bank by the two old-men bandits. If Edwin Polk was still with the bank, he would certainly remember the lengthy interview he had with Casey about the bank's time-controlled safe, among other things. They had gone too far on this business with Frank Carter to withdraw their offer to go to the bank on his behalf, however. So Casey took the loan papers and promptly said that he and Eli had to get back to the D&T to prepare for tomorrow's journey. Frank walked them all the way out to their horses, thanking them for what they were doing for him and his family.

As they headed back on the road to the ranch, Eli was the first to comment. "If that wasn't the definition of shootin' yourself in the foot, I don't know what is. That possibility never entered my mind. What if that sorry dog is still with that bank? You know he'll remember talkin' to you."

Casey considered the possibility of meeting with Edwin

Polk a second time and he tried to remember all they had discussed. "You know, there ain't no way he can tie us to that bank robbery. He thought we were cattlemen and we were thinkin' about openin' an account with his bank. We didn't go back the next day because the bank got robbed. There ain't nothin' wrong with us doing some business with the bank for a neighbor. And we'll be givin' him six thousand dollars. He won't be thinkin' about a bank robbery. Our problem is gonna be when he sees Elmer and Oscar. First look he gets of them and that's the end of us. So if he's there, we'll just have to pay back Frank's loan and explain why we didn't come back to open an account. He'll just be talking to the partners of D and T Cattle Company."

"The hell he will," Eli reminded him. "He'll be talking to Bob White and his brother, Tom."

"That's right! I forgot that."

The news about the possibility that the new Wells Fargo Bank was actually the old Fort Worth Investment Bank brought about another problem for the two bank robbers. If they were going to rob just one more bank, as they had decided, then what bank would it be? Wells Fargo was the only bank they felt they could hit without hurting the local people directly.

"We shoulda found out about all this before we gave away six thousand dollars," Casey said.

"You reckon we ought to turn around and go back and tell Frank to take the money up to Fort Worth himself?" Eli asked. "And tell him he's got one year to pay it back, instead of one hundred."

"You know," Casey replied, "I don't think so. I'm thinking about why Wells Fargo bought that bank. Don't you reckon it had something to do with the bank robbery by two old men? And it mighta had something to do with the bank not gettin' possession of the Woodward House Hotel property, too. Why would a big outfit like Wells Fargo keep somebody like

Edwin Polk there to manage their bank, with a record like that? I'll bet chances are, they sent in some fresh upstart to manage their new bank and Edwin Polk is long gone. There ain't but one way to find out and that's to go up there and pay Frank's loan for him. Besides, I still wanna go spend a night or two in the Woodward House Hotel. I kinda miss those folks."

"I reckon we're going to Fort Worth in the mornin'," Eli said. "You reckon we might have a chance to get breakfast or dinner at the Potluck Kitchen? I wonder how Joy Black is gettin' along these days."

When they got back to the D&T, they turned their horses over to Davy Springer to take their saddles off and turn them loose in the corral. Then they stopped by the cookshack and told Smiley George to tell Monroe Kelly they wanted to see him when he came back to eat dinner. The rest of the morning was spent inspecting the packs they kept in their rooms, to make sure their disguises were in good shape, at least for one last time.

At dinnertime, they locked their packs up in the closet that held their safe. Juanita had long since refrained from asking if they had some clothes in there that could use a washing. When Monroe showed up, they went over the orders they had left him with the night before to see how much had been done. They told him that they would be going to Fort Worth in the morning for some meetings with a group of cattle buyers and what they wanted done while they were gone.

The next morning, they had breakfast with Juanita and Miguel, as usual, before leaving the D&T to follow the old Comanche Trail east, until striking the Fort Worth–San Antonio Trail where they turned to the north, each man leading a packhorse. They figured to make the trip in two and a half days, with an arrival at the Potluck Kitchen sometime around noon. Their trip was without problems of any kind, except for the difficulty of deciding what kind of masquerade they were going to attempt for their final act. They eventually decided it was a waste of time until they had an opportunity to see if there were any changes to the old bank, especially in the matter of employees.

A little before noon on the third day of travel, they came to the creek they had used on two previous occasions to change into their disguises and leave their packhorses. Anxious to see if the creek had been used by other campers since, they rode their horses up the creek to the spot they had favored. There was no sign of anyone having been there anytime recently, which was encouraging. But there were tracks that suggested a single rider and a packhorse, probably, that were quite old. There was no sign of a campfire, which led to their imagining that someone just rode back up the creek, looking for signs himself. Colton Gray came to mind immediately.

"By the time he rode back here, we were halfway back to the D and T," Eli said.

"I hope to hell he's in Waco, where he belongs, and not in Fort Worth," Casey commented.

Back on the road, they passed Hasting's Supply in less than a mile as they approached the cattle pens at the edge of Fort Worth and the small cluster of businesses. They tied their horses up in front of the Potluck Kitchen and walked inside.

"Well, I'll be . . ." Roy Black started. "Howdy, boys. Ain't seen you fellers since I don't know when. Joy! Come see what the wind blew in the door!" The few customers seated at the long table all stared expectantly, anxious to hear who they were.

Joy Black stuck her head through the doorway, her lopsided grin fashioned to hide a missing tooth. "Eli and Casey," she murmured, and pushed her chunky body on through the doorway. "Eli and Casey!" she said again, this time with genuine pleasure. "We was just talking about you two the other day, wonderin' if you'd ever get back up this way again."

"We stayed away as long as we could stand it," Eli said. "Then we just had to come and get one of your dinners."

"He ain't lyin'," Casey said, grinning. "We wanted to see if you can still cook like you used to."

"Well, sit yourself down," Roy said, sitting behind the cash register as usual, his wheelchair still with no wheels, "and you can decide for yourself."

Eli and Casey sat down at the table and turned the plates right side up. They exchanged friendly remarks with a couple of the diners, and the others just continued to stare. Joy went back into the kitchen to fetch some more potatoes and beans. When she came out, she filled their plates first, before offering any to those already eating. "You boys gonna be around for a while?" she asked when she came back from another trip to the kitchen for the coffeepot.

"We ain't sure," Casey answered her, "just business as usual. We've got some meetings with some people we have to do business with on the other side of Fort Worth. Might even have to go on over to Dallas. We never know for sure."

"One of these days, when you have the time, I'd like you to explain what kinda business you're in," Joy remarked. "We thought you owned a cattle ranch."

"That's right, we do," Casey said. "But nowadays, with the cattle market the way it is, it ain't like the old days when you just got the cattle ready for the market, then drove 'em north to the railroad." He looked at Joy, who was staring back at him with a look of amazement on her homely face. Then he glanced at Eli, who was grinning, amused by the mess he was making in his attempt to explain why they were so busy. Afraid he was going to become even more entangled in his explanation, he tried to sum it up by saying, "Half the time, I ain't sure what we're doin'. We just go where we have to." He avoided making eye contact with the grinning Eli.

After a leisurely dinner with Joy and her brother, Casey and Eli promised they would try to stop by at least once more before going home. Then they climbed back up into the saddle and rode on into Fort Worth, heading for the old Fort Worth Investment Bank. They spotted the bright new sign from a block away that proclaimed it to be WELLS FARGO BANK.

"Looks like they're addin' some rooms on the back of it," Eli remarked. An addition was definitely under way, for they could see several carpenters framing up the walls. "They might not even be open for business."

"Won't that be a helluva note?" Casey responded. "I sure hope we ain't rode all this way just to eat dinner with Roy and Joy." They continued on up the street to the front of the bank, where, to their relief, they found an OPEN sign on the door. "Let's go on inside and see if we can find our old friend, Edwin Polk," Casey said.

They dismounted, tied the horses up in front of the bank, and walked inside, where they were greeted by a uniformed guard. "Welcome to Wells Fargo Bank," he said.

When Casey and Eli just stood there, looking around to see if anything was different, the guard asked, "Can I help you gentlemen?"

"This is the first time we've been in here since it was bought by Wells Fargo," Casey told him. "I reckon we need to see Mr. Edwin Polk. We wanna pay off a loan."

"The person you wanna see is Mr. Brewster. He's the loan officer," the guard said. "Mr. Polk is no longer with the bank."

"Polk's gone?" Casey responded. "I thought he was the bank manager."

"Yes, sir, he was," the guard replied, "but he's no longer with us. Mr. Branden Cooper is the bank manager now."

"Well, that's bound to be an improvement," Casey remarked. "I guess we need to see Mr. Brewster."

"Yes, sir," the guard said. "If you'll just take a seat over there, where those chairs are, I'll let Mr. Brewster know you're waitin' to see him."

"'Preciate it," Eli said, and he and Casey walked over to a small group of stuffed chairs on one side of the lobby, while the guard went to the door that used to be Edwin Polk's office.

"They're sure enough makin' changes in the buildin'," Casey said when they sat down. They could hear the sound of hammers and saws on the other side of the wall that separated the lobby from the back part of the bank, where the safe room was located. "They still just have the two teller cages, and, I swear, I ain't too sure, but they look like the same two tellers."

"I think you're right," Eli said, "but they don't seem to be payin' any attention to us. Don't know if it would make any difference if they did. We ain't the ones who robbed the bank."

Chapter 17

They sat there for about five minutes before a tall man, thin, with graying hair and wearing glasses, came out to greet them. "I'm Stephen Brewster. You need to talk to me about a loan?"

"Pleased to meet you, Mr. Brewster," Casey said. "We're here to pay off a loan for a friend of ours." He handed Brewster the loan papers he had gotten from Frank Carter. "The loan is for Carter General Merchandise in Little Bow. The amount due on it is six thousand dollars, which I have right here." He held a small canvas sack up for him to see.

"Why don't we go into my office, gentlemen," Brewster suggested, and extended his hand toward his office door. They filed into the office in front of him and he closed the door behind him. "Have a seat," he invited, and they sat down while he read quickly through the loan papers. "And you gentlemen are . . . ?"

"Casey Tubbs and Eli Doolin," Casey answered, thinking it best not to use fake names, since they were acting in good faith for Frank Carter. "We're the owners of D and T Cattle Company in Lampasas County. Little Bow is about a hundred miles south of Fort Worth, and since we had to be up here, anyway, we thought we'd save Frank the trip."

"I see," Brewster said as he kept reading the loan papers Casey had given him. "There isn't any mention of you gentlemen in this agreement."

"Nor should there be," Eli said. "We're just deliverin' the payment for him."

Casey took the money out of the sack and put it on the desk.

"I'll have to count that to make sure it's the right amount," Brewster said.

"I know I would," Eli said with a chuckle.

Brewster went to the door, opened it, and called one of the tellers who was not with a customer at the moment, "Julian, can you come and make a money count with me?"

In a minute, Julian walked in, nodded politely to Casey and Eli, then went to the desk to do a money count. Eli looked at Casey and nodded. Casey answered with a nod as well. They both remembered Julian as one of the tellers when they were there before. They sat there patiently waiting for the two bank employees to count the stacks of money. Julian finished first, wrote his total on a slip of paper, and waited silently for Brewster to finish. When Brewster finished, he said, "I make it six thousand and twenty dollars."

Julian handed him the slip of paper on which he had written the same total.

Addressing Eli and Casey, Brewster announced, "You have six thousand and twenty dollars. That's twenty dollars too much."

Casey looked at Eli and shook his head. Eli shrugged and took the twenty from Brewster.

"You can return that to Mr. Carter and I'll give you the papers certifying the loan is paid in full before you go." Since he still held on to the official papers, they figured they were going to be subjected to an attempt to sell them on the benefits of banking with Wells Fargo.

So they were not surprised when they got up from their chairs and walked out the office door and Brewster asked where did they do their banking. Casey told him they banked with the First Bank of Lampasas.

"It's a lot closer to our ranch," Casey said.

"That may be," Brewster said, "but I'd like to show you some of the advantages of banking with the advanced capabilities of a nationwide institution like Wells Fargo."

"Sounds like you're tearin' the whole back of the bank out," Eli said when the sound of hammers on nails started up in earnest again.

Brewster laughed. "Yes, we'll all be glad when the carpenters finish in the back. They're tearing down some old walls and putting up new ones to make some more offices. And they're expanding the old safe room into one that will better protect our customers' money."

"Is that a fact?" Eli asked. "I'd like to get a peek at that. The room where they keep the safe in our bank ain't much bigger'n an outhouse."

"Well, you should take a look at this one," Brewster said. "The safe is built right into the wall. A thief would have to move the whole back wall to get the safe out. And then he wouldn't be able to get it open until the time lock let him." The hammers went quiet for a while, so he said, "Come take a look. It sounds like they're taking a break."

He led them over to the door to the back part of the bank, opened it, and stuck his head in to make sure they weren't walking into the middle of something. Seeing that the men were carrying in some more studs from outside, Brewster signaled Casey and Eli to follow him.

Once inside the door, they could see that the existing walls that had formed the small safe room had been torn down and there were chalk lines on the floor where new walls were going to be built.

"You see these lines here?" Brewster asked. "That's where

they're going to install iron bars, just like a jail cell. When the door is locked, you can burn the building down and that safe will still be locked tight inside those iron bars."

"Yes, sir," Casey said, "that's really gonna be watertight when they finish all this up."

He and Eli were taking it all in, the milling about of the carpenters, the open back door as their helpers carried lumber inside for the partition walls, and the unlocked safe with the bank guard now standing guard while Brewster put Mr. Carter's money in the safe. Unfortunately, it was obvious that their usual ploy of watching the bank manager put their money into the big safe was not going to work here. They were going to have to put on their thinking caps to come up with a plan. And they were going to have to come up with it pretty quick before the carpenters finished their work.

They went back to Brewster's office then and waited while he finished writing the statement of the loan's satisfactory repayment and the cancelation of the lien on Carter General Merchandise.

"Please thank Mr. Carter for his payment and let him know that Wells Fargo would be happy to work with him on his future projects." He finally handed Casey the papers.

"We'll do that," Casey said.

"And you and Mr. Doolin might think about the kind of service Wells Fargo is ready to provide for the larger cattle operations in Central and West Texas."

"We'll keep it in mind," Casey assured him.

When they walked back to their horses, Eli held up the twenty-dollar bill, and Casey said, "You couldn't help yourself, could you?"

"I wanted to see," Eli said.

It was still fairly early in the afternoon, but they decided they'd check by the Woodward House Hotel to get a couple of rooms. So they rode back to the hotel and tied their horses out front while they went inside to check on availability. They got no farther than the front porch, when they were stopped by the sight of the two big rocking chairs, one with the name *Casey* painted on the headrest, the other with the name *Eli*.

With a howl of delight, Eli went straight to his chair and plopped down. Grinning like a dog eating yellow jackets, Casey followed his lead and plopped down in his. That's where they were discovered minutes later when Rose heard the noise on the front porch and went to see the cause. One look at the two men rocking back and forth like two young'uns and Rose went in search of Emma Woodward.

With no patience for nonsense, Emma marched out to the front porch, but stopped in her tracks when she immediately recognized the two overage schoolboys. "I knew you'd come back one day," she murmured to herself. "What a sight to see."

Then, in her best impression of a stern schoolmarm, the gray-haired lady threatened, "You break those chairs and there's gonna be hell to pay. Those chairs are sacred."

Unaware until that moment that she was behind them, they both jumped up out of their rockers and turned to greet her. She didn't wait and hurried to put her petite arms around both of them.

"Welcome home," she said. "Are you gonna stay awhile?"

"That depends on whether you've got any vacant rooms or not," Casey answered.

"I've got two vacant rooms," she said, "but even if I didn't, I'd kick somebody out and give their rooms to you."

"Bless your heart," Eli said, "we wouldn't ever want you to do that. You can't make no money doin' stuff like that. Me and Casey would just go down to the stable and sleep with our horses. We've done that many a night."

"Well, I don't want you doin' that when you come to see us," Emma insisted. "Rose, run tell Pearl we've got special guests for supper tonight, so she better mind what she's doing."

When Rose hurried to the kitchen, Casey told Emma, "We'll take those rooms for two nights. So I reckon we'll get our saddlebags and take 'em to the rooms, then take the horses down to the stable. I expect Mr. Plunket is still down there."

"Why, yes, Donald's still at the stable, and Walt Evans's blacksmith shop is still next door to the stable," Emma said.

"If you two ain't a sight for sore eyes!" Pearl sang out before they had time to go get the saddlebags. "We were talkin' about you two the other night and wonderin' when you might come this way again."

"How have you been gettin' along, Pearl?" Eli asked.

"Good as a woman my age can ask for, I reckon, tryin' to keep Emma and Rose outta trouble, and that's a full-time job."

"I expect it is," Eli said with a grin. "Everywhere me and Casey go, we like to go eat where they're supposed to have good cooks. And we ain't found no place yet that comes close to your cookin'. Ain't that right, Casey?"

"It's a fact, Pearl," Casey confirmed.

"Ah, you're just tryin' to make an old lady feel good," Pearl said proudly. "I reckon I'd better go see if I can get supper started, or you won't have nothin' to eat."

Casey and Eli took their saddlebags and rifles off their horses and Emma went upstairs with them to make sure rooms six and seven were clean and ready for guests. This, even though she knew she could trust that Rose had done a good job. Once they assured her that everything was satisfactory, they left then to take the horses down the short street to Donald Plunket's stable. On the way, Walt Evans saw them when they passed his blacksmith shop, so he came out to the street and followed them the short distance to the stable. When they pulled up in front of the stable, they were met by Donald and Walt at almost the same time, one in front and the other behind.

"Casey Tubbs and Eli Doolin," Donald sang out as they

dismounted and found themselves confronted by the two grinning faces, and another reunion began. What struck both Casey and Eli was how much their welcome was like that of a family reunion. It would be easy to think this show of affection was nothing more than that, a *show*, an effort to gain more gifts of money. But they had made no gifts of money to either Donald or Walt. They were just genuinely grateful for what Casey and Eli had done for Emma and Woodward House.

The reunion continued a little later when they gathered at the supper table and a couple of more recent guests at Woodward House were confused by the reception given the two strangers.

"Likely as not, we wouldn't be settin' here eatin' this fine supper, if it wasn't for Casey and Eli," Walt Evans told one of the new guests who asked who they were. "They own the D and T Cattle Company, which is a big ranch about a hundred miles south of Fort Worth in Lampasas County. But they're two of the most ordinary and decent men you'll ever meet."

When Casey and Eli were sitting in their personalized rocking chairs later that night, talking about the reception they had received, Eli said it best. "They say you can't buy love or happiness with money, but I don't know as how I can agree with that. That three thousand dollars is the best money we ever spent. It bought us a family and friends that are always glad to see us come home."

"Three thousand one hundred and twenty-five dollars, to be exact, to pay that loan off," Casey said. "And you're right, it bought us a family."

Pretty soon, the conversation had to turn toward the task that brought them to Fort Worth and the dilemma facing them with the target chosen for their next, and supposedly, last bank holdup. The construction work going on at the bank was especially ill timed, and might make it impossible to pull off a typical old-man robbery. The question facing them was

whether or not to call off the planned holdup until the construction was completed. Either that or choose another bank
to target, a choice that was not a popular one since their con-
science-stricken decision to avoid targeting the smaller banks.

"No," Casey declared, "Wells Fargo is the only bank we can
hit without endangerin' the savings of the local people."

"Maybe that construction work goin' on might make it easier for us to get in the back where the safe is," Eli suggested.
"Why don't we go to the bank tomorrow and set on the back
of it."

"I don't know," Casey said hesitantly. "That don't seem
very likely." He shrugged then and said, "But what the hell,
we might as well take a look. They can't arrest us for lookin'."

So they retired for the night, and after a big breakfast the
next morning, they said they had some business to attend to.
When Pearl asked if they would be there for dinner, they told
her they weren't sure. It would depend on how their morning
went, but they would be back by suppertime, for sure.

After breakfast, they walked down the street to the stable to
pick up their horses.

"You want your packhorses, too?" Walt asked, and they told
him they wouldn't need them today. He was curious about
what they were carrying in the packs, since they seemed
rather bulky, but he wasn't nosey enough to ask. They saddled Smoke and Biscuit, told Walt they would see him at supper, and rode off toward the main part of town. They rode
down the street behind the bank and discovered a vacant lot
directly behind the bank, which was being used at the present
time by the construction company doing the work at the bank.

Casey and Eli pulled up at the edge of the lot to watch
some of the workers carrying lumber into the back door of the
bank, and they could hear the busy sounds of construction
coming from inside.

"You know," Casey commented, "that fellow we talked to, Brewster, said they still don't open that safe until twelve o'clock. I wonder what time these carpenters knock off for dinner. And I wonder where they eat it, inside the back of the bank, or outside on the grass?"

"That might be real interestin' to know," Eli said, "interestin' enough to take another ride by here at noon to see what's goin' on." They rode on down the street then, before they might attract attention. To kill some time, they rode on down to the Acre, the popular name for the red-light district of town that was designated as Hell's Half Acre.

When they rode by the Ace Of Spades, a dancehall, Eli remarked, "I remember this place. Last time we went in there to get a drink of likker, two fellows followed us out and tried to rob us. Is it too early for a drink of likker?"

"It is for me," Casey answered.

Eli shrugged and they kept on riding. They finally came upon a vacant lot with good grass growing on it. So they stopped there and let their horses graze while they sat on the grass and talked about the possibility of robbing the bank by going in the back door.

Finally the time passed. Casey looked at his watch and said, "It's time to go. They oughta be openin' that safe about the time we get there."

When they got back to the vacant lot behind the bank, it was a couple of minutes past the hour of twelve, so the safe was unlocked. The carpenters and their helpers were filing out the back door of the bank, carrying their food sacks and metal buckets, to sit down on the wagons or the ground to eat.

"That makes me hungry," Eli said.

"I wish I could see inside that back door," Casey said, his mind captured by what might be happening inside the bank. "With that back door open, they probably send the guard to accompany the manager to unlock the safe, and maybe stay there till the tellers have reloaded their cash drawers." He let

that image continue in his mind. "That means we need to dis-
tract that guard back to the front of the bank long enough to
take the money and walk out."

"That sounds like we're gonna need a healthy portion of
good luck," Eli declared.

"You got that right," Casey agreed. "Whaddaya think? You
think we ought to forget about this bank? 'Cause if you ain't
sold on it, we'll just forget about it. This ain't the same as
when we first started this bank-robbin' business, when we
didn't have anything to lose. It's different now. Now, we've
got a helluva lot to lose, and a lot of people depending on us to
provide their livin' for 'em." He was thinking about everybody at D&T Cattle Company and what would happen to
them if he and Eli were taken down.

Eli understood what Casey was concerned about, for he was
struck with the same thoughts. Their nothing-to-lose attitude
in the beginning had given way to caution at some point. And
they had already agreed that this last caper was the stopping
place.

"I'll answer your question this way, partner," Eli said. "I'm
willing to go ahead with this job when we decide exactly how
we're gonna do it. But at any point, and I mean when we're in
disguise and ready to make our move, if either one of us ain't
sure, we give the signal to call it off and walk away. It ain't
against the law to dress up like an old man, even in the bank."

"That suits me just fine," Casey said. "Just give the signal
and we turn into two law-abidin' old men, right? What is the
signal?"

"'Jaybird,'" Eli said. "Just say jaybird."

Casey chuckled. "Jaybird," he repeated. "I can remember
that. So, now, let's go somewhere and get something to eat.
I'm hungry. And after that, I think it wouldn't hurt to ride
back out the San Antonio road to take another look at our secret camp, to make sure nobody's using it. Whaddaya think?"

"Wouldn't be a bad idea," Eli said. "Matter of fact, we've

still got time to make the Potluck Kitchen before dinnertime is over."

Roy and Joy were both happy to see Eli and Casey again. They greeted them as if they hadn't seen them in months. So they took their time over their dinner, making small talk with the brother-and-sister partnership, when a random thought occurred to Casey.

"I think I'll drop in that saloon next door and pick up a bottle of cheap whiskey before we leave here."

"I ain't sure I wanna see you startin' on a bottle of whiskey right at this particular time," Eli started. "Like I said, if you ain't . . ."

That's as far as he got before Casey stopped him. "Hold your horses! I ain't plannin' to drink it. I just had an idea that we might decide to pour a little whiskey on one or both of our clothes in case we need to act drunk for some reason. Then we can drink it *after* we get away with this one."

"Might not be a bad idea," Eli agreed. "We'll have to decide tonight how we're gonna try this one."

When they left the Potluck Kitchen, after promising they'd try to stop by again before leaving town, they went next door to the Roundup Saloon. Casey bought a bottle of rye whiskey, since that was always Eli's preference. Then they rode out the San Antonio road, making a quick stop at Hasting's Supply to buy twenty feet of clothesline, since they didn't have any. And they almost always needed some.

Floyd Hasting was glad to see them. And he always liked to joke about the deputy U.S. marshal who came asking questions about them because they bought black powder from him to get rid of a nest of yellow jackets. They visited for a little while, then told him they were on their way home and left. They figured it a good idea for him to testify that they left town that afternoon, in case someone might ask him questions after what was going to happen tomorrow.

Leaving Hasting's, they rode south a short distance before coming to the creek, where they were happy to find no signs of any hoofprints leaving the road on either side of the creek. So they rode up the middle of the creek to check their campsite one more time. There were no new signs of any visitors.

"We've been mighty damn lucky about this creek," Eli said. "I swear, I'm afraid our luck's gonna run out one of these times. And we'll come back to find our packhorses gone without a sign of a thank-you note. And we'll have to ride back to the D and T in our old-men disguises."

"Well, that would be better than havin' 'em waitin' for us to show up with the bank money," Casey said. "Come on, let's go back to Woodward House now and sit in our rockin' chairs. We've gotta come up with a final plan tonight."

When they left the creek, they continued riding south on the road to avoid riding back past Hasting's Supply. They rode about half a mile before coming to a small cross trail they had discovered on a previous trip to Fort Worth. It led them to the Waco road, on which they turned back toward town.

Chapter 18

Knowing they were leaving that morning, Pearl made an extra special breakfast with pancakes and maple syrup, along with the eggs and sausage. Casey and Eli both made the proper fuss over her efforts to please them. They had made it a point to ask Walt Evans and Donald Plunket how Emma was getting along with her hotel and they were happy to report that she was very busy. They said that it was extremely lucky that she had two vacant rooms at the time of their arrival.

"Oh, there are some things she's trying to save up some money to do," Walt said, "like fixin' up the bathroom a lot nicer and maybe some new beds. But the hotel is makin' it."

They had come prepared to help Emma out a little, and when they had said their goodbyes to everyone at the breakfast table, they came to Emma to settle their bill.

"I'm not going to charge you angels anything," she told them. "I owe everything I have to you two."

"I'm afraid you don't have any choice, Emma," Casey said. "I'm claiming my right, the same as any citizen in Texas, to pay the asking room rate in this here hotel. Now, how much is it?"

She just remained firm and shook her head. "I'm not charging you. It would be a sin."

"All right, if you ain't gonna tell us how much we owe for two rooms for two nights, we'll just have to guess at it," Casey said. He took an envelope out of his vest pocket and laid it on her desk. "I'm guessin' that'll cover it. You take care of yourself and we wanna thank you for your hospitality."

She couldn't find words to convey her feelings. She stared at the envelope lying on her desk and tears began to form in her eyes, for she knew what was in the envelope. She stepped up to Casey and hugged him. Then she hugged Eli and whispered, "God bless you both and keep you safe."

Casey looked at Eli and said, "We'd best get goin'. We've got a lot to do today."

They picked up their saddlebags and rifles and went out the front door. Eli reached out and poked the rocking chair bearing his name with his rifle to cause it to start rocking as he passed by.

She watched from the window as they went down the steps and headed for the stables. *There they go, Robert,* she said to her dead husband, *the two angels you must have sent to take care of me.* With trembling fingers, she opened the envelope containing five thousand dollars.

They settled with Donald Plunket for boarding their four horses, then rode down the street behind the Wells Fargo Bank to make sure the construction work was still going on. Then, satisfied that the situation was still the same as when they went in to pay Frank Carter's debt, they committed to the plan. To avoid the possibility of being seen passing the Potluck Kitchen or Hasting's Supply, they rode out the Waco road and took the long way back to their camp on the creek. After carefully checking to make sure no one had been there since the day before, they tied a rope line between the same two trees they had used before to enable their two packhorses to get to the water. Then they began the procedure, now well familiar to them, of transforming their appearances to that of much older men.

"I wish we coulda found some old work clothes," Eli said. "It woulda made it easier to walk in the back door of that bank." They usually bought old clothes from the undertakers, but no one kept the dirty old overalls and work clothes to re-sell. "We might be hollerin' jaybird before this plan even gets started."

With a close eye on Casey's pocket watch, they applied the actor's makeup that gave their faces the darkened appearance of old skin. Each of them worked on the other's face, since they didn't have a mirror. "It's a good thing this is gonna be our last job as Elmer and Oscar," Casey said, "'cause this is the last of this cream. And I don't know where we can get any more of it."

When the whiskers and the wigs were fixed in place, they went through a range of movements of their heads to make sure none of their real hair peeked out from under the fake hair. This test was inspired by the memory of seeing the tiny black line of real hair underneath the wig of the would-be rob-ber of the Lampasas bank.

"Well, Elmer," Eli said, "you look like you're ready to go."

"You think so, Oscar?" Casey replied. "I reckon you do, too." He looked at his watch. "It's about time for that safe to open. So by the time we ride back there, the tellers oughta have their cash trays filled and the carpenters oughta be quit for dinner."

They climbed on their horses and rode back down the creek to the road, hoping their packhorses would still be there when they returned, but certain they would attract more at-tention with four horses, instead of just two. Holding their horses to a fast walk, they rode along the back street until coming to the corner of the empty lot behind the bank. As they expected, the building crew was spread about on the empty lot, eating their noontime meal. Casey and Eli got down from their horses and tied them to a small tree growing there.

"You ready?" Casey asked, and Eli said he was, so Casey took the bottle of whiskey from his saddlebags and sprinkled it liberally about his shoulders and sleeves. "How's that?" he asked.

"Not bad," Eli said. "You smell like a drunk, all right. If we get through this without gettin' caught, I'd like to have that sleeve to chew on." While he talked, he was looking the situation over when he saw a prop he might use, since his part was to go in the back door. "Let's move the horses over across the street and tie 'em at that back corner of the bank. They ought not be noticed there and they'll be closer when we come outta there." Then he pointed to the other thing that caught his eye. "See that big bucket outside the back door? That looks like a mop handle stickin' up out of it. I can use that."

Casey was in agreement with his suggestions, so they untied the horses and led them across the street to the back corner of the bank building and retied them. They stood there for a few seconds to see if anyone had noticed them. It seemed no one had.

"All right," Casey said. "You wantin' to call jaybird?"

"Hell no," Eli answered, "I can handle my part. You just get rid of that guard for me. You got your check?"

Casey reached inside his duster and pulled out the check he had asked Emma Woodward for and held it up for Eli to see.

"Get goin' now before I start chewin' on the collar of that duster you're wearin'," Eli told him.

Casey hurried around the corner, heading for the front of the bank. Eli remained with the horses for a short while before heading for the bank's back door. When he got to the bucket, he found that it was empty except for a mop that was propped inside, so he picked it up and casually carried it with him.

Meanwhile, Casey walked through the front door of the bank, purposely stumbling a little as he crossed the threshold. He uttered a few strong swearwords to the threshold, attracting attention right away, and surged toward one of the teller windows. He stopped close behind a woman standing in line, close enough for her to feel his breath on the back of her neck. He was also close enough for her to smell the whiskey soaked in his clothes. Her natural reaction was to pull away and turn to give him a look of genuine disgust, especially when she saw how old he looked.

"Do you know where you are?" she demanded. "This is a bank, old man. This is not a saloon."

"Thank the Lord for that," Casey slurred. " 'Cause if it was a saloon, I was afraid all the whores looked old enough to be my mother." He paused to place his hand over his heart and mumbled, "God rest her soul."

"Well, if you aren't the most disgusting old drunk I've ever seen," the woman said, and stepped over in the line for the other teller.

A man standing in that line politely motioned for her to step in front of him. Then he gave Casey a stern look and said, "Old man, I expect you're about old enough to give up drinkin' whiskey."

"Is that so?" Casey asked, acting genuinely surprised. "How old do you have to be?"

"You know what I mean," the man said. "You obviously can't handle it. How old are you?"

Casey threw his hands up in the air wildly and slurred loudly, "Twenty-one, last time I gave a damn!"

The man who had been at the window in front of the woman finished his transaction and stepped around Casey, obviously not wishing to become involved.

So Casey stepped up to the window to confront the teller, a MR. BRUCE LOGAN, according to his nameplate. Casey was happy to see he had not been employed there when he and Eli were there before.

"Can I help you, sir?" Bruce asked politely.

"You sure can, Sonny," Casey replied, and reached inside his duster for the check. He slid it under the gate and said, "I wanna cash this check for five dollars and sixty-five cents. And I'm in a hurry. I've got a powerful thirst."

Bruce took the check and, after one quick look, slid it back under the gate. "This is a canceled check and it's a Fort Worth Investment Bank check. I can't cash this check."

"I don't see why in the hell not!" Casey responded. "This here's the same bank. You just changed the name of it. I might be old, but I ain't stupid. Gimme my money."

"It's a canceled check," Bruce tried to explain. "It's already been cashed by the Woodward House Hotel. Where did you find this check?"

"Someplace that ain't none of your business. Now . . . I ain't leavin' here till I get my five dollars and sixty-five cents."

"Sir, that check is no good. I'm going to have to ask you to leave. You're disturbing the other customers."

"To hell with them!" Casey growled. "I ain't goin' nowhere till I get my money!"

Bruce looked over at Julian. "You better go get Andrew. He's still in the back with Mr. Cooper."

At that particular time, Mr. Branden Cooper, the bank manager, was standing in front of the bank's open safe. Andrew Locke, the bank guard, was standing beside him as they both confronted a strange old man who had wandered in the open back door of the bank carrying a bucket and mop.

"You don't understand, sir," Cooper explained very slowly, having already surmised that the old man's simple mind was confused. "You aren't supposed to be back here in this part of the bank. Our customers don't even come back here."

"But they told me to go clean up the mess in the safe room," Eli insisted. "They said I could earn a dollar if I cleaned up the mess, put it in this bucket, and bring it back to show 'em." He looked back and forth from Cooper to the guard. "I know I'm old, but I can do a good job. I've cleaned up all kinds of messes in my life. And I could sure use that dollar."

Cooper started to speak again, but hesitated when sounds of a loud argument drifted over the wall from the lobby. He started to speak again and was stopped once more when Julian ran in the door and exclaimed, "We need Andrew up front! There's an old man raisin' hell at the teller cage and he won't leave!"

"I've gotta stay here till Mr. Cooper closes the safe," Andrew said.

Julian looked desperate, so Cooper told the guard to go along with him. "I'm almost finished here. You go take care of the disturbance up front."

"But what about this old fellow here?" Andrew whispered. "Don't you want me to get rid of him first?"

"I'll get rid of him," Cooper whispered. "I'll pay him a dollar to take that bucket out of here."

"You're the boss," Andrew said. "I'll try to be quick about the trouble up front." Cooper followed the guard and the teller to the door when they left. When he turned around, he found the old man standing right in front of the safe, his back turned to him. He was obviously staring at all the money.

"Whoa, there, old fellow," he said, laughing. "Looking at all that money might make you go blind." He hurried back to the safe. "I'm gonna give you that dollar somebody out there had promised you for a joke."

"I'm gonna need a little more than that," Eli said as he turned to face him, his Colt .45 aimed at Cooper's chest. "I'm not going to take it all. You see that sack on the floor, the one that says 'Wells Fargo' on it? You're gonna fill that sack and I'll leave you the rest."

Cooper was shaken, right down to his shiny black shoes, but he gradually regained his composure in the face of this ancient-looking man. "Old man," he said, speaking as calmly as he could manage, "you're making the biggest mistake of your life. One shout from me and you'd have that guard and everyone else who works for me in here to stop you."

"That's most likely true," Eli conceded. "But let me tell you the true facts of life that you may learn to appreciate—if you happen to live as long as I have. Here's what will really happen if you shout for help. I will shoot you in the heart and you will be dead. My partner, who caused the disturbance out front, will hear the shot. So he will shoot your guard and anyone else who is a threat. The reason we have an agreement like this is because we are both in the final years of a long and hard life and we don't have that much to lose. You'll understand if you live to be old enough." He reached into the safe and pulled out a thick stack of fifty-dollar bills. "Start fillin' that sack."

Cooper was convinced that the old man would do what he threatened, but he still thought he might be smart enough to bluff him. "What if I refuse to fill that damn sack?"

"That would be a mistake on your part," Eli answered. "You're wastin' my time."

"That's right and I'm not going to fill that damn . . ."

That was as far as he got before Eli suddenly rapped him on the side of his head with the barrel of his Colt, hard enough to knock him senseless. Then he jammed the thick stack of fifties in Cooper's mouth before he could make a sound.

While Cooper was lying dazed on the floor, Eli reached inside his duster and pulled the bow knot holding the clothesline wrapped around his chest, allowing it to drop to the floor.

He stepped out of the rope and proceeded to tie Cooper's hands behind his back, then tied his hands to his feet. Once the manager was secured, Eli wasted no time stuffing the sack with money from the safe, all the while hearing sounds of the confrontation in the lobby between the guard and Casey. When the noise began to calm down, he took that as his signal to withdraw. He picked up the nearly full bank sack and put it in the bucket.

"Thank you for your generous donation. Hope the rest of your day goes a little better." Then he picked up the bucket and the mop and casually walked to the back door. He paused there before stepping outside to make sure there was no one around his and Casey's horses. When it appeared that none of the carpenters were paying any attention toward him or the bank, he went out the door and walked unhurriedly toward the horses waiting at the corner of the building. He dropped the mop and bucket, where he had found them, and tied the drawstrings of the bank bag on Biscuit's saddle horn. Holding Smoke's reins, he climbed up on Biscuit and waited for Casey.

After a loud argument with the bank guard and Stephen Brewster, who was prompted to come out of his office when sounds of the confrontation reached his ears, Casey was taken by the arm and escorted to the door. "Next time you come in here makin' a fuss like that," Andrew told him, "I ain't just gonna walk you to the door. I'm gonna march you right down to the jailhouse. You understand?" He opened the door for him.

"I understand," Casey answered, still in his best imperson-ation of an old man's voice. "I promise, you won't see me again. Sorry for causing you a problem." Then he walked away toward the corner of the building and disappeared around it, leaving Andrew puzzling over the sudden change of attitude.

When Eli saw him come around the corner of the building, he led his horse to meet him. Casey took his reins from him and hopped up into the saddle and they rode away at a comfortable lope. They headed north so any of the construction workers who saw them leave could tell the posse they went that way. When they were out of sight of the bank, they doubled back on a side street and rode the long way back to their creek hideout. When they reached the creek, they took their usual precaution upon entering their camp, but there was no sign of trespass. So they set to work immediately to erase all signs of their disguises. Upon a prior agreement between them, they built a fire and threw each article of clothing upon it as they stripped down. There was some hesitation when it got down to the wigs and whiskers, since realistic ones were extremely difficult to replace.

"We made a pledge," Casey reminded Eli.

"Hell, I know it," Eli responded.

"We've got all the money we need," Casey said, even though they had not yet counted the money Eli managed to stuff in the sack.

"We were damn lucky to get away with this one," Eli declared. "This one could have gone wrong a dozen different ways."

"If we can't make it in the cattle business now, we don't deserve to survive," Casey opined. "And we got too many people dependin' on us to keep the D and T operatin'."

"And if we try another stunt as crazy as this last one, we're gonna get caught," Eli said, and threw his wig and whiskers on the fire. Then he reached over and jerked Casey's wig out of his hand and dropped it on the fire. Casey started to grab it back at first, then shrugged and pulled his whiskers off and tossed them in as well. Stripped down to their underwear, they went down to the edge of the creek with soap and washrags to remove all traces of their disguises.

When each man passed the other man's inspection, they put their clothes on and went about the business of repacking their packs to try to hide the money as best they could. The temptation to count it was strong, but they figured they were taking so much time doing more important things, like destroying all evidence of Elmer and Oscar. They knew they had to dig a hole to bury the final evidence because the fire wouldn't completely burn up the boots and the hats in the time they were willing to wait it out.

"I almost left this at home this time," Eli said as he took the short spade off the packsaddle. "We ain't never had a use for it before."

They took turns working on the hole with the short shovel until they had one deep enough to hold all of the remains of Elmer and Oscar.

Standing over the finished grave, Eli said, "Rest in peace, boys. We had a helluva time with you."

"Amen to that," Casey added. They reached across the grave and shook hands. "Now, I expect we'd best get along on our way home, partner. I'd rather stay around long enough to celebrate a good day's work with supper at the Woodward House Hotel. But I don't think it's a good idea to take a chance on Colton Gray finding out we were in town the same day the bank was robbed." So they loaded their packhorses, climbed aboard Smoke and Biscuit, and rode down the creek to the road, where they turned south and headed for Lampasas County.

Behind them, they had left the Wells Fargo Bank in a state of general disbelief, especially when they came to realize that they had been struck by the old-men bandits for a second time. For it was plain to see now that it was the two old men who had come back for a second helping. The one employee who had worked at the bank on both occasions, Julian Scott, had not recognized the old man who had caused the distraction in the teller lines. Julian claimed that it was because it was just one of them.

"If the two of them had come into the bank together, I'm sure I would have remembered. But I didn't pay that much attention to that one by himself," he justified.

"Moron," Branden Cooper declared, a makeshift bandage tied around his head, "if you had paid attention to the people in line at your window, the whole robbery could have been stopped right then and there."

Cooper was especially stressed over the robbery because part of the reason he had been sent down to Fort Worth to manage the bank was because of the ridiculous robbery that Edwin Polk had allowed to happen the first time. Cooper's reputation would be flawed by the fact that he was now the manager of the bank that the old-men bandits robbed twice.

"How much did they take you for?" Sheriff "Longhair Jim" Courtright asked.

"We don't know yet," Cooper replied. "We'll have to make a count of everything that's left in the safe before we'll know how much they took. If a posse had been formed and they were caught in a reasonable time, it would be a lot easier just to count that."

Courtright caught the hint of sarcasm in Cooper's tone. "Yeah, I reckon that's right," he responded. "'Course, it's a whole lot easier to call out a posse when you know which way they went. Maybe if your bank guard hadda watched that one feller after he left, instead of leavin' him at the door and sayin', 'Have a nice day.' A couple of the carpenters who saw the two of 'em ride away from the bank said they rode north. So I checked everybody I came to on the road to Denton, thought they might be headed for Injun Territory, but I couldn't find a soul who saw them two old men. So I reckon they cut back in some direction after they got outta sight of the bank. That left three directions they coulda gone, and not much sense in mountin' a posse."

"In other words, they got away with it and there's nothing anybody can do about it," Cooper said.

"Sorta looks that way, don't it?" Courtright said. "'Course, I'm sure the U.S. Marshal will most likely send Deputy Marshal Colton Gray up here to look into it. And since this bank belongs to Wells Fargo now, I wouldn't be surprised if they was to send a detective down here to investigate it."

Chapter 19

Longhair Jim Courtright was not inaccurate in his speculation about Wells Fargo's reaction to the news of the robbery of their newest acquisition in Texas. Wells Fargo president, Lloyd Tevis, was more than a little irate when he received the wire from Fort Worth advising him of the holdup by the equivalent of two circus clowns dressed up like old men. He was told by one of his assistants that the Fort Worth bank was not the only bank robbed by the two men, and some believed they really were two old men. To Tevis, that was even worse.

"This cannot happen in a Wells Fargo Bank," he said. "I want those two clowns captured and punished. Who is responding to these bank holdups down there? Is it left up to the town sheriffs?"

"No, sir. The U.S. Marshal Service has been working the holdups. It was turned over to Marshal John Timmons of the Waco court and he has assigned one of his deputies to investigate the old-men robberies full-time. He hasn't been able to track them down as yet."

"So now this deputy marshal will have to travel from Waco to Fort Worth. What's that? About ninety miles? Before he can even look for a trail! Isn't there a marshal in Fort Worth?"

"Yes, sir, Marshal Quincy Thomas and the Western District Office is in Fort Worth."

"Why isn't he handling the case? He's in Fort Worth. Explain that to me, Braxton, because I'm havin' trouble understanding how the law business works down in Texas."

"I was a little confused about that myself," Braxton said in his defense, "so I asked that same question. I was told that the first holdups they refer to as the 'old-men bandits' took place in the Waco area. So they assigned the cases to one of their deputies full-time."

"Well, we need to get a wire to the Fort Worth Marshal's Office and tell him this is Wells Fargo, not Mom and Pop's Community Bank. And we demand they put out some effort and catch these two-bit crooks."

"Yes, sir, I'll tell them," Braxton said, and backed out of Tevis's office.

Colton Gray was already on his way to Fort Worth, sorry to hear that Casey and Eli were still up to their evil ways, but happy to be sent out of the office again. *They're going to slip up,* he thought, *and leave me the evidence I need to arrest them.*

He realized that he dreaded that day because he definitely admired the good the two old cowhands had done with the money. And the only thing keeping him from becoming a close friend was the fact that they gained their wealth unlawfully and he was committed to enforcing the law.

He rode into Fort Worth just before noontime and pulled up in front of the sheriff's office just as Courtright was walking out the door.

"Well, howdy, Colton," the sheriff greeted him. "I was wonderin' when you might show up."

"Howdy, Sheriff Courtright," Colton returned. "Thought I'd check in with you before I go bother the folks at the Wells Fargo Bank."

Courtright chuckled. "Seems like another useless trip, don't it? Those boys are too slick to catch. I was just goin' to get some dinner. If you ain't ate, why don't you go with me and we can talk about this last holdup of your friends, the old-men bandits."

Colton thought it ironic that Courtright referred to the robbers as his friends. He wondered if Casey and Eli would think the same.

"That sounds like a good idea to me. I'm ready to eat."

"Good," Courtright said. "You can just tie your horses here. We're just gonna walk right down the street there." He pointed a little farther down to a building with a sign identifying it as HARDING'S. So Colton left his horses at the sheriff's office and walked down to Harding's with the sheriff.

When they walked into Harding's, the owner, Wade Harding, yelled, "Sheriff's here, Trudy!" Then he waited for Courtright to explain the man with him.

"This here's Colton Gray, Wade," the sheriff said. "He's a deputy U.S. marshal outta Waco. If he don't like his dinner, he'll arrest ya."

Wade laughed in response. "Welcome, Deputy Gray. The sheriff always eats a steak, but you can have beef stew if you druther." Colton said he'd have a steak, too. "Sheriff don't want his hurt too bad. How do you want yours?"

"Just so the center's warm," Colton answered.

"Sheriff's got company, Trudy!" Wade yelled again. "He'll have the same, but he wants the center warm."

Colton followed Courtright past the one long table to a smaller, two-person table by the window. Wade followed soon after with two cups of coffee.

"Up here from Waco, huh?" he asked as he set the coffee down on the table. "Come up because of our latest bank holdup?"

"No," the sheriff answered for Colton, "he came up here because he heard about your famous steaks."

Wade just chuckled and walked away when another customer called him.

Courtright got right to the point then. "This latest job was a real humdinger. I thought the first one, when it was the old bank, was a real show they put on. But this time, they didn't go in together. One of 'em went in the front door and the other'n went in the back door. You'll see what I mean when you go to the bank."

He went on to explain how the whole thing went down, with one of the old men making a disturbance up front to draw the bank guard away from the safe in the back. He was interrupted briefly when their steaks were brought to the table, but continued right after they both cut a big bite off to test the meat.

"What gets me is, one of the tellers, Julian Scott, was workin' in the old bank when those two hit it the first time. And he said he never recognized that old man when he came in," the sheriff observed.

He paused to work on his steak before it got cold, so they both concentrated on the meat for a while before resuming his report.

"Now, I'm sure you're gonna hear the same song outta Branden Cooper that you heard outta Edwin Polk," Courtright continued. "Why didn't I form up a posse and go after those two little old men? I'll tell you what I told them. Those two birds were long gone before the folks at the bank even knew they'd been robbed. And it was a helluva long time after that when anybody thought about tellin' me. Well, I went down there right away, but nobody knew which way they went. Couple of people behind the bank said they saw two fellers riding away from the back corner of the bank buildin' goin' north. But when I checked up that street, I couldn't find anybody else that saw 'em. So there ain't much use to get up a posse when you don't know which way they went." He looked at Colton and waited for his comment, his face a big question mark.

"No, you're absolutely right," Colton assured him. "There ain't much you can do in a situation like that. I'll go to the bank and let them lead me through the whole robbery, just to see if they remember anything that might help identify the robbers. But these two fellows are pretty darn good at pullin' the wool over your eyes. I have to wonder about their concentration on Fort Worth," Colton commented. "This is the third time they've hit Fort Worth, two banks and a cattle buyer. What is it about Fort Worth that keeps them comin' back here? This ain't the only place they've hit, but it's the only one they've hit three times."

"If you figure that out, maybe it'll give you a clue about who the robbers are," Courtright said. "But I'd be surprised if it was somebody who lives here."

"So would I," Colton said.

They finished eating and Colton paid for both dinners. Courtright protested, insisted that he should be the one paying for their dinner. But Colton wanted to maintain a friendly relationship with the sheriff just to ensure future cooperation. They walked back to the sheriff's office and Colton got on his horse and rode to the Wells Fargo Bank.

He saw right away why the sheriff had said that one of the robbers just walked in the back door carrying a bucket with a mop in it. The carpenters were busy at work in the back of the bank as he pulled up in front and dismounted. When he walked inside, he could see changes in the lobby. He noticed right away that there were two office doors in the far wall, instead of the one when he was last in the bank. Since he stood just inside the door, looking around, the guard came over and asked, "Can I help you, sir?"

"Yes, thank you. I need to talk to Mr. Cooper. I'm Deputy U.S. Marshal Colton Gray and I'm here to investigate the recent robbery."

"Yes, sir," Andrew responded. "I'll go get Mr. Cooper for you." He turned and went immediately to the first of the two doors and knocked. Then he stuck his head in, and in a couple of minutes, the door opened wide and Branden Cooper came out to meet Colton.

"Deputy Gray?" Cooper asked, to be sure Andrew had remembered the name correctly.

"Yes, sir," Colton answered. "I'm here to find out as much as I can about the robbery. I wonder if you could just walk me through it."

"Actually, I can't tell you firsthand what happened out here at the teller windows because I was in the back of the bank in the safe room when the one robber came in. You'll get a better picture of what happened from one of the tellers."

"Looks like you got a pretty good lick there over your eye," Colton declared. "Did that happen during the robbery?"

"Yes, it did," Cooper answered. He went on then to tell Colton that he and the guard were at the safe when this strange old man walked right in the back door carrying a mop and a bucket. "I tried to tell him that he was not supposed to be in the back of the bank, but I couldn't make him understand."

Cooper told Colton about the disturbance that caused one of the tellers to come to get the guard, leaving him alone with the old man and the safe open. "That's when he pulled a gun on me and threatened to shoot me if I made a sound, and I think he meant it."

"When did he hit you?" Colton asked, knowing that if it was truly Casey and Eli—and he felt sure that it was—it was not typical for them to use any kind of violence.

"When he told me to fill a canvas sack with money and I refused to do it. He struck me with his pistol and stuffed a stack of fifty-dollar bills in my mouth to keep me from making a sound. Then he produced some clothesline rope from somewhere and tied me up. And that's all I can tell you about what I remember about the robbery."

"Yes, sir, I understand. I'll talk to the tellers to get an idea about what happened out front. I'm sorry you had to take a blow on the head. I'm pretty sure the two men who held up your bank are, in fact, the genuine old-men bandits and not copycats. And that lump you got on your head is the first reported case of any show of violence on their part. I'm sure it's a distinction you'd rather someone else had accomplished."

"That's certainly an understatement," Cooper replied. He walked Colton over to the teller cages. He wanted to talk to Julian Scott for sure, but Julian was busy with a customer, so the other teller, Bruce Logan, told Colton about the one old man's disgusting behavior that ended up in a major disturbance bad enough to necessitate sending for the bank guard.

"He reeked of alcohol," Bruce said. "He insulted one lady in line in front of him. He was loud and cursing. When he got to my window, I asked him what he wanted. He had a canceled check he must have found somewhere and wanted me to cash it for him. I tried to explain to him that it was a check that had already been cashed. But he couldn't get it through his brain that it was no good and that's when he really started getting wild. And that's when Julian ran to get Andrew to escort him out. He argued with Andrew for a while after that."

"That's right," the guard said. "I thought I was gonna have to use force for a while there. Then the strangest thing happened. He suddenly calmed down and didn't resist at all when I took him by the arm and escorted him to the door. When I walked him outside and turned him loose, he said I wouldn't see him again and he was sorry he had caused a problem. I ain't never seen a drunk sober up that quick before. Then he just walked calmly away and disappeared around the corner."

Colton could picture Casey Tubbs walking casually away after the end of another one of his performances. Julian was finished with his customer then and was listening to Bruce and Andrew's accounting of the incident. It occurred to Colton that he didn't seem very eager to add any comments of his own.

So Colton asked, "What about you, Mr. Scott, you got anything you want to add to that? You're the only one who's gone through two of these robberies."

Julian clenched his teeth and blurted, "It happened just like Bruce and Andrew told you. I should have recognized that old man who made all the fuss. I didn't realize it was one of those two that robbed us before, until it was too late. They were already gone. It's just that the first time, there were two of them and they didn't act anything like this belligerent drunk. It didn't even occur to me who he really was. Maybe if the two of them had come in together, it might have triggered my memory. I could have prevented the robbery if I had just recognized him."

Colton glanced at Branden Cooper, who was glaring at Julian.

"You shouldn't beat yourself up too much for that, Mr. Scott. In crimes like these, it's pretty hard to tell all the outlaws apart." It was a weak attempt, but it was all Colton could come up with at the moment. In an effort to get Cooper's mind off Julian, Colton said to Bruce, "You say the old man tried to cash a canceled check?"

"That's right," Bruce answered. "It was an old Fort Worth Investment Bank check, at that. No telling where he got it."

"You still have it, or did he take it back?" Colton asked.

"No, I still have it. I don't know why I didn't throw it away. Do you want it?" He opened his drawer and took the check out and handed it to Colton.

"Yeah, I'd like to take a look at it," Colton said as he took the check. "Made out to 'Woodward House Hotel,'" he said, "five dollars and sixty-five cents. Woodward House Hotel," he repeated. "Is that a place here in town?"

Cooper just shrugged, still thinking about Julian's failure. Cooper was new in town, so he was not familiar with it, but Bruce answered. "Yes, that's a little hotel owned by a woman named Emma Woodward. It's one street over and north, five or six blocks."

Julian spoke up then. "She used to have an account here when it was Fort Worth Investment Bank."

Colton could feel his mind warming up. "If you don't mind, I need to keep this as evidence," he said to Bruce.

"Sure," Bruce said, then repeated, "I don't know why I didn't throw it away."

Colton folded the check and put it in his vest pocket. "I suppose I've taken as much of your time as I need to. I think I've got a pretty good picture of how the robbery went down. I would like to take a quick look at the back where the second man came in."

"Of course," Cooper said. "Come with me." He started toward the door to the back, when the second office door opened and Stephen Brewster almost bumped into him. Cooper stopped and said, "This is Stephen Brewster, loan officer. Stephen, this is Deputy Marshal Colton Gray. He's here about the robbery."

"Glad to meet you, Deputy Gray," Brewster said. "If there's anything you need from me, I'm glad to help."

"There was one thing I wanted to ask," Colton said, since he had both bank officers there. "On the day before the robbery, do you remember if you might have talked to two strangers who were interested in opening a company account, or asked to see your safe for any reason?"

Cooper and Brewster looked at each other, both shaking their heads. "No," Cooper said, "I don't remember talking about that the day before."

Colton wasn't really surprised. He hadn't thought about asking before because he suspected the robbers were Casey and Eli and they didn't need to ask questions about the safe. They had been there before, but he decided to ask, anyway, just to be thorough.

"To the contrary," Brewster said, "I talked to two strangers the day before the robbery, but they came in to satisfy an overdue loan of six thousand dollars. The loan was to Carter General Merchandise in some little town called Little Bow."

That statement grabbed Colton's attention. "Do you remember who the two men were that paid off the loan?"

"Not right off hand," Brewster said. "But if it's important, I'll look on my desk calendar. I'm sure I wrote their names down."

"I would appreciate it," Colton told him, and he and Cooper stood outside the door while Brewster went back to his desk.

In less than a minute, he returned. "The two gentlemen who paid the loan were Mr. Casey Tubbs and Mr. Eli Doolin. Does that help you any?"

Colton wanted to shout it, but he restrained himself and

calmly said, "It helps a whole lot. Thank you very much. I think I've got all I need for now." Brewster turned around and went back into his office.

Cooper and Colton continued on to the safe room, where Cooper reset the scene for him and showed him where he had lain, tied hand and foot.

"Is that the rope you were tied up with?" Colton asked, and was told that it was. "I'd like to take it along with me."

Cooper shrugged and said, "Help yourself."

Back in the lobby, Julian told Bruce that he hoped the deputy could catch up with the two old men before they spent all the bank's money.

"Or before they die of old age," Bruce replied. "One thing for sure, if this building ever catches on fire, somebody's gonna have to remember to go in ol' Brewster's office and tell him."

Andrew overheard him and said, "He don't miss a thing, does he?"

After leaving the bank, Colton decided to visit the Woodward House Hotel. He had a strong feeling that there might be something important about it. But he needed to take care of his horses. Had he known he was going to spend as much time as he had before resting them, he would have taken them to a stable first. He looked Scrappy in the eye and said, "One more call and I'll find you and Joe some water and grain. I promise."

He found the Woodward House Hotel easily enough, so he looped the bay's reins over the white picket fence out front and climbed the steps to the front porch. He started for the door but was stopped dead in his tracks by the two big rocking chairs with names prominently displayed on the headrests: *Casey* on one, *Eli* on the other. His thoughts were piling up, one on top of the other now. Had he just accidentally walked into a hideout for the two old-men robbers? He noticed a sign beside the front door that listed the times for breakfast, dinner, and supper, and another advertising single- and double-room rates. So he walked in the door to find a small registration desk at the head of a hallway.

There was a little bell on the desk, sitting on a sign that said RING FOR SERVICE, so he rang. In a matter of a few seconds, he heard footsteps in the long hallway beyond the desk and a little lady with graying hair soon appeared.

"Good afternoon, sir. Can I help you?" Emma Woodward asked.

Making a quick decision, Colton answered her. "Good afternoon, ma'am. I'd like to rent a room for tonight, if you have a vacant one."

"As a matter of fact, we do, Mr. . . ." She paused for his answer.

"Gray," he responded. "Deputy U.S. Marshal Colton Gray." He watched her carefully for her reaction when he said it.

She did react, but not with fear or panic. "A deputy marshal," she said with interest. "Are you in town because of the bank robbery?"

"You know about the bank robbery?" Colton asked.

"Everybody in town knows about the bank robbery," she informed him. "It's the second time that bank has been robbed. And I should ask you, was it really by the same two old men who robbed it the first time?"

"Yes, ma'am, I think it was."

"My goodness!" she exclaimed. "You have to wonder why they would come back to the same place they had robbed before."

She's good, he thought. *Either that or she really doesn't have a clue.* He decided he'd try her on another question.

"I couldn't help noticin' when I walked up on the porch. You've got some curious names for those two big rockin' chairs. 'Casey' and 'Eli'? Are they two guests who live here?"

"No, I wish that they did," Emma replied. "Those two chairs are named for two men who are the closest things to real angels that I've ever been lucky enough to meet here on earth."

"Is that a fact?" Colton asked. "Why do you say that?"

"Because this hotel wouldn't be here today, if it wasn't for those two men, and Lord knows where I'd be."

"Do you get to see them often?" Colton asked.

"No, only when they happen to be in Fort Worth and that's not very often," she said. He started to ask her if they happened to have been here around the time the bank was robbed, but decided it might cause her to become cautious with her answers. He need not have worried, however, for she promptly volunteered the information. "They were in town for a couple of days last week."

"So they were here when the bank was robbed, I reckon."

"No," Emma laughed. "They just missed it. They left town the day it was robbed."

She's totally innocent, he decided, *but Eli and Casey are guilty as sin.*

He was certain at this point that Emma Woodward and her hotel were among their special charities. He was aware that he probably had enough to make a case against them. But a good lawyer might still have grounds to argue coincidence. He decided to take the room and see what else he might uncover.

"I need to leave a few things in my room and go find a stable before my horses decide they want to find another job," he said.

"That shouldn't take you long," Emma said. "You'll find a good stable at a reasonable price a couple of blocks down the street that runs beside the hotel. The man who owns it is Donald Plunket. He's a permanent guest here in the hotel and he'll take good care of your horses."

"That is handy," Colton said, and walked out to get his saddlebags.

She waited for him, and when he came back in, she told him about Walt Evans, too, in case he needed a blacksmith or a farrier. Then she took him to his room on the second floor. They met Rose coming down the steps when they were going up. Emma paused long enough to introduce them.

"Deputy Gray, this is Rose Pigeon. She's my helper." To Rose, she said, "This is Deputy Gray. He'll be staying in number five tonight."

"I hope you enjoy your stay with us," Rose said to him.

"Pleased to meet you, ma'am," Colton returned, then continued up the stairs, unaware of the exaggerated clenched-teeth grin Rose gave Emma or the eyes raised to the ceiling and slow shaking of the head Emma responded with.

Emma opened the door to room number five, then handed him the key and waited in the hall while he went in and took a quick look around. When he came out, she went back downstairs with him and showed him the dining room and the kitchen, where she introduced him to Pearl before taking him to the washroom.

"Now, you can just come and go as you please," she said.

He decided to go a step further with her, since he was convinced of her innocence. "About those two rockin' chairs on the front porch, I'm gonna guess if you had room on the head-rest for the last names, too, they woulda said, 'Casey Tubbs' and 'Eli Doolin.' Am I right?"

"Why, yes, you are," Emma replied. "Do you know Eli and Casey?"

"As a matter of fact, I do," Colton said. "I consider myself a friend of those two characters. I stop by their ranch, the D and T Cattle Company, every time I happen to be down in that part of Lampasas County."

"Well, for goodness' sake," Emma gushed. "It is a small world, isn't it? And here I am, telling you all about them, everything you already knew."

He took his horses to the stable then and found Donald Plunket out by the corral.

"Howdy," Colton offered. "Are you Mr. Plunket?" Donald said he was. "I'd like to leave my horses with you for the night," Colton continued. "I'm stayin' in the hotel. They've been traveling for a few days, so they need water and some grain."

"Well, I'll be glad to take care of 'em for you," Donald said. "Is that a marshal's badge you're wearin'?"

"That's right. Deputy Marshal Colton Gray," he said.

"The bank holdup?" Donald asked.

"Right, I've already been to the bank and also met with Sheriff Courtright, so I know it was done by the genuine old-men robbers."

"Ain't that something?" Donald responded. "Don't that seem like a dumb thing to do? Going back to the same place they robbed before?"

"Seems like a dumb thing, but they got away with it," Colton remarked.

"'Course it weren't a Wells Fargo Bank the first time they hit it," Donald said with a chuckle. "Maybe those outlaws thought they were at a different bank and they ain't as smart as we give 'em credit for. I didn't feel sorry for those folks at Fort Worth Investment Bank when they got robbed. They were trying to run poor Emma out of business so they could get their hands on that property. But Emma found a source of money that paid off her loan and she owns that hotel free and clear."

"Yeah, I saw the rockin' chairs on the front porch," Colton said. "I told Emma I've known Casey Tubbs and Eli Doolin for a long time. They're friends of mine."

"Well, then you know that Emma thinks they're really two angels sent down to help her. And I ain't totally sure she's wrong."

Chapter 20

He talked to Donald Plunket for quite a while, and by the time it was approaching the hour to get ready for supper, he had met Walt Evans as well. So he was well aware of the golden reputation Casey and Eli held with all things associated with the Woodward House Hotel. He had also decided it worthwhile to stay over one more night to continue collecting words and evidence. Both Walt and Donald promised him that Pearl's cooking was reason enough to stay over one night longer than planned. He was well received by a full table of guests of the hotel and found that Walt and Donald had been accurate in their praise of Pearl's cooking.

Pearl, Rose, and Emma interrogated him to the point where they were satisfied that he was not married, nor had he ever been, and he was not currently involved in any relationship with any particular woman. The women knew not that it could ever lead to anything in the future, but the fact that he was a friend of Casey's and Eli's drove his stock up quite a bit, for he must have important connections. The obvious assets of a youngish body, tall and strong, with a face not unpleasant to gaze upon, were all pluses on Rose's rating sheet.

After supper, Walt Evans brought a bottle of homemade scuppernong wine he had made himself and the men sampled it out on the front porch. Donald and Walt insisted that Colton should occupy one of the large rockers, since he was a personal friend of Casey's and Eli's. It was a pleasant evening, and Walt and Donald were regaled by Colton's telling of the time when Casey and Eli captured the copycat bank robbers of the bank in the town of Lampasas. The evening ended too soon, but all hands had to work the next day, so they retired for the night. Colton enjoyed it almost as much as Walt and Donald, in spite of a definite feeling akin to that of a Judas, since his mission was to acquire evidence to arrest their heroes.

The next morning after a fine breakfast, Colton walked to the stable with Donald and saddled Scrappy. Not sure if he would be back in time for dinner or not, he said he would definitely be back for supper. He rode out toward the west-side cattle pens and the road to San Antonio. They had used the same creek to camp by, on two previous robberies. He felt certain that if the bank robbers were Eli and Casey, they would use the same place again, since there was never any evidence that anyone had discovered it. So he rode past the Potluck Kitchen and Hasting's Supply and continued on to the creek. When he reached it, he didn't see any tracks leaving the road to follow the creek. If there had been, he would have known they weren't left by the two bandits, for they would have ridden upstream in the water.

He didn't bother riding Scrappy up the middle of the creek, for he had no need to hide his tracks. He rode along the bank until he reached the campsite he had found before and dismounted. He remembered it well, the two trees where they had tied their packhorses while they hit the bank, the hoofprints between the trees and to the water. They were recent, he told himself, so he knew there had to be the remains of a fire. He began a careful search of the ground, in places where it would make sense to have a fire. With his fingers, he scratched leaves and loose dirt away, clearing a large area of the ground. When it was as bare as he could make it, he stepped back a few feet to look at the whole area he had cleared. And then he saw it, an area about three feet square that looked like it had dropped maybe half an inch. "That's where they buried their fire," he murmured. "But why bury the fire in the first place? They never did that before."

Unless they had something to hide, he thought.

His skinning knife his only tool, he attacked the square of earth, trying to loosen the dirt as best he could. After he worked for about a quarter of an hour with minimal results, he decided to ride back to Hasting's and buy or borrow a shovel. He had planned to stop there, anyway, so he didn't wait to give it a second thought. He climbed up into the saddle and rode back to Hasting's Supply.

Floyd Hasting recognized him when he walked in. "Deputy Marshal Gray! I wondered if you'd be back in Fort Worth after that bank robbery at Wells Fargo."

"Howdy, Mr. Hasting," Colton said. "Yep, I'm back up here, lookin' around for answers. I need a couple of things, if it wouldn't be too much bother."

"Why, sure," Floyd replied. "Whaddaya need?"

"First, I wonder if you could tell me how much rope I've got here."

Floyd looked at the coil of rope, puzzled. "Clothesline," he pronounced. "You wanna know how long it is?"

Colton nodded.

"Well, that ain't no problem." He took it over to the counter where he kept rolls of rope and twine. He straightened the clothesline out along the scale he had on the counter where he cut rope. "There you go. That's twenty feet of clothesline." He wound it up again and handed it back to Colton. "What else can I do for you?"

"Do you remember selling twenty feet of clothesline to anybody within the last week?" Colton asked.

Floyd shrugged and scratched his head. "No, I can't say as I do."

Colton was disappointed. He would have bet on it.

"Wait a minute!" Floyd said then. "I did sell twenty feet of clothesline to those two cattlemen. I forgot all about it. I remember now. That was all they bought, twenty feet of clothesline rope. They were the ones I sold some black powder to, to get rid of some yellow jackets. Remember them?"

"Right," Colton said, "I remember. Now, I need to dig a hole and I haven't got a shovel, so let me see your cheapest one. I just need it for one little hole."

Floyd led him over to a bin with several different kinds of shovels. He pulled one short-handled model out and said, "This is the cheapest one I carry, four dollars and fifty cents. Is this what you're looking for?" He paused and waited while Colton thought it over. "You just want a shovel to dig one hole?" he finally asked. "You just wanna borrow a shovel?"

"I'd sure rather do that," Colton replied. "Maybe I could just pay you some rent for it."

Floyd had to chuckle. "No need, just bring it back when you're through. Looks like I can't make much of a livin' offa you or the D and T Cattle Company."

"I would like to buy one of those big canvas sacks there," Colton said, and pointed to a stand on the counter displaying laundry bags at fifty cents each. "And I appreciate the loan of a shovel. I won't keep it long."

He rode back to the creek with a standard-length shovel and a sack to hold whatever he might find buried in the ground and went to work immediately on the hole. He dug down through quite a bit of dirt before his shovel struck something more resistant. Clearing away most of the loose dirt, he discovered that what he had struck appeared to be a half-burned hat and some burned parts of heavy clothing. Something metallic in the loose soil turned out to be a pair of spectacles with the glass missing. There were bits and pieces of clothing and two pairs of charred boots, and Colton would bet those were the sizes that Casey and Eli wore.

When he got to the bottom of the hole, he had to wonder, *Does this mean they're giving up their lawless life?*

Why else would they burn their disguises? It gave him much to think about. He spent some time sifting through the dirt as he filled the hole again, and he stopped to examine a patch of gray hair that had miraculously escaped the flames. A piece of beard or wig, it was hard to say, since he had never seen the two in disguise. But it still caused him to wonder again if it signified the end of the two original old-men bandits. Realistic toupees and fake beards would be hard to find and would probably not be casually discarded.

He finished filling in the hole and paused to look around him at the little campsite by the creek and imagined seeing Casey and Eli hurrying to get out of their disguises. He realized he now held the rest of their lives in his hands. It was a mistake robbing this bank in Fort Worth again. For it was pure happenstance that provided him with the solid clues that pointed straight at them. The twenty feet of clothesline in his possession was enough to hang them. The check that led him to the Woodward House Hotel, the rocking chairs, all pointed to Casey and Eli.

And to crown the whole blunder was the visit to the bank by Casey Tubbs and Eli Doolin to pay Frank Carter's debt the day before. It was typical of the two men to rescue a neighbor in danger of losing his business to a bank because he couldn't repay his loan. It was also typical of them to reimburse themselves at the expense of the bank threatening to foreclose. But it was ironic that they felt it necessary to use their actual names in case Wells Fargo or Carter General Merchandise had any question.

There couldn't be any tighter case than the one against

Casey and Eli, so he tied his sack of physical evidence on his saddle horn, grabbed the shovel, and climbed aboard his horse. He figured he could still make it back in time to eat with his new friends at Woodward House. But he decided to put the final period on his evidence of the bank robbery by stopping to eat at the Potluck Kitchen. He returned the shovel to Floyd Hasting on his way back. And since the merchant wanted to hear how the investigation was coming along, Colton told him that he had enough evidence to prove it was the same two men who pulled the first two robberies in Fort Worth, but he didn't identify them. He said he wanted to get to the Potluck Kitchen before they closed for dinner, so he thanked Floyd for the use of the shovel and departed.

"Well, how you doin', Deputy?" Roy Black greeted him when he walked in the door. "I can't recall your name right now, but if you give me a minute, it'll come to me."

"It's Colton Gray," Joy said with a warm smile. She walked up beside her brother. "I remember your name."

"I remember yours, too, Joy and Roy, but it has been a long time," Colton said. "How's business? You folks still stayin' busy?"

"Can't complain," Roy said. "We're stayin' ahead of the bill collector."

"There you go," Colton said. "Long as you can keep doin' that, you ain't doin' bad. What you got cooked for dinner, Joy?"

"Chicken and biscuits," Joy said. "Set down and I'll get you a plate. You want coffee, I reckon."

"I reckon," Colton answered. He found a place at the long table between two men who looked like cowhands. They both favored him with a nod, which he returned.

"You seen our two friends from the D and T Cattle Company lately?" he asked Joy when she brought him a plate.

"Matter of fact," she said, "they was in here 'bout a week or so ago. Ain't that right, Roy?"

Roy said that was right.

"Next time they come in, ask 'em if they've arrested any more bank robbers," Colton said. That story went over so well at Woodward House the night before, he thought it would be equally enjoyed by Roy and Joy. They were curious to hear what he was referring to, so he told the story again about the time Casey and Eli ambushed the two bank robbers in Lampasas. It proved to be as entertaining to them as it had been at the hotel, especially the part about the loosening of the cinches. The rest of the people at the table enjoyed it as well.

When one of the regular customers asked Joy who it was that they were talking about, Joy said, "Two of the best men God ever put on this earth. Ain't that right, Colton? You know 'em better than we do."

"That's right, Joy," Colton answered. *And it's my job to put them in prison for the rest of their lives.*

When he finished eating, he remained for a little while to have another cup of coffee while he thought about what he had to do. He suddenly realized he was sitting alone at the table, so he got up and left a quarter extra for the coffee he drank.

"You don't have to pay for the extra coffee, Colton," Joy told him. "You looked like you was off in another place somewhere. Is everything all right?"

"Yeah," he answered. "I was just thinkin' about a job I gotta do, that I'd rather not do. It happens all the time in my job. The food was good as usual, and the company was better. You two take care of yourselves and I'll see you when I see ya." He went out the door, climbed on the bay gelding, and headed for town and the Woodward House Hotel.

When he got back to the hotel, he took Scrappy back to the stable and repacked his packsaddle to fit his evidence sack in. He wanted everything ready for his trip to Lampasas County after breakfast the next morning. Then he spent some time in the washroom to clean up a little from his work with the shovel. After that, it was the rocking chair on the front porch with Casey's name on the headrest. He talked a while with Walt and Donald when they came for supper, and when Emma rang the supper bell, they left the porch and went inside.

When Colton was asked where he was off to in the morning, he said that he was pretty sure he had picked up the path of the two bank robbers' escape. They had not gone north, as was first suspected, but south, out the San Antonio road.

"You be careful," Emma told him. "We've decided we'd like to have you come visit again. So we don't want anything to happen to you."

"Why, thank you, Emma," Colton replied. "I appreciate that. I'll be careful."

After another excellent meal, courtesy of Pearl Pigeon, there was a little more time spent on the porch before Colton retired to his room.

He said his goodbyes after breakfast and was on the road to Lampasas County and the D&T Cattle Company before the sun was above the treetops. He had one goal in mind, to stop the old-men bandits and bring them back to face the justice fitting their crimes. He had sworn to the state of Texas that he would do just that and he was a man of his word. As he rode south on the San Antonio road, he thought about Casey and Eli, and he regretted the fact that there was so much good in them. His job would be so much easier if they were like the common thieves and murderers he normally faced. He warned himself to quit thinking along such lines.

Just do your job, he ordered.

Two and a half days was the time he expected to spend to make the trip to the D&T Ranch. It was a day's work for his horses to do forty miles, but Scrappy and Joe were accustomed to it and he wanted to arrive at the D&T at midday. He stopped for his noon meal at a little stream that was strong enough to keep fresh water moving. He relieved his horses of their saddles and packs and left them to graze in and about the stream while he made coffee and cooked some bacon and hardtack. After a good rest for his horses, he loaded them up again and rode until almost dark before he found a decent campsite to spend the night.

The next day was almost a duplicate of the first day. The horses were in good shape, and after the noon rest, he had his mind set to camp that night on a nice creek that was only twenty miles from the D&T. He had used it before and there was good grass and lots of trees for firewood. On prior trips, he could count on a good meal when he reached the D&T, either from Juanita at the main house or Smiley at the cookshack. On this trip, he was not sure he would be fed at all.

He figured he was no more than four or five miles from the creek and his camp for the night, when he spotted the smoke. He could have easily missed it, had he not happened to be looking in that direction. It looked to be no more than a hundred yards or so west of the road he traveled and it didn't look big enough to be a brush fire. Probably a campfire, and it was pretty far away, he figured, so he dismissed it. The trouble that caused the fire was closer than he thought, however.

"Now, I wonder where he's goin'," Del Haywood mumbled to himself as he sat on his horse about thirty yards from the road behind a thicket of juniper. "Got a packhorse loaded down pretty good, too. He's gotta be lookin' for a place to camp. It's gittin' pretty late."

Then he thought, *I bet he's headin' for the creek.* That would be the same creek his partner, Otis Sikes, was butchering a young cow beside. The creek curved around and crossed the road about three and a half miles up ahead and was a popular camping ground for folks traveling the road. Since it was getting dark already, Del had decided to ride on up to the crossing to see if there were any campers setting up for the night. So he had left Otis butchering the calf while he was gone.

He was about to ride out of the trees beside the road, when he caught sight of the single rider leading a packhorse just coming into view in the distance. He had quickly backed his horse behind the screen of juniper bushes and waited to watch him pass. In the growing darkness, it was hard to see the rider closely, but he sat tall in the saddle, so it might be a good idea to wait until Otis could help him.

The rider's horses looked like they were in good shape, and there was no telling what he was carrying on that packhorse. This would be a lucky day to rustle a fat calf and catch an unsuspecting traveler as well. He decided he would follow him to make sure he stopped for the night at the creek. And if he didn't stop there, he would simply shoot him in the back, then go back for Otis. He waited until the stranger was almost out of sight before Del gave his horse a kick and rode out of the trees and onto the road. In the rapidly deepening darkness, he found he was able to keep the rider in sight with little chance of him turning around to see that he was being trailed.

When Colton came to the creek, he left the road and rode about thirty-five yards upstream before coming to a small grassy clearing. Even in the darkness, he could see the evidence of a couple of prior campfires. He unsaddled his horses and set them free to water and graze. Then he went about the business of making camp, starting with the chore of gathering wood to make his fire, unaware that he was being watched. Scrappy was uncomfortable with it, however, and whinnied a request for identification a couple of times, but never received an answer.

Colton was aware of the bay's discomfort, but figured it likely a coyote or possibly a fox snooping around the popular campsite. He would keep his weapons handy, just in case he was wrong.

Del continued to watch for a while, trying to make a decision. He was tempted to shoot him while he was still in the process of making camp. But there were so many trees between him and his target, he was afraid he didn't have a clear enough shot. And after just a short time of watching, it was impressed upon him the man looked to be well able to handle himself.

Feeling a bit scrawny in comparison, Del decided it was more of a sure thing if he went back to get Otis. The man wasn't going anywhere. He and Otis could wait until he went to sleep, then slip in his camp and cut his throat while he was sleeping. That was more to Otis and Del's style, anyway.

Besides, Del thought, *I'm hungry and I want some of that beef Otis is cooking.* He backed carefully away to get his horse.

Scrappy calmed down again, so Colton figured that whatever critter had been snooping around his camp had backed away. To be sure, he drew his six-shooter when he walked down the creek bank with his coffeepot, his gaze sweeping back and forth on both sides of the creek. When he squatted at the water's edge to fill the pot, his focus shifted from spot to spot in the trees lining the banks.

They would have taken the shot by now, he thought, and went back to his campfire to cook something to eat.

"Where the hell have you been?" Otis Sikes asked. "You ain't been a helluva lot of help butcherin' this calf. Where'd you go? I needed you to look after that meat cookin' on the fire."

"Quit your bellyachin'," Del responded. "You ought not need no help takin' care of that one little ol' calf. I had more important things I had to look after."

"Like what?" Otis demanded sarcastically.

"Like a little midnight party I got planned for tonight that's gonna be worth more than that little calf," Del answered. He pulled a slice of meat off the fire and started chewing it, at the same time filling Otis in on his plan. "I figure we can slip right up the creek and take that feller without even wakin' him up. He's got two good-lookin' horses, a heavy packsaddle, and a handgun and a rifle that I could see."

"Shoot! Why wait till midnight?" Otis responded. "Let's go get him now."

"I don't know 'bout that," Del said. "He's a pretty stout-lookin' tree. He might be tough to chop down. I druther he was asleep."

"Well, I reckon I'll take your word for it," Otis said. "We'll give him time to turn in, then we'll visit him." He chuckled and joked, "Maybe we oughta take him a slab of this fresh meat so he can fill his belly up and go right to sleep."

"I think I'll fill my belly up, instead," Del replied.

"If he's camped on this side of the road at the crossin', we can just walk down the creek till we get to his camp," Otis said. "Then we can ride his horses back here and see what we got."

Chapter 21

Colton poured the last of the coffee out of his little coffee-pot into the cup and leaned back against the trunk of a cottonwood tree while he thought again about what he was going to do tomorrow. He was only about twenty miles from the D&T Ranch, so he figured he would have breakfast before he started out in the morning. He did not tell his boss, Marshal John Timmons, what he planned to do. And he wasn't sure what to expect from Eli and Casey, but he thought he owed it to the two men to come here alone.

Hearing Scrappy making inquisitive sounds again, he turned to set the coffee cup down beside his blanket. The first shot caught him in the left shoulder, forcing him to continue turning toward the creek. He rolled, over and over, down the creek bank, and heard the second shot snap as it passed over his back. He kept rolling until he was almost in the water and low enough to take cover below the top of the creek bank. He pulled the Colt .45 from his holster and cocked it. The trouble was, he didn't know where the shooter or shooters were, but they knew exactly where he was.

So he had to move from there. He didn't know how badly he was wounded, but at least it was in his left shoulder. At this moment, his whole shoulder felt numb. The creek bank was not that high, so all they had to do was walk closer to the creek and they would be able to see him lying there. So he started dragging himself backward, only able to move himself inches at a time. Still, he struggled to try to reach a gully about ten feet behind him.

"I got him!" Del exclaimed excitedly. "I got him! He rolled down into the creek!" He ran toward the creek, cranking another round into the Winchester '66 rifle he carried.

"Watch yourself, Del!" Otis warned. "He might not be dead!"

"I got him!" Del repeated as he ran directly to the spot on the bank where he saw Colton roll over, his rifle aimed down because he expected him to be lying in the water. But when he reached the bank and looked down at the water, Colton was not there. He turned immediately, bringing the rifle up as he did, but not in time to beat the .45 slug that impacted his chest. Otis, who had started running after him, stopped in his tracks when he heard the pistol shot and saw Del collapse, then go headfirst down the bank.

"Oh, hell," Otis swore. "I toldja, you dern fool. I knew you didn't kill him." Instead of advancing any farther, he took a few steps backward and took cover behind a tree.

Meanwhile, Colton never stopped dragging himself backward, until he finally reached the gully. He dropped down into it. The gully had been formed by runoff after heavy rains, the result of which had left a space around three feet deep. Ignoring his wounded shoulder, which was no longer numb, but rather a throbbing pain, Colton crawled on all fours, following the gully into the trees. When it became shallow to the point where it would no longer hide him on all fours, he crawled out and sought the cover of a cottonwood, while he tried to determine where Otis was. But he strained to search the patch of trees between himself and the creek, to no avail, until Otis spoke. Then he heard Otis call out to him and realized the gully had taken him out behind the dead man's partner.

"Hey, in the creek!" Otis yelled. "Ain't no use for any more shootin'. You done killed my partner, but I ain't holdin' it against you. He weren't shootin' at you. He was supposed to fire a warnin' shot over your head, and I reckon he just aimed too low. We thought you was rustlin' our cattle. Terrible mistake. How bad are you hurt? Maybe I can help get you to the doctor. There ain't no hard feelin's." He edged slowly out from the tree he was hiding behind and crept cautiously toward the creek, his rifle ready to fire.

Amazed by the stupidity of the man's attempt to draw him out, Colton waited until the man was clear of the trees before responding. "Stop right there and drop the rifle," he commanded.

Startled to find Colton behind him, Otis turned and fired two wild shots before Colton stepped away from the tree to place two shots that staggered him and dropped him to his knees. Because of the distance, and he was using his handgun, the second shot was required to finish him after the first one stopped him. Otis remained on his knees, holding his rifle in one hand and staring lifelessly, so Colton approached him cautiously. He didn't want to end this bizarre encounter by being shot by a dead man. The mission he was on had been difficult enough without this unfortunate encounter and the addition of a piece of lead in his shoulder. He was going to have to treat his wound as best he could until he was someplace where he could get some help. And that would be two days at the least, if he started back to Waco in the morning.

Cursing his luck, he walked up to the corpse still on its knees, and with a little shove, he pushed it over on its side. His horses had darted at the sound of the sudden gunfire. They now wandered back to his camp. He looked at the bay gelding and said, "Next time you try to tell me something, I'm gonna pay more attention." Then it occurred to him that the two men who attacked him had no horses. "They must have sneaked down the creek on foot," he told Scrappy. "The fire must have been their camp," he said, remembering the smoke he had seen before reaching the creek.

He took a quick look at his shoulder and decided the major bleeding had stopped, although his left sleeve was soaked. He found a small towel in his saddlebag, so he stuffed that inside his shirt to help contain the bleeding. Seeing that he had no other choice, he decided to walk back up the creek to find their camp and he could ride their horses back to his camp. So he tied his two horses to a tree limb to keep them from following him and started walking up the creek.

He figured he had walked over a hundred yards, when he picked up the smell of roasted meat on the breeze. At once concerned that there might be someone in addition to the two would-be assassins, he became a little more cautious as he approached the camp. When he got close enough to see into the camp, he saw the fire, which was dying down considerably. And there was meat extended over the fire on an assortment of green tree limbs. He saw their horses. There were only two and they were tied next to the water. Beyond the fire, he saw the remains of a half-butchered calf.

Rustlers, he thought. *Well, at least I've done some rancher a favor tonight.* He walked on into the firelight. "That's far enough right there," a voice came from the other side of the fire. "Put your hands in the air, you no-account, suck-egg dog."

Finding it hard to believe that he had walked into the second blunder of the night, Colton stopped and stuck one hand up in the air. "If you don't mind, I'll just raise my gun hand. The other one hurts like hell to raise."

"Before you get any ideas about what you're gonna do," the voice came back, "you might wanna know there's four of us watchin' you. And we're in the mood to lynch a low-down cattle thief."

"It might not make any difference to you, but I think you

oughta know, what you'll be lynchin' is a deputy U.S. marshal and not a cattle rustler," Colton said. "I just shot your cattle rustlers. There were two of 'em."

All four men stepped into the firelight, all with their six-shooters in hand. The older one, the obvious leader, said, "Mister, that's a damn good story. I hope it's the truth. You got any proof of that?"

"Can I take my hand down?" Colton asked, and the man said he could, but to move it real slow. Colton took his hand down and pulled his vest aside to reveal his badge. "I'm Deputy Marshal Colton Gray," he said. "I just came back here to get their horses to transport their bodies."

"I swear, I didn't have any idea there was a deputy marshal trackin' the no-accounts who've been livin' off my beef. My name's Gary Corbett, my ranch starts on the other side of this creek. We expected they would be rustlin' our cows tonight or tomorrow night, but we didn't know what part of our range they'd work on. Then we heard the shootin' and that's how we found their camp."

"To be honest with you, Mr. Corbett, I wasn't trackin' these two rustlers here. I was just on my way from Fort Worth to the D and T Ranch. I just happened to camp on this creek where it crosses the road. These two jumped me and put a bullet in my shoulder. I didn't know they were cattle rustlers until I walked up here and saw that beef cookin' on the fire."

Everybody relaxed then. One of Corbett's men pulled a strip of beef off the fire and took a bite of it. "This meat's gonna be too done to eat in a minute, boss." The other two men chuckled and helped themselves to a strip of beef as well.

"Where's your manners, Charley?" Corbett said, and invited Colton to sample a slice of meat. "No sense in lettin' it go to waste."

"I don't mind if I do," Colton said. "That little slab of

bacon I had for supper is long gone." He took the strip off of a limb that Charley extended toward him. He took a big bite and chewed it thoroughly. "I've gotta hand it to ya, Mr. Corbett, you raise some pretty tasty beef."

"Glad you're enjoying it," Corbett said. "Reckon we ought to take a look at that wound in your shoulder?"

"Well, I don't know if there's much we can do for it, until I get someplace where a doctor or somebody can probe around in there and loosen that slug. It stopped bleedin' for the most part, so it'll most likely be all right till I find somebody."

"You say you're headin' to the D and T Ranch?" Corbett asked. Colton said he was. "Well, they've got a chuck wagon cook named Smiley George who's pretty good at doctorin'. He used to work for me, so I know he's near as good as a real doctor. D and T ain't but twenty miles from here. I'll bet he'll take care of you." He laughed, then added, "Unless you're on your way there to arrest the owners. In that case, he might try to finish you off."

"I expect you're right," Colton said. "It'd be kinda hard to arrest Casey and Eli, especially since I count them as friends of mine."

And I find that ironic as hell, he thought.

"Oh, you know Casey and Eli?" Corbett asked. "I'll tell you one thing, without those two men, I wouldn't have a cow to worry about losin' to rustlers. You'd think they'd be worried about competition in the cattle business. But not those two. They're the first ones to help if help is needed."

"Well, I expect I'd best take those two horses back to my camp, so I can load those bodies on 'em before they get too stiff to bend," Colton said.

"You want us to go along with you to help you load 'em?" Corbett asked. "I mean, you with just one good arm and all."

Colton could tell that Corbett wanted to see the two dead rustlers for himself. "I could always use a hand. And as far as

I'm concerned, you can search their bodies and saddlebags for anything valuable that might help pay for the loss of some of your cattle."

That satisfied Corbett, so they followed Colton back to his camp. A couple of Corbett's men stayed behind long enough to put the fire out before coming along. With plenty of manpower volunteering, the two bodies were quickly laid belly down across their saddles. Colton confessed he was going to leave them there until they stiffened into that position before he took the load off the horses.

"You ain't got but twenty miles to go in the mornin'," Corbett said while his men searched the bodies and their saddlebags. "Then you can rest their horses." He stroked his chin as he thought. "Are you gonna take those bodies all the way back to Fort Worth?"

"No, I'll be goin' to Waco from here," Colton said, "but that's almost as far."

"Why don't you just leave 'em for the buzzards, or dig a hole and dump 'em in it? Shoot, nobody knows who those two are, or cares what you do with 'em."

"I agree with you," Colton said. "But rules are rules."

"I sure don't envy you the trip back, Deputy. Those bodies are gonna get pretty ripe. Tell Casey and Eli that I said howdy." He started to walk away, but an idea struck him that he thought might interest the deputy. "If you really don't want the bother of hauling those bodies all the way back to Waco, why don't you just take a picture of 'em and take that back?"

"That would do just as well, I'm sure," Colton answered. "I reckon I don't do that for the same reason I don't just put 'em on the train and ship 'em back. There ain't no railroad here abouts and I ain't got one of those photographic cameras."

Corbett laughed. "Yeah, but I know where one is, and it's between here and the D and T."

Colton seriously doubted that. "Where?"

"Little Bow," Corbett said. "There's a fellow that's been in town for about a week. His name's Johnathan Guiese and he's been takin' pictures of the town and the country around Little Bow. Frank Carter let him set up a little shop in the back of his store. He travels around in a wagon he says is his darkroom. I bet he could take a picture of those two. He took a lot of pictures in the Civil War. You can go into Frank's store and look at 'em. Me and my wife saw 'em."

Colton was interested. A picture would surely beat leading two rotting corpses all the way back to Waco. "I've never been to Little Bow," he said. "You say it's between here and the D and T?"

"Yeah, it is, but it ain't on this road. There's a little trail that leaves this road . . ." He paused to estimate. "It's about eight or nine miles from this creek. There ain't no sign or nothin' that says Little Bow, but you just pass a little trickle of a stream and there's a couple of little pine trees with a broke wagon wheel on the ground between 'em. It'll trail off to the west. Like I said, it ain't much of a road, but it'll take you straight in to Little Bow."

"I'm much obliged," Mr. Corbett. "If that fellow is still there, it might save me one of the worst trips of my life."

"He'll still be there," Corbett said. "My wife's plannin' on havin' a picture of me and her made. I oughta tell you, though, my wife's mother is dead set against it. She says those picture-takin' things will capture your soul. I don't reckon you'd worry too much about that with those two cattle thieves, though. Anyway, Little Bow ain't but four miles from the D and T's front gate, and anybody in Little Bow can tell you how to get there. By the way, I 'preciate you takin' care of my cattle rustlers."

His two corpses were already stiffening up when he crawled out of his blanket the next morning after only a few hours' sleep. One look at the bodies and he said, "I don't feel much better than you look." Feeling no desire for food, he settled for some coffee before he got back on the road. He started looking for the trail to Little Bow after he had ridden what he figured to be around six or seven miles. It was not long after, he spotted the two pines. He wasn't surprised that he had never noticed the trail before when he had traveled this road. Even had he noticed it, he would probably have assumed it to be the path to a farmhouse back off the main road.

He figured he'd been on the trail for about three hours when he came to a small farm, and just beyond that, he saw the gathering of buildings that told him he had reached Little Bow. It was hardly a bustling little town, so when he rode up the middle of the street, he only passed a couple of people in front of the shops. They were stopped in their tracks by the sight of the man riding by, leading a string of horses, two of which had bodies lying across the saddles.

The largest building in town was the one with the sign that read CARTER GENERAL MERCHANDISE. When he reached it, he rode around to the back and tied his horses beside an enclosed black wagon that looked like a stagecoach with no windows. That had to be the photographer's, he figured. He walked back around the building to go in the front door, where he saw the display of photographs Corbett had talked about. Frank Carter had arranged a nice little area for the photographer to arrange his display.

"Can I help you, sir?" Frank asked when he glanced up from the counter and saw the tall young stranger in the doorway.

"Mornin'," Colton replied. "I'm lookin' for the photographer who took all those pictures you've got over there." He pulled his vest aside to show his badge.

"Mr. Guiese?" Frank asked, immediately concerned that the law was looking for the photographer. The fact that the lawman had obviously suffered a wound, evidenced by the bloodstained sleeve of his shirt, contributed to his concern.

"That's right, Mr. Guiese," Colton said. "Is he here?"

"Yes, he's here. He's in the back havin' a cup of coffee," Frank told him, not sure if he should have or not. What could Guiese possibly be mixed up in? "Mr. Guiese ain't in any trouble, is he?"

Colton smiled. "Not that I know about. I'm Deputy Marshal Colton Gray. I've got a couple of dead outlaws in back of your store and I want Mr. Guiese to take a picture of them."

Frank relaxed at once. He grinned guiltily and said, "I'll go tell him you want him." He turned and went through the door to the back of the store.

Colton took that opportunity to look at some of the Civil War photos on display. He decided right away that a photograph would suit his needs in this situation.

In a few minutes, the store owner returned with Guiese in tow.

"Deputy Gray, Mr. Carter tells me you are inquiring about purchasing a photograph of some dead men," Johnathan Guiese said.

"That's right," Colton replied. "I need to take a picture of these outlaws to prove that they're dead, so I don't have to haul their bodies all the way back to Waco. If you could make a picture as good as you made of those army officers on the table over there, that would do just fine, if they'll hold up till I get back to Waco."

Guiese smiled and said, "Those pictures you're referring to are albumen prints. They held up since the war was over. They're the same process I'm using today. I would have to charge you three dollars for one print, however. There are certain chemicals I have to purchase to develop the negative, fermented chloride, silver nitrate, special paper, and such."

"Fair enough," Colton said. He had actually thought it would cost more than that. "Can you go ahead and take the picture now? I've got places I need to be this mornin'."

"Where are the dead men?"

"They're out back of the store," Colton said.

"Well, let me get my camera," Guiese said, "and we'll set it up to shoot right away, but it will take a while for me to develop the picture and make the print." He paused, then asked, "Do you need to find a doctor for your shoulder?"

"I doubt if there is one in this little town," Colton replied. "I'll see if I can find somebody after we get this picture done."

While Guiese was getting his camera set up, Colton pulled the subjects of the photograph off their horses and arranged them as best he could. By this time, word had gotten around the small town about the two dead outlaws and the photograph to be taken. So a sizable group of spectators had gathered to witness this historic event. When Guiese was ready to shoot, he suggested that Colton kneel between them.

"I don't need a picture of me," Colton said. "I just need a picture of the two dead men."

"If you are in the picture," Guiese explained, "there is no question who the two men are. If you're not in it, then it's just a picture of two dead men that you could have gotten anywhere."

"That makes a lot of sense," Colton decided, so he stepped in between them and knelt on one knee. After the picture was taken, he asked those standing around gawking at the dead men if anyone knew who they were. No one did, until Jim Watts, owner of the Texas Rose Saloon, said they had been in his saloon a couple of times. One of them was named Otis, the other one Del. He didn't know their last names.

Colton thanked him, then asked Carter if there was anyone in town who did any doctoring. Carter told him there was no real doctor, but the barber Lawrence Taylor did some minor doctoring, and had been known to work on a bullet wound. So while Guiese was developing his film and making the print, Colton took the horses down to the creek that ran behind the town and watered them. After that, he paid a visit to the barber.

"I'll take a look at it," Lawrence told him, "and see if I can get to it." Colton sat down in the barber chair and Lawrence removed the towel he had stuffed in his shirt. "Least I can do is clean it up, so you won't get it infected. It's a miracle to me that it ain't got infected yet. Take your shirt off." He watched Colton get out of his shirt and commented, "You didn't look like you was having much trouble moving it. Can you raise your arm up like this?" He demonstrated by raising his arm straight up over his head.

Colton raised his, although he grimaced a little when he tried to straighten it all the way.

"I believe you were pretty lucky. That bullet must not've damaged any bone or nothing."

"If I'd been lucky, he would've missed," Colton said. "I can raise my arm up like that, but it hurts like hell when I do."

"So my advice to you is, don't raise it up like that no more," Lawrence said, then quickly added, "I'm just japing you. I expect it's just the inflamed muscle around that bullet that makes it hurt, but it'll get better in a few days and it'll numb up around that bullet."

"You saying you can't dig it outta there?" Colton asked.

"That's what I'm saying. What'd he shoot you with?"

Colton told him, a rifle; then the barber said, "That's what I suspected. That bullet is in there too deep for me to get at. That muscle is already closing up around it. I'd really make a mess of your shoulder if I was to try to dig it out. You might take a shot at me before I finished. You won't be the first man to walk around with a bullet in him somewhere."

"I reckon not," Colton said.

"But I can clean it up and put some disinfectant on it and put a clean bandage on it," he said. Colton told him to go ahead. So he reached in a counter behind the chair and pulled out a bottle of whiskey. "You want a drink of this before I pour it on that wound?"

"No, just pour it in th . . . Damn!" He yelped before Lawrence gave him time to prepare for it.

"Now, it's all over before you even had time to dread it," the barber said. "Ain't that better than watching me pour it in that wound?" He cleaned all around the wound and applied a clean bandage, and when he was finished, he charged him a dollar. "Twenty-five cents of that was for the shot of whiskey. You're gonna be sore around that wound for a few days, but after a week, you won't even know you've got that chunk of lead in your shoulder. Just remember to lean a little to the right when you're fixing to shoot at somebody," he japed.

Chapter 22

When he went back to Frank Carter's store, Johnathan Guiese was still working on his print, so Colton got his other shirt out of his saddlebag and exchanged it for the bloody one. While he waited for his photograph, he talked with Frank and his son. Then with the son's help, he loaded his dead outlaws back on their horses. He asked Frank for directions to the D&T Ranch, which launched the shop proprietor on a high-praise speech for the two owners of that ranch.

Finally, Guiese came back in the store to show Colton his finished photograph. Having never seen one of himself before, Colton was unable to recognize himself. He looked at Frank and asked, "Do I look like that to you?"

"Exactly," he answered.

Colton turned and held the print up in front of Frank Jr., who said, "That's you, spittin' image." Colton still wasn't sure. He studied the faces of Otis and Del and they looked accurate, so he carefully wrapped the picture up in the protective paper wrap Guiese gave him. He paid Guiese an extra fifty cents for a protective envelope with a string tie. Then he thanked everyone for their help and left Little Bow, figuring that somewhere along the four-mile trail to the D&T there would be a good place to leave Otis and Del.

He had not ridden far when he noticed that a couple of buzzards high overhead had taken a curious interest in him. About halfway to D&T, he came to a thickly wooded area and decided he wasn't going to find anything better, so he turned Scrappy off the trail and made his way through the trees, until satisfied he was far enough off the trail. Then he dismounted and, with his good hand, jerked the bodies off the saddles.

He looked up to see maybe a dozen buzzards circling above the treetops. "Where did you boys come from?" He climbed back on his horse and headed back to the trail. "Dinner is served," he announced.

Davy Springer was the first to spot the rider approaching the barn, leading a packhorse and two saddled horses. He recognized him at once. "Hey, Smiley, yonder comes Colton Gray and he's leadin' a couple of horses with empty saddles."

Foreman Monroe Kelly heard Davy, so he came out of the barn to see. "Better run up to the house and tell 'em Colton's here," he told Davy.

Davy ran up to the kitchen to let Juanita know so she could tell Casey and Eli. Then he hurried back to the barn to hear what Colton was doing out this way again. He got back to the barn just as Colton pulled up before Monroe and Smiley, who were waiting to greet him.

"Deputy Colton Gray," Monroe announced grandly. "What brings you out this far from Waco? Do I need to tell any of the boys they better slip out the back?" he japed.

Colton was the only one who could find the question ironic, since their bosses would be the most likely. "Howdy, Monroe. I just had some business out this way, so I thought I'd stop by the D and T Cattle Company to see how you boys are gettin' along."

"Musta been some serious business," Smiley commented, "judgin' by them empty saddles." He watched Colton as he stepped down from the saddle. "Is that a bandage you're wearin' under your shirt?"

"Yeah, I caught a slug from one of the owners of these horses, so I thought your bosses wouldn't mind if I let 'em rest a little bit before I take 'em back to Waco with me. I worked 'em pretty hard before I got here."

"That bandage looks new," Smiley said. "Who put that on for you?"

"The barber over in Little Bow," Colton answered.

"Lawrence Taylor?" Smiley asked.

Colton nodded.

"Did he get the bullet outta there?" Smiley asked.

Colton told him that the barber said it was best to leave the bullet in his shoulder.

"You want me to take a look at it?" Smiley asked. "Ol' Lawrence is a little bit shy about goin' too deep under the skin."

"Why, sure, you can take a look at it, if you want to. I'd druther not be totin' it around in my shoulder, if it would be just as easy to get it out."

"Come on over here to the cookshack and sit down on that stool," Smiley said, "and I'll get my tools."

"Let me take care of my horses first," Colton said, but Davy volunteered to take care of them for him and turn them loose in the corral.

"I'll put your saddles and your packs in the barn," Davy told him.

"Much obliged, Davy," Colton said, and went to the cookshack, took his shirt off, and sat down on Smiley's stool. This was the way Casey and Eli found him, with Smiley probing around in his shoulder.

"Are we too early?" Eli japed. "Should we have waited till Smiley finishes killin' him off?"

"Yeah, Smiley," Casey added, "it'd be a whole lot quicker if you'da just shot him."

"Mr. Tubbs and Mr. Doolin," Colton came back. "It ain't polite to be disrespectful to my doctor, especially when he's workin' on me."

"Well, if there's anything left of ya after Dr. Smiley's through with ya, Juanita's expectin' you to join us for dinner up at the house," Casey said. "You picked a good time to come for supper. Miguel killed a hog this mornin', so Juanita's cookin' pork chops."

"I accept your invitation," Colton said.

"You come over this way from Waco?" Eli asked.

"No, I came down here from Fort Worth," Colton said.

"Is that a fact?" Eli asked. "What were you doin' in Fort Worth?"

"Wells Fargo Bank up there got hit by the old-men bandits last week and their trail led down this way," Colton answered, watching the reactions on both faces. There was no more than a slight twitching of the eyes of both men, but they exchanged a quick glance.

"How'd you get shot?" Casey asked. "You musta caught up with 'em."

"Oh, I caught up with 'em," Colton declared, "but this bullet hole was just something that happened on the way to catchin' up with the old-men bandits. This had to do with those two empty saddles on those extra horses I brought with me."

"All right, I'm fixin' to go in and dig that bullet outta there," Smiley stated. "So you better find you somethin' to hold on to."

Colton just clenched his fists and motioned for him to proceed. To Casey, he said, "Let me get through with this business and we'll talk."

"It'll be about dinnertime by then," Eli said. "So just come on up to the house when Smiley's done with you and we'll eat some of those pork chops."

"Thank you," Colton uttered painfully when he felt the first prick of Smiley's knife. "I'll do that." Then he turned all his concentration on an effort not to cry out in pain as Smiley wasted no time diving in and extracting the bullet. He went over to the pump by the horse trough and rinsed the spent bullet off; then he handed it to Colton and told him it was a lucky piece for him.

Walking back up to the house, Casey and Eli were already deep in conversation. "He came here from Fort Worth," Eli said. "There weren't no damn trail to follow. What did he come here for? He knows. That's why he's here."

"If he's sure, then why didn't he come right in and try to place us under arrest?" Casey asked. "I think he still just thinks it's us, but he ain't got nothin' to prove it. And he ain't gonna get any new evidence to point to us because we've retired from that business. It's his tough luck. He's too late to catch us and I know we're lucky we got away with that last one. I don't know about you, but I've suddenly gotten too old to do crazy stuff like that."

"Yeah, and I still can't believe we got away with forty thousand dollars," Eli said. "We don't need to steal any more money. Maybe we shoulda spent some of it to tell Smiley to cut Colton's throat. You think he's gonna try to haul us outta here under arrest? He wouldn't be that dumb, you think?"

"I don't think the men would stand for it," Casey said. He thought about that for a few seconds. "You know, he mighta come here from Fort Worth, but maybe he's got a posse of deputy marshals coming to meet him here from Waco. Maybe that's the reason he's still actin' all friendly-like."

"And maybe he's just bluffin'," Eli suggested, "hopin' we'll slip up and confess something. Let's call his bluff and don't give him any reason to think we're spooked."

Eli stroked the whiskers on his chin as he thought about the possible results of Colton's surprise visit. Even now, Smiley might be casually mentioning that he and Casey were away from the ranch last week. Did they tell the men they were going to Fort Worth? At the moment, he couldn't remember.

"Where did we tell everybody we were last week?" he asked Casey.

"Waco," Casey answered. "We said we had to see some people in Waco. I'm pretty sure." He studied Eli's worried expression and said, "I swear, I never thought it would come down to this. I figured we might end up gettin' caught in the middle of a robbery, if we pushed our luck too far. But I never once thought we'd end up gettin' arrested by Colton Gray. I declare, I got to where I genuinely liked that boy—considered him a friend. I know he joked about you and me being the old-men bandits, but I never figured he'd try to prove it. Thought he was just japin' us. Didn't you?"

"Yeah, I know what you're talkin' about," Eli said. "Kinda feels like gettin' turned in by a friend. Like I said, we'd best play innocent and call his bluff, 'cause you know he can't have any real evidence to hold against us. He's still fishin' for something."

"Is Colton not coming to dinner?" Juanita asked when they came in the back door.

"Yeah, he'll be here," Colton answered. "Right now, Smiley's takin' a bullet out of his shoulder. Then he'll come up to the house."

"He is wounded?" Juanita was at once concerned.

"Yeah, but don't worry," Casey told her, "it ain't that bad. Don't look like it's slowed him down any. He'll be up here pretty quick."

"Dinner be ready in about fifteen minutes," Juanita said.

"That'll be fine," Eli said. "You just holler when it's ready.

We won't wait for him." He and Casey went to the study to wait for her signal.

When Juanita called for them to come to dinner, they went into the kitchen to find her talking to Colton. He turned to face them. "I could smell those pork chops in the skillet when I was halfway here," he said.

"He say he gonna start without you, you don't hurry up," Juanita said, and chuckled. "Sit down and I pour the coffee."

"What's that you're holdin'?" Eli asked, pointing to a stiff folder with a string tied around it in Colton's hand.

Colton grinned. "That's something I thought I'd show you after we eat. It might spoil your dinner if you look at it now."

"Oh, all right" was all Eli could say. He looked at Casey and received a puzzled stare, much like his own.

As was their usual custom, Juanita's husband, Miguel, joined them at the kitchen table, and he and Colton exchanged friendly greetings. Dinner was somewhat quieter than on typical days, with much of the light conversation occurring between Juanita and Colton. Juanita could not help but notice the lack of the usual lighthearted chatter between Casey and Eli and whoever their guest happened to be. She wondered if there was something wrong. When dinner was over, the two owners of D&T Cattle Company and the deputy U.S. marshal retired to the study to digest and discuss.

Eli was unable to restrain himself. "You said before we ate that there was another bank robbery in Fort Worth and you think you know who the bandits are?" He ignored the frown his question caused on Casey's face.

"As a matter of fact, I do," Colton replied. "I went up to Fort Worth to investigate the robbery because it was another one done by the old-men bandits. Well, this one was the real old-men robbery and not a copycat attempt. By the way, that was a mighty fine thing you two did, goin' into the bank the day before the robbery and payin' off that six-thousand-dollar loan for Carter General Merchandise. I talked to Frank Carter and he said it most likely kept him from losing his store." He paused, noticing that he had the rapt attention of both partners, so he continued.

"By the way, I stayed in Fort Worth two nights. Stayed in a little hotel called Woodward House Hotel. Really nice folks there and they really took me in when I told 'em I was a friend of yours. They surely think the world of you two. I had to laugh when I saw the rockin' chairs on the front porch, 'Casey' on one, 'Eli' on the other. Emma said those chairs belonged to you, and nobody but you two could sit in 'em when you were there. She said they oughta belong to you, since you gave her three thousand one hundred and twenty-five dollars to keep the bank from takin' Woodward House from her." He paused as if recalling. "Yes sirree, nice folks, Emma and Pearl and Pearl's daughter, Rose. I told 'em about the time you two stopped a bank robbery in Lampasas. They sure got a kick outta that, especially Walt Evans and Donald Plunket."

By this time, both Casey and Eli were somewhat in shock as Colton related their complete story regarding the holdup of the Wells Fargo Bank. He wasn't through, however. "It was kind of easy to follow the bank robbers' trail after they left the bank. Of course, I knew where it led, anyway. I stopped in the Potluck Kitchen to say hello to Roy and Joy. They said to tell you howdy when I saw you, so howdy from Roy and Joy." He paused, waiting for some response. There was none, so he went on. "When I left Potluck, I rode on up to Hasting's. I had twenty feet of clothesline the robbers tied Branden Cooper up with at the bank. And Mr. Hasting said, yep, he sold it, and he remembered who he sold it to. That pretty much wrapped it up right there. I knew who the robbers were, but I figured I might as well pick up some more evidence. Because you can't ever have too much evidence. So I rode on out the road to that little creek the two robbers had used before, when they did a couple of robberies in Fort Worth. And I found the hole they dug to bury what the fire didn't burn up, when they decided to get rid of their disguises. You know, when I found that hole, I had to wonder if they had decided to give up this robbery business and go straight."

Casey could see the writing on the wall, and after hearing the wealth of evidence that led Colton to Eli and him, he was appalled to think they had left such an obvious trail. "Sounds like you finally got on the right trail. What are you gonna do about it? You gonna arrest 'em?" He glanced at Eli and read panic in his eyes.

"Oh, I've already arrested them," Colton replied. "And you and Eli are gonna be the first to see the real, original old-men bandits." He untied the string on his folder, pulled the picture out, and laid it on the desk. They both rushed to the desk to see what the picture was.

They stared at the grim photograph of him kneeling between the two dead men. "That's you!" Casey finally said. "But who the hell are they?"

"I told you," Colton said, "they are the two old-men bandits. They resisted arrest, so we shot it out. That's where I got the bullet in my shoulder. I don't know their last names, but their first names are Del and Otis. I don't reckon we'll ever know who they really are. But that doesn't make any difference. I didn't want to carry their rotting bodies all the way back to Fort Worth, so I took a picture of them to prove they're dead. And I've got plenty of evidence to show they're who I say they are."

"But how the hell did you take a picture?" Eli blurted.

"I've got your friend Gary Corbett to thank for that. He told me the famous photographer Johnathan Guiese was in Little Bow makin' pictures. He was set up in Carter General Merchandise and he made a picture for me. He's the one who said

I oughta be in the picture with 'em, otherwise it would just be a picture of anybody and not necessarily the bank robbers. That made sense to me. Sure makes it easy to transport 'em to Fort Worth. The main thing is that the original old-men bandits are through. They won't ever rob another soul." He paused and looked each one of them in the eye. "That is a fact. They are through robbin' banks, aren't they, boys?"

Casey and Eli stared at each other for a moment before Casey blurted, "Absolutely!"

Eli nodded frantically. "You bet. They're dead. That's the end of those boys in the bank-robbin' business."

Like Eli, Casey felt as if he had just been released from prison, and then it occurred to him the magnitude of what Colton was doing for him and Eli. It struck him that the young deputy was going against his entire sense of honesty, because he evidently felt that he and Eli were worth saving.

"I swear, Colton, I don't think there's any way I can repay you for what you're—"

"You might want to wait a minute before you start to thank me," Colton stopped him. "It's gonna cost you. You took forty thousand dollars out of that bank. When I go back with my evidence and the picture of the two men I killed, the first question is gonna be, 'Where's the money?' So I need to return some of the money. I'm not talkin' about all of it, or even half, but I need to take at least fifteen thousand or so, instead of zero. All they have is my word on the whole story. They'll have to take my word for it that the amount I give them is all that they had on them when I caught up with them. Evidently, they must had hidden some of it or given some of it away. Who knows what they did with it in the time they had to get rid of it? They might suspect me for a while, but eventually they'll see that I don't have any money."

Casey and Eli were both still trying to believe what he was telling them was what he was actually going to do. Ever since they created the characters, Oscar and Elmer, their plan had been simple, they had nothing to lose. So ride it until it goes lame, then take the consequences. Shot, hung, or imprisoned, as long as they enjoyed the ride, the cost was worth it.

But what they had not anticipated was the simple pleasure they enjoyed in being able to help some of the people who couldn't help themselves. And it was especially satisfying to strike a blow against the banks that squeezed the life out of the little man. It was their good fortune that they were able to prosper because of their ill-gotten gains. And they built a cattle ranch that was big enough to survive the ups and downs of the markets, while providing a good living for more than a dozen people. So the difference in their thinking now from when they first began this wild ride was now they had too much to lose.

"Colton, I've always known you to be an honest man," Casey stated. "What you're proposing to do is not what an honest, hardworking lawman would do. You were onto me and Eli from the first and I always figured you'd get us before it was over. What changed your mind to the point where you would go against your own principles?"

"That's a question that has caused me a lot of hard thinkin' since I first had any contact with you two characters. You're right, I suspected you and Eli early on, just because you always seemed to be in the vicinity of the latest robbery. And I fully intended to arrest you as soon as I was able to find indisputable evidence to back it up. The trouble was, I also kept finding evidence of all the good use you put the money you stole to. And I've come to the conclusion that you've really done more good than harm, and I didn't think you deserved the punishment your arrest would sentence you to. I reckon I just decided that, basically, you and Eli are two good people who have done some bad things. And if you just quit the bad things, you'll do more good for society as free men, instead of as prisoners. Other than that, I guess I got to the point where I considered you two as friends of mine. I'd like to keep it that way, and as long as your career as bank robbers is done with, I don't see any reason why it should change."

Neither Casey nor Eli knew exactly what to say in answer to Colton's unexpected confession. They were totally surprised to find that he, like themselves, could operate on both sides of the law at the same time.

Finally Casey suggested, "I don't see no reason for it to change, either. Why don't you set here for a few moments while Eli and I go down the hall to have a little parley, okay?" Colton said that was fine with him.

They walked down the hall and went into Eli's room, where they kept one of the safes. "That was kinda touchin' back yonder," Eli said. "Good thing we got outta there when we did. I was fixin' to start bawlin' any minute. You too, huh?"

"Hell no," Casey responded. "I wanted to come outta there so we could decide how much money we're gonna give back to the bank. You know they're gonna suspect him of keepin' part of it, if he goes back with only a little bit of that money. How much you think we oughta give back?"

Eli thought about it for a minute. "You know, us giving him money to give back to the bank is a confession to the crime."

"He's got enough on us to prove we done it," Casey said impatiently. "Now, we've got to decide how much we'll give back to keep them from thinkin' Colton kept most of it. Whaddaya think?"

"Well, in the first place," Eli answered, "we didn't have no idea there was that much money in that sack. We figured there was twenty thousand in the sack, and thought that was plenty when we added it to what we've already got. So I say half it with 'em. Give 'em twenty thousand. Whaddaya think?"

"I agree," Casey said. "Open the safe." When they went back into the study, Casey handed Colton a bag. "We decided we'd half it with the bank. Here's twenty thousand, make up a story about the rest."

Colton was pleasantly surprised. "You boys were more generous with the bank's money than I expected. This'll make it a lot easier to sell my story."

"I reckon we coulda done the right thing and given it all back," Eli said. "But we had certain expenses when we took on the job, don't you know? And we had to hold a little money back in case we run into another needy soul who ain't being treated fairly."

"Ha!" Casey blurted. "I reckon we're outta that business, too."

Chapter 23

Three and a half days after the secret pact with Casey Tubbs and Eli Doolin, Deputy U.S. Marshal Colton Gray led a string of three horses into the town of Fort Worth. He rode down the street to the sheriff's office, where he pulled up and dismounted. He was about to go inside when the sheriff hailed him from across the street. He had just come from dinner at Harding's.

"Whatcha got there, Colton?" he asked when he saw the empty saddles.

"Howdy, Sheriff Courtright," Colton answered. "I've got a couple of horses I want to leave at the stable and some money to take to the bank."

"No foolin'?" Courtright responded. "You caught up with those two old men who robbed the bank?"

"As a matter of fact," Colton replied, "I tracked 'em as far as Little Bow, but they elected to shoot it out, instead of goin' to jail. I had to kill both of 'em. I got away with one shot in my shoulder. I was lucky. One of those photographers, fellow named Johnathan Guiese, was makin' photographs at Little Bow. He made a picture of the two of 'em and I paid him to make me a print. And I'm glad I did, 'cause I ended up stayin' there overnight to get the bullet took outta my shoulder. And, boy, I'm tellin' you, by the second day on the way back here, those two ol' boys got so ripe, I decided to let the buzzards have 'em. I figured I didn't need 'em, anyway, since I had a picture of 'em. I asked everybody in Little Bow if they knew who they were. Nobody did, but the owner of the saloon said they'd been in his place a couple of times. Didn't know their last names, just knew one of them was called Del and the other one's called Otis, but he didn't know which was which. But they had the money when I caught up with them, so I reckon there ain't no doubt they were the old-men bandits."

"Well, I'll be," Courtright stated. "I'll be honest with you. I didn't think anybody was ever gonna catch those two. I thought your boss was just wastin' your time sendin' you all over the place after the robbers were long gone."

"To tell you the truth, Sheriff, I think it was just his excuse for gettin' me out of his hair." He stepped back up into his saddle again. "I just always like to check in with the sheriff whenever I hit town. I'll go to the bank and the stable and I'll be out of your way."

"Always glad to see you, Colton," Courtright said. "Did you get all the money back?"

"No, sorry to say, they only had a little over half of it when I caught 'em. So I've got to go give Mr. Cooper that piece of news." He rode away toward the bank before Courtright could ask any more questions, afraid he might come up with one he hadn't figured out an answer for.

When he got to the bank, Branden Cooper was even more surprised to see him than the sheriff had been. "Deputy Gray, we didn't expect to see you again. What can I do for you?"

"You can take this sack of money off my hands," Colton said.

"You recovered the stolen money!" Cooper exclaimed.

"Not all of it, I'm afraid. When I caught up with the two men who robbed your bank, they only had a little over half the stolen amount in their possession. Those are their horses out front. There's not another penny in the saddlebags and they didn't have a packhorse. They could have done anything with the rest of that money—given it to somebody, dug a hole and hid it somewhere, or maybe it's on a packhorse somewhere that wasn't with 'em when I found them. I counted the money. It's a couple dollars over twenty-two thousand."

He almost smiled when he said it as he recalled Casey changing his intentions and telling him it would be more believable if they didn't divide it *exactly* in half.

"Could you not question the thieves as to where the rest was?" Cooper asked.

"No, sir, I didn't get a chance to. When they realized I was onto them, they set up an ambush and we ended up in a gunfight. I got this wound in the shoulder. They weren't so lucky. They backed me into a corner and I had no choice but to kill 'em."

Cooper took the sack and dumped the money on his desk.

"I'm sorry they didn't have more of it," Colton said.

Cooper looked up at him, realizing he had been staring at the money, obviously disappointed by the amount. "It's not your fault, Deputy. I should be appreciative of the fact that you stayed after the thieves and recovered this much of the money. So thank you for your diligence in going after them."

He offered his hand and Colton shook it, knowing Cooper was probably wondering how much of the money he had taken for himself. As was his usual practice when personally returning stolen money, he had Cooper give him written confirmation on the amount he had returned to the bank.

He left the bank and made one more stop before he was finished, and that was at the telegraph office, where he sent the following message: *Caught bank robbers STOP Both bandits killed STOP Returned money to bank STOP Return Waco Monday.* He was sure the telegram would serve to infuriate his boss, because Timmons would probably have preferred to have him return to Waco with the two fugitives and the bank money. Colton wasn't sure at what point he decided to return directly to Fort Worth, instead. It just seemed the right thing to do. And besides, he now had friends there. So he headed for the Woodward House Hotel, where he thought he might still be in time to eat dinner after he dropped the horses off at Donald Plunket's stable. Then, if Emma Woodward had a room available, he would stay the night and start for home in the morning to see if he was still employed as a deputy marshal.